THE POET'S STORY

Edited by

HOWARD MOSS

A Touchstone Book Published by
Simon and Schuster

Reprinted by arrangement with Macmillan Publishing Co., Inc.

Manufactured in the United States of America

1 2 3 4 5 6 7 8 9 10

Library of Congress Cataloging in Publication Data

Moss, Howard, date.   comp.
   The poet's story.

   (A Touchstone book)
   CONTENTS: Moss, H.   Introduction.—Berryman, J.
The lovers—Bishop, E.   In prison.—[etc.]
   1. Short stories, American.   *2.* American fiction—
20th century.   I. Title.
[PZ1.M839P05]   [PS648.S5]   *813'.01*   *77-8444*
ISBN *0-671-23082-4*

FOR

William Maxwell

Contents

Introduction

In Gorky's *Reminiscences,* he tells of having read some scenes from *The Lower Depths* to Tolstoy. Tolstoy wasn't pleased. He said, "Most of what you say comes out of yourself and therefore you have no characters." And that simple statement says more clearly than anything I know why poets attempt to write fiction. For the self—the *I*—is most typically the viewpoint from which a poem is conceived and written. With a few important exceptions—Homer, Chaucer, Browning—*they, you, he,* and *she* stand outside the poet—the net of reality, a huge temptation. And in time, I think, most poets fall into that net. It takes courage to enter one's own world with any degree of truth. It takes a different kind of courage to enter the worlds of other people—and, for a writer, a different kind of skill. Poets bring to the task one advantage and the defect of that advantage: though they have learned to search for the truth, because that search has been directed toward themselves, their interest tends to be parochial or narcissistic or limited to the landscape and the psychology of the ego. That tendency must be overcome before a writer can produce poems of dramatic tension, a legitimate dramatic poem, or fiction. If writing could be conceived as a religious matter, poets would be admired for being devout and scorned for having committed themselves to the wrong faith.

It would be difficult to make a list of fifty poems of this century that exhibit a true interest in character—character as I think Tolstoy meant it and demonstrated it. Psychology, yes—psychology is all over the place. But it is not the same as character. In fact, the very existence of the word *psychology* reinforces the fragmentation of character. Though we use the word commonly, it was not always at the tip of everyone's tongue. Psyche was a character in a story before she became an attribute of everyone. Psychology can be dispersed: ring true in abstract statement, in insights and perceptions, strike home in a passing observation, and even be demonstrated in figures essentially hollow. And that is not only true of the figures in poetry, when they appear at all. A great deal of what passes for fiction consists of puppet plays; yet the puppets may ring true psychologically. The trouble is they don't necessarily ring true any other way. The shadings are off; if they're emotionally believable *and* interesting—almost anyone can be emotionally believable and dull—there's something wrong with their minds, or they don't walk properly, or they don't speak understandably, they can't swim, some of them can't even drive. I'm not speaking here of the mechanics of fiction, or true-to-life fiction, that low order, where the characters are merely accurate and live on streets that have real names and use the right golf clubs and eat the right entrails. No, I mean something like a mystery story where everything is obviously false, with the exception of the motives of the people in it—themselves false.

Psychology, then, is the key to character but it is not character itself; after all, a key unlocks the door leading to something else. What is it, then, psychology unlocks? I think you might say that psychology is general and that character is specific. The door must be recognizable in order to be opened. But the room it opens on is capable of infinite variation. It is the credibility of each variation—the ability on the writer's part to describe precisely the individual room and to make it felt—that becomes his task and his difficulty. A chair's a chair . . . but *this* one? The wall is blue . . . but what *kind* of blue? The distinctions become increasingly difficult as one moves from psychological abstraction to characteristic experience. This is not only true of the so-called realistic novel but of any novel, for no matter how fantastic the variation or exquisite the conception, the novelist ultimately tangles with personality. The poet has already fought an analogous battle with imagery, having progressed from the general outburst to the specific metaphor. The struggle with character is similar. The amateur poet fails by making experience general. The amateur novelist universalizes character and displays his not very fine Italian hand by allowing each character a dominant trait: Gloria is angry, Tom is sad, Helga is weatherbeaten.

Yet if psychology is general and character specific, something further needs to be said. General things are diffused; the specific usually has a direct impact. But in the case of psychology, because it is a medical discipline as well as a word that stands for human insight, the reverse is true. Psychology defines, character eludes—you'd think it would be the other way around. Though it categorizes, psychology tends to be increasingly cautious in its definitions. We now know that a word like *schizophrenia* covers more territory than language permits. Hardly meaningless, it nevertheless demands more and more qualification. And it is precisely in art that those qualifications already exist. Character cannot flourish in the abstract. What may be symptoms to a doctor are ways of behaving to a writer. Take Nicole in *Tender Is the Night*. Dr. Dohmler, at the Swiss clinic, makes a definite diagnosis: schizophrenia. But Nicole is more than a schizophrenic. Her charm, her anger, her sexuality, her selfishness, her terror are all made manifest despite the label. And in Chekhov's "Ward No. Six," Ivan Dmitritch is classically paranoid. Dmitritch would have no force or conviction if he were not subtle, penetrating, and masterful in argument.

Fitzgerald's novel and Chekhov's story are less concerned with mental illness than with its effects on other people, and they have certain resemblances. The leading characters in both are doctors dealing with psychotic behavior, and each of them reverses positions with the very character he is "treating." Nicole drains Dick Diver. Dr. Ragin ends up in Ivan Dmitritch's place. But these likenesses are superficial. The overtones of the Fitzgerald novel are psychological, romantic, nostalgic, and, to a limited extent, social. The thrust of "Ward No. Six" is philosophical and political. It profoundly concerns itself with the difference between being a victim of evil and the luxury of rationalizations about it. It takes the enforced incarceration of Dr. Ragin in his own psychiatric ward to make him see what no amount of learning or training or observation or thought or imagination has been able to illuminate before. Evil is concrete and immediate: it is more than a philosophical abstraction. The sufferings of its victims are real and those who do nothing in the face of it abet it. "Ward No. Six" opens up an abyss. An attack on the passivity of Tolstoy's moral theories and a product of Chekhov's trip to the prison colonies on Sakhalin Island, it is a work of conscience—the most overtly political of all of Chekhov's stories.

"Ward No. Six" anticipates R. D. Laing by almost half a century. Both Chekhov and Laing test common assumptions, but Dr. Laing is shedding light on a problem Chekhov already understood. It would be false to confuse art, necessarily enigmatic and mysterious—it is always about to utter the unutterable—and science, which must describe, classify, and predict. My point is that I would still go to Chekhov, who died in 1904, rather than to Dr. Laing, an expert in the field, to understand the human dimensions of the problem. I learned more about the unconscious from reading Proust than from reading Freud.

People who are summed up in a word are people we are lying about. Art questions that lie constantly by showing us how things really happen to people and, on a more profound level, by its shadings, by the intelligence that fuels its emotional force, and by its range.

Character is elusive not only because it is truly reflected from life, where it is hopelessly enigmatic, but because character always has something left over, something not used by the author in the course of the story, novel, or poem. No pool is truly a pool once it has been drained. And so a character must exist outside his framework—before and after the action. If he has no past or future in the reader's mind—no matter how unconsciously—he hasn't registered completely. Stories are read for thousands of reasons, but anyone who appears in a story has a pre- and a post-reality. An author has one limitation any mother transcends: he cannot give birth to a character; at best, he can catch the baby in swaddling clothes. He *can* kill a character off. In which case, he risks, like all of us, immortality or oblivion.

Immortality and *oblivion*—like *ecstasy* and *glory*—were once fairly common words in poetry, at least in romantic poetry. The poet progresses from lines without imagery meant to convey great feeling, like "the sky is full of joy," to something as specific, say, as Eliot's description of the sky as "a patient etherized upon a table." Vague exultation has become no exultation at all. A poet may reverse the process in the way Stravinsky, after *Le Sacre*, embraced neoclassicism—a very sophisticated embrace—but one might note that, for all its oddness, Eliot's image is supported by the most conventional of iambics. Simplifications of style, leanness of syntax, this or that new kind of poetry, always point up the inescapable: after all is said and done, the poet is stuck with the image in the same way the novelist or storyteller is stuck with character. For both, memory is the great source; one doesn't set down—even in the present tense, at whatever level of consciousness—something that is not memorable. For a poet, memory connects—the very function of metaphor, where one thing reminds you of another, or rather, one thing *enlivens* another. For a fiction writer, memory accretes and sums up— the function of meaningful action. But because one term of a metaphor must precede the other and because accretion involves process, memory is a function of time. That would seem obvious, but time is different for the novelist and the poet. The fiction writer is dominated by the clock and the poet by the metronome. They are just dissimilar enough— metronomes can be sped up, slowed down, or stopped—to provide a fertile field of transaction.

From the beginning of this century, poetry and fiction have borrowed from each other, imitated each other, and in some cases become each other. Whitman and Rimbaud, an odd couple at first glance, are the godfathers of the prose poem. As prose moved into poetry—Ezra Pound and William Carlos Williams are crucial figures—so poetry moved into prose. Whenever poets escape from meter—Marianne Moore comes to mind—they approach the conditions of prose; the metronome becomes almost inaudible and one glances up at the clock. What is syllabic writing but a counting out? Counting out is not the same as measure, where duration and stress are more critical than number. Whenever prose writers depend heavily on cadence or the image, they move toward poetry.

In Cocteau's film, *The Blood of a Poet,* the poet is spewed out of a mirror—Narcissus is being ejected by the pool. A mouth opens in the palm of the poet's hand and cries, *"L'aire! L'aire!"* That plea for oxygen implies a window. As I remember it, the poet breaks a windowpane and sticks his hand out into the air to let it breathe. But he never bothers to look out. His true adventures occur later when he is swallowed up by the mirror and enters "a hotel of follies." Nevertheless, the point has been made. The mirror is the totem of the poet, who looks *at* and *into* himself, who creates himself, as it were. And I would say the window belongs to the fiction writer, who looks *out* and *around*, and is a product of the world. In the love affair that has occurred in this century, the novelist has flirted with mirrors and the poet with windows. The increasing prominence of confessional writing in poetry and the number of fiction writers drawn to documentation suggest a new hardening of positions. Attempts to get at the truth may also, I suspect, be forms of camouflage. In telling all, the poet frees himself to deal with character —having been merciless toward himself, he is free to be merciless toward everyone. And the fiction writer—finding plot, character, and relevance pre-empted by clever mystery writers, excellent film makers, and exploiters of the topical—is increasingly drawn to the actual. Where is reality really to be found? In the blood and guts of one's own experience? In the external event examined with the same meticulous detail, the same concern for form, often, one would bring to fiction?

The twentieth century is rich in great writers, but because Proust is as much an epic poet as a novelist, he is, to my mind, its key literary figure. He saw the significance of windows very clearly and the importance of mirrors by implication. Is there any other book that so strangely combines plunges into the interior of the self with so faultless a portrait of the external world—natural and social—as *Remembrance of Things Past*? It is obsessive in both directions. And it would be hard to explain away the fact that every crucial sexual scene in *A la Recherche* . . . is seen through a window. I include in that grouping two scenes not ordinarily considered sexual: that one where Marcel looks out at the garden through his bedroom window and sees his parents dining with Swann, the first clue to the subject of voyeurism in the novel, and his playing with the magic lantern in his bedroom, which shortly follows. The theme of the voyeur—which is spun for us slowly— as well as the device of the magic lantern tells us more or less the same thing: for the voyeur, the distinction between windows and mirrors is psychologically nebulous; the outward scene merely activates the inner compulsion of the viewer; what he sees is not the reality of the act but a fantasy implicit in himself. The disturbed psyche mirrors what is viewed through the window; the seeming observation is a narcissistic turning inward. The voyeur doesn't look at people in order to examine, understand, or know them but because they perform—like marionettes of the unconscious—in a certain way. The *character* of the actors has no meaning, though their physical attributes may be of great significance. And the magic lantern, projecting images of others, is manipulable. Not only can the images be chosen but they can be projected at will, and in Marcel's case, the characters he *thinks* he sees (he later finds out more about them) do not conform to the fantasies they at first evoke. Moreover, he projects those images where he pleases: on the door, the wall, the doorknob, and so forth. Through the magic lantern, Marcel sees fragments of the history of France. That is its window side. It has a mirror side. In its repetition of chosen images that lead to fantasy, its ability to frame a person, an image, or an act (the way a window frames a voyeur), and by being physically manipulable, it is, by analogy, a masturbatory device.

In Proust, intelligence has emotional force, but the sexual scenes often lack sensuality—Albertine and Marcel seem strangely hermetic, as if the act of going to bed together, the heart of their struggle, had somehow become metaphysical before it was consummated. Swann and Odette exude a more gamey flavor. With Marcel and Albertine we are analyzing feeling rather than experiencing it. We are being tortured, but tortured so intelligently that following the argument almost prevents us from feeling the pain. It soon becomes clear enough that that's what feeling is: pain. Proust was no fool; the window and the mirror, in the hands of the right magician, are interchangeable. That cup of tea out of which Combray is evoked is a mirror of the past but opens a window onto the future. What are mirrors and windows but the glassy fields of dissolution and envy? In the one we watch ourselves decay; through the other we see those things we long for and can never attain or become. What Marcel sees reflected through a window becomes his utlimate reflection—a word almost too luringly usable in Proust's case. In the end the dirty pictures become focused: Marcel turns out to be as sexually compulsive as Mlle. Vintueil, Swann, and Charlus.

Using the images that Cocteau and Proust provide as clues, I would say that the distinction between fiction writers and poets is becoming obsolete, that it might be more useful to think of authors as mirror-writers or window-writers. In the same way that liberal members of opposing political parties may be closer to each other in thought and spirit than to the conservative members of their own parties, so certain prose writers are closer to poets than to each other.

In America the two schools stem from two major figures, both poets, who may be viewed as their source: Emily Dickinson, the mirror, and Walt Whitman, the window. If it is confusing to have a poet—Whitman —stand for the generic prose writer, one can at least say that Whitman brought the devices of biblical prose into poetry: repetition, cataloging, and cadence. It would be hard to find, in any case, another figure who so clearly illustrates what I mean.

Take two superb poems: Dickinson's "Because I could not stop for death" and Whitman's "When lilacs last in the dooryard bloomed." They have in common the subject of death, but it would be inconceivable for Emily Dickinson to have written an elegy on the death of a public figure, an event external to her life and a theme whose magnitude derives partly from the power and importance of the subject it mourns. The Dickinson poem, in spite of its intensity, reflects a smaller world. It is measured, literally and figuratively; it is compressed, whereas Whitman's poem is expansive and comes to include, finally, the entire United States. Both are poems of great feeling, perfectly true to themselves, and typical. Whitman's poem, for all its length, is organized around a few images: the star for Lincoln, the lilac for seasonal rebirth, the hermit thrush for Whitman himself. In the course of the poem, Lincoln's body is moved by train across the country. The Dickinson poem uses a similar idea: a carriage ride, sufficient to its scope, and the figure of Death is appropriately a courtier or suitor.

Who is a window? Who is a mirror? Proust may seem too much a mirror, but then one thinks of the party scenes, those gargantuan satires on middle-class and upper-class social life, and a window opens. Chekhov has a house full of windows. Strolling around, one becomes aware that two or three of the panes are mirrored. And in our time, Mr. Nabokov is a fine example of both. In spite of being the master depictor of motel life in America, he is essentially a mirror writer. He said: "time is a fluid medium for the culture of metaphors." Norman Mailer, despite the obvious egotism, is a window writer. Can one imagine Mr. Nabokov—or Emily Dickinson—covering a moon launching, the conventions, or a prizefight? It is not inconceivable, though, to think of Whitman in the role of the evangelical journalist. Good writers hover, like angels caught in a magnetic field, between the mirror and the window.

Some writers hover between, and some are caught between. The poet may decide that not everything can be got down in poetry. And he begins a story or a novel. It would be interesting to make an anthology of the beginnings of poets' novels, especially the unpublished ones (unpublished *novels*, not unpublished poets). I would make a fairly safe bet that the first two pages consist of description in ninety percent of the cases.

We are at a railroad station in Malaya and the sky is turbulent and suffused. In fact, it is raining. It keeps on raining for a long time, because the poet is afraid—with good reason—to begin the action, to introduce the inevitable character. Sooner or later, he has to, and Malaya pales before the all-too-recognizable instructor's wife, editor's lover, or professor's mistress. There she is, at the bar, in the hotel, at the counter, and little falsehoods begin to pile up. Some of them are merely the plague of fact. She says she has just had her hair done. Where would she get the hair rinse? The travel book informs us that there are no hairdressers in Malaya and customs specifically forbids the importation of hair rinse. Or she has just finished a lemon ice. The latest issue of the *National Geo-*

graphic tells us that lemon ices have never been introduced into Malaya. But the real difficulty is that she is obviously not the person she is supposed to be. She is either too recognizable or not recognizable enough. Either she changes from minute to minute or she is hopelessly consistent. Just as conversation is not automatically dialogue, people are not necessarily characters. Who *is* she? She is red-headed and envious. Then she is more envious. And her hair seems to get redder. Later she is in an absolute rage of envy and completely rubescent. We find out, finally, that she is basically kind. We leave Malaya.

The Malayan novel has not been published—I hope. But poets' novels *are* published, and they stand a better chance than most of ending up at one end of the spectrum or the other. When they're bad, they couldn't be worse, and when they're good, they're superb. Fitfulness and experiment aside, the inner urgency that can lure a poet to prose can, paradoxically, produce work that closely resembles poetry itself. William Faulkner, Malcolm Lowry, Herman Melville, D. H. Lawrence, and James Joyce all started out as poets. Giving up poetry's official title, they continued on its secret missions. Are there really significant differences in the originality of conception, the play of language—the bolt of the imagination in general—between *Moby Dick* and *The Cantos*, between *Ulysses* and *The Waste Land*?

Ernest Hemingway, Willa Cather, and Muriel Spark started out as poets, too, but in their work the parting of the ways between fiction and poetry is clearer. The interest in words stays steady but the language is stripped down, or at least grows sparer; a concern with dramatic structure develops and becomes individual. The metaphor ceases to be central, though the motif may take its place—that double threading of language and concept that grows significant by repetition.* In Muriel Spark's *Girls of Slender Means*, the words *slender means* take on a double meaning. During a fire only those characters slim enough to squeeze through a tiny bathroom window survive. The title of *A Farewell to Arms* says good-bye to two things at once, love and war. But they crop up again in tandem in *For Whom the Bell Tolls*. What is unique in each of these writers, so different from each other, is the unmistakable sound of a voice. Words exhale temperament. We expect that individual voice—we demand it, in fact—in a poet. And though great fiction writers develop who are not poets to begin with—Proust, James, Tolstoy—they each have two qualities we assign to poets: a singularity and an authority of the imagination. Great novelists may be visionaries or enigmatic or focus on a social sewer, yet they must do two things at once:

---

* It is of interest to note how often motif is expressed in metaphor in the titles critics give to their works: *The Hovering Fly* (Tate); *The Wound and the Bow* (Wilson); *The Double Agent* (Blackmur); *Stewards of Excellence* (Alvarez); *Masks and Mirrors* (Bewley); *A Sad Heart at the Supermarket* (Jarrell), etc.

produce a recognizable world and create one of their own. The ability to make the official document personal is the true link between the novelist and the poet, for each stamps experience uniquely. A literary convention is a passport, but like the real thing, it can bear only one signature. When people say that something is Chekhovian or Proustian, it is odd, when you think about it, that they don't say, "That's pre-Revolutionary Russian," or "That's pre–World War I French," the stigma of long-windedness aside. They don't say it because that is not quite what they mean, though what they mean may certainly include the historical perspective and the period flavor. The social, political, economic, and military worlds of Russia and France are documented in many places. It is Chekhov's version and Proust's version that are so telling. What those worlds once were—the very sense of what it meant to be alive in them— has been re-created for us, yet belongs, in each case, to a single writer. It belongs to him because he has transcended it. We don't read Chekhov or Proust only for glimpses into worlds at a remove; we read them for glimpses into ourselves. No one is as egotistical as a reader.

There is the poetry *of* fiction, that quality of magic that comes from the demands of the medium itself, and there is poetry *in* fiction—two very different matters. The latter is an inferior brand if what is meant is merely "poetic prose." Hundreds of writers are labeled "poetic" for the wrong reason, a gift for description. It consists often of being partial to adjectives. At any rate, a gift is not an art. It is the mastery of a theme, a viewpoint, and a language that makes a superb writer. Poets may come to fiction for any number of reasons, but poets *of* fiction, as well as writers who come to it *through* poetry—window or mirror or both— invariably have one thing in common: they have style.

The purpose of this anthology is easily stated. It is an attempt to save valuable work from oblivion, to collect those stories written by poets who do not write, or have not yet written, enough of them to make up a book. Many poets write a story or two that appears in a magazine, but all too often the life-span of the magazine issue becomes the life-span of the story. The stories get lost, end up in private files, in anthologies that go out of print, or languish unread in a library. Because the point of this book is to make unavailable material available, one of its ground rules was fixed from the beginning: no poet would be included who had published a book of short stories. That meant leaving out stories by writers I admire: Conrad Aiken, Howard Nemerov, Robert Penn Warren, Delmore Schwartz, and William Carlos Williams, among others. Poets, trying to remedy the situation, have taken to including a short story or two in a book of poems. Any story published in a book of poems was also out of the running.

Then the writer had to be an American. Stories written by British poets was too large a field to cover and the materials too unavailable, for with the British came (and went) the Irish, the Australian, the Canadian, the New Zealand, and the Indian. That meant leaving out stories I like by Stephen Spender, Dylan Thomas, Ted Walker, Leslie Norris, and others. Even with these two firm rules, there was more material, in the end, than I had room for. One inclusion may seem an exception, the story by W. S. Merwin. It is not, but it *is* a special case. Mr. Merwin published a group of prose pieces, related in method, called *The Miner's Pale Children*, but he did not include any of the fine short stories he had written prior to the book. "Return to the Mountains" is one of them.

The stories in this anthology divide themselves roughly into two categories. In one, the poet abandons his usual subjects and methods of procedure and focuses on the classical ingredients of fiction: plot, character, and suspense—tiny thrillers might be a description of them. They are stories that try for the *frisson*. They are window stories. The Millay is a classical example, and under that heading I'd put the stories by Muriel Rukeyser, Donald Justice, Josephine Jacobsen, and possibly the one by Carolyn Kizer. And perhaps W. S. Merwin, though that story ends with a *frisson* of a different kind: horror and mystery rather than the catharsis of drama. And, in the other category, there are those stories— mirror stories?—that seem to me to explore or extend the writer's characteristic preoccupations: the ones by Jon Swan, Jean Garrigue, Anne Sexton, and John Berryman.

The "memory" stories going back to the writer's childhood or adolescence are interesting for the divergent ways they handle what once was, and may still be, difficult emotional material. Something of the fable marks them all. In John Berryman's "The Lovers," the stranger we know practically nothing about achieves an extra dimension. His character is not to be one. His is the fate the narrator is about to unwittingly suffer, that of the enchanted lover who, in order to save himself, must remove himself from enchantment. The stranger bears the knowledge the narrator is on the verge of learning, and, as such, he has something of the function, though none of the qualities, of the serpent in Eden. He is the unwelcome tarnisher, experience's bitter messenger. It is not *because* of him but *through* him that the narrator comes to the end of innocence. By the time we finish the story, we realize that its title refers not to the young couple at its center but to the two hopeless men, who love and are not loved back.

The boy in the tree in Richard Wilbur's "A Game of Catch" is an uneasy, painful Cain, who strikes out at others from a desperate isolation, the awful brother, the outsider whose only way of joining is to gain attention by being hateful. In Jean Garrigue's "The Snowfall," only the dead and the rejected embody the perfect realizations of love. Like the mother and the grandmother in Mona Van Duyn's "The Bell," some of the characters in these stories seem larger than life—by their oddness, the glancing intelligence by which they are perceived, the undertow of metaphor that waits in the shallows. Transmutations of one kind or another extend their meanings. The two nameless lovers in James Schuyler's "Life, Death, and Other Dreams," for instance, seem less like characters than archetypes. In the story's small coda, where the lovers lie side by side in their graves, it is significant that the narrator suddenly makes himself evident. Is he warning us—or himself?—against the pretensions of art in an attempt to preclude falsity? Is he simply admitting, through his "characters," that he hopes this story will be read? Self-consciousness is suborned by being included, like the stage manager's asides to the audience in a Chinese play—as much a part of the convention as the action. Using awareness of the medium in the medium itself can result in parody—like bad movie music signaling the action ahead—but in Mr. Schuyler's sad and funny story, I take it to be a form of ironic honesty, like saying "Dear reader" to a reader one almost holds dear.

Objectifications can teeter between confession and materialization. In Elizabeth Bishop's story, the fantasy of being in prison tells us not at all who the narrator is but very clearly the kind of person she'd like to be and allows the writer extraordinary moments of landscape engraving, imaginative leaps—the description of the walls and the courtyard—leaps that seem more daring in a story so obsessed by confinement. And there is that moment, too, in the Kenneth Koch story, where the narrator suddenly breaks the thread and says to an offstage character we don't know, "I love you"—a break that both undercuts and highlights the speculation the postcards give birth to. In that switch of viewpoint, something is being said about life and art in the simplest and yet most complicated of ways. For the utterance is banal and direct, as if the author were saying, "Enough of all this artifice and theory—the plain truth is 'I love you.' " Yet the postcards, created by artists of a kind—there are little poems on the reverse sides—are sent by, and to, real people whose stories the writer is trying to reconstruct from the stained, defaced, and half indelible messages. They are artful communications within an artful communication; they are at the heart of the story the writer is writing—a piece of artifice in itself. The postcards may be artifacts, the story a work of art, but the writer makes one thing clear: *he* is real. Life is getting back at scholarship. And there is that moment in the James Merrill story where the driver, after a mystical revelation that reveals very little, reveals a *real* mystery to us: he is sixty years old. In the Louise Bogan story, how far the journey goes from a fixed position, how much it takes in simply by meticulously describing a single room! And then there is a slight undercurrent: is this the way all journeys end, with the traveler confined to a space, and memory the only clue to how he got there?

There are other mysteries. The one that pervades the way of life of the mountain people in the W. S. Merwin story—all presented, it seems, rather realistically and yet with that mountain shimmer, that discrete secrecy that lets us know that what might seem obvious is not quite within our grasp. When the animals turn, like natural compasses, and point in one direction, and the narrator comes upon the strange, ballet-like action of the old women sewing cauls, we are moved by . . . what? The venerableness of the symbols? The secret of life withheld from the narrator, as it may well be from us? The strange mixture of the exotic and the mundane that gives the story its flavor? Like Merwin's poems, "Return to the Mountains" is visionary, in that the use of the eye is the paradoxical key to what cannot be seen. It makes us aware that there is more than we can see, the revelation of which can never be final. The significant figures in Merwin's story are not characters but a chorus, and it appears with the force of a vision at the end.

Stories written by poets usually take place somewhere between the window and the mirror—stories of revelation objectified to a point, but not to the point of realism. They bear the poet's particular badge: the mysterious and the real held in suspension. You know more when you finish these stories than you can say. If they could have been reduced to statement, there would have been no point in writing them.

JOHN BERRYMAN

The Lovers

He used to come to see us one summer when we lived on the Island. As I reached the corner of the house wheeling my bicycle, which I was not permitted to ride on the lawn, dirty and hot in the late afternoon, he would be the first person in view if he was there, sitting stretched at full length but hardly at ease in a beach-chair just at the edge of the tulip-bed, balancing his drink on its wooden arm, when his head lifted staring out towards my mother and listening to my father, who sat invariably a few feet away in an angle formed by the house and garage, also facing the cannas bordering the lawn at the back. No matter how quietly I approached, my mother always heard me and had turned from her care of the cannas by the time she came into sight as I advanced, her face pale above the blooms, her inexhaustible brown hair blowing, her garden-glove dark against the orange sky, raising a hand to me. I never waved in reply without a twinge, an impulse of remorse for my absent day, the anxiety I knew she was feeling,—for this was the year when what she called my violent indolence first showed itself. It was the summer I was in love with Billie. Billie was an interesting blonde girl who lived half a mile from us, the daughter of a notable playwright; but the relation, if it had lost none of its tenacity, was complicated because her mother had left him—they had been the centre of an artistic set in some middle-Western city, and she had then written a book about him— and was now married to an ace of the last War, a small shattered man, a European, who was kind to me and seemed nearly invisible in the rambling noisy suburban mansion filled night and day with hangers-on, suitors, unclassified cosmopolitan guests. The unsubstantiality, for me, of this menage was enforced less by its confusion, or my shyness, than by my

sense of wonder at its names; Mme. Durand had living with her her
mother, Mrs. Austin, and in a reaction of feeling after her last divorce
she had changed Billie's name—the playwright's—to the irrelevant name
of another former husband, Neville; so that of the three women in this
family still dominated by the memory (and the existence, productive
erratically of extravagant gifts for Billie, nearby in New York) of the
excommunicated celebrity, none bore his name, and their own names
senselessly differed. 'Billie,' too, which I knew as I knew my biceps, flexed
and felt endlessly in hope, would disappear for minutes into its incomprehensible original, Wilhelmina; and I loved her as against a set of
uncertain troubled lights. Of Madame I remember little except her in-
tolerable fatness, the nascent snobbism in Billie which I associated with
her, and a luncheon described to me long afterwards by my mother, one
of Mme. Durand's large hen-parties, at which one of the guests, a tall fair
woman who had been told by her psychiatrist that she could attain
normality only by giving way immediately to her impulses, of whatever
sort, amazed the assembly of fifteen women by suddenly reaching into
the centre of the table, snatching up the odd-appearing main dish, sniffing it, and making loudly a remark so atrocious that I only after years,
with the greatest difficulty, learnt what it was. Repeated hesitantly, with
recovered horror, in my mother's charming voice, it seemed at the moment of shock nakedly to score the tone of that society of the distant
summer of the executive class, a society abrupt and sordid enough—the
weekend parties in the Clubhouse, the sleeping, the desertions—not
much to suffer under a symbol of such concise ferocity; only my father
and my mother were distinct from it. But he too, our visitor, and aside
from the accident of my not liking him, appeared to stand somewhere
else, apart from the Lennoxes and Clouds and Gores, the people who
lived along the Lane and their friends who would be drifting and drinking and flowering on the lawns when I returned in the afternoon. The
sun was setting always behind them in my mind, because I rarely saw
them at any other time. I left the house at eight-thirty every morning on
my bicycle, raced to Mme. Durand's and waited restlessly on her drive
below the grove of trees for Billie to come out, and off we went. We
made this arrangement because I avoided entering her house. The sense
of unreality which in itself it gave me was heightened by a feeling, which
I began to have that summer, that I was not appearing in my true
character. Although I could have given no account of that character, I
was aware of the discontinuity between my life at school, absorbing if
horrible, and my frenzied useless vacations; and I had an intermittent
consciousness of guilt. My English master had given me a list of books to
read during the summer, 19th Century novels for the most part, and I
remember I went faithfully to the public library every few days and
brought volumes home, two or three at a time, returned them, and

brought others; but it was my brother who read them; and the advantage, although years my junior, he then established over me he has never relinquished,—in our discussions of fiction he still assumes a tone, dating from that summer, of immeasurable experience and superior judgment.

What our visitor thought of the life we led, or of the life rather which at my level I shared and in the midst of which my parents had their different life, I doubt that it occurred to me to wonder, self-absorbed, going and coming. I saw him at most, every few days, for an hour at five or six o'clock; save once, he never came in the evening, and he never arrived before my father, who drove out from the city, changed at once, and was facing the cannas, armed with that admirable brand of Scotch which I have scarcely tasted since illegal days (our porter's charge for 'bringing it in' was invariable and so heavy that with the indulgence of despair my father ordered liquors and wines more expensive and rare than seemed sensible later across a counter), ready for anyone, by five o'clock. My mother adjusted her time between the guests and the flowers, never appearing distant, although when she tossed, as now and then she hospitably did, a comment from across the lawn, it came to us with a diminished sound. The Clouds and Parkers would be there, perhaps Justin and Margaret, perhaps Macomber and Mrs. Tench, or the Dimmings. Or he would be there alone. I sat on the edge of a porch with a limeade, if I was not indoors following the dancebands, and listened to my father's familiar, ever-changing accounts of the life of his young manhood, his leaving college at his father's death, the Continent before the War, old Baltimore, old New York; of conditions on the Market—it was an unsettled but promising summer; of hunting, and the theatres of the past, restaurants and women. Our visitor listened also; I watched him, for I had already learnt that these stories which interested me, no matter how frequently told, so intensely—so spacious and free the life in them seemed to me, so daring and rich their recital by my father—could be tedious to others; I watched him for a sign of disloyalty, and I never saw one. Yet I thought that somehow they did not deeply engage him. His mind in the immense head kept on working; when he looked at me I saw it, and I thought sometimes I could see pain, or longing,—although it may be that my father's reminiscence interested him more than I imagined, for one afternoon, coming when my father had stayed in town for dinner, he seemed restless with my mother, and left at once.

He said little, at any rate; of himself, nothing. We did not understand clearly what he 'did,' and he never, although my mother several times suggested it, brought anyone with him. This was why I disliked him, perhaps: he seemed singular,—independent, as no one else I knew was. And then he looked at me, he looked at all of us, most at my mother, when his chair was turned as my father's was, with uncomfortable intensity; he looked at me sometimes as if he did not believe I

existed. Again, when I would be included in the talk and he turned to
me with his slow, holding glance, I felt the obscure pressure of a real
interest, and I avoided his eyes. To his rare questions about Billie, whom
he met one afternoon when I brought her home, although they were put
with the gravity which was habitual with him and with which I was
unfamiliar in such questions, even was pleased by,—I replied as shortly,
with as great nervousness, the same tortured grin, as to anyone else's
questions. What he said to my father, however, often fixed my attention
and remained with me for days. He spoke deliberately, with a kind of
constraint which gave his words unnatural, memorable emphasis. One
day, on my father's referring to an unexpected Congressional vote of the
day before and asking his opinion, he said instantly, almost with impatience, that politics did not concern him. 'What does concern you then?'
asked my father, more nearly indifferent to politics himself than any
other man in his set, but surprised to hear the blank disclaimer which he
could never have made and would have contradicted had it been made
of him. 'Work!—a wife, and work!' our visitor said after a pause, during which Billie's face hovered so vividly before me, its round brows and
low forehead conjured by the question, that his reply reached my ears to
stun me; I did not understand the words in their starkness—'work'
particularly fell into my mind like a word unknown, with its special
weight from the idiom of workers in science and art—I did not understand them, but I recognized that their energy and sentiment were inim-
ical to the beloved face which they had caused to vanish, as I felt them to
be utterly strange to any answer which I might have made to the question, and I resented them, at the same time that their formality charmed
me into the wish that I might have summoned, or might sometime sum-
mon, such a response myself to another question at another time.

Often thereafter this reply recurred to me, always mysterious, with
incomprehensible reaches behind its bluntness, evoking dissonant emotions, and always with the power, which nothing else possessed, of ban-
ishing the face which haunted me; or if, after a time, not quite of
causing it to disappear, of driving it to a certain distance,—at least of
touching the springs of its ghostly force. No doubt I was in love with
Billie; I said so a thousand times daily to her with my lips, with every
emotion, every impulse, I carried it to myself at night, lying uncovered
on my bed sweating, lively with ecstasy; but the undiscriminating violence of my feelings would be better suggested by saying that she obsessed me. She was a torture, an enchantment. Her figure running, loose
in its short light dress, her golden hair tossed in the morning light as she
flew towards me down the turn of the drive, made me weak, like a
repeated blow upon the muscle of my upper arm. My whole body,
braced, eager and weak, at once shrank and yearned towards the moment
of meeting, when we would cling kissing, hidden by the trees above and

the wall below, for the first time that day together. Childish those em-
braces certainly were, in their crude clouded view of what union might
be, in their awkwardness, restlessness, such that at any second either of us
might break causelessly away; an adult, watching, might have found us
absurd or pretentious, experiencing the emotion with which a professional man in the audience observes, smiling, the efforts of an actor who
is impersonating a member of his profession, and how badly. Yet as we
pressed together our lips and breasts helplessly, wantonly, we were in
darkness—the darkness of touch and magnification of sound, the splitting of the ear-drum at a murmur, the precipitation of the soul into a
palm. The delicacy and the flow of darkness; the darkness broke—not
when our bodies parted—long before, when the possibility, the far view
of parting lighted my mind again with the abruptness and brilliance,
blinding the eyes, of a switch pressed. In a second it will be over! I
thought agonized, and the irresolutions of pleasure and pain which are a
child's first lesson in the world hung over me anew, so that I could not
have told whether I was glad or sorry when at last we drew apart, her
face smiling already and hot, my hands trembling, and I said 'Get on.'
She jumped on the crossbar then, her arms inside mine on the handles,
her hands on mine in an old joke that she steered better than I, and
leaned back swerving against my left shoulder—the unnerving moment
of each day,—while her massed hair brushed my neck and cheek; I got
the bicycle-rest up; we started slowly in the gravel and picked up suddenly, coasting down the steep final turn of her drive into the road.

The days passed like a coasting, a hot wind. They were Billie agile in
the glare of the beach, shouting above the Sound pounding the sand,
Billie across the net bent forward, balancing from foot to foot, waiting
for service, Billie bounding away towards the sideline, turned for a backhand, Billie's throat going back for a lob, her eyes gleaming as she
grinned out at me from a tunnel in the fortification we were building,
her voice, her weight against my shoulder and arm, her small breasts we
examined on the porch in darkness, marvelling and tremulous, with the
fearful anxiety of the traveller who lingers in a strange city and rushes to
the next and lingers again, waiting for news—what news? what news?—
from his half-forgotten, absorbing home. Late in the summer, the worst
days, when nights held the heat still, the pavements never cooled, the
float dried as we dived and burned us when we climbed back,—we were
bold and wild. Of the famous innocence of first love, celebrated and
remembered with desire by the poets whose childhood was solitary, we
had never much, or if in the beginning we were so, I lose it now in
memory; what I recall is a plunge down, deeper daily in forbidden
complex experience, hesitations and curiosities and indulgences of the
porch in darkness. But late in the summer we passed feverishly into
regions so wicked and pleasant, that we seemed to ourselves by August's

end old in vice: by the time of the masquerade at the Clubhouse it seemed to us that we had no more to learn—not that we were exhausted, not that we did not suffer our privations, but the capacity of our selves was measured. Purity of feeling, selflessness of feeling, is the achievement of maturity; we begin in the slime, the naked beating self. Yet in a civilized view our diversions that summer left us unsoiled, and Billie went back pure, intact to school, an image of tan youth, with candid eyes,—to be violated next year, perhaps, casually across the kitchen table of a fraternity house, tipsy in the vague light from a door half-opened into the passage, the dance music faint at this distance, by a boy who did not know her name, her magical name, against which no fatigue or incantation had power to preserve me except our visitor's grave words, repeated by me to the ceiling, like a rite, with envy and relief, as meaningless as for some stray from the street, crept into a church for a moment out of the sun, the Elevation of the Host.

It may be that he preserved me, or was able to provide my only aid, because he preserved himself—I did not know from what, but I had a sense, related to his solitude, that he did. Not from feeling, certainly: I had the testimony of his phrase and the weight of his eyes when I intercepted their glance flowing across the lawn while my father talked. Perhaps from the expressions that others used, the forms men's feelings regularly take; these he seemed to avoid as by nature; he never greeted my parents, never thanked them when he left; he made no effort that we could see,—was not, as we say, involved,—and when he walked into our living room on the night of the masquerade dressed merely in a white linen suit, I was not surprised, although with what emotion I could spare from my own excitement I exulted over his mistake. This was the first year I was allowed to go to the great September party which closed the season in the Lane; it was known as 'the masquerade' but was simply a fancy-dress ball, very fancy, to which everyone looked forward for weeks; Billie was going too for the first time—all the day before she had talked of nothing else, intoxicating herself with it, her first grown-up dance. We would meet there. Now our guest was late, and my mother was keeping us. My father, dressed as a musketeer, from the figure of Athos in the illustrated volume of Dumas he had given to me at Christmas, posed amiably at the mantel and said nothing about our guest's lack of costume. I sat tense and silent. But they talked while we waited for my mother to come down, and it struck me, through my distraction, that our friend was in an extraordinary mood. It was impossible not to listen to him. I never at any other time heard him so little reserved. His voice, even, as he swung up and down the room, talking rather rapidly, not loudly, was rich with anticipation and what, to me who knew him, was almost recklessness, although to a stranger he would have appeared controlled enough. The burden of his talk I forget; he made images, he recalled, he dallied, he soared, and the unaccustomed tide of that wonderful voice—stilling quite, during the spell, my dislike—filled our rooms like the beating of wings, the leap of the heart in devotion and hope.

'Ah!' said my father. I turned, and there on the stairway, in gold, queenly and strange, stood my beautiful mother, taller and younger, smiling down at us. She stood for a long moment in the bright lamplight, triumphant, happy in our gaze, before she continued her descent. 'Good evening!' she greeted us. 'But you don't look the man for a party—' Her tone and startled air turned me again to our friend—another stranger—his face rigid, with such despair in the passionate eyes, such black depth as a vision of Hell, that I could have struck him. It was as if the room darkened and whirled with bitterness. In another second his features had softened, his glare died out. What I had seen seemed phantasmal as he came a step forward and said in his normal serious voice that if his astonishment had surprised her he was sorry: it had been, really, a tribute, and should be forgiven: 'You *are* magnificent,'— turning to my father, 'I congratulate you!'

The expectations of youth are its oblivion. I had forgotten my amazement, forgotten the incident five minutes later, when we mounted to the open floodlit doorway of the Clubhouse, where groups and couples in motley costumes, outrageous, exquisite, clownish, passed and repassed, shouting, laughing, the orchestra sighing from within a sweet lament. 'Here are the brother and sister,' someone said as we entered the light— Mrs. Lennox. My father bowed. At this moment, however, the pleasure which I never failed to take in this compliment—in that the metaphorical relationship seemed closer, for my mother and me, than our familiar one, and made me appear to myself older—was blocked as it rose. Across the ballroom by a table I caught sight of Billie, in a blue dress, waving a glass, not at me; she was gesturing, talking with three boys, or men, grouped before her. My breathing seemed oppressed. I started around the dance-space. Halfway, she laughed—I could not hear her above the music—and handing her glass to one of the men, danced away with another, a Spanish gentleman. Danced away with another—danced away with another—while I followed, disappointed and anxious. When at last I got her attention and cut in, she merely said 'Hello' without surprise or warmth, we danced ten steps, another man cut in. I leaned against the wall for a moment while the music rose and fell. Then as I followed, my heart throbbing and sick, my brain hot with betrayal, dominoes, slaves, gentlemen, warriors swarmed in my sight towards her,—divided her,— the room turned on the blue dress like a wheel. The tunes changed, the noise increased, my terror grew. She seemed not to see me, stared past or looked carelessly across as if I were a little boy with whom she played once, years ago. And she herself seemed to me strange. While night before last . . . I tried to call up and hold an image of the porch, but it slipped from me in my distress, the gathering unreality. What I wanted at last was to go outside and weep, but I dared not leave, hoping still for change, at any instant—turning in a glide-step there, ten feet from me, radiant, blind—a sign, recognition, our love, made once more whole. I wandered back and forth, trying to control my face, confused, more and more tired, watching my mother whirling and shining like a shower of gold and gold-brown hair across the room, waiting, waiting. Several times I saw our friend against the wall near the doorway, and once he beckoned to me. I edged my way around the dancers, trying to catch a glimpse again of Billie, whom I had lost.

'Why are you not dancing?'

'You aren't dancing yourself. I haven't seen you once,' I said, too sick and desperate for manners.

He looked out into the throng with a curious expression, as of an intensity of search which had ceased to be personal—the expression he has in most of his photographs of recent years, and the one I remember, since we never saw him again. 'That's true,' he said. 'But you can hardly have my excellent reason.'

'What's that?'

'I am in danger,' he said looking down at me seriously.

I was puzzled or angry: 'You keep out of everything, don't you?'

'Keep out?' he was startled. 'Here I am: I came! But the arrangements are not mine.'

His answer, although I did not try to make it out, touched another bitterness in me. 'Is that why you haven't got a costume on?'

He smiled. 'I have. I wear it against danger.'

But as he spoke I had seen Billie again, and muttering something quickly, I left him on my hopeless terrible quest, blown from corner to corner by the music of the dance. It is my fate, I thought: to follow her, to be near her if I can. As I went, the part of my mind which was not eyes tried to recall the sign I had had, the phrase, of which his last words had almost reminded me; but I could not, and in any event—while my eyes fixed her glowing face and my heart heard her name—I knew that it would be of no use to me now.

ELIZABETH BISHOP

In Prison

I can scarcely wait for the day of my imprisonment. It is then that my life, my real life, will begin. As Nathaniel Hawthorne says in *The Intelligence-Office*, "I want my place, my own place, my true place in the world, my proper sphere, my thing which Nature intended me to perform . . . and which I have vainly sought all my life-time." But I am not that nostalgic about it, nor have I searched in vain "all my life-time." I have known for many years in what direction lie my talents and my "proper sphere," and I have always eagerly desired to enter it. Once that day has arrived and the formalities are over, I shall know exactly how to set about those duties "Nature intended me to perform."

The reader, or my friends, particularly those who happen to be familiar with my way of life, may protest that for me any actual imprisonment is unnecessary, since I already live, in relationship to society, very much as if I were in a prison. This I cannot deny, but I must simply point out the philosophic difference that exists between Choice and Necessity. I may live now as if I were in prison, or I might even go and take lodgings near, or in, a prison and follow the prison routine faithfully in every detail—and still I should be a "minister without portfolio." The hotel-existence I now lead might be compared in many respects to prison-life, I believe: there are the corridors, the cellular rooms, the large, unrelated group of people with the different purposes in being there that animate every one of them; but it still displays great differences. And of course in any hotel, even the barest, it is impossible to overlook the facts of "decoration," the turkey carpets, brass fire-extinguishers, transom-hooks, etc., —it is ridiculous to try to imagine oneself in prison in such surroundings! For example: the room I now occupy is papered with a not unattractive wall-paper, the pattern of which consists of silver stripes about an inch and a half wide running up and down, the same distance from each other. They are placed over, that is they appear to be inside of, a free design of flowering vines which runs all over the wall against a faded brown background. Now at night, when the lamp is turned on, these silver stripes catch the light and glisten and seem to stand out a little, or rather, in a little, from the vines and flowers, apparently shutting them off from me. I could almost imagine myself, if it would do any good, in a large silver bird-cage! But that is parody, a fantasy on my real hopes and ambitions.

One must be *in*; that is the primary condition. And yet I have known of isolated villages, or island towns, in our Southern states, where the prisoners are not really imprisoned at all! They are dressed in a distinctive uniform, usually the familiar picturesque suit of horizontal black and white stripes with a rimless cap of the same material, and sometimes, but not always, a leg iron. Then they are deliberately set at large every morning to work at assigned tasks in the town, or to pick up such odd jobs for themselves as they can. I myself have seen them, pumping water, cleaning streets, even helping housewives wash the windows or shake the carpets. One of the most effective scenes that I have ever seen, for color-contrast, was a group of these libertine convicts, in their black and white stripes, spraying, or otherwise tending to, a large clump of tropical shrubbery on the lawn of a public building. There were several varieties of bushes and plants in the arrangement, each of which had either brilliantly colored or conspicuously marked leaves. One bush, I remember, had long, knife-like leaves, twisting as they grew into loose spirals, the upper side of the leaf magenta, the under an ochre yellow. Another had large, flat, glossy leaves, dark green, on which were scrawled magnificent arabesques in lines of chalk-yellow. These designs, contrasting with the bold stripes of the prison uniform, made an extraordinary, if somewhat florid, picture.

But the prisoners, if such they could be called,—there must have hung over their lives the perpetual irksomeness of all half-measures, of "not knowing where one is at." They had one rule: to report back to the jail, as "headquarters," at nine o'clock, in order to be locked up for the night; and I was given to understand that it was a fairly frequent occurrence for one or two, who arrived a few minutes too late, to be locked out for the night!—when they would sometimes return to their homes, if they came from the same district, or else drop down and sleep on the very steps of the jail they were supposed to be secured in. But this short-sighted and shiftless conception of the meaning of prison could never satisfy me; I could never consent to submit to such terms of imprisonment,—no, never!

Perhaps my ideas on the subject may appear too exacting. It may seem ridiculous to you for me to be laying down the terms of my own imprisonment in this manner. But let me say that I have given this subject most of my thought and attention for several years, and I believe that I am speaking not entirely from selfish motives. Books about imprisonment I like perhaps the best of all literature, and I have read a great many; although of course one is often disappointed in them in spite of the subject-matter. Take *The Enormous Room*. How I envied the author of that book! But there was something artificial about it, something that puzzled me considerably until I realized that it was due to the fact that the author had had an inner conviction of his eventual release all during the period of his imprisonment,—a flaw, or rather an airbubble, that was bound by its own nature to reach the surface and break. The same reason may account for the perpetual presence of the sense of humor that angered me so much. I believe that I like humor as well as the next person, as they say, but it has always seemed a great pity to me that so many intelligent people now believe that everything that can happen to them must be funny. This belief first undermines conversation and letter-writing and makes them monotonous, and then penetrates deeper, to corrupt our powers of observation and comprehension—or so I believe.

The Count of Monte Cristo I once enjoyed very much, although now I doubt that I should be able to read it through, with its exposure of "an injustice," its romantic tunnel-digging, treasure-hunting, etc. However, since I feel that I may well be very much in its debt, and I do not wish to omit or slight any influence, even a childish one, I set the title down here. *The Ballad of Reading Gaol* was another of the writings on this subject which I never could abide,—it seemed to me to bring in material that although perhaps of great human interest, had nothing whatever to do with the subject at hand. "That little tent of blue, Which prisoners call the sky," strikes me as absolute nonsense. I believe that even a keyhole of sky would be enough, in its blind, blue endlessness, to give someone, even someone who had never seen it before, an adequate idea of the sky; and as for calling it the "sky,"—we all call it the sky, do we not; I see nothing pathetic whatever about that, as I am evidently supposed to. Rather give me Dostoyevsky's *House of the Dead*, or *Prison Life in Siberia*. Even if there seems to have been some ambiguity about the status of prisoners there, at least one is in the hands of an authority who realizes the limitations and possibilities of his subject. As for the frequently published best-sellers by warders, executioners, turn-keys, etc., I have never read any of them, being determined to uphold my own point of view, and not wanting to introduce any elements of self-consciousness into my future behaviour that I could possibly avoid.

I should like a cell about twelve or fifteen feet long, by six feet wide. The door would be at one end, the window, placed rather high, at the other, and the iron bed along the side,—I see it on the left, but of course it could perfectly well be on the right. I might or might not have a small table, or shelf, let down by ropes from the wall just under the window, and by it a chair. I should like the ceiling to be fairly high. The walls I have in mind are interestingly stained, peeled, or otherwise disfigured; gray or whitewashed, blueish, yellowish, even green—but I only hope they are of no other color. The prospect of unpainted boards with their possibilities of various grains can sometimes please me, or stone in slabs or irregular shapes. I run the awful risk of a red brick cell; however, whitewashed or painted bricks might be quite agreeable, particularly if they had not been given a fresh coat for some time and here and there the paint had fallen off, revealing, in an irregular but bevelled frame (made by previous coats) the regularity of the brick-work beneath.

About the view from the window: I once went to see a room in the *Asylum of the Mausoleum* where the painter V——— had been confined for a year, and what chiefly impressed me about this room, and gave rise to my own thoughts on the subject, was the view. My travelling companion and I reached the Asylum in the late afternoon and were admitted to the grounds by a nun, but a family, living in a small house of their own, seemed to be in charge. At our calls they rushed out, four of them, eating their dinner and talking to us at the same time with their mouths full. They stood in a row, and at the end of it their little black and white kitten was busy scratching in the dirt. It was "an animated scene." The daughter, age eight, and a younger brother, each carrying and eating half a long loaf of bread, were to show us around. We first went through several long, dark, cellar-like halls, painted yellow, with the low blue doors of the cells along one side. The floors were of stone; the paint was peeling everywhere, but the general effect was rather solemnly pretty. The room we had come to see was on the ground floor. It might have been very sad if it had not been for the two little children who rushed back and forth, chewing their bites of white bread and trying to outdo each other in telling us what everything was. But I am wandering from my subject, which was the view from the window of his room: It opened directly onto the kitchen-garden of the institution and beyond it stretched the open fields. A row of cypresses stood at the right. It was rapidly growing dark (and even as we stood there it grew too dark to find our way out if it had not been for the children) but I can still see as clearly as in a photograph the beautiful completeness of the view from that window: the shaven fields, the black cypress, and the group of swallows posed dipping in the gray sky,—only the fields have retained their faded color.

As a view it may well have been ideal, but one must take all sorts of things into consideration and consoling and inspirational as that scene may have been, I do not feel that what is suited to an asylum is necessarily suited to a prison. That is, because I expect to go to prison in full possession of my "faculties,"—in fact it is not until I am securely installed there that I expect fully to realize them,—I feel that something a little less rustic, a little harsher, might be of more use to me personally. But it is a difficult question, and one that is probably best decided, as of course it must be, by chance alone.

What I should like best of all, I might as well confess, would be a view of a court-yard paved with stone. I have a fondness for stone court-yards that amounts almost to a passion. If I were not to be imprisoned I should at least attempt to make that part of my dream a reality; I should want to live in a farm house such as I have seen in foreign countries, a farm house with an absolutely bare stone platform attached to it, the stones laid in a simple pattern of squares or diamonds. Another pattern I admire is interlocking cobble-stone fans, with a border of larger stones set around the edge. But from my cell window I should prefer, say, a lozenge design, outlined by long stones, the interior of the lozenges made of cobbles, and the pattern narrowing away from my window towards the distant wall of the prison-yard. The rest of my scenery would be the responsibility of the weather alone, although I should rather face the east than the west since I much prefer sunrises to sunsets. Then, too, it is by looking towards the east that one obtains the most theatrical effects from a sunset, in my opinion. I refer to that fifteen minutes or half an hour of heavy gold in which any object can be made to look magically significant. If the reader can tell me of anything more beautiful than a stone court-yard lit obliquely in this way so that the shallowly rounded stones each casts a small shadow but the general surface is thickly sanded with gold, and a pole casts a long, long shadow and a limp wire an unearthly one,—I beg him to tell me what it is.

I understand that most prisons are now supplied with libraries and that the prisoners are expected to read the *Everyman's Library* and other books of educational tendencies. I hope I am not being too reactionary when I say that my one desire is to be given one very dull book to read, the duller the better. A book, moreover, on a subject completely foreign to me; perhaps the second volume, if the first would familiarize me too well with the terms and purpose of the work. Then I shall be able to experience with a free conscience the pleasure, perverse, I suppose, of interpreting it not at all according to its intent. Because I share with Valery's *M. Teste* the "knowledge that our thoughts are reflected back to us, too much so, through expressions made by others"; and I have resigned myself, or do I speak too frankly, to deriving what information and joy I can from this—lamentable but irremediable—state of affairs. From my detached rock-like book I shall be able to draw vast generalizations, abstractions of the grandest, most illuminating sort, like allegories or poems, and by posing fragments of it against the surroundings and conversations of my prison, I shall be able to form my own examples of surrealist art!—something I should never know how to do outside, where the sources are so bewildering. Perhaps it will be a book on the cure of a disease, or an industrial technique,—but no, even to try to imagine the subject would be to spoil the sensation of wave-like freshness I hope to receive when it is first placed in my hands.

Writing on the Wall: I have formulated very definite ideas on this important aspect of prison life, and have already composed sentences and paragraphs (which I cannot give here) I hope to be able to inscribe on the walls of my cell. First, however, even before looking into the book mentioned above, I shall read very carefully (or try to read, since they may be partly obliterated, or in a foreign language) the inscriptions already there. Then I shall adapt my own compositions, in order that they may not conflict with those written by the prisoner before me. The voice of a new inmate will be noticeable, but there will be no contradictions or criticisms of what has already been laid down, rather a "commentary." I have thought of attempting a short, but immortal, poem, but I am afraid that is beyond me; I may rise to the occasion, however, once I am confronted with that stained, smeared, scribbled-on wall and feel the stub of pencil or rusty nail between my fingers. Perhaps I shall arrange my "words" in a series of neat inscriptions in a clear, Roman print; perhaps I shall write them diagonally, across a corner, or at the base of a wall and half on the floor, in an almost illegible scrawl. They will be brief, suggestive, anguished, but full of the lights of revelation. And no small part of the joy these writings will give me will be to think of the person coming after me,—the legacy of thoughts shall leave him, like an old bundle tossed carelessly into a corner!

Once I dreamed that I was in Hell. It was a low, Netherlands-like country, all the marsh-grass was a crude artificial green, lit by brilliant but almost horizontal sunlight. I was dressed in an unbecoming costume of gray cotton: trousers of an awkward length and a shirt hanging outside them, and my hair cut close. I suffered constantly from extreme dizziness, because the horizon (and this was how I knew I was in Hell) was at an angle of forty-five degrees. Although this useless tale may not seem to have much connection with my theme, I include it simply to illustrate the manner in which I expect my vision of the outside world to be miraculously changed when I first hear my cell door locked behind me, and I step to the window to take my first look out.

I shall manage to look just a little different in my uniform from the rest of the prisoners. I shall leave the top button of the shirt undone, or roll the long sleeves half-way between wrist and elbow,—something just a little casual, a little Byronic. On the other hand, if that is already the general tone in the prison, I shall affect a severe, mechanical neatness. My carriage and facial expression will be influenced by the same motive. There is, however, no insincerity in any of this; it is my conception of my role in prison life. It is entirely a different thing from being a "rebel" outside the prison; it is to be unconventional, rebellious perhaps, but in shades and shadows.

By means of these beginnings, these slight differences, and the appeal (do not think I am boasting here, or over-estimating the power of details, because I have seen it work over and over again) of my carefully subdued, reserved manner, I shall attract to myself one intimate friend, whom I shall influence deeply. This friend, already an important member of the prison society, will be of great assistance to me in establishing myself as an authority, recognized but unofficial, on the conduct of prison life. It will take years before I become an *influence*, and possibly, —and this is what I dare to hope for, to find the prison in such a period of its evolution that it will be unavoidable to be thought of as an *evil influence*. . . . Perhaps they will laugh at me, as they laughed at the Vicar of Wakefield; but of course, just at first, I should like nothing better!

Many years ago I discovered that I could "succeed" in one place, but not in all places, and never, never could I succeed "at large." In the world, for example, I am very much under the influence of dress, absurd as that may be. But in a place where all dress alike I have the gift of being able to develop a "style" of my own, something that is even admired and imitated by others. The longer my sentence, although I constantly find myself thinking of it as a life-sentence, the more slowly shall I go about establishing myself, and the more certain are my chances of success. Ridiculous as it sounds, and is, I am looking forward to directing the prison dramatic association, or being on the base-ball team!

But in the same way that I was led to protest against the ambiguity of the position of those prisoners who were in and out of prison at the same time (I have even seen their wives washing their striped trousers and hanging them on the line!) I should bitterly object to any change or break in my way of life. If, for example, I should become ill and have to go to the prison infirmary, or if shortly after my arrival I should be moved to a different cell,—either of these accidents would seriously upset me, and I should have to begin my work all over again.

Quite naturally under these circumstances I have often thought of joining our Army or Navy. I have stood on the side-walk an hour at a time, studying the posters of the recruiting-offices: the oval portrait of a soldier or sailor surrounded by scenes representing his "life." But the sailor, I understand, may be shifted from ship to ship without so much as a by-your-leave; and then too, I believe that there is something fundamentally uncongenial about the view of the sea to a person of my mentality. In the blithe photographs surrounding the gallant head of the soldier I have glimpsed him "at work" building roads, peeling potatoes, etc. Aside from the remote possibilities of active service, those pictures alone would be enough to deter me from entering his ranks.

You may say,—people have said to me—you would have been happy
in the more flourishing days of the religious order, and that, I imagine, is
close to the truth. But even there I hesitate, and the difference between
Choice and Necessity jumps up again to confound me. "Freedom is
knowledge of necessity"; I believe nothing as ardently as I do that. And I
assure you that to act in this way is the only logical step for me to take. I
mean, of course, to be acted *upon* in this way is the only logical step for
me to take.

LOUISE BOGAN

Journey Around My Room

The most advantageous point from which to start this journey is the bed itself, wherein, at midnight or early in the morning, the adventurous traveller lies moored, the terrain spread out before him. The most fortunate weather is warm to cool, engendered by a westerly breeze, borne from the open window toward the ashes in the grate. At midnight, moonlight lies upon the floor, to guide the traveller's eye; in the early morning, the bleak opacity that serves the traveller in this region as sun brightens the brick wall of the house across the yard, and sheds a feeble reflected glow upon all the objects which I shall presently name.

This is a largish room, almost square in shape. It faces east and west, and is bounded on the north by the hall, which leads, after some hesitation, to the kitchen; on the south by someone's bedroom in the house next door; on the west, by backyards and the Empire State Building; on the east, by Lexington Avenue, up and down which electric cars roll with a noise like water running into a bottle. Its four walls are chastely papered with Manila paper. Its floor is inadequately varnished. Its ceiling bears all the honors away: it is quite lofty in pitch, and it is clean, absolutely unspotted, in fact, save for a little damp over the fireplace, which, from some angles, looks like a fish. A fireplace, resembling a small black arch, occupies a middle position in the south wall. Above it, a plain deal mantelpiece of ordinary design supports a row of books, a photograph of the News Building taken from the Chanin Building, four shells from a Maine beach, and a tin of Famous Cake Box Mixture. Above these objects hangs a Japanese print, depicting Russian sailors afflicted by an angry ocean, searchlights, a burning ship, and a boatload of raging Japanese.

The initial mystery that attends any journey is: how did the traveller reach his starting point in the first place? How did I reach the window, the walls, the fireplace, the room itself; how do I happen to be beneath this ceiling and above this floor? Oh, that is a matter for conjecture, for argument pro and con, for research, supposition, dialectic! I can hardly remember how. Unlike Livingstone, on the verge of darkest Africa, I have no maps to hand, no globe of the terrestrial or the celestial spheres, no chart of mountains, lakes, no sextant, no artificial horizon. If ever I possessed a compass, it has long since disappeared. There must be, however, some reasonable explanation for my presence here. Some step started me toward this point, as opposed to all other points on the habitable globe. I must consider; I must discover it.

And here it is. One morning in March, in the year 1909, my father opened the storm door leading from the kitchen to the backsteps, on Chestnut Street, in Ballardvale, a small town in Massachusetts, on the Boston & Maine Railroad. A bare March sky with wind in its shed its light over the street; the gutters ran with melted snow under ice as thin as a watch crystal; last year's maple leaves lay matted on the lawn. My father and I walked down the hill toward the station, and said "Hello, how are you today" to Mr. Buck, to Mr. Kibbee, and to Stella Dailey. Old Jack Leonard had backed his horse up in front of Shattuck's store. A bag of potatoes, a ten-gallon kerosene can, and a black hound sat in the wagon, and a yellow cigar ribbon, tied to the whipstock, fluttered in the cold air. Across the tracks, the willows by the bridge let fall into the foaming water a mist of reddening boughs. The mill dam roared. The windows of the mill sparkled in the March sunlight falling without warmth. The station platform was empty. Above our heads the station master's wife shook her duster out the window, under the scalloped eaves. On this platform, for nine hundred mornings, I have said goodbye to my father, and each morning he has given me a kiss smelling of cigar, and a penny, and I have looked carefully at the Indian on the penny's head, and at the wreath on its tail, and have remarked the penny's date. But now I am older, no longer at the age when one looks at the dates on pennies. I am going away. I shan't ever see again old Leonard, or Shattuck's store, or the hydrangea bushes in front of Forrest Scott's house that in autumn spilled dusty-blue petals over the grass, or the mill dam, or the mill, or the swing in Gardners' yard, or the maple tree in my own, or the hedge of arbor vitae around the Congregationalist church. Or hear, in the night, the express whistling for the crossing, or, in the daytime, the Boston train, and the train for Lawrence and Lowell, braking down for the stop, ringing its bell around the curve. Now, this morning, the Boston train is coming in from the fields beyond the river, and slows and brakes and stops. The steam shrieks out of the engine and smoke trails out, into the clear morning, from the smokestack, blotting out the willows and the mill dam. The conductor lifts me up to the step. That is the reason for my presence here. I took the Boston train in March, 1909.

Granted, then, that the traveller is here for an assigned, an established reason, the journey may proceed due west by slow degrees from the fireplace. Here I come upon two chairs that look worn to the bone, and a large, square green bureau, in execrable modern taste. The surface of this last is scattered over with objects of little real or artistic value. A sharp turn to the right brings me to the window, giving onto the brick wall before mentioned, and tastefully draped in dotted swiss. Then the entire west wall unrolls before the eye. The window is flaked to the immediate northwest by two pictures: one of a thunderstorm, and the other of a small bunch of violets. I then come upon a hanging shelf whose well-proportioned but inadequate interior can house nothing larger than a 16mo. So that here all the 16mos in the apartment lie down together, the lion and the lamb: "La Madone des Sleepings," "Apologia Pro Vita Sua," Whitehead's "Introduction to Mathematics"; the poems of Baudelaire, William Drummond of Hawthornden, Waller; the plays of Chekhov and Thomas Middleton; "Walden; or, Life in the Woods"; "The Turn of the Screw," Montaigne's Essays, and "Taras Bulba." Beneath this truly horrifying array of literature is situated a large and comparatively unused desk, on which stand displayed pictures of myself and several other people, a pot of pencils, largely decayed, a cashbook that serves as a bill file, an inkstand that serves as a letter file, and a letter file that serves as a bill file. Also a lamp, an ashtray, a stamp box (empty), two postcards, a paper knife made out of a cartridge and bearing the arms of the city of Verdun, and a large quantity of blank paper.

The north wall contains nothing of interest save the bed and the traveller moored therein, a table, a lamp, and a picture of a water jug, a bowl, two lemons, and a pear (by Vlaminck). The east wall, on the other hand, is filled by an object of immense interest and charm, an object that combines service and beauty in unequal parts. It is an armoire; within its doors lie shirts, towels, pillowcases, and sheets, but the doors themselves—what serviceable quality could dare to compete in importance with this beauty! Vertically, along the edges of the doors, carved from wood, two garlands fall, composed of roses, rose leaves, pine cones, grapes, sunflowers, bursting figs, and lobster claws. The size, the stability of this piece (which has been lent to me by a friend until such time as she can find a purchaser for it), should hearten the traveller. On the contrary, it is at this point, precisely when the end is in sight, and the starting point almost gained, that the catastrophe of the journey invariably occurs.

For it is here, as I nearly complete the circle set, that at midnight and in the early morning I encounter the dream. I am set upon by sleep, and hear the rush of water, and hear the mill dam, fuming with water that weighs itself into foam against the air, and see the rapids at its foot that I must gauge and dare and swim. Give over, says this treacherous element, the fear and distress in your breast; and I pretend courage and brave it at last, among rocks along the bank, and plunge into the wave that mounts like glass to the level of my eye. O death, O fear! The Universe swings up against my sight, the universe fallen into and bearing with the mill stream. I must in a moment die, but for a moment I breathe, upheld, and see all weight, all force, all water, compacted into the glassy wave, veined, marbled with foam, this moment caught raining over me. And into the wave sinks the armoire, the green bureau, the lamps, the shells from the beach in Maine. All these objects, provisional at best, now equally lost, rock down to translucent depths below fear, an Atlantis in little, under the mill stream (last seen through the steam from the Boston train in March, 1909).

JEAN GARRIGUE

The Snowfall

She was very good-looking: anyone would have to admit that. But her good looks had come to her as a surprise for even through high school she had been thin and sharp-faced. The chagrin of her looks had so impressed her then that she had really never had time to adjust to the new face in her mirror. She still really saw a girl with big cat eyes and a cat-thin face, straw-colored hair lying in wispy uncertainties over the top of her head where sharp ears should have stayed. Her good looks had, in fact, come late: not really appeared until she was twenty-one or so. Suddenly then the hungry boniness of her had disappeared: her shoulders seemed less narrow and hunched, there were amazing tendernesses of contour at the waist, her hair had deepened in color and she had let it grow long.

She had gone through high school and college indifferent and cold, scornful of the tomfool, meaty boys so interested in games and machinery. At twenty she was still actually a child: her social vanities needed no reassurance for she was trying to be a good painter and succeeding—her teachers praised her. But then she had grown up into beauty. It made a great change in her life. She met Tom, who was determined to take her over and scout the nonsense out of her head. They spent an out-of-door summer together. She was good with a gun and had no squeamishness about breaking one syllable of a sparrow's note in two, bursting it midway in air. She was even better than Tom and he had gone to military school and worn royal blue capes! This prowess which—it is true—she bragged of, irritated him and he had set out to break her will in other ways: he realized that she was aloof, physically, not caring to be touched. So he was determined to get her that way, and he did. He was absolutely

21

ruthless and remorseless, he did not care if he nearly broke her arms and
when she would bite him because there was nothing else she could do, he
was filled with such a pleasant rage that he nearly loved her more than
ever.

She herself was painfully and bitterly confused, for she was able to
mock him intellectually, to deplore his tastes and ambitions, and yet to
welcome the savagery that exerted itself between them. Not that she ever
admitted that she liked his callous way of saying: "Yes, you will," but the
tension was harshly alive and exciting. Couldn't she admit that? It was
exciting. She liked, suddenly, the contours of his mouth: heavy and wide,
his hair falling flat over his eyes, the strange fur on his shoulders and
back that made her feel as if she were touching a beast.

But the struggle exhausted her—this pure blank hatred she felt for
him because he managed to be stronger than she and could pin her down
like any sickly insect—and yet, on the other hand, this desire to struggle
with him that her hatred might be inflamed so that later it could be
subdued. Well, wasn't that it?

It worried her, as well, that there was no sweetness attached to her
feelings: no kind of joy. He tormented her, taunted her, bullied her; he
never spoke of her painting and she never permitted him to see anything
she had done, as if that would be a last sacrilege. It was not until after
she had known him for a year that it occurred to her that there was
really a kind of immorality at hand, that she was bossed by him not
because *she* loved him or even desired him, but because some black
motion in her drove her toward him. Once she realized this, she considered it as an abasement and then at last was able to break it off. But the
need for reassurance by the male had become a hunger she could not do
without, and she had a series of affairs: getting great gifts, records and
fountain pens and books.

This energy of interest served to extrovert her. She had not become
proud of her looks but interested in them as if they were some distant
favor conceded to her, like a newly discovered and romantic relation. Yet
profoundly at heart she remained celibate and distrustful, distrustful not
of those boys she knew who were incapable, in fact, of tricking or shocking her, for she had made certain, after Tom, to pick those more tract-
able; but distrustful of the good of the feelings they aroused in her.

She was wary, alert, high-strung, in short, a light sleeper, subject to
sudden disorders, and picked at her food. On parting with Tom she had
developed an illness that puzzled two doctors. They hesitated, actually,
to call it only "nerves" and had put her to bed for a month. During that
time she had wept regularly, had been unable to sleep or eat, had lain
back against herself, a light shadow on the substantial bed, her lids
protecting her eyes. "What is it, what is it, can't you tell me, if only you
would tell me!" her father implored. He had taught her to beat him at

tennis and shoot better than Tom. He took a presumptuous, passionate interest in her.

But she had not known herself: shaking her head slowly, as the tears seeped vulgarly out, the color of lilac or shadow, she had not been able to say.

She had met Nicholas in Chicago where she was teaching in a private school and at first she had believed that she might very possibly be able to love him. For he was an artist: she no longer had the problem of trying to make herself understood: he knew what subtleties might awake that gratitude so infrequent in her, and counted on the small: the flower or a print, the right silence, to accost her with the appreciation that was the nearest to love she had come. He was not always yearning at her feet. He was intelligent and immensely talented: a violinist, he played in the Symphony. This was the first man worthy of her, she might admit to herself! She had scorned and ridiculed those others until they had learned to ridicule themselves.

How near she was to love for Nicholas! But what was it—at some mysterious last point the reservation had to be made, the dread qualification. "I love you, however . . ." However, it was true that he was plain and underfed. However, it was true that she admitted once to a friend that she could not quite see taking him into a nightclub. But you never go to nightclubs, her friend answered, and that was true, she never did. She should be ashamed for making so feeble an excuse! Then what was it? What was it that stopped in her, on the threshold of declarations? She had no virginal reluctances, no qualms about committing herself to the long escapade of a love affair, bout after bout, sorty and sally and volley of wills. What was it that balked like the mule at that suggestion of the permament? She could not say, except that it was the instant that had always moved her, never the funereal threat of continuity. It was the necessity of the endowed instant. As if music were suddenly remembered inside her when the right time for wooing occurred, when she, that is, willed it. She realized that the immense virtue of Nicholas lay in just his sensitivity to her: he actually waited for her first stalking move. His love was so strong and fearful that he dared not risk forcing what he valued upon her. She had to be willing and ready: he had to be sure of the fact. She had become, in her own nervous and resonant way, her own clanging, brisk and jaunty, cocksure fashion, the male and he the compliant, watchful, studious female. He reflected, then, her directions, and it was his task and cleverness to do so. This she immensely admired, and for the first time in her relations with any man felt strong and free. Luckily, too, he tempered his praise of her with occasional outbursts of chill and spare invective. She was not the bitch and louse of criticism's usual hurt spendthrifty. Those criticisms were but another way of expending admiration!

and demanded but laughter or the return of insult: bloody, murderous hacking: "You've got nothing in your head." "You're cold and dull." "You fool, you."

But his was reflective, bony comment. She feared his insights because they came from profundities in him that shamed her. She wished she could see him so clearly. It made her feel jealous and slightly inferior. At the same time, it was a consolation (despite her resentment of it) to know that he so had her "interests at heart." She really felt that he knew her better than she knew herself with whom she lived so irregularly. She asked him advice as she might have asked her father had he glossed her with as much clarity of love.

Yet she had taken the job at Yellow Springs, had precipitantly, in the month of September, left Nicholas to be alone in a small town to teach young girls the amenities of water colors.

In her heart she was fearful of going. Once she had made the decision she seriously wondered why she did not stay in Chicago and marry Nicholas. She did not really want to be alone. She felt that she should be but she did not want to be. She was forcing herself into a difficulty. And yet the decision was not a calculated one. A restlessness had made the decision. It awoke her at night and turned her from Nicholas. It criticized and belittled. It made Nicholas a foreign, slavish little dog. It detached her from him, making her cool to his enthusiasms. It made her think: no, this isn't my life yet. Besides, his parents hate me (which was true) and my parents think he is a lame duck (which was also true). It forced all kinds of ridiculous, out of the way and untrue judgments upon her. But in the end it remained that she had to get away.

She was even prepared to hate Yellow Springs. But that inland, sweetened country took her by surprise. It was morning-like and new. She felt that for a long while she could be content with her new, abstemious life: living in a girlish room in somebody's house, teaching classes and holding conferences, painting and saving her money so that soon she could take a year off and study seriously in New York. (Nicholas would come too.)

For as she had grown up belatedly and with a certain amount of aversion to the process, so she had timidly approached her talent, one hand held in back of her. Time? She had an infinite amount of it and as for those powers in herself—well, she firmly and uncritically believed that life would see to it that she deepened and darkened. So, at the age of twenty-three, she was not yet ready for the responsibilities of her desires and possibly Nicholas' eager willingness to assume responsibility for her, to wrap her around with his verities and hopes and to support her intellectually by all the thinking he had done on history, poetry and philosophy, had driven her from him. Possibly she had feared that she might not grow up with him. Possibly she feared that his love stood between her and the blows actuality had not yet given her. For she did fear the laziness in her that might prevent her from feeling all that she should feel. Oh, she had fine ways of protecting herself from the full consequences of situations! A healthy convenience for black-outs! How well the obdurate memory failed when the ego could profit therefrom!

Well, looking back upon it now, walking through the bitter-bright rindy leaves of first windfall, she could not really understand why she had left Nicholas. He had been the first not to force reproaches upon her, not to make her feel that she was lacking in primal femininities. Looking back over the laundry list, the library catalog of boys she had known since that unlucky initiation with Tom, she realized that she had permitted all of them to make love to her so that afterwards she would be unable to forgive them for it. But with Nicholas that action had not seemed a disguise for the attainment of blunt supremacy. But especially! she had not felt humiliated by being exposed to her own coldness. At last she did not feel that she was being the dupe of others' desires, the ready jewel-eyed player queen, a stake for others but heartless to herself. So she could then "afford" to be kind to him, could then relax for the first time, since she trusted him. The competitiveness and hostility, the sardonic allegations could be given back to their falsities. He loved what he saw and did not see. Indeed, how interesting to herself his love made her!

But yet—she had had to be free. His love still kept her away from the world. It was still the petition to her vanity, it was so pure and warm, so devoted and sorrowful—a kind of less complicated father-love.

Yes, she had bolted like a thief. Why did Nicholas allow her to go so easily? Possibly because he had reasoned: she is going to a small college town, to teach in a girls' school where they specialize in horseback riding and by the end of the year, after having met only young faculty darlings who sway as they walk, and young well-wived husbands and old salt and pepper deans, and having seen America's sons of the filling station and fire department, ruddy, agog young men born on another planet, she may know that, after all, is is I she has been searching for all her life and I who have accounted for all her unusual lonelinesses in the middle of her fashionable popularities.

And, parting with her, he casually turned over to her his battered but racy and strong Ford coupé. I would simply be paying garage rent here, you know, he said. Now that you won't be here to take rides I'll practice instead. What about other girls, Nicholas? she asked. They can walk, he said.

He wrote her daily, long journal-like letters. Sometimes he felt that he was the curator of a remarkable bird, the last of its species! Would not this account for his watchfulness? But the bird in order to live must go away, must understand more of the world before it could thrive in the great cage of air where he had willed that it must "settle." It must not be hungry for freedoms whose emptinesses it had never tested.

Yes, watchful Nicholas was also cunning, with the foresight and insight of great desire. It was as if his humility and generosity were not character traits but mere extracts and, at the same time, mere placations of the necessity she had become to him. Her ignorant wilfulness, her errancies—merely the excess of her charm! The headstrong moodiness with which she protected her sensitivities—it had frightened all away from that which she truly was. Let him be the Pygmalion to startle her soul!

And she, walking on streets of little houses where pear leaves, dark brown and red, like pyres of light were heaped, was happy and at peace. His letters like literature came, budding with comparison of her to the dark summer. It was wonderful to be away from him and to have only his letters, his thoughts and her memories. Could she not see him now in his true magnificence? She need never look up to find his eyes, full-lidded, mournful and black in the boniness of his face, fixed on her with an expression that was—really—spaniel-like. The way he dressed need not disparage him now—those shirts with flabby collars, the trousers that were always too long and the coat that made his shoulders narrow. Some people could not learn to dress. Nicholas was one. It was the same with his room. Cigarette ashes and dust. Unwashed milk bottles. Discarded razor blades. Month-old newspapers. Torn window blinds. And yet he lavished such care on a phrase, he would work hours to perfect a trill. There was no correlation, she knew, as he had told her. Nevertheless, it disturbed her, and always his slight smell of violinist's nervous sweat, the way he could get his fingers ashy putting out a cigarette! But now, in the absence of those irritations perhaps she could begin to see him with the joy of the soul's eye, she thought, having been educated by him to this.

And indeed she did. She even considered seriously for the first time fidelity. More than that, his ever-recurring appearance by letter fed and sustained her, an aerial diet delicately intoxicating! She went from letters to classes, zestful and proud, and, walking on the old Victorian campus, thought for the first time: I can really dispense with all but the world! Watching the bees stupefied by the rank sweetness of pears gone soft and brown, and grapes in arbors split open by the warmth of the sun, she was tenderly content as if the autumn promised improbable happiness she did not have to run to.

She went to her first party in Yellow Springs with a red-haired Professor of Radio, a spotty, conceited character lording it over with his voice as if every individual were a crowd. On meeting her he had decided immediately that she was to be his girl for the year. And she, observing distantly the standard ways he took to indicate his liveliness, thought: how it is that once I took pride in leading a fool by the nose?

At the party she was introduced to Luke Banford, who sat on a thin chair in a corner, idly fiddling with a pad of paper on which, as she noticed quickly, he had drawn a few caricatures. On seeing him in a gray checked suit which fitted so aptly his moderate tallness and flatness, on seeing his hair, black as a seal's wet fur, his high, polished dark forehead, his eyes, aloof and steely as a bird's with a glance that cut because of its brilliance, his full, wide mouth, so amply balanced and darkly molded, she felt a sudden anger of distaste. Male beauty, made by a watchmaker!

The party bored her and she soon acquired a headache. Do let us go, she said to the Professor who had been cracking jokes with Banford which she had not bothered to listen to. I suggest we all take a ride, the Professor said munificently. What about Starr Lake? It's the last night of Indian Summer they say. She looked up warily to intercept Banford's black glance like ice. Why not? he said, looking at her without smiling. She noticed then a deep, blunt scar on his forehead.

But she said: "Why not?" and turned away. The dark man flushed and the Professor frowned. A moment later he drew her away into the center of the room and said: "Hey, take it easy. He's really a nice guy. I knew him in New York."

"Then what's he doing in Yellow Springs?" she asked.

"He was in a crack-up last year. His wife was killed."

"A sad story," she said.

Riding in the Professor's roadster, a hostage between the two men, the Professor leaning warmly toward her, Banford drawn tautly into a corner, she suddenly felt enormously energetic and cruel. As her father had squeezed through the barbarities and inanimities of domestic depressions and business failures by kidding Existence, so she at such times took it out on the world with a brazen, vaudeville wit. Usually her excitement came from ambivalences of tensions, deploying between the erotic and sudden confusing memories that enraged her. She felt herself to be on a ferris wheel then, circling, lifting and dropping over areas of the unknowable. Frightened, she laughed it off, reforming and socializing the nightmare. At such times she wished to turn on herself and kill or mutilate and so chose the world as a worthier object. Nicholas had hated her in such moods but Tom had always laughed with her. Now she noticed that the Professor did too, though he was awkwardly interrupting to lean across her to say to Banford: "She's really got a heart like ducksoup. She's the kind to want to stop a car if she hears some animal crying in the woods."

But even to this Banford, for all his wealthy politeness, scarcely responded and the Professor laughed alone but perhaps more out of relief than enjoyment, for usually he was a part of the world her surgical humor gashed.

But as they stood out in the wind by the lake her jokebook mood dropped away. She was aware of the handsome man's silence and remembered what Nicholas had said of those parties of malice: "It is a way of defaming the world." The wind roughly blew at her and she wished to run straight to the cold mouth of the water.

Sometimes she would meet Luke Banford on the campus. He walked Indian straight, stepping as lightly, with narrow feet, usually his wrist-watch hand in his pocket. He never wore a hat but the wind did not seem to touch him; his hair was always of a piece with his head, black and shining like mica, and his eyes so critical, so glittering beneath the evenness of his proud eyebrows. Occasionally he walked with her, but they never seemed to manage to say much—talking with him was like talking against a waterfall, difficult, as against frightful pressures he built up against her: of silence, of formality, the niceties of caution. She was ready to give it up, simply to pass him by briefly when they met. Besides, she thought, he must really be stupid. And she decided that he had no character.

Then she thought the more of Nicholas, hurrying to his image as if it were an icon in a corner. What an ample and noble life he lived! Always at the heart of sound! But she began to harry his image; she began to drive and hurry it. Less frequently would it appear between unexpected interstices of time, the rough dark head. And sometimes at night, thinking of him, she could find no flavor of joy at all. The image could then assume no life nor body of its own, could neither rustle with sound nor burn with light. My heart must be empty, she thought fiercely, putting her hand against it. And her mouth felt dry.

Suddenly the year began to hurry to its death. A cold wind one morning cut all the leaves down. Rain followed, to soil them. Midway from classes that afternoon she met Luke.

The melancholy of the day had quieted and humbled her. She shivered in the wind as she stood talking to him. He said: "Will you have a drink?" and took her by the arm. The warmth of his hard, delicate hand pierced through her coat and dress sleeves. The abrasive effect of his misfortune had, up till then, made him seem cold and self-insulated—as if by vanity, she had even thought! But now, walking in the sodden afternoon, he seemed less brittle, incalculably more free and direct with her. Perhaps the sadness of the rain!

And sitting with him in the dark light of a tavern she evasively looked from his scar to his mouth and then to his crisp collar. She noticed his fingers, pointed for a man, and the few small hairs on the back of his hand. Suddenly the sight of his scar pained her. The imper-

fection on perfection. And it seemed that from that short, blunt mark his
pain must flow. For surely his silences covered over a dark space of
what—some suffering no one could get to! And it seemed remarkable to
her that so handsome a man should be so dark and unreachable—so
alone, for instance, at the party!

The subtle and petty resentments she had held against him—those
neat marriages of color in ties and socks, the hardness of his head and
eye, the rebuke of his distant and impersonal indifference, were then
revoked. Looking at his scar, she began to marvel as if he had been
accused of some grotesquerie. Certainly it then distinguished him. Pity,
pity! This is what she exclaimed later. I learned to pity him!

As he was lighting her cigarette, his hand touched hers, and the
effect, as though he might have held the flame to her fingers, made her
heart freeze with subtle fear and anticipation. They talked in many
directions eagerly but carefully, until he said: "I had been planning to
leave this town until I met you."

She trembled but sipped her martini as if she were concealing a tear.
When finally she looked up at him his eyes were still on hers: black and
tense as an animal's. She could not see beyond their surfaces of light.
The black kept out the color of his thoughts.

From then on she saw him constantly, for dinner, for long walks, for
drives in Nicholas' Ford to the show parts of the state. Those with whom
she had been about to make friends she forgot had ever interested her.
She went from classes to him. His looks made him seem remarkable, like
some foreign trophy of war and honor. She felt that he wore armor,
delicate, invisible, and his aloneness gave her a superstitious belief in his
integrity. This exhilarated her because she felt that he had been
wounded.

He did not mention what had—as she understood from the Professor
—changed his life. He had only told her that he had moved around for
the last year, had been up and down the West Coast, in Wyoming, St.
Louis, all kinds of places he had never seen before. But it was those very
allusions, intensities of gaps between the unfinished accounts of years,
that touched her. What time she did not spend with him she spent in her
mind with him, finishing out his history, supplying connectives between
small anecdotes he related about Hartford, Connecticut, where he had
grown up and the year he'd gambled in Wall Street and lost his shirt.
But he treated his past gingerly as if it were unfriendly to him and so she
too politely pretended to herself that she did not wish to know about it.
Yet she conventionally wished him to move in her head sequentially
when actually he seemed to have been born from the scar on his forehead. His Spanish eyes and English nose. His sad, cool blood and hawk-
like heart.

In a month she was completely in love with him. It did not shock her when he asked her to marry him. She had been so taken by surprise that it seemed inevitable that at last she had pulled out of her sleeve the ace of hearts. In fact, for the first time in her life she did not think about herself. Luke's image completely objectified her. It concentrated her as well. All thought and emotion ran from her to him. She could have been fanatically happy. For at last she was directed, caught up in a single purity of attention and desire. But yet she would be threatened by tears as, sitting by Starr Lake on Saturday afternoons, geese flew over. Uncontrollable, unreasonable sadness! Was it because he was restless with his measly job and talked of Wall Street deals, thereby frightening her? She could only see money gained as money earned.

She wished to put her sadness to some practical cause. For her heart beat so fast, with such elation! And his delicate Indian tread, the steel in the center of his breast so compelled her to moody symbols. She dreamed of ways in which to paint him: with red silk scarves, a blasphemy of softness, tied round his throat.

In that month her looks changed. She grew rosy, and moved so tenderly that everyone remarked: She's a changed person—for one thing, always so gay! She put up her hair, which added a city dignity to her pointed, child-like face. But it was not that! A look in the eyes! The points of her pupils had been absorbed, as if she were always looking into the sun, and all the green of the iris suffused her glance.

Yes, for a month she had no time to think about herself and indeed continued to write to Nicholas as if nothing had happened to her or as if, rather, Luke had given her a new self which had nothing to do with the selves Nicholas had known. Then, in middle November, when he wrote her that he was coming down to see her, she awoke with a start and wired him that it was impossible for her to see him. After that she tried on several occasions to write him the letter that would cut him off from her but each letter was too blunt and exultant. She did not want to boast about her new-found happiness for then it seemed unreal. Actually, she did not want to talk about it at all. It was too private a revelation. When Nicholas finally called her long distance she was rude and stormy. He who had believed he could best keep her by leaving her alone when she made it clear that she wanted to be left alone, broke out into great anger and vowed that he was coming straight down to see what had happened to her. Freed by his rage, she was finally able to write him the letter that told him it was all over and that she was to be married soon. With that gesture she turned her back on all her past and made Luke the king of her eye.

Yet, had she not been able to pity him, who knows what would have happened? Pity was the solvent. The glamor of the automobile wreck! His wife killed by that! He, exempt, but not from remorse and pain, cast out like any wanderer by the guilt he felt. Yes! Pity for this aloof, metallic, glittering man who seemed, physically, as incorruptible as a statue, lent impulsiveness to caution. He was elusive. He was mysterious. He was not knowable because his very appearance so satisfied the eye that the eye wished to stop there, content with the secrecy and reserve that the beautiful must have for protection. As the thorn must safeguard and give dignity to its rose!

Commonplaces, homelinesses, like their cow-licks and ingenuously large ears, had been all the deeps of those she had known before she met Nicholas. Goodnesses and practicalities and shrewdnesses. That kind of single-hearted devotion, intent, possessive but also detached, she had known in Nicholas. But in Luke, there was the great feeling of the pit, that steep fall, that downward rush into perils and dangers, the gambled card, the risked life, the conquering contempt, the disdain, the destruction.

In a few weeks they were always together: she deserted her studio save for those occasions when he would come there to let her sketch him. He was in a dream, a masked dream, filled with loathing of what he had come to, teaching a class in radio in Yellow Springs after years of sail-boating off Long Island and commanding stone houses on the seacoast. But the sickness still so hidden by his hard breast she would cure, she believed. That sense of responsibility for so obscure a charge exalted her. And he was good to her in a purely self-absorbed and penitent way; he permitted himself to be taken care of by her. When suddenly he had to go to New York on business he accepted the loan of Nicholas' car and even some money she jokingly gave him although he had flushed and had said crisply: "My poor foolish proper girl."

The week that he was gone she hated the canvas color of the sky and the bare, ruined trees and could think only of the fanciful, proportioned life he would, with casual elegance, ordain for her. And when he returned, having wrecked Nicholas' car on the way, she was only so glad that he had not been hurt that she could not fret over the embarrassment, to say the least, of the loss.

Of course he did drive ninety miles an hour!

But the car could be repaired. "Think nothing of it," she said. "I don't."

Yet her effort to steel herself against such concern robbed for a while her joy of some of its energy. This did vex for she was immoderately anxious to have everything perfect between them. She was as determined to have him as perfect as he could be and what he had done and had been did seem, in many ways, an intrusion upon the joy his presence brought her. Simply to be in the same room with him! Whereupon she remembered that her mother had said to her: "I just like to be where you are." Ah, well! Then she had turned disdainfully away.

And as when she talked about her own childhood she did not expect

him to tell her about his, so she did not expect him to tell her why it had
been so necessary for him to go to New York. He had the most subtle
ways of keeping such areas of his life fenced off. A silence contacted
around him which anguished her but for which she had total respect. He
seemed, really, divested of background. She was certain that he had had
an easy boyhood but this was simply because he dressed so well and had
such fine, easy manners and, moreover, because he had such a talent for
letting money go by him, out the window of hopes! This scornful uncon-
sciousness about money worried her for she did feel that he might be the
sort of person to get himself into trouble over what he, in his piratical
dignity, deemed trifling, the care of bankclerks and prudential knaves.

So she had soon learned to live with a small, cold dread for him,
unnamable, based upon nothing but fluctuations of intuition. Those
fears accounted for sudden tendernesses toward him that were her own
miracle. She had never before been so human, so "womanly." But those
others had presented solid, impermeable surfaces; the face-hardened
opinion, the dogged conviction. She in her uncertainties had had to
proceed against such certitudes, her footing untenable on such resistant,
tensile bluffs. But he was dark shade, the cool and fear of subtle caves.
His silences were stony and hawk-like but softness also spread out from
them. There were things he did not want to say. There were strengths he
wished to preserve from glaring speech. He did not have to be anything
with her but a breathing thing: a dark object of blood and black hair
and bird-black, icy eyes.

Yet he saw that, at occasional parties, she did not drink too much,
and he studied minor landscapes of hers or those sketches she was always
making of him with long care and interest. "The sky is too cold here," he
would say, or "if you could make this corner more interesting, I should
like to hear the *sound* of the bells." "Now the value of El Greco's
crooked beards—you make this face too symmetrical." It was his own, a
fact both ignored.

Such criticisms seemed gilded. She saw him as the prince of good
taste. She admired the disinterestedness with which he listened to scraps
of her past: the rebellions at ten, the death of her grandmother, games in
which she had won all the marbles from little boys. He was not anxious
as Nicholas had been to verify an interpretation of her, painfully anxious to catch more light on the coils of her soul.

She invited him home for Christmas vacation. On Christmas Eve she
was so excited, so happy, for snow had begun to fall at twilight and late
that night they had gone out for a walk, running into bushes like children and throwing soft, tender bullets of snow at one another, that she
said to herself: I fear: this joy brings me too close to sorrow. And at three
o'clock that night had gone to his room, once her grandmother's.

"My dear!" he said, "this is incestuous," as he found her weeping beside him.

"Luke!" she begged, "do not leave me."

When Nicholas came down she was immediately outraged to see his dark face like her conscience against the general white.

"I hope you came to get your Ford," she said.

"You can keep the Ford. I wanted to see you."

"There's nothing worse than post-mortems. I said what I had to say in my letter."

"I know you did," he said, "but I didn't believe your truth. But it's true that you've changed. You're all dolled up. Let's see your finger nails."

He seized her hands. She tried to pull them away but he held on to them savagely. There was an intense, invisible motion about him. His rough, black hair looked uncombed. His shirt collar was, as usual, wilted and smudged. He looked into her face as if he held a bright light against it. She avoided his eyes and suddenly he let her hands go with a show of great disgust.

"Yes, I would say," he said methodically, "that there is a change. You have that well-loved look that pretty women around thirty so often get."

"You're insulting," she said.

"But where's the candidate?" he asked. "No pictures around?"

For a moment he paced up and down the room. How undersized and bony he looked! How shabby and hungry! She felt triumphant, thinking of Luke's long, flat and beautiful back, the wide wings of his shoulders. And his delicate, narrow ankles!

Suddenly Nicholas stood before her. "Why have you done this?"

"I am in love."

"But you have made a mistake," he said studiously. "There is only one for me and that is you and there is only one for you and that is me."

Her heart hardened. "I could never love you," she said.

"What does he want to give you? A house in Indian Hills?"

"Keep him out of it," she said fiercely.

"How could you have changed?" he asked thoughtfully. "I believed you wanted to be a painter. It seems you want to be a wife. Just a beautiful doll of a wife. Just a loving, fatuous spouse."

"Get out," she cried, pained and hurt.

"Now I have made you angry. But what have you done to me? You are going to make me suffer. I don't like that. Can you understand how I wish to protect myself and how I would do anything, anything, to make you realize that I am the one for you?"

"I have found the man I love," she said stonily.

"Was it such deception?" he asked, grimacing.

"Did I ever tell you I loved you?"

"But you might as well have. We might as well have been married. No one could have known you better than I! You allowed me to know you. All your miseries, ambitions and memories. If you can forget, do you think I can?"

"It was all a mistake."

He paled. "Then you are killing our two years. Two years is a great deal of space and time to kill. I don't think you will succeed."

"How dramatic you are."

He went on as if he did not hear her: "In the winter there is only One. Is it because the streets are so cold? The world shrivels up like an old orange. Passion becomes so inward, it is in all the pores and secret veins. It *is* the body. In the spring it is different when the world expands and goes outward. The wits of the heart get crafty then. Do you want me to forget you? Is that what you want?"

She looked at him hurriedly and then turned away. In her heart she could not find it possible to say yes! forget me! The way in which she knew her was a consolation! Even his ridiculous manner of treating her as a museum piece. Stay! Just that way! he had commanded her, just so against the light!

She looked out to the snow. Did she want him to forget her? He had discovered so much of herself for her.

He came up to her. She saw a heavy sorrow standing in his eyes. He took her by the shoulders. But the instant that his nervous touch was upon her she was glad. Oh, I cannot really love him, she knew. False sympathy! Senitimentality! He's nothing to me! He was never my soul. It's that he talked so well. His rhetoric bewitched me.

Please go! she said, and moved away from beneath his hands.

He said no more but looked at her. For a moment yet the reasonableness of his pain struggled with her. But suddenly realizing that what she wanted to do she did have the courage to do—but yet not want to do and cringed to do when he did not touch her but only looked at her—she said:

"Here are the keys to the Ford."

She threw them at his lank chest, and walked out of the room, leaving him there.

This then, more than anything, gave her completely and wholly over to Luke. She need not be obliged to remember Nicholas' nose when she admired Luke's; to think how both men were so dark, but Luke so golden dark and Nicholas so blackly dark, like a coal-miner; she need not remember that sometimes—such was the sad universality of language!—Luke said the phrase that Nicholas had once said.

But there was a difference! She felt obliged to consider the relation anew, from a distance. Nicholas' leavetaking had robbed her of some very imperceptible but dense and alive background. Now no one stood in the mirror but Luke and herself. That older, obscure penumbra of image, the subtle prod to her conscience, now gone, left her all the more dramatically alone when Luke was away. Now she was feverish, her body felt alone and abandoned. For two months the sun did not shine and Luke had resigned his job at Yellow Springs and had taken a job with the new radio station in her home town. It paid him better and he needed money, he jocularly confessed. He had debts in New York that might catch up with him.

But then he had turned around and bought a brisk and handsome second-hand roadster for them, as he put it. Every weekend he drove its wheels off to see her; two hundred miles each way. She knew how fast he drove and how destructive his impatience could be. But yet! the winter was so black and arid! What would she do without him? She had made no friends in Yellow Springs. She was absolutely dependent on him. The Professor, sternly disapproving of the choice she had made, avoided her. Two casual acquaintances—serious but charming young women—had said to her on separate occasions: "But he seems so superficial!" She had darkly thought that they had conspired together to present the same judgment to her, and had been bitterly offended as she had violently distrusted her father after he had said one night when Luke had gone out for cigarettes: "Are you sure he will make you happy?"

"Am I sure I will make him happy!" she had rejoined.

"No, my dear," he had begun with his best Polonius air, "a man does not depend on a woman for happiness. What a man wants is the difficult. He wants to fight. He wants to buck up against stone. He wants to feel his courage and muscle. Now Luke: are you sure he wants that? Are you sure he isn't looking for the perpetual golf course?"

Oh, she could have turned upon him! She could have said: You old cotton-mouthed fool! You kill-joy you! But she had not. Her father, for all his insulting sententiousness, loved her piously and wanted to see her well married to a home, wanted for her all the safeties he had sought so feverishly, and all the dullnesses. But that he had dared to speak of Luke! No one dared use his name but as she allowed them to. Oh! to answer him, to say: You don't even know whom you're speaking of, please dismiss the subject, I will not have the ignorant speaking of what I love—it was rude, too shocking. It would rankle in her conscience afterward. Thank God, at that minute Luke had come back, the brim of his hat holding snow like daisies. "Darling!" he had exclaimed. And that word, fallen so clemently, with the effect of propitiation, between them, a word he rarely confessed to before her parents, exposed the full humiliation of the injustice done him. She had gone up to him, kissing him straight on the mouth, and had stood there, against the tight glances of the two. Luke had stiffened beneath her kiss, which had increased her anger that he should have had to feel its apology.

So she was alone and every Friday night he raced like a speed-king to her. She was alone but yet she could have begged him not to come. For every late Friday night she felt gripped by some agony as if the car were driving through her brain. Occasionally she dared say: "I hope you want to live long, Luke."

"I'm careful," he would state. "I'm an expert."

And then she would be blankly silent.

Yet what would she do, she asked herself, if he did not come every week? For she was quite alone. Nicholas had been right. In the winter there was only One. The world contacted to One. And she waited each Friday for his arrival so that she might come alive.

At first Luke had said: "Let's marry at Christmas." But then she agreed with him later on that it would be better to wait until the summer.

"Why not a house in Indian Hills for a while?" he suggested.

"Oh, Luke," she had replied, abashed. "What do you want from life?"

"You," he had answered conventionally. "I'm spoiled. You're really all I want."

But looking up with the instant delight that statement had borne, she was oppressed by the look in his eye which had not become more brilliant from the influence of those gold words, and as he drew her to him was disappointed by the regular clop of his heart and his beautiful, bitter odor.

And what did he mean, that he was spoiled? she thought anxiously, remembering much later that quality of his voice which seemed to come through from another time, as if the words were too well known to him, through which, it could seem, another voice was speaking? Or was it merely the repetition of that ironic malice he had employed once before when he had said to her as she stood in a doorway in a green dress, putting up her hair: "How strong you are! It doesn't matter if I'm weak, does it?"

It was afterward that she thought: why did he choose February? Of all months dead in the calendar, when hope had been exhausted by the winter, when the long effort against the withering cold had all but mummied the flesh and the heart could do no more than keep up its life against the north, of all times, why had he told her then that it was not his wife who had been killed in the accident but a girl he had been in love with and that it was her death that had nearly knocked him in and that his wife was still in New York.

Oh, Luke! she had said. Oh! the lie! she had thought. The dishonor! she had thought. He had said she must understand: how the story had got started that it had been his wife; the Professor had got it wrong.

"I never wanted to talk about it," he said. "He didn't hear it from me. It was my business. I didn't want the blabbings of others about that. Their questionable condolences: O my God, I've just heard . . . That's why I got away. Everyone saying: tough luck. Her mother. Her sisters."

"You loved her," she said.

He looked up as if she had, in that withdrawn moment, touched him. "Yes."

"Then you met me," she persisted quietly.

He had not heard her. Sweat was on his upper lip.

"It was all useless," he said, "useless."

"Luke, tell me," she said. "I've got to know."

"Oh, the filthy details," he said, striking at the table softly. "Icy road. March.

"She lived in New London. I'd gone up to see her. Sunday night I was going back to New York."

She waited.

"I wasn't going fast. There was a curve. I skidded. Another car was coming. It skidded. We all met. Of course she was with me. I was the only one in the whole bunch to get out alive."

She looked at his scar with horror but then had no more reactions.

A great snow fell. It was thick and strong and broke many branches. It fell steadily on Thursday, stopped on Friday, and began again on Saturday, when Luke was with her in her studio. It made the whole world look like the inside of a great soft tomb, and what Luke had told her was jailed in it. She felt stunned, but by the snow.

Yet she listened to him as she watched the white grains fall over the sky panes. Were they not falling through? Could the glass stop them? The world was white like the inside of a tomb.

He was saying that he would save money like hell and get a divorce in six months. Idly she thought: he exaggerates. It will take a year. And he will never save the money. He cannot save. He's a prince with money. I can save. I'll buy his divorce.

But she lifted her hand and let it fall, imitating the descent of one particular flake.

"I am not jealous of your wife," she said. "She's a legal dear."

He smiled uneasily.

She looked at him but preferred the snow flakes. They were brilliant. His face had gone inward. In the gray light those individually bright and sharp flakes made, his face was blurred as if a heavy beard covered it over.

"I'm jealous only of what is like myself," she went on. "What was your girl like, Luke? I think she was like myself."

"She was," he said.

"But she's faceless. What was the color of her eyes? Was she tall?

"Luke," she said, starting, "did you like me because I was like her?"

"O God," he said.

She saw that he was bored.

As well he might be! The girl was gone!

She wanted to weep because the girl had died uselessly. Luke had loved her, had he not? He had gone up to see her on weekends. The girl had loved him. She too had feared his recklessness and had driven back with him on that icy night. Simply to save him from excesses of speed. But she had not! And she had not saved him! He had concealed the noble fact of her death for so long!

"If I am like her, Luke," she said, "I'm not real, am I? I'm the second-hand parody of her."

"You're out of your head," he said, smiling, and trying to touch her hair.

She averted her head quickly. "How can you love me if you loved her?" she cried. "I'm jealous but she's more jealous! The jealousy of the dead is lasting!"

He sought to take her hands. "Anybody loves more than once."

"But there is only One!" she answered. "In the winter there is only One. But in the spring too. In the summer too when swimming is the season and the natural sensuality of the pleasure-seeking will."

He smiled, attempting to draw her close and away from such abstractions.

"No," she said, "she makes you dead too. She loved you and you should suffer and you've not and that makes you dead too."

But he was still smiling, attempting to take her hands.

"Nicholas was right," she said. "Go away, Luke, I am very tired."

"You're sick," he said. "You've got to have a fever."

"I love you," she answered, "but your girl haunts me and I love her more."

Obediently he left. She locked the door of the studio which the school had so kindly given her. The gray, philosophic light of the snow came down.

That girl's the mercury for my looking glass, she thought. Now I know how cold, how practical, how shrewd his heart. I see now how he cares for me, she thought. He cannot care, she thought, as I could not care. Love is the image of ourself until ourself destroys us.

And she wept for the perfect love of the girl and for the perfect love of Nicholas.

JOHN HOLLANDER

In the Creep Block,
One Was Observed . . .

There was no doubt about it. I personally thought that it was the clock that was rigged, but the majority view held for one of the skylights in the ceiling, and groups of men huddled together under the blank panels between the areas of leaded glass overhead as if to get out of a downpour. Particularly when anything peculiar was going on, on which occasions I would usually sit down on the floor, with my back against the wall, whistling all the verses of something and tapping on the floorboards. Sometimes I thought that it was the noise of the tapping that had landed me there in the first place. The other tapping, I mean; but looking back on it, it was probably the white cane that got me arrested.

The more authentic aluminum one (I had bought it weeks before at one of the five Truss and Surgical Supplies in the neighborhood) I had left in a cab on the previous day. The mirror sewn into the peak of my cap had shown such an engrossing sight in the front seat that I had completely forgotten the cane. Beside the driver were an oak barometer, lying on the seat, a ball of twine and what looked to be an odd volume of Pope's Homer. I was dividing my attention between holding my head at the proper angle and rolling my eyes up right, apparently unseeingly (I'd had to take off my smoked glasses in the cool darkness of the cab), and actually trying to puzzle out what the driver's little kit could possibly be *for*. By the time the cabby said "OK, Sixth and Alvarado," I could only push a bill at him, await his scrupulous return of change, go through all the jazz about pretending to feel out its denominations, and finally plunge across the hot expanse of sidewalk into the musical interior of QUIMBY'S A CLEAN PLACE TO EAT. Only halfway through my Quimburger and Thick Frappe did I remember the cane. But by then it would have been risky as well as too late to do anything about it.

But the next day I wanted to go out again. I got an old cane with a crook from the Salvation Army, carefully painted it white, made a broad band of red six inches up at the bottom, and out of some raffish impulse added two red rings on the handle. Then I laid out all my regalia: cane, heavy dark glasses, an old and ulcerous white enameled cup, and the sign that hung around my neck. On dirty yellow cardboard, lettered in labored Gothic script was the announcement "BLIND, BUT VERY MERRY." Fully turned out, I was free to work any well-crowded street with my most penetrating stare.

For a full, fixed, frank gaze is the moral equivalent, in public, of the private glance that steals visions through keyholes. In any open crowd of strangers, a certain kind of candid but relaxed staring is the most ill-advised of acts. It must be camouflaged to be effective. Walking, waiting, milling, hurrying or dawdling citizens meet your open gaze with various reactions; but the blushes, the raging, the sudden twitch of terror or sneer of resentment have in common one thing. They are the same signs of inner disturbance that the recipient of your stare might evidence when, sealed in his bright, tiled bathroom, fresh from the indulgence of some private and idiosyncratic little ritual, the medicine chest were to fly open, and a face (yours, or Harpo Marx's, for instance) were to appear through a sliding panel in its back, wearing a bland tool of studious concentration. Even at best, the citizen would turn away and then you would have to work up the stare all over again. Ronnie Gocart, who in my late childhood would share with me two blocks of homeward walk after school, used to advise me with confidential seriousness: "Always look 'em right in the snatch and then they can't turn away." I remember taking the advice very seriously, but it was some years before I realized that the young ladies in question probably thought, if anything, that I was staring at the ground as I trudged sloppily along. I mention this now only as an object lesson: here intention was thwarted; that it was successfully disguised was insufficient consolation, that they didn't turn away became unimportant.

But in Los Angeles I learned to see much through the mask of darkness. I never pretended to be blind in New York, for reasons that I still don't fully understand; but within a few weeks after I'd come West, the good weather would occasionally see me, like the eager subjects of the newspapers' inquiring photographers, in "various spots," tapping at long and aperiodic intervals, jingling the coins in my cup, studying faces and necks and shoes, among other things. And all this with no embarrassment or other harm. Was it for nothing that I had been reared in a real City, one of the very few, and that its priceless lessons had been taught me early? Glimpse: *Myself, fifteen, in high school. Running with a*

sweetly innocent cabal, reading coterie books but struggling for unneces-
sarily high marks and not getting laid at all at all. Listening to string
quartets in the dark (it was better that way). Now we are at a Stadium
concert: darkness is starting to curtain a not-long-since yellow sky. The
opening measures of the Rachmaninoff Paganini Variations *are greeted*
with scorn by those of us of more advanced views; the music dims under
the sound of a passing plane. Enter, a porky thug of a since-exhausted
vintage: Truman shirt, huaraches, little tummy pressing out against the
pleats of mocha slacks (what was he doing there?), crossing us awkwardly
to take his hard, stone seat. Some mutterings come from us; says thug:
"You wan' I should rap your teeth down your throat?" (Please, may
there be no real ugliness, here, now.) From us, nothing. He turns to
another, a stranger on his left: "And yours, too, shithead?" Other:
"What did I do? Why?" Openwork shoes (whose attribute I am eyeing
now with more practical calm; they are like the openwork privates of an
Etruscan, an Ajax' toe; I can stomp if it comes to anything): "BECAUSE
YOU'RE LOOKING AT ME." *My silent riposte, "Indeed, who isn't?" is*
now unneeded; the whole tempo has changed. A Person has become a
Scene, and it is all right to look. Huaraches has lost, and accepts the
stares of the surrounding benches. They are no longer the penetrating
public peeping that I am at this moment considering for the first time:
"Because you're looking at me," the urban slight when administered
under all but decreed occasions. Only at what are properly spectacles is it
all right to look. A drunk shouts obscenities at a busdriver, a baby is
smashed in a revolving door, a suicide on a ledge discovers that she really
isn't one and dies by what is, in the last analysis, an accident. It's okay to
look, lady. But don't look at me.

Hence, in later years, my blindness, that I might better see. I don't
want to traffic in paradox, if I can at all help it. But there it is: seeing is
a funny thing at best. Whatshisname unscrews his 20–20 eyes, after he
knows what he couldn't possibly have known all along, and says:
"Thanks, I can see better without them." "I see many things," croons the
blind old Village Bore in the Bulgarian movie that one has been trapped
by urging friends into seeing; she turns out to be the Oversoul after all.
"A man of great public vision" reads part of the inscription on the statue
of Mumble McMumble, but any child can see that his patined bronze
pupils stare out sightlessly across Central Park, cataracted with bird
droppings milder even than Tobit's. I make no apology for my own
remark: seeing always seems to mean knowing.

I was blind, then, in order that I might better see. At any rate, there I
was one day, starting out on the fringes of my own neighborhood, observing the set of many mouths and the pace of many gaits, cataloguing
obscure blemishes (two ancient tracheotomy scars in five blocks, etc.).
Just after successfully navigating a street corner (successfully for me, that

is: my dangers are not those of the blind), I made a fatal blunder after all. A phony blindman with a peculiar nervous twitch, far less sure of himself than such minor grifters usually are, engaged my attention for a moment. Then suddenly a thing in plainclothes had emerged from behind smoked glasses and tin cup, clapped me on the shoulder, and thrust a crude but shiny badge under my eyes. I regret not having been able to see what must have been the magnificent moment when two owlish pairs of eyes atop two waggling, crane necks were attempting at once to assess each other and to remain apparently vacant.

"Okay, Flurch, I'm taking you in." His manner suddenly adjusted itself to his new legitimacy of appearance.

"My name isn't Flurch and I don't even think it's funny."

"No lip, now. You were on the flurch and I know it. I specialize in this sort of thing. Get a move on."

"But Officer," I began as we started moving, it seemed to me, more swiftly than we were actually doing, "I was merely engaged in my researches." A gentleman, I had been taught, treats everyone else as if he were also one; rationalists are not born, but rather create themselves; one must not always work at treating others as if they, too, had minds.

"Shove it, now. What do you think, I'm a mark too? And how much do you pull down? Come on, drag it up."

At this display of technical jargon, I could only show him the entire contents of my cup, which contained an English threepenny bit, tax tokens from various Southern cities, two slugs and a pierced amusement-park Lucky Piece, stamped with the incomplete message "TOM AND MATILDA SEE AL . . . ," my own collecteana, all. "Never have I drawn a grivenik's profit, Officer, from my attentive wanderings."

"Are you shitting me? Where is it?"

"Search me!"

He did. "What is it with you people? The crumbiest little con that doesn't even cover unemployment maybe and you think you're Yellow Kid Weil." This man was full of the lore of his specialty. I had by now concluded that "flurching" involved feigned blindness for the coin of it. And I remained resolute.

"Officer, I've done nothing wrong—I haven't really begged at all, and I've bothered no one. I'm too old to be part of some initiation prank and I don't feel like lying about what I'm doing, anyway. I was merely studying the passing parade, you might say. I pretend to be blind so that nobody I stare at will be offended or overly uncomfortable. I—"

"Okay, Flurch. I've had it. Let's go."

But I hardly needed this injunction, for we were by then involved in an adroit series of calisthenics and mutterings, ending up handcuffed together, while headquarters was telephoned. In a very few minutes a car had arrived and we were being finessed through traffic to some sort of district station. The matter of booking me required quite a bit of huddled consultation between the bunco cop, as I later learned that he was called, and a detective sergeant. I surrendered my paraphernalia, coin collection, wallet, money, keys, belt and shoelaces and started to protest again. This time, the sergeant listened me out.

"Who is this guy?" he asked my captor.

"I don't know for sure yet. I'll research it later. Wandering Grew is still in Quentin and all his friends have left town. This one's got a new story and a nutty line, but I'll crack it yet. My files—"

"Check his prints!"

"Ah, why can't I do it my way? In a couple of hours, I'll trace these coded bands on his cane here right back to the source. This guy looks to be of the old Saratoga Sam school, which means he must have grown up in, or at least spent a good while in Baltimore. Christ, it's written all over him, the—"

"Forget it. If he thinks he's so special, and if you think he's so great, put him in the creep block. We've got no time to waste on all your fancy postgraduate work. But we'll book him on a vag tonight. You'd just better have something tighter than all this in the morning."

The sergeant was comforting, if not refreshing; he sounded exactly like one of his calling who had served manfully on a radio program that, as a child, I had dutifully listened to at 5:45 every afternoon. He turned to another officer: "How much did he have on him?"

"Okay for vag."

"Well, let him take a load off his feet until tomorrow." (See? The man might have been reading from a script.)

"But Sergeant Felsenkopf," began the expert again, "I can really trace him in an hour or so. This is an age of specialization you know. Your old, brutal police methods aren't going to work with what I like to call, uh, the modern criminal. He— Look here," he broke off, turning to me again. "Here, you, read this sentence on this card out in a normal way not changing your normal way of speaking in any way." All this was said very mechanically, as, seemingly from nowhere, he produced a rather soiled card. I held it before me and stared at the union printers' label at the bottom, letting my eyes go out of focus in the glare of the white, overhead light.

"Come on, now!"

I began to read in a normal way: "Merry Mary got married to a lawyer with wens on his forehead that he kept purple with an ointment of tin and an analgesic balm prepared by a—"

"My sweet Christ!" This was Felsenkopf in mingled displeasure and disbelief.

"But sergeant, it's only my dialect test. I want to find out where he—"

Felsenkopf held up his hand gently and winced. I suppose that I giggled. He called out to two loitering figures across the wide room: "Take this, uh, Kooker here and put him on creep block for tonight."

The creep block was not really a cell block at all, although it may once have been one. It was a long, high, brightly-lit room, lined on three sides with newish, shiny green tiles that ran up to a ceiling that looked, in the glow of the fluorescent lights that outlined the skylight panels, to be mauve in color. The fourth side ended in an unusually complicated wrought-iron framework in which was set a perfectly ordinary barred door. It was a little too low, one realized on being pushed through it. The lights were recessed in the ceiling and covered over with a heavy grille, as in a gymnasium, and a large clock set high in the wall opposite the door was covered in the same way. Around the sides of the room were wooden benches, not so narrow as to be really uncomfortable, but tipped, I soon learned, at such an angle to the wall that the eventual impulse was to get up and run toward the center of the room. A rather soft, dark-brown asphalt-like material gave the floor an illusion of yielding, yet without any real resiliency. In many ways it was a very nasty room in which to plunge some twenty or so nondescript males, the immersion accompanied in each case with a clanging reminder, as the door swung shut, that much as it resembled a junior high school gym, this was really a jail.

I picked my way across the floor. Standing and squatting shapes lounged about among a few prostrate ones; I made for one wall and tried out an empty section of bench. Without quite realizing why, I got up after a few seconds and walked toward the wall opposite the door. A faint drone of echoing conversation drilled through the room, obscured from time to time by the amplified shuffle of feet, the brushing noise of bunched clothes dragging across the floor, an occasional cry or groan. A burst of frenetic whistling emanated every so often from a short, nervous one with absolutely no hair. Of the more than thirty men in the room, he seemed to be the only one with any obvious physical defect, although most looked, in some way or another, to be ailing. The tune that he whistled, so rapidly and so high that it could hardly be made out, was the first strain of "Take Me Out to the Ball Game."

Spalding, or so the other men called him, had little to say. I remember him for his near-idiocy and for the constant intrusion of his whistling. He was the only man I cared to single out for any attention at all. I had no wish, you must see, to come to terms with the place at all, particularly since I should be out of tomorrow, none the worse for the boredom. The other men's shapes remained shapes only as I kept focusing my eyes on the dreadful green tiles of the walls. Finally, I sat down on the floor, stretched myself out on one side, curled my arms about my head, and half shut my eyes while I indulged in the minor restorative of

watching a man standing nearby make a furious run at pocketpool with
his right hand probably reaching down through a good-sized hole, while
with his left he made elaborate gestures to accompany his conversation
with another man, both hands in his pockets, rocking back and forth on
the balls of his feet.

"Surely," I told myself in the manner of narrators of ghost stories,
"I'll be out of here in the morning." And, tired by the utter uninterest-
ingness of the whole business, I fell asleep. It was a few hours later that I
snapped awake. Whether it was the new noises and unaccustomed order
that followed the distribution of the box lunches, or whether it was in
fact the sudden realization that I probably wouldn't be out of there
tomorrow at all, I don't know. I had been having a dream in which Jiggs
Bannon came and bailed me out with crisp, new fifty-dollar bills, carefully licking his right index finger under his long upper lip to count
them out. His hat was on and he was looking very solemn, and his
advanced age alone seemed faintly reproving. I was saying to him, almost
as I awoke, "I'm sorry I had to call you so early in the day, Jiggs. I know
you like to keep night hours." And then I was glumly realizing that I
hadn't called anybody, Jiggs or some lawyer or even Mr. Vel at the hotel
desk; that nobody knew where I was; and that the police hadn't booked
me on a vagrancy charge but had put me into a kind of legal limbo.
When Jiggs finally did come for me, three days later, by the way, there
wasn't the least bit of reproof. Only regret did he voice about having to
wait another day for an amenable bondsman; it was only then that I
discovered that, with great wit, Sergeant Felsenkopf had booked me on a
Peeping Tom charge. My only one.

Maybe it was only the noise of the lunch distribution that woke me
up. But here I was, strained and aching, wondering how long I'd be
there, watching two guards depositing a little pile of cardboard boxes on
some of the unoccupied benches. Then they withdrew, allowing hungry,
bored and crazy men to approach the pile in various ways. Graduate
students in various subjects, meanwhile, glanced at watches and took
scrupulous notes in their little dugout overhead, peering down through
the one-way glass of the artificial skylights. I ambled over, committed
now to life as it seemed to be shaping up for a while, and selected one of
the lunch packages. It contained the picnicky version of institutional
slop: a bright orange-colored rubbery slab of plastic cheese between two
pads of cotton batting, an unsucculent chip of grayish pickle, a boring
apple and a container of milk. A small group had gathered near the
lunch bench, eating grimly and staring with disdain at the vocal gripers.

"Yummers!"

"You could eat better in any shiddy liddle coun'y can."

"If you don't want it, could I . . . ."

I joined the little community, grateful for their silence. Everyone seemed to be sharing the effort of chewing; all five men were the other side of fifty and dressed pretty much alike, in faded and stained suntans and fairly clean white shirts, open at the neck. But that, and what struck me as the salutary tone of their morale, was all they seemed to have in common. Maybe it was only for me, or maybe only, because of what happened, for me now, that Hagestolz dominated the group. He was certainly bigger, older, sadder-eyed and more heavily bearded than any of the others; he alone wore his shirt sleeves unrolled, the cuffs neatly buttoned. And awkward, stooping a little, he was the last to speak.

"You new here?" He barely seemed to have looked me over.

"Yes. I came in today."

"Then move over toward the other corner after you put your lunch tray back. You're being studied." He said this with a kind of nonchalance that puzzled me. I had heard of the tight politico-sexual organizations inside prisons, and was a little chilled by what looked like their lack of ceremony. But I decided to be innocent.

"Who by?" I inquired, inquiringly.

"What say?" said Hagestolz, who had turned to a muttered conversation with the others.

"Who am I being studied by?"

"Psychology students from UCLA. Those skylights are one-way glass." This was before the days of closed-circuit television.

"Why?"

"Modern police methods"—Hagestolz started imitating the tone of the scholarly cop who had arrested me. The others sniggered. He gave them a look of disgust and resumed his own manner. "They keep bringing Spalding back in for a few days every month so a new batch of students can hear him whistle. They don't even bother to cook up a charge any more. Just 'habitual offender.' What are you in for?"

I considered this; after all, I was in the creep block. "I got caught watching my landlord giving it to the girl who lives upstairs from me. I had a periscope rigged from my own window, so I could watch her room without getting out onto the fire escape. Well, the landlord, a little guy with glasses, came in to fix the back burner. On her stove; but I know they've been doing it for weeks, so I sent up my periscope and I saw him come in and take off his coat and they start to fool around and they get onto the bed and bang! the lights go off. But there's a streetlight shining in, and I think I can make out a few things, and suddenly it gets brighter and I can see her face while she's lying there, as clear as anything, with her eyes shut and mouth working around. It's almost as if there's a spotlight on them. And then I found out that there was, a spotlight I mean, and on me, too, and a couple of cops had come up the fire escape and seen me and I got pinched."

"First offense?" One of the men standing next to Hagestolz was clearly not impressed.

"Yes. They pull in a lot of guys for this?"

"All the time. That's why they set up this place, like for observation. They keep you here until you're bailed out. Half these guys are in here for Peepin' Tom. Then they peep at them. Pretty good, huh?" We had been ambling down the long side of the room, and stopped to sit, away from the others, on one of the benches for a few moments.

I asked, "What's Hagestolz here for?"

"That's different. Him and me are trusty. We're up five years for a con, but the psychologists had us sent here from upstate to sort of be constant factors they call it. We get interviewed about all you guys twice a week. It's better than one of the goddam minimum-security boyscout camps and we get a better shot at parole. But you guys aren't for real."

"What do you mean?"

"In, out. Then get it hushed up by your family. There was a guy here, head of the school board someplace, got caught in a tree with a pair of eight-by-fifty glasses looking in a window of a girls' dormitory at the college. In two days, then somebody fixes it, and there's nothing on the blotter even. Or bigger guys than that; they got Vontzel Gold in here once on the nuttiest deal in the world. Even the tax guys can't get him, but he had this weird piece of gash, Elaine, and he was laying out all kinds of fancy money for the bug doctor for her; she can't stand being alone, she says, she can't stand it when she just ain't."

"Just ain't what?"

"Like not there for real. 'I mean I don't exist,' she always was saying, 'unless some guy's looking at me, unless I can feel him looking at me, then I can feel like I'm here.' I don't get it, and the Vontz never got it, but he was stuck on her and stuck *with* her, you know what I mean, and one night they're in bed and Vontzel is sleepy, but she's awake and gets the heebie-jeebies. But he won't look at her. So she goes to the window and pulls up her nightie and sits out on the ledge and lets the streetlight shine on her quiff so you could see it from a block away. Vontzel gets screaming mad and yells at her to get back, like anyone can see her. But that's what she wants, she says, she wants to be *there*. So Vontz knows what he's putting up with and gets foxy and says she should come back to bed, nobody can see her there, he can't even. So she turns and gives him a crazy eye and says 'God sees, you pig, God sees.' He gets even madder, and starts yelling even louder, and he's just about to give her a clop in the chops when the cops walk in. And that nutty Elaine starts coming over all sweet and pulls her skirt down and tells them it was Vontzel made her do it, that he can't raise one unless he can see somebody looking at *her*, like from across the street. So off they carted him to the creep block. Vontzel was wild; they kept him here three days before they fixed it up downtown."

"What happened to Elaine?"

"Yeah, so they'll probably let you out on bail in a day or two, and then your folks can fix you up. Look, I gotta go now, Sonny, I have to report to the psychologists. If you got any questions, ask Hagestolz." So saying, my nameless informant sauntered down to the door of the room, where a uniformed shape awaited him with a bored look barely discernible, in that awful glare of overhead lighting, on its face. I was left alone for the moment, and although Hagestolz looked to be a man of knowledge and power, I decided to remain where I was and devote myself to the business of being watched. Except for that one picture that Virgilia took of me long ago, and that I only discovered some years later, I cannot recall being aware of being spied upon myself. That knowledge didn't bother me in the least, and I was only perplexed about how to go about dutifully being an event. An event in my sense, of course; a piece of reality, just happening, unprepared by frame or arrangement or selection for the eye of a beholder. It became, suddenly, very difficult to do anything at all. I wandered about until I found a place on one of the benches that seemed to be at a good visual angle from one of the spyholes: I had no desire to be unduly foreshortened, or to look too imaginatively grotesque by reason of some brute trick of perspective. So. There was a good chance that what would be seen would be really me. There is always a problem about what visual version of one is really oneself; Matilda used to tell me of the time, the only time, she herself ever sat for a portrait.

It had been when she was still in art school in Boston, and a fellow-student who wanted to be a society portraitist and who thought she looked like a Sargent did her painstakingly in oils. "After we'd agreed on the prose, a sort of a three-quarter-view, I-am-more-subtle-than-my-more-beautiful-frothy-sisters thing," she told me once, "I began to feel as if the part of my face he was looking at, trying to get *right*, was gradually roughening up. In texture. It felt like a piece of concrete block, but from *inside* the face, not as if I'd rubbed my hand over it. Then it began to swell up, and go ballooning out toward him, across the room. But he didn't seem to notice." Matilda always thought that this sort of thing had to do with why people shy away from their own profiles, whenever they see one that's been decently drawn.

In any event, I just wanted everything to be nice, as far as my watchers were concerned. I started groping for routines, but they all became, under the silly lights, somehow implausible. What to do? What to do? This could, I realized, lead to panic, and I was already starting to sweat at the roots of my hairline. I considered picking my nose systematically, going at it like a miner, assembling one of those considerable nuggets which, with a half-hour's admixture of dust, gets to be like old plasticine, and surrepitiously (ha ha!) depositing it somewhere, such as under the wooden lip of one of the benches. But it hardly seemed worth the effort. I got more and more uneasy, knowing all the time that it was an uneasiness that came from being free of the usual burgherly cares about being seen. I have often made love by an open window, letting the sound of crickets or sirens wash over me and mine in waves, feeling the scratches of dropped milk-bottles on a neighboring stoop against my back. And all this with perhaps a shaded lamp, filling the room with soft light. All right, so look. Some girls are nervous, though, but I think that this has little to do with what Others might see. But in general, pulling shades down has nothing to do with ensuring privacy. It's a kind of orderly tic.

Here I was, though, unable to do right by my observers. All around the huge room, the other prisoners were being garrulous, creepy, sullen or demented, but *being* so, *out there*, not imprisoned, like me, inside what seemed to be a huge papier-mâché head. But not papier-mâché; mind, rather, a confining chamber made out of what I know, what I know I don't know, and what I know can be known. I must have sat there, fretting and stewing, for hours. Being "under observation," most safe selves feel, is a little like being, say, "beneath contempt." I began to feel that it was more like being under water. Standing under some pious idiot's gaze, *under-standing* the whole thing at the same time, not being possessed of the comfy narcissism of an actor or a singer, I felt completely helpless.

In the end, it was easiest to surrender to the whole idea of the creep block. After a few hours, I became a creep, studiously and lightheartedly imitating the behavior of those about me. For a while I outdid even Spalding in scratching at my crotch and whistling "Have you see the muffin man?" Then I put my head in my hands and fled from the *thingness* of everything. Then I discussed current events with an aging urchin who had been picked up for soliciting outside an orthodox synagogue, and was therefore deemed worthy of observation. And so the afternoon passed merrily. I hardly noticed supper when it arrived (more tidy slop, I presume) and even forgot to be grateful when, at about seven-thirty, we were led out of the big room into what I gathered were perfectly ordinary cells. I was fortunate in having a private one, several prisoners having been transferred just that evening to other institutions. It was easy to stop being a creep, and to start wondering how I was ever to get out of the clutches of the Los Angeles police. But I also realized that after a few more days of this, de-creeping would get harder and harder. "Institutions," mental, penal, religious all work wonderfully well in urging people inside them to become each other. They have only to look about them and learn, but in no sense that I would want generally to accept. As I lay down to sleep I was comforted by knowing that crises like this one, which can distract one from the true path, causing one to construct all sorts of implausible views of the way things go in order to keep reasonably comfortable, don't happen every day. If they did, peeping at things would be impossible, for there would be no rich, quiet, eager darkness to peep *out of*, no dark, insatiable mind to fill with glimpses, patches of phenomena, stabs of the light of a true outside that nourishes and sustains.

JOSEPHINE JACOBSEN

On the Island

After dinner the Driscolls sat for a while with Mr. Soo, by the big windows looking out and down over the bay. There was nothing to close: they were just great oblong unscreened openings, with all that fantasy of beauty spread straight before them. Mary had not learned to believe in it, any more than she had learned to believe that the shadowy, bamboo-furnished, candlelit room behind them wouldn't be invaded by insects—even perhaps bats, or one of the host of hummingbirds. For storms, there were heavy shutters. But nothing ever seemed to come in; only the air stirred, faintly sweet, against their faces and their flaccid fingers; it grew spicier and more confused with scent as the dark strengthened.

Mr. Soo, in his impassive and formidable way, seemed glad to have them; or perhaps he was only acquiescent, in his momentary solitude. The inn was completely empty except for themselves, Mr. Soo, and the servants. This was rare, she gathered, even in the off-season she and Henry had chosen—and, indeed, their room had been occupied, only the day before yesterday, by another couple. A party of six would arrive after the weekend. Being here alone was part of their extraordinary luck. It had held for the whole trip: in Port of Spain they had got, after all, the room facing the Savanna; on Tobago they had seen the green fish come in, the ones that were bright as fire in the different green of the water; they had even seen, far off, on the trip to Bird of Paradise Island, a pair of birds of paradise, dim and quick through a great many distant leaves, but unmistakable in their sumptuous, trailing plumage.

This still, small place was their final stop before the plane home, and, just as they had planned it, it was beginning as it would end, hot and green, unpeopled, radiantly vacant. "It's the closest we'll get to real jungle," Henry said eagerly. And the jungle was no way away. The inn sheltered in cocoa bushes, shaded by their immortelles: Mr. Soo's plantation was a shallow fringe stretching for acres and acres, with the true jungle less than half a mile behind it. Mr. Soo, she felt sure, had never read one of Henry's books, but obviously was aware of his name, and this perhaps had led him to offer them brandy and sit by them in one of the gleaming, cushioned chairs, as they stared out to the disappearing sea. He did not look to Mary like a man whose pleasure lay in fraternizing with guests. Pleasure? His hair, in short, shining bristles, clasped his head tightly, giving the effect of pulling his eyes nearly shut by its grip. His face was the agreeable color of very pale copper; the mouth straight and thin, the nose fleshy. She and Henry had secretly discussed his age: thirty-eight? forty-four? thirty-seven? In the exhausted light he appeared now almost as though he had been decapitated and then had his head with its impassive face set, very skilfully, back upon his shoulders.

Mr. Soo had been born in Trinidad, but had come here to the island almost fifteen years ago, to raise cocoa. Mary was sure that the friends who had told them about the tiny inn had spoken of a Mrs. Soo, but she was not here and there was no reference to her. Arthur, the major-domo, had said only, "No Mrs. Soo," in response to an inquiry if she were away. Dead? Divorced? A figment of friends' imagination?

"Yes," Henry was saying, " 'like it' is too mild; they can't wait to come again. They're very bird-minded."

Mr. Soo looked at him in astonishment. "Your *friends?*"

"Yes. Very. Why?"

"They seemed to me," said Mr. Soo, obviously shocked, "very nice people. Intelligent. Not bird-minded."

Henry now gaped, baffled.

"Bird-*minded*, Mr. Soo," Mary said nervously. "I think you're thinking of how we sometimes say bird-*brained*. Bird-*minded*. It means thinking a lot about birds. Anxious to see new ones, you know."

Mr. Soo still had an offended air. "Very intelligent people," he said.

"*Very!*" said Henry and Mary simultaneously.

A rush of wings veered past the window, in the new darkness. "Very few here on the island, intelligent people," said Mr. Soo. "Just natives. Blacks."

There was a short pause. A faint yattering, like the rapid clack of unskilled castanets, came dimly from the upper reaches of an invisible tree.

"Haven't you any Chinese or Indian neighbors?" asked Henry, non-committally.

"Fifteen miles," said Mr. Soo, "is the nearest. I do not like Indians," he added. "But they are civilized. They come from civilized country. On Trinidad, all the shops, the taxis, all mostly Indians. They have an old civilization. Very few criminals. Except when they are drunk. The criminal classes are the blacks. Every week, choppings."

Oh, God, thought Mary, here goes our jungle holiday. Well, she decided immediately, we don't *have* to talk to him; we can go to our room in a minute. She caught Henry's glance, flicked to his wrist.

"Good heavens, it's after 10:00!" he announced like an amateur actor. "If we're going to get up early for the birds . . ."

Mr. Soo said quickly, "Lots of birds. Even at night. Pygmy owls. They fool the other birds," he explained. "That honey-creeper, green honey-creeper. The pygmy owl fools him. Like this." He suddenly puckered his lips and gave a tremulant, dying whistle; afterward, he smiled at them for the first time. "And you see cornbirds. Tody-tyrants, too. And mot mots, with long tails . . ." He sketched one with a quick hand on which the candlelight caught jade. "They pull out their own tailfeathers. And the kiskadee. That's French, corrupted French. *Qu'est-ce qu'il dit?* Means, what's that he says. Over and over. The kiskadee."

The Driscolls rose, smiling. Are the birds part of the inn, like the sour-sop drinks and the coconut milk and the arum lilies?—or does he like them? It seemed to Mary that he did.

"There was a bird this morning," she said, "on the piles . . ."

"A pelican," interrupted Mr. Soo.

"No," said Mary rather shortly. "I know pelicans." (For heaven's sake!) "A little boy told me what it was. But I can't remember. Like 'baby' . . ."

Henry and Mr. Soo said simultaneously and respectively, "A *booby!* That's what it was, a booby!" and, "A little boy?"

"The *nicest* little boy," said Mary, answering Mr. Soo. "He showed me the fiddler-crab holes and all the live things growing on the big rock, on the sea side."

"What was his name?" asked Mr. Soo unexpectedly. He had risen, too.

"I haven't an idea," Mary replied, surprised. "No, wait a minute . . ."

"A black boy," said Mr. Soo. "With a pink scar on his cheek."

Mary was not sure why the words she was about to say—"*Victor*, I'm sure he told me"—seemed suddenly inappropriate. In the little silence, Mr. Soo surprisingly bowed. "I am sorry," he said with obvious sincerity. "He is, *of course*, not allowed there. He has been told. This will be the last," he said quickly. "I am *so* sorry."

"Good heavens," said Henry, rather irritably, "he was fine—we enjoyed him. Very much. He was a bright boy, very friendly. He showed us how he would fight a shark—imaginary knife and all, you know."

"He was in the *water*?" said Mr. Soo with a little hiss.

During this contretemps, Arthur had approached; his dark face, lustrous in the candlelight, was turned inquiringly toward them over the brandy decanter.

"No, really, thanks," said Mary. She managed to smile at Mr. Soo as she turned away, hearing Henry say, "We'll be back for breakfast about 8:00," and then his footsteps behind her across the lustrous straw roses of the rug.

Later in the night she woke up. Theirs was the only bedroom in the main building except for Mr. Soo's apartment. Earlier, massed poinsettia, oleander, and exora had blazed just beyond their casement windows in the unnatural brilliance of the raw bulb fastened outside—now, by a round gold moon that was getting on for full, blue and purplish hues had taken over. The bunches of blossom were perfectly still.

She could see Henry's dark head on his pillow; he was spread-eagled with one foot quite out of bed. Very soon, familiar pressure would swallow them. Henry, even here, was immersed in his plots, manipulating shadowy figures, catching echoes of shifting dialogue. It had nothing to do with happiness, or satisfaction, but she knew that increasingly Henry's mind veered from hers, turning in patterns whose skill she admired. Henry believed in his plots. His cause and effect, lovely as graph lines and as clear, operated below all things. This island, which seemed to her full of hints flying like spray, yielded itself to him in information of tensions, feathers, blossoms, crops. More and more, like a god let loose on clay, he shaped and limited. She loved him for this, too: for his earnestness and the perfection of his sincerity; but sometimes now, she knew, her mind seemed to him disorderly and inconsequential, with its stubborn respect for surprises.

A breeze had begun to stir. The blanched crests of blossoms nodded beyond the broad sill and there was a faint rattle of palm fronds. Also, something moved in the thatch.

I will go to sleep if I think of the right things, she said to herself, and she set about remembering the misty horses, galloping easily over the Savanna track in the Trinidad dawn; she'd stood in her nightgown on the balcony to see their lovely, silent sweep. And the fern banks on Grenada: hills of fern higher than towers, deep springing hills of fronded green. And the surf, the terrifying surf, when they'd launched the little boat off Tobago for the trip to Bird of Paradise Island. The turquoise water had broken in a storm of white over the shining dark bodies and laughing faces of the launchers, the boat tipping and rocking, flung crazily upward and then seized again by dripping hands. She'd felt both frightened and happy; Henry had hauled her in and they'd plunged up and down until finally they reached deep water and saw ahead of them, beginning to shape up in the distance, the trees which perhaps sheltered the marvelous birds. "Nothing is known of the breeding-habits of Birds of Paradise," her *Birds of the Caribbean* said. She repeated this, silently, sleepily. Nothing is known of the breeding habits of birds of paradise. How nice.

Suddenly, she heard water, a seeping sound—though, on her elbow, she could see it wasn't raining. She swung her feet over the bed, but not to the floor. Luck had been good here, but in the dark she wouldn't walk barefoot and her slippers she kept under the sheet. She felt her way cautiously to the bathroom door. Inside, she lighted a candle—the generator went off at 11:00. The bathroom was immaculate, but water shone by her feet and seeped toward the depression which served as a shower-floor. The toilet was unobtrusively overflowing in a small trickle. Eventually the floor would be covered and water would ooze under the door. What on earth could they do about it tonight, though? Move in with Mr. Soo? She began to giggle faintly. But it was a bother, too; in remote spots things took forever to get themselves fixed. She put Henry's sandals on the window-ledge, blew out the candle, and closed the door softly behind her. Henry hadn't stirred. She got back in bed, thinking: It's a good thing I saw those sandals—they were *in* the water! The words set off an echo; but, as she remembered what it was, she fell asleep.

By morning, the water was in their room, reaching fingers in several directions; the heavy straw of the rugs was brown and dank. When they came out into the pale, fragrant sunlight of the big room, Arthur was throwing away yesterday's flowers from the two big blue vases on the low tables. Henry, dropping his binocular-strap over his head, stopped long enough to report their problem. Arthur looked at them with an expression of courteous anguish and ritual surprise and said that he would tell Mr. Soo.

When they returned two hours later, hungry and already hot, Mr. Soo had come and gone. His small table, with its yellow porcelain bowl filled each morning with arum lilies, was being cleared by Arthur, who brought them a platter of fruit and told them that after breakfast he would transfer them to Mr. Soo's room. They were astounded and horrified in equal proportions. "That's absolutely impossible," said Henry. "We can't inconvenience him like that. Why can't we go down to one of the beach cottages? Or up on the hill?"

Arthur, who at the moment represented all help except the invisible cook, did not say: Because I can't run back and forth and still do everything here. He said instead, "Mr. Soo did tell me to move you after breakfast."

Henry was anxious to talk to Arthur. Wherever they went, he ab-

sorbed gestures, words, inflections, as a lock-keeper receives water, with
the earnest knowledge of its future use. He was very quick at the most
fugitive nuance; later it would be fitted into place, all the more impressive for its subtlety.

Arthur had poured their second cups of coffee. Now he reappeared
from behind the red lacquer screen, carrying one of the big blue vases. It
was filled high with yellow hibiscus and he set it gently on one of the
teakwood stands.

Henry said, in his inviting way, "You do a bit of everything."

Immediately, Arthur came to the table. "Only I am here now," he
said. "And the cook. Two boys gone." He held up two fingers. "Chauffeur is gone."

On short acquaintance, Mary did not particularly like Arthur. He
had a confidential air which, she noticed, pivoted like a fan. At present it
was blowing ingratiatingly on Henry. "Mr. Soo had a lot of trouble with
help," said Arthur. Mary saw with a rather malign amusement the
guest's breeding struggle with the writer's cupidity. The victory was
tentative.

"Now *we're* upsetting things," said Henry, not altogether abandon-
ing the subject. "It's ridiculous for him to move out of his room for us."

"Won't upset Mr. Soo," said Arthur soothingly. "He can shut the
apartment off, sitting room, library. Another bath, too, on the other side.
Used to be Mrs. Soo."

Mary could see the waves of curiosity emanating from Henry, but he
gallantly maintained silence. "There is a sleep-couch in the sitting
room," Arthur went on. "Mr. Soo does want you to be comfortable, and
so." He pivoted slightly to include Mary in his range. His eyeballs had
crimson veins and he smelled of a fine toilet water. "Mr. Soo is very
angry with that boy," said Arthur. "Mr. Soo does tell he: Stay away from
my beach, ever since that boy come here."

In spite of herself, Mary said irascibly, "But that's ridiculous. He
wasn't bothering anyone."

"Bother Mr. Soo," said Arthur. "Mr. Soo is so angry he went last
night to go to see he grandmother. Told he grandmother, that boy does
come here again, he beat him."

"May I have some hot coffee, please?" asked Mary.

Arthur did not move. He swept his veined eyes from one to the other.
"Mr. Soo does not own that beach," said Arthur. "Can't no mahn own a
beach here. Mr. Soo's beachhouse, Mr. Soo's boat, Mr. Soo's wharf. But
not he beach. But he don't let no mahn there, only guests."

"Why does he like this beach so much?" said Mary, for it was small
and coarse, with plenty of sharp rocks. "The boy, I mean."

"Only beach for five miles," Arthur told her. "That boy, Vic-tor,
come with he brother, come to he grandmother. They live topside. Just

rocks, down their hill. Very bad currents. Sea-pussy, too. Can't no mahn swim there."

"May I have some hot coffee?" Mary said again.

Arthur stood looking at her. At this moment a considerable clamor broke out in the kitchen behind them. Voices, a man's and a woman's, raised in dispute, then in anger. The woman called, "Arthur! You come here, Arthur!"

Arthur continued to look at them for about two seconds; then, without haste, he went away, walking around the screen toward the kitchen.

"All right, all right," said Henry, answering a look. "But you know perfectly well we can't come here for five days and tell Mr. Soo who he must have on his beach."

"It isn't his beach."

"It isn't ours, either."

Something smashed in the kitchen. A door banged viciously. Outside the window went running easily a tall, big boy. His dark, furious, handsome face glared past them into the room. He dived down the wooden steps past the glade of arum lilies. His tight, faded bluejeans disappeared among the bushes.

"What was *that* in aid of?" said Henry, fascinated.

Arthur appeared. He carried the faintly steaming enamel pot of coffee, and, coming up to them, poured a rich stream into Mary's cup. Then he said: "The big brother of Vic-tor, he's a bad bad boy. Daniel. Same name as the man fought the lion." He bowed slightly, thus reminding Mary of Mr. Soo, turned to the other teakwood stand, lifted the empty blue vase, and went off with it behind the screen.

"'*Fought* the lion'?" said Mary, inquiringly, to Henry.

"Well," said Henry, "I suppose Arthur places him in the lion's den, and then improvises."

That was the last of the excitement. They were transferred quickly and easily from their moist quarters; the toilet was now turned off and not functioning at all. Mr. Soo's room lacked all traces of its owner, unless a second bed could be viewed as a trace. It had a finer view than their abandoned room, looking all the way down the series of log terraces to the small, bright, rocky beach.

Greenness took over; the greenness of the shallows of the bay before it deepened to turquoise, of the wet, thick leaves of the arum lilies, soaked each morning by an indefatigable Arthur, of the glittering high palms, and the hot tangled jungle behind the cocoa bushes shaded by their immortelles. Mary had—unexpectedly to herself—wanted to leave before their time was up. She had even suggested it to Henry right after breakfast on that second morning. But Henry wanted to stay.

"It *isn't* Mr. Soo," she said, trying to explain. "It hasn't anything to do with that. It's something else. There're too many vines. Everything's looped up and tangled. The palms rattle against the tin and give me dreams."

"Don't be fey," said Henry rather shortly. "We'll be away from palms soon enough."

Mr. Soo continued cordial in his immobile fashion; he talked to them from his small table when, at dinner, their hours coincided. Once, he had Arthur make them each a sour-sop, cold and lovely as nectar, when they came in brown and sweaty from the beach rocks. But by some obscure mutual assent, there were no more brandies. After dinner, the Driscolls sat on their tiny terrace, watching the moon swelling toward fullness, and drank crème de cacao in tiny gourd cups provided by Arthur. They knew they were destined to share their final hours on, and their first off, the island with Mr. Soo. He too would be on the biweekly plane to Trinidad. Mr. Soo said he was going to Port of Spain to procure plumbing fixtures. Arthur said Mr. Soo was going to procure a number two boy and a chauffeur. Where on earth did Mr. Soo wish to be driven, over the narrow, pitted, gullied roads that circled the island? Through and through his plantation, perhaps. Arthur took no note of coldness in relation to his comments on Mr. Soo; also, Mary felt, the most ardent questioning would have led him to reveal no more than he had originally determined. His confidences went by some iron and totally mysterious auto-decision. She had absolutely no idea how his sentiments stood in regard to his employer.

On their last afternoon, the Driscolls went for a walk. Just before dusk, they decided to go deep along the jungle path. This was the hour for birds; all over the little island they were suddenly in motion. Almost none, except the hummingbirds with which the island fairly vibrated, flew in the golden hot midday, but at dusk the air was full of calls and wings.

Mary and Henry went along the middle ledge, above the arum lilies. Down on the beach, the fiddler crabs would be veering, flattening themselves, then rearing to run sideways, diving down holes into which fell after them a few trembling grains of sand. From here, the Driscolls could only see the white waves, leaping like hounds up at the rocks. They went along slowly, musingly, in the fading heat, up the steep path back of the garden sheds, below the giant saman, the great airy tree with its fringed, unstirring, pendent parasite world. With its colony of toe-hold survivors, it was like the huge rock on the beach, half in the tides, to whose surface clung and grew motionless breathers.

They turned up the small, dusty road toward the solid wave of tree-crests towering ahead. They had been this way twice before; they remembered a goat tethered up the bank at eye-level, a small scrubby cow standing uncertainly in the ditch. They would pass a cabin, half up the slope, with its back to the bay far below, its straw roof smothered under rose-colored masses of coralita. They walked in intimate silence. The road was daubed with the fallen blossoms of immortelles and their winged pods. Once, two laborers passed them, stepping quietly on their tough bare feet, the shadows of leaves mottling their dark erect bodies and bright blue ripped trousers, their machetes in worn scabbards swinging gently from their heavy belts.

Around a curve, they came on a dead, long snake, savagely slashed. Just before their path struck off the road there was a jingle and faint creaking, and around a tangle of scarlet blackthorn rode two native policemen, their caps tilted against the sunset, their holsters jogging their elbows. They pulled their small horses, stained with sweat, into single file; one raised his hand easily in a half-salute and both smiled. These were the first horses the Driscolls had seen on the island, and the first police. Of course, there had to be police, but it was strange how out of place they seemed. When the hushed fall of the hoofs in the dust died away it was as though horses and riders had melted.

Later, sitting on a fallen tree in the bush, Mary thought idly about the snake, the laborers, the policemen. Henry had gone further in, but she had felt suddenly that she couldn't walk another step. She sat on ridged strong bark coursed by ants and thought about the policemen, their faces, their small dusty horses, on that peaceful, hot patrol. Surely there must be almost nothing for them to do. And yet the idea of violence, she realized, had come to the air she breathed. Not violence as she knew it in Henry's books, or in the newspapers at home—riot, rape, murder, burglary. This violence seemed a quality of growth—the grip of the mollusks on the wave-dashed rock, the tentacles of the air plants flowering from the clutched saman. It oppressed her with its silence, its lack of argument. Perhaps she responded in some obscure portion of her feminine heart. An ant ran silently and fast over her hand. She shook it off and stared into the green that had swallowed Henry. His preciousness to her appeared not enhanced but pointed up by her sense of the silent violence of growth around her, as if, among the creepers, windfalls, sagging trees, his face, clear to her love, defined itself as the absolute essential. Of the rest, blind accidents of power, and death, and greenness, she could make nothing. Nothing they might do would surprise her.

There was a wild cocoa bush not ten feet away, dropped into this paroxysm of growth, thin, tall, struggling for light. She could see the pendulous gourds in their mysterious stages of ripeness: cucumber green, yellow, deep rose-bronze, and plum-brown. That plum-brown was on the voluptuous poles of the bamboos, the great, breeze-blown, filmy, green-gold stools of bamboo.

She listened for Henry. There was provisional silence, but no real stillness; hidden streams ran with a deep, secret sound in the throat of distant ravines, and the air was pierced and tremulous with birdcalls, flutings, cries, cheeps, whistles, breaks of song; response and request; somewhere away, lower than all the sounds but that of water, the single, asking, contemplative note of the mourning dove.

All at once, there was Henry. When she saw him, she realized that some portion of her had been afraid, as though, like the police on their little horses, he would melt into the greenness for good.

"Did you realize I'd forgotten my binoculars?" he asked, infuriated with his stupidity. "Of all idiotic times!"

Suddenly, she flung herself at him, winding her arms about his neck, linking their legs, covering his face with quick, light kisses. He held her off to look at her, and then folded her tightly in his arms, as though she too had come back from somewhere. "We haven't a flashlight, *either*," he said, "and, if we don't look out, we'll be plunging about in the dark, breaking everything."

On the way home, they went more rapidly. The birds were almost completely silent. Now and then one would flash in the tree-crests far above them, settling to some invisible perch. We've left this island, Mary thought. There came a turning point—on a wharf, on a station platform, in the eyes of a friend—when the movement of jointure imperceptibly reversed. Now they were faced outward—to their suitcases, to their plane, to the Port of Spain airport, to Connecticut and typewriters. Mary began to worry about the dead snake, in the thick dusk; she didn't want to brush against its chill with her bare, sandaled feet. But, when they came to the spot, she saw it at once. It seemed somehow flatter and older, as though the earth were drawing it in.

As they rounded the bend to the final decline, a sound came to them, stopping them both, Mary with her hand digging into Henry's arm. They thought at first it was an animal in a trap, mistreated or dying. It was a sound of unhuman, concentrated, self-communing pain, a dull, deep crying, with a curious rhythm, as though blood and breath themselves caused pain. "What *is* it?" cried Mary, terrified.

"It's a human being," said Henry.

He was right. Drawn close together, they turned the bend in the road, and saw the group from which the sound came: just up the steep slope to their left, in front of the cabin. Raw light from a kerosene lamp on the porch fell on the heads of the men and women, in an open semicircle. Around this space crawled on her hands and knees a woman. Her head was tied in a red kerchief and the light caught her gold earrings. She pounded the earth with her fist, and round and round she crept in short circles.

Dark faces turned in their direction, but the woman did not stop; on and on went the sound. Alien, shocked, embarrassed by their own presence, the Americans hesitated. Then Henry caught his wife's elbow and steered her, stumbling, down the path.

"Oh, Henry, *Henry* . . ." she whispered frantically to his shadowy face. "Oughtn't we to stop? Couldn't we? . . ."

"They don't *want* us!" he hissed back. "Whatever it is, they don't want *us*."

She knew he was right, but an awful desolation made her stumble sharply again. The sound was fainter now; and then, in a minute or two, gone. Below them, they could see the lightbulb lashed to the trunk of the saman tree, like a dubious star.

Later, Mary was not sure why they said nothing to Mr. Soo. Neither, strangely, did they discuss it between themselves in their bedroom, showering, dressing for dinner. It was as though its significance would have to come later. It was too new, still, too strange; their suspended atmosphere of already-begun departure could not sustain it.

This sense of strangeness, and also, perhaps, the sense of its being their last evening, seemed to constrain them to be more civil to Mr. Soo. Arthur, bringing their Daiquiris, told them there would be a cold supper; the cook was away. His air was apologetic; this was evidently an unexpected arrangement. On the terrace, he set their drinks down on the thick section of a tree bole that served as a stand, and looked through the open casement window into their room, now transforming itself again into Mr. Soo's room: at the open, filled suitcases, the range of empty hangers, the toilet bottles on the dresser.

"You sorry to go?" asked Arthur. "You like it here, and so?"

"Very, very much," said Henry. "We hope we can come back."

"You know, one thing," said Arthur. A gong was struck imperiously. Arthur took his empty tray back through the toom. The door closed behind him.

Perhaps it was too late for a more cordial response; perhaps Mr. Soo, too, felt that they were no longer there. Above his arum lilies in their yellow bowl, he was unresponsive. After one or two attempts at conversation, the Driscolls ate their cold supper, talking to each other in tones made artificial by several kinds of constraint. Over coffee, Henry said, "I'd better see him about the bill now—it's all going to be so early in the morning."

Mary waited for him by the huge open window-frames, where they had sat on their first evening, discussing with Mr. Soo their bird-minded friends. The moon, which tonight was going to be purely full, had lost its blemishes of misproportion; it was rising, enormous and perfect, in a bare sky. She could hear very faintly the sound of the tide as she stared out over the invisible bay to the invisible sea.

Behind her, Mr. Soo and Henry approached, their footsteps hushed by the straw, their voices by the silence. Turning, she was confronted by Mr. Soo's face, quite close, and it struck her that the moonlight had drawn and sharpened it, as though it were in pain.

"I hope you and your husband have been happy here," said Mr. Soo.

"Very," said Mary. (Now we're in for a drink, she thought.) "The birds have been wonderful . . ." she began, but Mr. Soo was not listening.

"The driver from the airport will be here at six o'clock," he said. He turned and left them, walking slowly over the gleaming rug.

The moon hadn't reached their terrace. Arthur, arriving with the crème de cacao, had to peer at the tree-bole before setting down the little cups. He did not go away, but stood and looked at them. Finally, he said: "Do you remember Vic-tor?"

"Of course," said Henry, and Mary added, "The little boy."

"He's gon," said Arthur.

Henry said with interest, "Gone?"

"Dead, gon." Arthur stood there, holding his tray, and waited for them to speak. When they still did not, he said, "He did go off those high rocks. Back down from he house, those high rocks. He did go to swim in that sea-pussy. Like he grandmother told he not to. He is gon, out to sea; no body. No body a-tall. He was screaming and fighting. Two men fishing, they tried very hard to grab he up, but couldn't never get to he. He go so fast, too fast. They will never have no body—too much current, too many fish. He grandmother told he, but that boy, he gon to swim. He won't even mind he brother, brother Daniel, brought he up," said Arthur, turning away and continuing to talk as he left, "or he grandmother, took he in. The cook is gon," said Arthur, faintly, from the distance. "Now Mr. Soo, Mr. Soo is all alone." The door closed.

Mary got up, uncertainly; then she went into the bedroom and began to cry very hard. She cried harder and harder, flinging herself on the bed and burrowing her head in the pillow. She felt Henry's hands on her shoulder blades and told him, "I can't even think *why* I'm crying—I didn't even know the child! Yes, he showed me the crabs, but I didn't *know* him! It's not that . . ." She was obsessed by the mystery of her grief. Suddenly, she sat up, the tears still sliding down over her lips. "That was his grandmother," she said.

"It's a pattern," said Henry miserably. "We saw it happen all the way from the beginning, and now it's ended. It had to end this way."

She touched his face. His living body was here beside her. She slid her hand inside his shirt, feeling his flesh, the bones beneath it. The room was filled like a pool with darkness. She ran her finger over his chin, across his lips. He kissed her softly, then more deeply. His strong, warm hand drew her dress apart and closed over her breast.

"I love you," he said.

She did not know when Henry left her bed. She did not, in fact, wake until a sound woke her. Her bed was still in darkness, but the window was a pale blaze from the moon, now high and small. It struck light from the palms' fronds, and against it she saw the figure on the ledge, in the open window. Young and dark and clear, and beautiful as shining carved wood, it looked against all that light, which caught and sparked on the machete's blade. It was gone; she heard a faint thud on the earth below the window. She raised herself on her elbow. In Mr. Soo's moonlit room she stared at Mr. Soo's bed and at what she now made out on the darkening sheet. It was Henry's dark head, fallen forward, and quite separate. His eyes were still closed, as if in an innocent and stubborn sleep.

DONALD JUSTICE

The Lady

It was while young Dr. Will and his Yankee bride were honeymooning that the old Macready place burned down.

Only the two Negroes were there at the time. Boards had been nailed every which way across the windows, but the Negroes were not the kind to notice that, or mind it much if they did. They had, adjunct to the kitchen, a room of their own—more a cell than a room, really—that had been theirs while they cooked and waited on Will's father. Will, coming home to bury his father the winter before and finding them there, in that room, had made his first mistake. It was no doubt pity to begin with, because they had absolutely nothing. Even the clothes he found them in he recognized as his father's, though not the old castoff pants and patched shirts that might have been expected, but broadcloth and serge that, given a good scrubbing, might have passed well enough for even the old man lying dead upstairs to be buried in. And where could they go anyway?—the old man that had been a slave too feeble at eighty to be hired anywhere else, the runt of a boy too tongue-tied and foolish and lazy to be wanted anywhere no matter how cheap his feed was. Will left them there, in the cramped eight-by-eight kitchen room, and explained to the last living aunt that had cared enough to drive the twenty miles from Paris for the funeral how somebody had to be there to take care of the place. He sold the land the afternoon of the funeral, but not the house or the field around it, and that night got on the train Northbound again for the degree he was going to take one week in June and the wife he was going to take the next. But Will did not let pity—or whatever it was—keep him from locking the doors before he left, taking it for granted that the Negroes who had not known enough to stay out of the clothes trunk would not know enough to stay out of the big poster bed upstairs either, or the eighty- or ninety-year-old silver and plate, or anything else they would appreciate only enough to use. Still, if they ever got tired of the sun outside, there was room enough left them to wander about in: up and down the stairs, for example, with the sun cracking through the boards across the oval staircase window. And even if they stayed in the kitchen, there was more than enough room to get the fire started.

They probably did not mean to. Capus, the old one, swore that he was driving the cows toward the barn, and the boy with him, when he glanced up and saw the smoke, and one wall already sagging, about to go. Whether or not Will let pity make him believe that, he never laid any of the blame on them.

The afternoon he got the telegram from his aunt, he and his bride simply set out from the hotel in Washington, D.C. By the next afternoon they had covered the nearly three hundred miles to Wassahoochee in their new A-model. So before dark, the second day after the fire, Will and Amy Macready were out surveying the ruins.

The chimneys remained. Slender stone chimneys they were, tall, and blackened a little with the smoke, looking like gateposts. Behind these was the barn, for some reason not destroyed, though its paint had curled up from the heat. Amy took one deep glance and shut her eyes. Later, no longer frail in appearance, no longer even dainty, she thought: Had it not been for the fire. But then she was a frail woman still, with spots of rouge for color on her cheeks, one of those women so convinced by thirty that no man would ever marry her that she could not understand Will when he did. She had neither a handsome face, nor any money of her own, nor any family name to speak of, and he had all these. There was only the one thing about him she could not really admire: His large freckled hands, with light reddish hair across the back of them, which he did not mind because these were the "family" freckles and the "family" color, but she thought them ugly. Large and awkward as he was, he had always been gentle and considerate and soft-spoken with her, as with everybody, and if she could have understood him she might have loved him. But she was having to look at those chimneys. And when she saw her husband begin to poke about in the rubble, lovingly almost, with a stick he had picked up, and a little smoke or dust rise out of it, she felt that she would never understand that about him.

She could not say it was his fault exactly. But certainly, during the faraway winter of their courtship, he had led her to expect somehow a fitter welcome. "Good God," she said later, "at first I thought he was about to propose that we set up housekeeping in that barn. And then I saw that somebody else was already living out there. If you could call it living." Amy meant the Negroes. Capus she saw first, hobbling out of the barn to greet them. She saw the boy too, following him out. What she never got over was the way Dr. Will gathered the boy's neck into the crook of his arm and dragged him near, with a show of familiarity, and the way the kinky head rubbed against the doctor's dark travelling suit. For the doctor it was nothing but the joy of homecoming, even to a heap of rubble and two Negroes he had seen once before in his life. But for her it was something else. "I thought we had all gone mad and back a hundred years in time," she would say, when she had learned to laugh about it.

There was nothing to do but accept the aunt's invitation, and so they went to share her house in Paris while theirs was being raised again. Macready's aunt was elderly and slept much in the afternoons. The family albums and mementos could not have lasted long, nor the shop-windows, of which even in Paris there were not many. Amy was soon bored, and when Dr. Will, tired of driving to Wassahoochee every day to supervise the reconstruction, suggested that they take rooms at Mrs. Billy Kyle's boardinghouse, there wasn't any quarrel. There, while the doctor drove out to the house in the country, she sat on the front porch and read magazines in the mornings, and in the afternoons paid her first calls on the ladies, in a silk dress the first day, and in a new cotton print thereafter, mastering quickly one of the small details of life in Wassa-hoochee though already she despaired of ever comprehending the larger. She did not talk much those afternoons (that came later); she sat dream-ily on the front porches and in the shady parlors, her hands clasped in her lap as though she were in a schoolroom, listening to lessons. And all this while, no one—the doctor included—had got one hint of what was on her mind.

The house, at the doctor's insistence, was to be a replica of the old Macready place. She might have favored something more up to date and maybe fancy, but she said nothing. When they moved from Mrs. Billy Kyle's to the completed house, which smelled within and without of fresh white paint that gave Amy one of her headaches, no one could have told that it was new, except for the paint. It was the same as ever: a squarish two-storied box, without style or ornament, with matched chim-neys on either end like sticks holding a woodpile in. Except that the doctor had had wire strung and pipes laid, at considerable cost, so that his wife should at least not suffer the want of electricity and plumbing. For he was always a considerate man.

"So it was like that?" Amy must have thought, but she said nothing, and stepped in through the door the doctor held open for her.

By a mistake, the furniture had not arrived. Amy had to stand, after marching through the bare rooms. Then she sat in the car with the door open to what breeze there was—this with a patience he was too busy to see. And with the same patience she allowed her husband to conduct her over the grounds (in high heels) which she had already seen once too often that first day. For the Negroes were there. She saw them along with the stock in the barn on the tour, and saw them talking with the doctor in the back yard, and saw them, closing her eyes back in the car again, pressing her fingertips into her forehead. By then she knew it could not be postponed any longer. Through the weeks at the boardinghouse she had not quit hoping that they would be gone when she had to return, that they would have drifted on God knows where, just as the doctor told her they had drifted up; and she had not questioned him about it, for fear of having to know once and for all that they were there. And that he meant them to stay. So she had not accompanied the doctor on his daily inspections, no doubt inventing some woman's reason—"No, I would rather wait and see it all at once, finished. You understand that, don't you dear?"

About noon the furniture arrived and was all afternoon being moved in. Old Capus and the boy helped as best they could, carrying in this or that—the kitchen chairs, struggling with the trunks. But because she would not let them touch one precious thing, not one thing that could be broken, it was dark before the last piece was in place. Under such circumstances, on the electric stove that had never been used, with the aluminum ware and china and silver that had been wedding gifts, Amy managed to prepare her first meal for her husband of nearly three months.

The linen tablecloth, a wedding gift too, had not yet been unpacked. So she bore supper into the dining room (it had to come from cans) and set it on the long, shiny, bare table. She had heard the back screen door open, and she did not have to glance into the darkness of the back porch to know they were there. Yet still she did not let on.

The doctor had to speak first. "Amy, aren't you forgetting something? Or is that just one more thing I forgot to tell you?" And he inclined his head toward the back porch.

"Oh dear, and must we feed them too?" She sank into the chair.

"Amy! Stop and think if they heard you!"

"May I ask where they've been eating up to now? Or haven't they been?"

"Why won't you understand! I wouldn't think of making that poor old Negro man walk all the way over to colored town when we can——"

"Then tell me this, Will, just this. What do they eat?"

"The same as us," the doctor replied and, as Amy reported later, he began to laugh. ("I thought he was laughing at me," she would say, shaking her head with affected bitterness, "and so I thought I had him then. But little did I comprehend the depths of that man I had tied myself to.")

So she got up from the chair, saying, "Then they might as well have

mine!" And before the doctor could cross to stop her, she had taken up
her plate and started for the back porch.

Evidently she had been meaning, if it came to that, to force the
doctor to one of those dramatic and unnecessary choices women are
always posing—a choice between herself and the others. But the doctor
had reached the door before her and, standing there in her path, he—
very gently—seized the plate in both his freckled hands and peered down
with no expression whatever into her set face. Whatever it was that
happened to her then—maybe courage, like the heart, skipping a beat—
it was enough for her grip on the plate to relax. And if it was not
courage, it was a kind of instinct that told her once he had stepped
through the door with the plate in his hands, he would never again be
willing to stand between her and any door. No matter what, she said
nothing, and had to stand there, and had to watch the doctor carry her
own supper out to the man and boy on the stoop, and had to hear them
eat in darkness, and had to see the doctor return to his place at the other
end of the long table and finish the meal she had got out of cans for him.
She did not even cry.

The doctor said one thing more that evening. They had not had time
to unpack the new linen napkins either, but he waited till he had arranged the silver on the empty plate, and touched his lips with his fist
once or twice. "We will get you a cook first thing tomorrow, love," he
said. "Yes, we will."

Amy had not understood then, and so she had not smiled. But remembering it, she could smile. "I swear," she would say, "he had kept
silence through that whole horrible dinner out of nothing worse than
pure and simple consideration for my feelings. And believe me, sometimes there isn't anything worse. He said that, on our first night in the
house, and when he had just polished off the first meal I had a chance to
fix him—he said that, mind you, out of the same consideration. Oh yes.
Hah!"

In a way Dr. Will was unlucky. She might not have planned to sleep
late the next morning, but she did, and the doctor learned to make
breakfast alone without complaint. It was the first act of a prolonged
contrition Amy and his own obliging nature contrived to exact from
him. Perhaps it was with no more conscious purpose that she did not
rouge her cheeks that morning, or paint her lips, or comb her hair, or
put on the pretty cotton frock. What woke her finally was the sound of
wood being sawed, and she went straight to the window. Leaning on the
sill, she looked out beyond the barn, across the pasture where the two
cows stood. What looked like a path ran through the high ragged grass
and at the end lay a pile of lumber. Three men were there. One, in
overalls, was moving the saw, his bent knee holding the wood in place on

a sawhorse. Another stranger, also in overalls, sat on the pile of lumber beside the other man. The third man wore a gray felt hat. This was her husband. At that moment she felt she had begun to understand what he was. He was a man who would pay carpenters to build a cabin for a pair of utterly helpless Negroes he felt some queer responsibility for, and for not one visible reason but their very helplessness. Yet at the same time he would have it built in the very farthest corner of the property. That was, no doubt, for her sake.

She came downstairs after seeing that, and in the kitchen found the ugliest colored woman she had ever seen. That would be the cook. Amy did not speak to her, and though by then she had not eaten for more than twenty-four hours, she did not enter the kitchen. When the doctor came in for lunch Amy was still in the housecoat, the honeymoon housecoat. He explained what he had done, evidently expecting her to be pleased that he was having the cabin built so far from the house.

But Capus and the boy, she knew, could still walk up the path at mealtime.

That first cook stayed only a month or so and was followed by a succession of others that Amy could scarcely tell apart. But it was the duty of every one of them to leave the ham and sweet potatoes and grits and cornbread out on the back porch table for the old man and the boy. After a while Amy sometimes brought herself to say good evening to them from the dining room. But she did not go out on the back porch, even when they were nowhere near.

The first present with which Dr. Will did not surprise Amy was an organ, a little one that fitted in a corner of the parlor. He must have known that would not be enough. He bought her a new A-model to go visiting in, and used the old one for his own calls. It was about that time, sitting in one parlor after another in the new frock she would have driven to Paris for, that she began telling it by bits and snatches, what would never be much of a story till she would begin, and sometimes was not much then. ("Well, Will did not get home last night again, sitting up all night with a sick darky—that is what you call them down here, isn't it?—or maybe it was a sick cow. I never ask, you know. Now another man I would not trust, but Will . . . So there I am in that big house all by myself, scared to death, and you know what I did? I got up and turned on every light in the house, and he won't complain about the light bill either. After that I slept like a baby and didn't think of them once. You know who I mean, whachamacallem and that idiot boy.") Other times she told it with such breathless ardor that no one stopped to think till after she was through talking and had commenced with her way of laughing that here was Amy Macready violating her own privacy —and this their right, not hers. It was always the one story, and it had something to do with the Negroes which she could never quite make clear. But in the end she must have realized what it was: that she had only been waiting for the old man to die.

But they were still in the cabin and nothing changed. Amy saw so little of them that once in a while she would almost forget. And then she would catch a glimpse through one of the upstairs windows, where they would be hoeing the garden perhaps (which she admitted they kept up very well, so that there were always the fresh peas, beans, collard greens). But she could never stay at the window long—there was something about the boy. He traipsed everywhere at the old man's heels, and he had not grown one inch since the day she arrived, and never would. If she saw his mouth working, she could not help imagining the sounds. They were like words, but what did they mean? The tongue-tie caused it, or part of it. Only Capus pretended to understand, was—as the doctor put it—the boy's *interpreter*. The work the boy helped with he must have done more by instinct than anything else, knowing how to squeeze a cow's teat and all the rest without having to be told how, just as the right kind of dog knows without training how to follow a scent. No doubt there would have been a hard time telling him anyway. All that could be done was to point out whatever it was—a cow, a pile of wood— and the boy did whatever was to be done. His yellow eyes looked straight at whoever was talking, or pointing. But probably not even the old man could guess how much or how little the boy understood of what went on around him.

She watched this way and remembered, waiting for the old man to die, knowing the boy would have to be sent away then. She waited four years, then five, and the old man did not even get sick. He took to using a stick to hop around with, but he did not get sick. He was there at the house, on the back porch, and the boy with him, every morning and every evening, although in the mornings she did not have to see them because she would not be up yet.

That was why when they were not there one morning it was noon before she heard of it. The cook told her. The present cook was a small surly black woman who padded about the kitchen making no more noise than if she went barefoot, and Amy was always turning around to find the woman standing just behind her, waiting to be discovered before she would open her mouth. But that morning the cook began telling her before Amy felt the dining room cloud with her presence. Somebody, it turned out, had come looking for the doctor at breakfast, and the doctor had driven off with him.

"Then you're sure the doctor didn't see them before he left?"

"No mam, but he say tell you not to worry, it don't mean a thing."

Amy did not want to believe that it did. Or she did not want to believe too soon, in the absence of proof. Nor did she want to put it to the proof too soon, just as she had sat on the porch of the boardinghouse with her ladies' magazines, preferring not to know rather than go all the way out with her husband to the half-finished house where she would have to know, and know finally. And just as she had not asked her husband then, she did not put any more questions to the cook. It was something not even to think about, but to be breathed in and out like a change in the air, till she was ready to be used to it.

But in the middle of the afternoon, when she sat down at the vanity to comb her hair finally, she discovered a note. It was not signed, but it was from the doctor. "Love" (it said), "a poor colored boy came for me this morning. His mama was in pain so I had to go. I assume it is another *youngun* (they won't listen to me) and it is way out in the country so I don't know when I can get back. I have to hurry, but I knew you'd worry if I didn't explain. Love."

She had started downstairs before she saw a purpose to the note: he hadn't mentioned the missing Negroes. It was like him not to want her to think anything was wrong, with them especially. Which was the beginning of proof that something was. All at once a picture bobbed before her eyes, and she had to touch the stairpost at the landing to steady herself. The picture was like a dream: the boy, babbling away, razor in hand, crouched over the sleeping old man. For just that moment she was certain he was capable of it, of anything, of worse even.

Downstairs by then, she found the cook on the back porch shelling peas. The cook got to her feet, gathering the hulls into her apron, but when Amy had told her what she wanted done, the woman shook her head. Amy asked her twice more—once politely, the second time with calm insistent rage—and each time the woman said "No mam" and looked at the floor. "You will either go down there this minute and find out, or else you will get out of my house for good." The cook stopped saying "No mam" then and shook the hulls out of the apron into the dishpan on the floor. Then she took the apron off.

By the time Dr. Will arrived home, just at dark, the cook was gone. He did not need to ask for an explanation. Amy let him sit down to supper before she commenced.

"Will, I think you had better run down to the cabin before it gets good and dark."

"It's already dark."

"Not outside it isn't."

"They'll be along for supper any minute, if that's what you're driving at."

"Why? Did you already see them?"

"No."

"Then you know they won't."

"Now, Amy, if you could have seen that poor suffering creature

where I was today, and the trouble she was having, then you'd understand how a man can be tired out though he doesn't have anything to do
but stand around and look at it happening, and maybe one or two other
little things after it's all over. I told her way last year she couldn't have
any more, even if they could afford it, which they can't. And I told her
how, I even gave her——"

"Will! That's just it. You're always so ready to help, and here you
won't even go out and see what you can do to help them, and them
living right on your own property so long. It looks like he could slit the
old man's throat and you wouldn't even——"

"What? What's that?"

"I said he could slit——"

"All right. Only let me finish this. I haven't had a bite since breakfast
and not more than one or two then."

"It will be dark by then and you know it."

He had already begun rising before she could say it, and was wiping
his hand across his mouth.

"Then if you promise not to worry about it, all right."

Amy followed him to the door and told him to be careful. He
laughed, a short laugh.

It was just that time between light and dark when what light there
was seemed to come welling up all around, coming from nowhere. The
dog that had taken up with the Negroes had been lying on the steps,
waiting to be fed. Now she raised her head from her paws and ran at the
doctor's heels. Amy watched them take the turn into the path through
the field. By that time they were nothing but shadows.

She went into the parlor, turned on the light, and sat down at the
organ so that she would not have to think about it. But she had not
begun to play when (as she told it) she felt the presence of another
person in the room. For a minute she sat there, her foot resting weight-
lessly on the pedal, her fingers tight on the keys. She supposed the doctor
would be just about reaching the cabin, but when the voice came, she
recognized it as his. "I recognized the voice," she said, "though I don't
think anybody had ever heard anything like that in it before—call it
harshness. And when I recognized that, then it came to me what a daze I
had gone through, not just then but the whole day, and how quick it was
all gone. And not that one day alone."

She spun around on the stool and recognized him too, where he stood
in the door, though he was not the same. It was something about the
face, and this time there was an expression around his mouth, but she
could not recognize that. She did not understand what he had said till he
repeated it.

"God amighty, Amy, I hit him.

"Yes, I dragged him out of bed and hit him. A boy like that. Why, he didn't know any better. He didn't even know any better than to let me drag him out of that bed and hit him. And the whole time he didn't shed one little drop. You'd think he could cry when I hit him anyway, even if he didn't know enough to before."

Amy knew what she had to say, though she had not yet begun to guess what he was talking about. "And you did right too, Will, I know you did."

"I didn't have to hit him, did I! I could have pulled him off the old man and let him go, couldn't I!"

Still she did not see, but that did not stop her from talking till she got him to sit down on the davenport. She sat down close beside him and waited till he was quiet enough to answer the questions.

He had found them on the bed. The cabin had the bed in it, and a cane-bottom rocking chair, and old newspapers for the dog to sleep on if she wanted to, and not much else. It wasn't clean and it wasn't dirty. But since it was summertime, there was one other thing about it—almost an odor, a little like musk, that the doctor had not realized he was smelling as he stood outside the door, knocking on it, the dog getting mixed up with his feet and beginning to whimper. For Dr. Will was the kind who would knock even on that door—but he got no answer.

He opened it anyway, and though it was not quite good dark outside, it was so dark inside that the doctor thought they were asleep. As the darkness took shape he saw they were fully dressed, not only in their overalls but with their work shoes still on. By that time the doctor was standing by the bed, reaching across the boy to lay his hand on Capus' shoulder, meaning to wake him. There was not time to notice that, with the whimpering stopped, not one sound in the room was coming louder than his own breath.

Just as his hand was poised there in mid-air, the boy gave a sudden lurch, his arms going around the old man, fiercely, possessing him, shielding him. So Dr. Will did not have to touch the old man's shoulder to realize that it would be cold. He only seized the boy with his two hands and started the struggle to pry him from the dead body.

The old man apparently died not long after coming back from supper the night before. The doctor explained to his wife why that must be: because otherwise Capus would have had his shoes off. Or even if he had collapsed that morning—sitting on the edge of the bed, knotting his shoes to come to breakfast—it would have amounted to the same thing. For what mattered was that the boy had been lying there in the one room, in the one bed, at least through one whole day if not the night, not knowing enough to come up to the house alone for his meals, and to say, or try to say, what had happened. Or not choosing to come, since, no matter what instinct would never have been able to tell him, it could tell him at least that they would want to take the old man away. The doctor could explain all that to his wife, but he could not explain why, as soon as he had managed to drag the boy upright, he had begun slapping him. He had slapped him into the chair and then he had stopped.

Amy said that she could understand it very well, that it was nothing but indignation, and no one could blame him. But the doctor said no, that was not quite the word. He said it calmly, and she knew it was safe to ask what steps he meant to take.

"I told him not to get back in that bed. That's all. I told him I'd get out the horsewhip if I caught him back there when I came down in the morning with the gravediggers."

"And do you think that boy could understand a word you said?"

"Yes. He is not all that dumb. You don't understand this kind of thing, that's all, nor can I blame you."

"And do you think that even if he understood the words, that that means he is going to do what you told him?"

The doctor was about to say something when he stopped. "By God, Amy! God amighty! That little yellow-eyed——" He was on his feet. "Where's my flashlight?"

Amy ran after him as far as the back porch door. "There's nothing you can do about it anyway. Will, listen to me . . ." He had taken the flashlight down from the porch shelf without breaking stride. "Will, come back in here, are you gone out of your head?"

It was a night without a moon. Amy had to try to follow the flashlight with her eyes. It did not look as though he meant to take the turn into the field path. She saw the flashlight disappear into the barn, and still she did not know what he had in mind. In that mood, according to her, he also would have been capable of anything, and for a minute she had the wild notion that he might keep a gun out there.

She watched in a kind of spell for the flashlight to reappear. By the time it did, she could see a little better. She was able to make out that he was carrying something and that he had struck out through the path toward the cabin.

It was only a shovel.

Amy saw that finally—but not till she had run up the stairs and taken her post by the window through which she had so often watched the Negroes at their work. Once there, she saw the flashlight again. It was set on the ground at the far end of the pasture, next to the cabin, and it was casting its beam on the doctor's pants legs. Already he had bent over and commenced digging; so there could not have been time for him to go back into the cabin and make certain that the boy was really in the bed again. Amy knew by that the doctor had not needed to, that he knew by then the nature of the thing he was dealing with.

"That," she said later, "was the second time I thought I had won. I didn't even stay at the window long enough to realize what a fool picture

it was—Will digging a grave for a dead nigger in the middle of the
night. Well, maybe not the middle, but it must have been before he was
done. So if I didn't stay there long enough to realize that, I don't guess I
stayed there any time at all. And of course poor Will didn't take the time
either to see what a fool thing it all was. Though I doubt if a little thing
like that would have stopped him."

After she left the window she made ready for bed directly, though it
could not have been more than a little past eight o'clock. She read a
magazine in bed for a while and went to sleep with the light burning.
Whatever time the doctor came in, he was careful not to disturb her.

The next day the doctor did not leave the place, and every day he did
not leave the place after that, it seemed easier. If the telephone rang he
would not let Amy answer it. When one of his old patients, a Mrs.
Wilbur, was driven out to the doctor's by her son, Amy met the boy at
the door. "The doctor says you had better take her over to Dr. Herbert
in Paris. Yes, that's right, he isn't feeling very well."

Amy did not try to find another cook. She rose early and was glad to
get her husband's breakfast. Though he had not milked a cow since he
was a boy, somebody had to, and he did not seem to mind. One day he
picked a mess of peas too, and another time swept the back yard. And
every morning and every evening he fried a little something on the stove,
placed it in a dish, covered that over with another, and carried it
through the pasture to the cabin. He would be gone perhaps half an
hour.

"He just sits there," the doctor said.

"Don't you think you'd better put a lock on the door?"

"No, he won't run away."

"I mean——"

"Oh no, that boy, he wouldn't harm a soul, if that's what you mean.
Don't you worry, love."

That lasted nearly a week before Amy drove in to visit anybody.
Then, sitting on one of the front porches, clasping and unclasping her
hands, she explained.

"I didn't know if I should let him out of my sight, but I had to see
another human being—I mean besides Will—before I began to question
my own sanity a little. You see, he won't let me touch that food he
prepares for the boy. Says it is not my place to. I keep telling him he did
right, and he says yes, he knows it's the only thing he could have done,
but that's no comfort. I am beginning to think he ought to be put away
someplace."

"The boy, you mean?" she was asked.

"Yes, the boy too. But I was thinking more about Will. I'd have him
put away in one of those nice rest homes for a while—we could afford
it—only I don't think I could get old Dr. Herbert or any of the others to

sign whatever it is they sign, and nothing short of law would budge that man I married."

The story would be over then, and she would be smiling as she rose to go. "I had better be getting back or else he'll worry his fool head off about me. He may not need me, but I like to think he does, a little. If only so he'll not have to stop worrying over me. It's such a habit with him by now, you know."

It was nearly twilight when she got into her A-model and turned back toward the farm and the man she probably did not even then understand wholly, though she had stopped not loving him. It was nearly twilight and soon it would be dark. It was about the time, she knew, that Dr. Will would be hurrying, as he always hurried in anything, through the field and toward the cabin, the dog running at his heels, and he would be holding the covered plate as preciously as he could between those large freckled hands of his.

CAROLYN KIZER

A Slight Mechanical Failure

I want to tell you about a series of incidents that began with an encounter in the terminal of O'Hare airport in Chicago. This woman of forty, tall, sunny and rather dramatic looking, sees someone she has known, casually, for a long time, whom she hasn't run into for years. Because she is nearsighted, every greeting is a surprise.

"Hello there! Are you on your way home? I'm in luck." Perhaps that is not exactly what he said, but more or less the idea. Her memory is not retentive, even over the short span of time since this encounter occurred, except for gists of things, old phone numbers of children who have vanished into other worlds, bits of case histories without proper names attached.

The man who addresses her is someone she has known for about eighteen years. That's easy: she was married eighteen years ago, and this man and his wife had been in the circle of her husband's friends. He was a lawyer, like her husband. As a young man he had been slightly moon-faced, his expression rather tentative, perhaps reflecting nothing less ephemeral than immaturity. At any rate, the impression he gave then had prevented her from signalling herself: *There*—that private announcement that we make when we are instantly attracted.

She herself had been tawny-haired—and still managed to remain so, an effort uncharacteristic of her. Rather tawny all over, carelessly assembled, graceful and gauche by turns, she put one in mind of a big cat. In the cell of her marriage—finished these ten years—she had seemed even more like a big, untamed cat pacing her cage with a long, steady lope, shaking her head impatiently from time to time, as if in a futile attempt to ease the chafing of an invisible collar. Some men are strongly drawn to

77

this kind of woman, but she was not aware that this man had ever been one of them.

But now, with his hand on her arm arresting her gently, as if afraid she would take flight (cats can't fly), she saw the changes in the half dozen years or so since she had last seen him. He retained the face of a man in his twenties, but now the features were utterly unblurred; there was a decisive set to the man's whole appearance. Also, she remembered him as characteristically pale. Now he was lightly and evenly tanned, the look bestowed by regular, brief sessions under a lamp. Or did he ski? Yes, she remembered now. The whole family skied. Her own children—off on weekends with their divorced father—had mentioned seeing them at Aspen or Sun Valley.

But what contributed most strongly to the almost crystalline presence of the man now was that his hair was pure white. Now, in his mid-forties, he was a distinctly handsome man. If that voice of her body did not now say, *There*, it was only because of being still a little muffled by preconceptions.

Still, there was some other change that seemed less the product of the years than of some recent happening. His expression seemed a little too fixed—fatigue, perhaps?—and the skin around his eyes and mouth was a bit white and pinched. She speculated about this, probably squinting at him slightly as they strolled towards the plane to which they both had changed, she from Washington, he from New York.

There was some complication about his ticket—evidently he had shifted to a later flight at the last minute, out of New York—so she went on ahead and quietly took her window seat, peeling off her suit jacket and slumping down in her fawn-colored sweater and skirt (with only one small spot on it, of breakfast syrup from that morning), fastening her seat-belt as loosely as she could. She gave a few precursory tugs to the arm rest next to her, hoping the flight would not be full, and that she could remove it and stretch out on the seat, the only way in which she could comfortably rest. A sprinkling of other passengers came down the aisles and ducked into the window seats. After a few minutes she was aware that he had seated himself about a third of the way back, on the opposite aisle. The DC8 took off, in one great smooth lift, and presently the seat-belts and no-smoking lights went off, and the aisle lights as well, for it was already fairly late at night.

A few minutes later, he was bending over her row of seats and inquiring, "May I sit with you?" And she smiled, and moved her magazine from the adjacent seat. A certain reticence had prompted her to leave him at the check-in counter and stroll on towards the plane: at the time of her divorce, which had been protracted, bloody, public and difficult, most of their common friends had dropped away. Their friends had been affluent, or about-to-be affluent professional men, with a few businessmen who thought of themselves as liberals, and one or two university instructors and their wives. Her husband had been something of a political dilettante at one time, and most of his friends shared his interest in local government, a preoccupation which, on the part of nearly all of them, had withered away as their careers made more and more demands on them, as their families grew ever more expensive to maintain, and as they suffered less and less gladly the actual boredom of local poltical meetings and their endless talk, talk, talk. The businessmen among them now used the word "liberal" about themselves automatically, without any real conviction. The instructors had become full professors, and, like the others, rather smugly identified with the upper middle class of the middle-sized city where most of them had grown up.

She had been one of the few outsiders. And then she was the only one of this circle to seek a divorce. None of the others had been divorced in the ten years since. Her divorce had been a shock to the community at the time, both because of her husband's position as the last scion of a pioneer family, and because he and she had kept up a careful front of politeness to one another over the miserable years, and a declination to gossip about each other even to their nearest relatives. As a rich, fastidious, inhibited only son with a dominating mother, her husband was actually incapable of discussing his own feelings. She had chosen not to, partly because it seemed unsporting to take advantage of his inability to express himself, partly to fend off the solicitude of her own watchful and anxious parents.

Even without these reasons, it seemed to her that divorce was always a shock, a traumatic shock. Sometimes she went even further, and insisted that both parties involved in a divorce become victims of temporary insanity. She felt it was the most charitable way of recalling her husband's behavior, and even her own, during that trying time. Their friends—acquaintances really, because they virtually had no intimates—had fled from them as if they spread contamination. And perhaps, she now was able to think, her bitterness long abated, perhaps they had. Disaster is catching. Insanity is contagious. And their friends had their own investments to protect.

Of course there had been certain exceptions. Now it sometimes amused her to think of them, a decade later. A number of her husband's closest associates, once he and she had established separate residences, came and hung about her door as if she were, indeed, a big cat in heat. All unsuspicious, she had welcomed them in at first, only mildly concerned that their wives did not accompany them. Then, when she understood what they were after, she phoned her mother long-distance, and asked her to come and stay with her for a month or two. Curious! None of them had ever seemed anything to her but her husband's rather pleasant, rather innocuous friends, supports if not yet pillars of their community, dutiful as fathers, faithful to their wives. Or was it that they were so conventional that the extraordinary fact of her divorce had converted her into some strange, symbolic being, a Scarlet Woman perhaps? Whatever it was, it was distasteful to her, even as she giggled over it.

Finally, there were the obscene phone calls, persistent, miserable, sometimes four or five in a single night. At first it didn't occur to her that this could be someone that she and her husband knew. One day she ran into a political friend of her husband's on the street, rather a prominent man, even then. She recognized the voice. By a casual word or two in the right places she might have brought about his ruin. But, other than having her phone number unlisted, she did nothing.

Of the men who had hung about her then, one was now a judge, still another a state official. All of them were wealthier. All of them paid lip-service at least to conventional behavior. So far, she had resisted the temptation, on the rare occasions when she met any of them, to embarrass them by reminders of that time when they had pressed her bell like eager bachelors.

The man sitting next to her now had been one of the bachelor husbands. He and his wife had merely dropped her, unobtrusively, while maintaining a casual association with her husband, for reasons of business. She bore them no malice for this—although, like Robert Frost, she did have malices to keep—but had continued to think of the couple, when she thought of them at all, as decent and amiable people. However, because of the business connections with her husband, she was sure that he probably knew more about her divorce, and its attendant agonies, than most people had. Having some idea of the rather Medean version of herself which her husband had projected then, and perfected since, she had felt a little shy about anything beyond an exchange of civilities.

However, here he sat, looking pleasant, but still rather pinched. He bought her a drink: she noticed his hand was trembling. They continued to divulge the kind of information about their respective families that friendly people share with each other after long and unintentional separations. Bill is still in his first year at Wesleyan. Sally broke her leg skiing last month. (Yes, they *did* ski.) Behind their casual words she sensed, with every breath, his particular attention.

Then he said, "Do you know, tonight I missed the Boston shuttle, just missed it? I ran out onto the field as they were taking the steps away, and I cursed them, and myself, and the cab-drivers of Boston. It had been the second section, so I had to wait quite a while before another plane came along, and I knew I would miss my connection to the coast.

Which I did, of course, or I wouldn't be here. I wouldn't be here. You know what happened?"

He had been holding her arm. Now he put down his drink and took her other hand. "The shuttle I missed collided with another plane over New York. The big plane lost a wing, but managed to land with only a few injuries. But they believe that everyone on that shuttle is dead. I know they are. When we landed, I saw the big plane sitting there with its wing sheared off. And I could see where the shuttle was still burning."

Of course she returned the pressure of his hands, murmured, "My dear, my dear Phil," and other things one utters in the kind of situation which makes it impossible to avoid clichés unless one is without a spark of human feeling. She murmured, and he murmured back, and he stroked her arm as if she were the one in need of soothing, and they had another drink.

She asked him about his trip (hers had been to visit a daughter in school in Virginia), and that led him into a discussion of his cases, quite unhesitatingly, remembering that she was used to lawyers talking shop, perhaps even recalling dinner parties of long ago when she seemed to enjoy it. There was no diminution of his tenseness; if anything, it seemed to be building in him. When she touched his arm, it was as if she put her hand on naked bone, with a thin overlay of cloth. She noticed the rope of tension in his neck, and the prominent corners of his jaw when he was not speaking showed that his teeth were clenched. Then, to her vast surprise, he asked her, as if it were a favor she could bestow, if he might rub her back.

"But of course! I love it. Doesn't any right-minded woman? And I can never get the children to do it." She turned sideways, slightly away from him, and he firmly grasped the back of her neck; she felt like a kitten that is being picked up. Then, with long, firm strokes, he began to rub her back through her tan sweater.

"I love it, I love it," she murmured, and began to purr. She stretched out her whole long length and let her hands fall open.

"Oooh," she crooned, "you do it so well. You must love to be massaged yourself."

"I do," he said, "but Anita won't let me touch her back. She says it makes her nervous. So of course I can't ask her to rub mine." He went on with calm, strong determination, never abating the rhythm of the strokes. Although her intense pleasure probably added to his, it was plain than his first motive was to give relief and comfort to himself.

Gradually she felt herself melting into the seat, now extended, like his, as far back as it would go. Almost involuntarily, she turned towards him; he gripped her gently by the shoulders, then began to caress her back again, while she rested against him. After a few minutes he stood up and took a blanket from the rack and wrapped them both in it, and for the rest of the journey they lay in each other's arms, kissing gently and deliberately from time to time, but holding quite still now, like one inanimate vessel containing their deep emotional excitement.

At one point he said, of course, "I want you." She could tell, from what he then said, and failed to say, that he would not know how to manage very well. "Poor man!" she murmured tenderly to herself. Aloud, she said, "I never thought of your even being the kind of man who would be . . . up to anything. Both of you have always seemed to me so . . . so virtuous."

"Did you mean to say 'conventional'?" he asked. But she did not reply. Instead, she was thinking ahead. Oh, it was apparent he would not know how to manage. "And if I help or plan," she thought to herself, "it will spoil it for him because it will imply so much experience of this sort of thing." She resigned herself to the clumsiness which she fancied lay ahead.

But even though she was prepared, she was a little shocked when the plane put down at the airport at home. "Thank God," she said to herself when they moved out into the aisle, and the other passengers stood up and put on their coats, because he did not look them over furtively to see if anyone recognized him. She had been sure he would, knowing the cautiousness and propriety that characterised him and his whole style. Instead, it was she who looked around, only from curiosity. Although she customarily behaved with circumspection, she had long ceased to care what the community she lived in thought of her. She was habitually as detached from it as she had been a few minutes ago, when the plane was separated from the ground by thousands of feet.

The shock came when they picked up their bags at the terminal. They both had their cars in the airport parking lot, but she had assumed that he would suggest that they rendezvous for a drink at one of the airport motel bars nearby. She knew that his wife and children were going to be at a ski resort until the next day. He had said that he planned on joining them for a day's skiing. But surely the simplest thing in the world would be to phone his wife and tell her that he was too exhausted for the long drive into the mountains. And he knew that her son was staying with friends. Instead, he shook her by the hand, gripped her upper arm briefly, and said goodbye.

"Well, I'm damned!" she thought, hoisting her bag and trudging out into the dark to search for her car. Ruefully, she thought, "It's probably for the best. This really wouldn't have been his kind of thing. And it hasn't been mine for a long, long time." Like nearly all her morality, her belief in the essential soundness of the seventh commandment had been learned from experience. She tended to be impatient with that sort of intellectual who, for all his brilliance, has never been able to arrive at the simple conclusion that to be reasonably happy you have to be reasonably good.

But what she thought was her final comment to herself on the experience, as she lay in what seemed her unnecessarily wide bed an hour or so later, trying without success to simmer down, was that the whole episode had been no more than a reaction, on the most atavistic level, to having missed death "by inches." She thought of stories she had heard about men in the war who, when the man next to them was killed, would have an erection. "He's probably come to his senses already. And that will be that."

An hour later, she climbed rapidly out of a cold bath into which she had lowered herself, laughing rather grimly at trying "the headmaster's remedy," to answer the phone. She knew his voice at once.

"I wasn't able to get the car started. What an idiot I was, not to see you to yours, and have you wait for me. I've become so used to these flights east that I've fallen into a routine. And yet I knew I was having trouble with the battery before I left."

"Where are you now?"

"At a gas station, where they've towed the car, waiting for a taxi I just called."

Then he wondered, was it too late to come to see her?

Yes, she replied, she rather thought it was.

"Goodnight, then."

"Goodnight." Oh, the idiot!

Over the next few days he phoned, a number of times. Her son answered the phone once or twice. Like her, he had an excellent memory for voices.

"Mother, Philip Graves is on the phone, for you, but for some reason he says his name is Mr. Smith." "Good heavens," she thought "this is even worse than I expected." Discreetly, her son had left the room.

"Philip, there are lots of quite plausible reasons why you might want to speak to me on the phone. We're both on the Opera board, even though I never go. We're both on the symphony board, even though *you* don't go. Our children see each other at dances and so on. For God's sake, let's not lie any more than we have to." Even as she said this, she realized she might as well be speaking into a dead phone. He went right ahead making nervous inquiries about when and where they could meet. Their schedules were incompatible, so they had similar colloquies the rest of the week. She could sense, behind each inconclusive conversation, the continuing strength of his obsession. It always surprised her a little.

Eventually, as "Mr. Smith" kept calling, she began to wonder if the false name, the nervous and unnecessary fibs, were becoming part of the obsession, even nourishing it. "Maybe I'm just being mystical about this because it annoys me so much," she thought.

Finally, they had a brief meeting in a dark cocktail lounge, at what normally would have been their dinner time. He seemed just as he had been on the plane: surprisingly unself-conscious, not staring into the dark to see if he was identified at the adjoining tables. Quite the man of the world, one might think. Her conversations with herself about him were becoming increasingly ironic.

The next afternoon he phoned her, to explain that he had suddenly been released from a previous engagement and would be free to see her that evening. She suggested that he come over about ten, when her son would presumably be asleep. However, the boy picked up, as children will, the tension which she felt but was careful not to express. He was in and out of bed half-a-dozen times on one pretext or another, until she was almost desperate enough to tell him, "Listen, Phil Graves is coming over here to see me, and I want you to get lost." He was a little old to be ordered to stay in his room. But at last he subsided, and she zipped herself into a yellow silk housecoat and waited for the discreet knock on the door.

"I'm sorry if I sound addle-pated," she said to a friend on the telephone the next morning. "I was up all night with a sick friend."

"Ah, there's a lot of 'flu around," was the reply. 'Flu, my eye! The man had been impotent. Now her ironies were, apparently, receiving a transfusion of old-fashioned vulgarity. She continued the conversation to herself: "I was the only one who was up." Good heavens, she was turning into a Molly Bloom! Faintly aghast with herself, she giggled silently for a long time.

"The worst of it is," she told herself wearily, "I shall have to let him come *back*. One can't just leave a man in this condition. To himself, he'd have the name without the game." She had felt failure too many times herself to want to wish the condition on another human being. "I'm bored with him now, I'm bored with the whole thing. But I'll have to give him his chance to prove that he can make it."

That night, sleepless again, she admitted to herself that what she had called boredom was rather more complex. She was irked, not so much by the ineptitude he'd shown since they disembarked from the plane, or by his actual impotence. She was sufficiently experienced not to be surprised by that, the first time. What was missing was the tenderness she felt had suffused them both as they lay together on the plane. The laying on of hands—quite literally when he'd rubbed her back—had succeeded, in part, in liberating them both: him from his death-inspired self-preoccupation, and her from an endless addictive dialogue with herself.

"He is," she decided, "frustrating me, and sexual response is only part of it." She realized she was angry with him. "Those ludicrous phone calls! And then the way he came over here, with his head lowered like a steer. No grace to him at all." She knew men were amused by the need women felt for tender notes, and flowers. But it was because they required some proof of grace or style, something to justify what might seem to others a meaningless sexual escapade, through what a Russian she had once read called mutual aid.

If she was being irrational about this, after all it had all been a bit irrational to begin with. "Brushing death . . ." she wasn't being very articulate about it, "brushing death made him different from what he had been, someone . . . someone more *unusual* than he was, and more imaginative." But as she had said before, in a sexual context, he couldn't keep it up. And the trouble was, their coversation kept turning back to the preoccupations of their ordinary lives.

"I love my daughter better than my son. My wife knows this, and keeps bringing it up, which makes it worse. I feel so close to my girl, such an intimacy. And it's all the more precious to me because I know it will only last a few more years. I had always thought it was a perfectly normal thing for fathers and daughters to be close at this age."

"Well, I don't think it's 'normal,' in the sense that it happens all the time, but I think you are very fortunate."

"Anita acts as if there were something wrong with me."

His conversation about children had been more interesting than hers. At least it had concerned something deeply important to him.

They talked, too, about the last time they had seen each other, before their meeting at the airport. It had been the funeral of the only intimate friend they had in common. She had died of cancer at thirty-five. Joan had been a woman of exceptional warmth and generosity. They spoke of Joan's funeral, where all the young husbands had wept openly. The violinist who played at the service had been a friend, and he wept, and his tears ran down his chin onto the violin he was playing.

That hadn't been too bad. Talk of love and death. The trouble was, it all concerned the world they had in common. Perhaps this was where she failed him, that she brought no mystery to him. She wondered if he too had once thought of her as the Scarlet Woman. Perhaps all their talk of family love and family life had, more than anything else, put him off.

She saw him only once more. She had composed most of the dialogue ahead of time, and it went predictably. All that remained was for them to speak the lines, lines of such a painful banality that it is difficult for her to reproduce them now. But nearly all their lines had been banal. It was only the thoughts which had gone on inside their heads which had been daring, passionate and original.

"I'm *terribly* sorry I was in such a hurry. I promise to be better next time." His protestations didn't hide the faint note of smugness. At least he had salvaged something.

"Really, it doesn't matter in the least." Just leave, leave!

"Is there anything I can do to . . . help?"

God, *no.* "No, thank you. I'm just fine, really." She noticed him looking towards his hat on the bureau. God, I haven't even known a man who wore a hat in ten years.

"I wish I could stay longer, but I'm afraid I have to get home. It's nearly two."

"It's all right." Now your dignity is restored. Now, without guilt I can let you go.

Later, she reminded herself of wild lovers she had known, uninhibited men, many of them artists and bohemians of one kind and another, many of them much younger than she because of those reservations— how right she had been!—about adultery. Of patterns building one another higher and higher until, in one great smooth lift, the human being abandoned, for a moment, his tenement of earth.

It was cold comfort. Philip could never have been that kind of lover, under the best of circumstances, nor she to him. She could, she was quite sure, acquire another marvelous young man. But, she thought drearily, without any particular confidence in that intuition which had seemed to her in her youth so infallible, with a little more daring, just a small helping of imagination, he might have released both of them into love.

KENNETH KOCH

The Postcard Collection

On the first card, which seemed to be a French one from around 1928, which had already been sent through the mails and had writing on the back, was a picture of an old woman in a yellowish-pink dress holding a watering can and bending over some flowers; the blossoms were red, blue, and purple, one of them yellow; most of the background of the card was yellowish-pink, though with a little more grey intermixed than in the old woman's dress. However, in the upper left hand corner was a splash of green shaped more or less like a leaf-mint, and over this green was inscribed in printed writing the word "Auvergne." The handwriting on the back of the card was slanted and thin, in dark blue ink. The words it contained were not all legible because someone had apparently spilled liquid (most likely water) on some of them and this had washed away certain parts of their letters, here the angle of a K, there the tall blue stem of a T. The message was written in French; what could be read of it was, roughly, as follows (translated into English): "Theo, my dear—The Auvergne is as beautiful as you have always . . ." (said? told me? No, not "told me" because then the objective pronoun "m" would have been visible before the "have," the "avez"). After this point the writing on the card was largely blurred. There was some clarity again toward the end: ". . . a large one" (masculine gender): "un grand"—or, possibly, "a great man" (no, in that case "grand" would be, necessarily, followed by "homme," which it was not); perhaps, "a big one." But a big or great or grand what? A kiss, perhaps, or a hug; maybe a drink—perhaps the writer was explaining that somone had given her (him?) a big glass (not cup, which is feminine) of delicious local Auvergne wine to drink; if the latter explanation is true, then the sentence could be reconstructed as follows: "We just wanted a sip of the local wine, and we asked the man for it, wanting a small glass, but he gave us a big one." On the whole, however, this sentence seems rather clumsy and long. If one accepts it as a more or less accurate reconstruction of the meaning, however, then one is forced to suppose that the writing on the card which precedes it and follows the words "Theo, my dear—the Auvergne is as beautiful as you have always (said?),'' that the words in the middle say something like "Or at least so it seems. Though it is rather hard for me to tell, I am so tipsy just now. Gerard and I just had a rather too-refreshing moment at the Caves Gibicault; I'm sure you know them, the ones outside of town. Well, you have told me how generous are the people here!" It is possible, of course, that the main body of the card is concerned with something entirely different; the sentence ending with "un grand" could very well be some such thing as "He has a little shoe and I have a big one." It is possible, too—and this would defeat all but the most painstaking and even inspired efforts—that in the blotted-out sentences the writer of the card was merely indulging in the free association of images or words; or even in the half- or super-conscious ordering of such free-flowing associations, which constitutes poetry.

Turning the card over again, it is possible to examine the picture with a view to discovering just what it is about it that has made us suppose, half-unconsciously, it's true, that it was written by a woman in her middle years, perhaps beyond, though most likely between the ages of 40 and 50. One notices on second perusal that the scene pictured on the card is not entirely the product of human imagination (ramifications of this problem suggest themselves at once but had better be resolved later); more simply, the scene is not entirely painted but is, aside from the green leaf-mint splash signifying "Auvergne," the lettering, and the coloration of the background, woman's face and gown, and flowers, a photograph—perhaps photo-montage would be a more exact description since one easily detects a sort of incongruity between the old woman in her bending position (she looks more as though she were stooping to water vegetables which grow very close to the ground) and the flowers, as well as, of course, and this phenomenon is common to so many words, suggesting as it does the limits, after a certain point necessary ones, of the skill and knowledge of the artist or perhaps indeed of his aesthetic intentions, between the woman-flowers cluster and the background, which has a generalized quality not present in the aforementioned. We have in some way (perhaps correctly) unconsciously identified the woman pictured on the card with the author of the message on its other side. This identification was partial, however, since we have supposed in the writer a greater degree of culture and urban sophistication than seems present in the old woman; in fact it's this "urban sophistication" in a rather naive form which is what appeals to us so little in the message we have figured out for the back. One gets the feeling that the writer might have led a happier life, full of more real satisfactions, if she had been more like the pictured old woman, whom she no doubt felt superior to when she purchased the card. Perhaps not; but that would suggest a sweetness and a calm in her one could not help but admire. We should in that case have to change our estimate of the contents of the message on the back; for the one we have constructed would never spring from a truly sophisticated yet serene and loving soul.

Yet, again, the last hypothesis—the the card was written from deep wells of sunlight and contentment—seems contradicted by the scene that is pictured on the card. That scene is, as we have already noticed, naive and even simpleminded. Then was the card sent to amuse the recipient? This possibility is rendered unlikely by the first and almost completely legible sentence on the back (see above).

Or was there a confusion in intention, a striking difference between the impulse to purchase that particular card and the emotions and cross-currents active in the purchaser at the time of writing the message? Was one meant to correct the other? How much of reality, of what we see, is born of that sort of connection, of that kind of need for the amendment of initial impulses—or is what I am talking about rather the working out of concealed realities by the use of half-understood contradictions?

Was the writer first moved by naive enthusiasm, then embarrassed by the simplicity of the card? If so, we have to suppose something ironic in the message, such as (after the Dear Theo sentence) "though it's nothing like this card, which has given me, a newcomer here, a little laugh, but which will probably give you a big one!" Or was it quite the reverse, and was the writer, actually liking the Auvergne and liking the recipient "Theo," yet moved by a self-destructive impulse only thinly veiled as an outwardly directed one, since it was always in truth directed at her warmest and most spontaneous emotions (perhaps this arose from a shame deeply felt in infancy or childhood), subtly (perhaps for "Theo" quite obviously) attacking, by the naive imbecility of the card, the presence of this spontaneous enthusiasm in herself. A fear, then, of being naive, or perhaps even a far deeper problem, a mistrust of all one's emotions—perhaps more accurately this: one great emotional scar, one terrible wound inflicted by and on one's feelings at some time in one's life—then, forever after, every emotion strongly or spontaneously felt, every feeling which seems to shadow these painful and primal ones, these huge feelings which did not work out, to shadow them as the light yellow-green of the front of the postcard in question might shadow the sunlight on the fields of the Auvergne, every such emotion then recalling the large

painful ones, thus every access of joy immediately corrected by pained
remembrance, by pain.

If all this is true, picture and card may be reconstructed to read
secretly somewhat like this: "Theo, my dear—how happy I am and yet
how miserable! Is the Auvergne a reality? If, at a moment, I find it such,
it then seems to me the most beautiful poetry there is, for just as for most
persons poetry, or beauty, is an adornment, an extension of reality, of
life, for me it is the peering through, even for the briefest moment, of
any piece of reality, a peering through, that is, of the black cloak of
death and fog which my unfortunate character at once pulls down to
cover, to suffocate everything. So the very falseness of this card, the
sentimental idiocy of flower-watering peasantry, the too-bright, too-color-
ful, too-improbable flowers, are but a mirror of the falseness, for me, of
any duration of an individual joy, of joy of any kind. I do not know if
this overhanging gloom of mine, this extended inner voice which whis-
pers always of death and dissatisfaction is an unfortunate product of
experiences particular to me, or if it is a generalized problem of ma .
Yours, in the hope of some solution during this life, Magda."
But here I think we may leave this hypothesis, for the moment at
least. For, given the "Theo my dear, etc." actually legible on the back of
the card, the hypothesis has to be somewhat modified.

On the basis of this sentence one would guess the writer not to have
been an intellectual capable of the subtlety of expression contained in
the hypothesized "secret message." However, does it matter? With what
are we really concerned? Doesn't there exist such an intellectual somewhere inside every human being, an "inward intellectual" who can be
brought into the light, from whom we can be freed only by what he is
continually urging us to: the fullest exercise of our intellectual and
above all our imaginative powers?

> *Is there not, inside every one of us,*
> *An "intellectual," who, when the bus*
> *Is ready to depart, says "Do I really*
> *Want to get on?" and makes us miss it nearly?*
> *And is not such a one at work in all*
> *The choices we make dressing for a ball*
> *Or walking down the quais to pick a card*
> *To send to someone? Though we try quite hard*
> *To sublimate him he is always there,*
> *Like the hair cell that underlies the hair.*
> *True, great and passionate experience*
> *Can so inundate every human sense*

> *With fire and glory that the "intellect-*
> *Ual" gets deader than one might expect;*
> *But once the passion's gone, then he arises.*
> *And thus great art with its so great surprises*
> *Like passion that endures is all that can*
> *(If even it can) change one to a man*
> *Or woman of whom the surface is as thrilling*
> *As Italy, and far more warm and willing*
> *To move about; and yet not constantly*
> *Is such great pleasure possible to me,*
> *So I regard these postcards, these half-arts,*
> *In nervous patience till the glory starts.*

Were I to put the card in a novel, I should have imagined its message as follows: "Thank you for the kiss. It is true, perhaps, that in the middle of the Auvergne I should not have noticed you, or rather *recognized*, had you not, just before kissing me, slightly tilted your straw hat to the left, then let me feel the warmth of your lips. Ann."

But this happy version would have come about because the intellectual inside of me has direct connections, and constantly, with the surface, and will not allow any nonsense. If you are attached to the sensual life, he would say to me, with its sunscorched hat-tilting, write it out, put it in, perhaps it will come true. We never know.

As if the evidence of any one thing we had seen were not totally damning!

The second card, which featured on its picture side the various kinds of French currency circa 1908 implanted on a heady blue, white, and green background of scenes from the Bois de Boulogne, had written on its back merely "Hi" in English, and after that "A toi" in French ("to you," or more properly "to thee"), and was signed very clearly in the purplish red ink that had written the rest, "Mary." This address is easy to make out: Mr. Alfred LaFont, 3836 Retreat Street, St. Paul, Minnesota, USA. There is no return address save for the words (a name) "Mary Ryan." Oh yes. Underneath it in very blurred writing is "Hôtel de l'Univers, rue Monsieur-le-Prince, Paris."

And who are (or were, for death strikes everywhere: and the date on the postmark is 1909) these two, Mary and Alfred, and how were they related to one another? I should like to look some more at the front of the card.

On one of the coins, which is colored silver and like all the rest somehow made into a kind of paper bas relief actually on the postcard, is pictured a woman whose long full dress seems to belie her youthful walk, her slim form, her clear cheek (her face is not visible save for the left

cheek). Her hair is voluminous and youthful-looking too, and is gathered
behind her head into a fat "pony-tail" type of hairdo. Her silver gown is
slightly raised up over her tiny left shoulder, probably chiefly to suggest
the fullness of the material, to add to the sense of richness one seems
meant to feel about this woman all round. Her little right arm is extended to the side as well as slightly behind her, as though its activity
could scarcely keep up with the pace of her stride; for the coin scene
catches the woman in a moment of movement and activity. Furthermore
her right arm is slightly bent at the elbow, the two sections of her arm
thus creating an angle of about 130°. Another angle is created by her
hand and wrist, which are tilted at from 95–100° away from the forearm. About 1½ times the length of the forearm away from the lowest
(the highest on the arm) point of the wrist, one eighth of an inch below,
though with its straight silver rays passing apparently under the arms
and wrist without really touching them, which presumably would burn
them, because it is a sun, is about 1/20 of a round object that seems to be
the sun; aside from sending out rays of its own, it is intercepted by a
straight line crosswise, which is thinner and has less body than the rays.
This interception, however, does not merely pass under or beyond the
sun as its rays pass beyond the woman's arm and hand—on the contrary,
it effectively cuts it off: there is no more sun beneath the line. This same
line, however, does not cut off the woman, but, like the sun-rays, seems to
pass under her or beyond her, at about an inch or two (according to
scale—actually as pictured it is a distance more like 1/1000 of an inch)
above her knees, or rather where one assumes her knees are beneath the
folds of the dress. There is thus a suggestion, of a purely mechanical
origin, of the superiority of the figure of the woman to the other elements in the composition: everything passes beneath or beyond her; and,
perhaps most strikingly of all, her body is the largest element in the
composition and the one that is by far the most raised up; her silver
figure triumphs in uninterruptibility, size, and volume. She is the highest, silveriest, and then she is moving too, which always catches the eye;
or rather she is sculpted as if in movement. Her left arm is extended
straight down and forward, creating an angle of about 40° with the
perpendicular line of her body. Its hand is holding something slightly
larger than her head, something polygonal in shape, which at first view
seems to be a small shield and even perhaps to be stuck to her arm in
some way rather than to be clasped by her fingers. Further observation,
however, coupled with intellectual reminiscences of what this scene is
probably supposed to represent, leads one to speculate that the held
object is probably a sack of some kind, most likely a repository (if true,
this would explain the position of the right arm and even the nature of
the woman's movement across the coin) for grain or seed. The woman's
right knee is slightly bent, yet the foot is flat on the ground; the left leg,

on the other hand, is bent slightly from the hip and again abruptly from the knee, in such a way that the bottom of the foot (shoe) makes an angle of 60° with the flat horizontal (in this case the bottom and top of the card). Around the circumference of the coin, at varying short distances from the moving woman, are letters which spell out "RÉPUBLIQUE FRANÇAISE."

I love you. It is ridiculous to try to hide this from you by going over the collection. When I see the blue on a card I see your eyes; they float into my vision and there is no more work possible for that day. Or if yes, if there still is work possible it is no longer work of the same kind, for all my clear observation is disturbed by an overwhelming desire to tell a truth which is not, so to speak, "in the cards." I want to say "I love you" over and over again, as if that somehow had a meaning which could sustain us. "Sustain us?" no, that is overdramatic; we are not falling. But we are deliberately exposing ourselves to the dangers of the air.

And to say that "is not in the cards" is perhaps wrong too. For isn't this card, with its complex and beautiful surface (of which I have described only the tiniest part), its lovable red-and-purplish ink, as well as the air of freshness about the spacing of the message, and that message itself, in its simplicity, its directness, its nearly John Donne-like force (what more "metaphysical" and direct can one say—Hi! A toi, America, France, you, I, the world, our love) evidence entirely to the contrary? Are we not, in fact, in the presence of one of the sweetest moments in the world, the conscious and unconscious moving together, in a single dance, or perhaps merely a striding along, which expresses in its mingling of absence and presence the irresistible nature of life's minutest failures?

For this I have to thank France. And I shall thank you too. And what of the manufacturers of postcards! far from my coin, to the right, and above the grand lac of the Bois de Boulogne, that cornucopia exuding pink and blue bank notes of fifty, one hundred, five hundred, and one thousand francs!

> *When you're free of indigestion*
> *Follow this divine suggestion:*
> *Let the richness of*
> *The earth enslave your love.*
> *I mean 'engage your love'*
> *But it is all no matter;*
> *Life is shapeless as a glove*
> *Yet a formal matter.*
> *Inside this five-fingered*
> *Easily-splayable form*
> *Poets who have lingered*

Find this to keep warm:
"Always let variety
Substantiate your feeling
And love's sweet society
Will pay you richly when the springtime's dealing.
Otherwise
Avoid horrible disease that flies
About.
Sit down sometimes. When you feel like it, shout.
And most of all
Do the impossible. Call
Sleep being awake,
And zero all you want to take."

Advice that's hard to understand,
But on the other hand
Come to me while I am sleeping
Dear zero in my keeping.

After a night of intensely various and gentle visions I return to the collection.

A floral decoration in blue, a decoration which is festooned around the outside of a blank white rectangle inside which is imprinted a poem, in French, entitled (in Latin) "Ultima Verba." The poem, which is printed in a sort of rounded type with little arabesques of branching ink between some of the letters, has twelve lines, and reads (translated loosely into English, that is, reading and translating one word at a time, as each word comes along, and not surveying and studying the whole in the attempt to make a perfect poem) as follows:

Beneath your eyes O adored woman
I've assembled all these materials
Which piled up encumbered on my table
Bearing the name "Little Floral Games"!

Metrical lines, prose sweet and pretty,
Lofty sonnets, or modest quatrains,
Words where wit and grace are joined—
All has more or less passed through your hands.

If, listening to you, lovable sovereign,
I had been able to award to the competitors
Gold and silver flowers, like a real Mycenas,
One would have seen me giving them handfuls.

Unfortunately, perhaps, the message is completely blotted off the back of this card; there is nothing but a small smear of red ink. It is doubtful that it was ever sent through the mails. There seems to be a certain amount of redness faded onto the poem-side of the card too, as though the card had perhaps been kept for a long time in juxtaposition with something red—a shirt pocket, a red velvet vest, hose, flower petals, a red-covered book. Perhaps there had never been any intention of sending it; perhaps there had. In any case, about this there is no evidence.

Printed in the bottom right-hand part of the card, and in slightly larger type than that in which even the title of Ultima Verba is printed, are the words (in French) "Little Floral Games."

The poem, which is signed (I forgot to mention this) in printed handwriting "Alfred Saurel," seems to me extremely bad, defective in technique as well as in thought; I have the impression that the author is saying something very banal, which he is trying to dress up with a selection of literary clichés from various epochs (such as calling his wife "aimable souveraine"). And what he seems to be saying is that he has gathered together a lot of material for a magazine or anthology and that he has not paid the contributors; he rather hopes, too, one would gather, that these unpaid poets and authors will be happy to accept instead of money the assurance that the editor's wife liked their works so much that she would have prevailed upon her editor husband to pay them if he had had any money.

A further study of the blank side of the card reveals that it was printed in 1888.

It is difficult to tell whether it was stupidity, technical ineptitude, or a mind enfeebled by old age or disease that could result in such a poem as this one—perhaps all three. It is possible too that Saurel wrote very quickly, in great bursts of enthusiasm, sometimes badly, sometimes well, and had not the critical sense or the patience to know when the products of his creative spasms were worth preserving. However, the badness and flatness of this poem are so remarkable as to suggest limits beyond which this poet's genius could not go.

There is another poetic card like the last, an encircled and decorated poem covering the outward face of the card; red and blue and green flowers are intertwined about its rectangular topside, falling down in gentle sweeping lines which considerately never touch the poem's words. This poem too is one of the Petits Jeux Floraux de Marseilles Series. The message on the back—and how old this one is too! the postmark is 1888—is written in brown ink, very hard to decipher, but says this (in French): "Dear Hal, The winter has come and gone. xxxxxxxxxxx umbrella. xxxxxx not at all by the sea xxxxxx Raspail xxxxxx will not xxxx sun xxxxx Gambetta xxx (signed) xx olphe." It is addressed to "M.

Alphonse de la Roche, boulevard du Temple, xxxxxxx France." (Undoubtedly Paris). Here is the poem (translated by the usual method):

> *When your beautiful eyes mount, O young girl!*
> *Toward the blue firmament sown with pearls of gold*
> *What dream you? Tell me? Your lip so* gentille
> *For this world of a day does she still murmur?*
>
> *Is it the butterfly whose wing so weightless*
> *Shoots out in twirling, on the evening breeze,*
> *Or the ravishing echo of a voice which to you is dear,*
> *Which is it that makes your eye gleam with a ray of hope?*
>
> *One would say that your breast palpitated at every murmur*
> *And that the crazy breeze and its enchanting breath*
> *Even up to the slightest shudder of immense nature*
> *Found something like an echo in the depths of your heart.*
>
> *Ah! If along the sounds which strike your ear*
> *There is one which dies and revives alternately,*
> *One which in the distance at each instant awakens*
> *Beautiful angel, it is a sigh of love from my heart.*

One turns this postcard over in amazement. Why did someone named Adolphe send this card to someone named Alphonse de la Roche? Is it, perhaps, within the possibilities of French names that Adolphe was a woman and not a man? But even supposing Adolphe to be a woman, it is hard to understand why she would send this card bearing a poem obviously addressed by a man to a young girl, to a man, to Alphonse de la Roche. If, on the other hand, Adolphe is a man, the selection of the versecard is, if understandable, somewhat reprehensible. Well, at the least unusual. But somehow from the contents of the card (what is written on the backside of the poem), one does not get the impression that there is any sexual meaning intended in the sending of this card (except, of course, the usual: impelling an object forcibly toward another who may be expectant but is by the nature of the situation passive; as what I am writing, beautiful and responsive reader, is intended to enter into your soul—and after?). One does not get this impression for the simple reason that the message written on the card (for all its gaps) seems very straightforward, newsy, and factual—though it is possible, of course, that one may miss, seventy-some-odd years after the fact, a long time for words and their associations to change, a certain esprit or double-entendre. However, I am not satisfied with what I now know, and I think some further research is necessary. Of course, the card could have been merely chosen at random, with the sender not noticing what was printed on the face, or observing merely that it was a poem and thinking "Oh, Alphonse (is Alphonse perhaps a woman too? No, there is the "M.") likes poetry! I'll send him this." In fact, there is one possibility which may save me a trip to the library if it turns out to be tenable—that is, that Alphonse was a child; in this case, if he were a child who liked poetry, and if the card were from a grown-up friend, member of family or no, man or woman, it seems in no way extraordinary that such a grown-up friend would be likely to send Alphonse a card with a poem on it—perhaps to correct his taste (as if to say, "Here's what your aunt Eliane thinks poetry is, not that beastly gutter-talk of Verlaine and Corbière which you are so fond of"), perhaps out of kindness and in ignorance of what his taste in poetry was, or again perhaps it was sent by a person with equal or superior critical standards who naively, but correctly, or else somewhat smilingly, and either tongue-in-cheek or tenderly, perhaps both, having discerned what little Alphonse's literary preferences were, had decided to satisfy him, come what may, with this pretty card.

This whole child hypothesis seems to me vitiated, however, by the discernible contents of the message written on the card's back: why, I should wonder, the reference to Gambetta? But it strikes me now that my objection is not very well-founded. For if Alphonse was an intelligent adolescent he probably had political views as well as poetical ones, and it may have been that the same aunt (or uncle—in fact, if this is true it seems more likely an uncle) who was satisfying his literary taste (either correctly or incorrectly, and either kindly or ironically) was at the same time twitting the boy about his political "heroes." "Well, what do you think, now," the card might have said before it faded, "of your Mr. Gambetta?" There is also the possibility, of course, a slight one but still made somewhat greater by the presence of another street name—"Raspail"—on the card, that the writer was referring not to the politician but to the street named after him, the Cours Gambetta. Then the chief content of the message might be the writer's eagerness to return to Paris.

What I am led more and more to believe, however, on the basis of this and the previous card, was that "Little Floral Games" was something more than an anthology or magazine and represented a kind of literary "movement." In this case, it must have had its zealots, and perhaps the person who sent this card was one, perhaps the person who received it was another; or perhaps it was only Alphonse who was a Petits Jeux Florauxiste (as they may have called themselves). In this case, the content of the poem on the card would be considered of much less importance than the fact that the poem there imprinted was a little floral game, *qu'il faisait partie du mouvement p.j.f.* The sender of the card, then, would not have selected or sent the card with the intention of its recipient seeing his (the sender's) thoughts and feelings projected into the actual lines of the poem, but merely with the idea of showing the poem's existence, as if to say "We (or you) (or I) have triumphed again. Here is Hern's (the poem in question having been written by Ludovic Hern) poem in print!" or "Alphonse, my dear, ah! what do you think of our movement now!?" Of course the possibility immediately suggests itself, too, that this card may have been sent, and the one preceding it bought, out of the same complicated and ultimately self-defeating motivations that prompted the sending of the first card, the woman-farmer-of-Auvergne. Certainly, though Hern's poem has a kind of delicacy and consistency within its own genre that was completely absent from the poem of his editor Jaurel, it is easy to conceive of the person who sent it feeling scornful of its rather sticky sentimentality, its too frequent platitudes, and, as well, its complete emptiness of any content that would interest a grown man except at certain very rare and half-conscious moments. In this case, then, we would imagine an Adolphe not a part of the Petits Jeux Floraux movement, if indeed there was one, and who had sent this card as a mere joke to a friend whose literary tastes were as sophisticated as his own, perhaps however with the same secret complex of reactions that we imagined may have motivated the sending of the Auvergne card. Was Adolphe secretly attracted, as it is indeed not difficult to be, by the somewhat sleepy beauty of the poem, for all its limitations, and then, scornful of himself for being so attracted, impelled to send, as a result of a self-destructive impulse, the card bearing the poem to Alphonse de la Roche? If one imagines a vicious relationship between the two, the self-destructive complex which then would have motivated the sending of this delicately tender and utterly sexless love poem seems even more apparent.

Perhaps the message read

> Dear Hal, The winter has come and gone. (So
> I fear has your) umbrella (and the wits of the
> poet of the verse on the verso ((The writing would
> have had to get very small here to accommodate
> itself to the space available))

> small here. Not at all by the sea, (a stone's
> throw, really, from) Raspail, (do I miss you? I)
> will not (say so in the) sun, (by Saint) Gambetta.
> (Viciously, Ad)olphe.

This message is especially obscure toward the end. What, for example, is the meaning of "Do I miss you? I will not say so in the sun, by Saint Gambetta"? Unless some very private allusions are being made, the sentence is nonsense. Perhaps, in fact, it should read (which would fit in

just as well with the available evidence—i.e. the remaining words and
blank spaces): "do I miss you? I need not, will not say—you are my
moon, my sun, my Jules Ferry, my Gambetta!" In the event our latter
hypothesized version of the sentence is correct (oh your beautiful lips,
your eyes, your clear cheek, I cannot resist them much longer, my imagination is already on the prowl, leaving behind the cards as an eagle
leaves the sun when he is struck by dark necessity; help! back!), then
there need be no dubiety whatsoever about the complex and self-destructive impulses that motivated this card's sending—card which as we have
it now shows a double desire to be direct and tender (in the poem and
in the message), and a desire both times mocked by the desirer, for the
inanity of the poem as applied to a mature and guilty passion is no
greater, surely, than the impropriety of evoking, in the name of such a
love, of any love, the presences of Gambetta and Jules Ferry, bewhis-
kered politicians who, no matter how effective their governmental poli-
cies might be, were not of a sort to set a lover's pulses spinning, universal
wheels in motion, spots darting from one flower to another, of the sun, as
if glass bees, not they, not at least on the basis of their names on the grey
austerity of a card.

But another aspect of the situation has to be considered, an aspect
which could not have been treated quite so clearly at the time of the
woman-from-Auvergne postcard. That aspect is simply this: given the
apparently necessarily defensive nature of the adult psyche (a defensive-
ness which may be no more protective, say, than a linen suit; but think,
even there, how much a linen suit does keep off—such damaging sun
((one could die for the lack of one's suit)), chilling rain ((only keeps off
a little, then can become damaging itself in being rain-chill retentive)),
fragments of dust continually hurled at us like postcards through the
mails, but faster and with what motive? a mystery of nature), given the
defensive nature of the soul, shall we not assume also that it is on its
guard against whatever is too obviously directed against it with an aim
of penetration? and will it not be actually pierced most easily by the
disguised, by the oblique? and does not, furthermore, each soul have at
least an unconscious awareness of this proclivity and weakness in other
souls and, therefore, select, when it wishes to effect a penetration, some
weapon so subtle or self-mocking as to pass unnoticed through those fibers
which, no matter how closely woven, are made of mortality and are thus
bound to be open to death and thus to love, desire, hopefulness, hopelessness? Brief, is not the disguised self-mocking avowal of such a card as
this perhaps the most effective means of communication, I will not say
between people, but between souls? It is true that about 95% of the
card's effectiveness would be cast off as follows by a sensitive recipient:
"Ha! irony, self-mockery; affection, yes, but inferiority, uncertainty of
deepest feelings, or shame about them, shall I never escape from this

monkey cage, my deepest feeling is not mockery, beyond this there is something, ha, hollow . . ." etc. The possible penetration of the other 5% is difficult to gauge, but its chances may appear in a clearer light if we imagine the chances of anything penetrating from an absolutely serious and soulfully loving card:

> I love you, darling. Do not let them torment you, mislead you. I am coming back. The great sun and the moon are witness that you are my only love, my apple, my Eden, my God, if you desire. Until that happy moment when, brimming with tears, these two poor eyes that stare at the empty you-less grey of this card will once again be fastened upon those eyes and other features for which they were created. Thine. Adolphe.

The thought of Adolphe writing this to a man is absurd but is the thought of his writing it to a woman any less repellent? In any case this message does not fit in with the words which actually remain on the back of the card.

The least one can say is that there are a great many human relationships and a great many situations inside other relationships in which there is no communication without disguise and self-mockery. Probably most of this disguise and self-mockery are so *built-in* to the situation and relationships, so *usual*, that they are rarely, except at the heights of hysteria or inspiration, recognized as such. For example, coming to call for you in an automobile is one, my dearest (which I can barely wait to do), or "talking to you" on the telephone.

From this built-in disguise and mockery, what way out? Because one feels all the same (remembering the pleasure of past occurrences) the superiority of absolute openness, lack of disguise (a kind of movement one is always trying to achieve in the ocean by throwing out one's arms, but waves cannot perfectly accomplish what only comes from the inside as prompted by another human being). Naturally it is very dangerous (*dit-on*); but given its absolute superiority, who could care? It is questionable that the way out could be found by means of a postcard, I mean by sending one, even by sending a great many. By sending enough, though, I suppose, an aesthetic pattern could be set up which might, if assembled in the atmosphere of right emotions, liberate the recipient from absolutely everything except—except what? But postcards themselves are a self-mockery and a disguise; so is all art; and so, for that matter, is talking through the vocal chords, the trachia, and the epiglottis.

Away! I am returning to my hypothesis that this postcard was sent by one member of the Petits Jeux Floraux Movement to another. In order to check up on this hypothesis I am going to the Bibliothèque de l'Arsenal (to its Provençal et littérature du sud de la France collection) to see if the name "Alphonse de la Roche" appears on any of the P.J.F. posters. If it does, then that I will take as sufficient evidence my hypothesis is correct. I sense I feel a certain need to be saved from the billowing abstractions and uncertainties which my previous hypothesis got me into. I also feel, in general, a kind of illness of having been too long away from the object of my research, the postcard itself, a condition which makes me aware that if I stay away from a specific object long enough I am bound to be carried away and then practically swallowed up by the same billowy clouds which begin by appearing as appealing abstractions which can take me away from a too dumb attachment to the dung on the cement (if that is what I happen to be looking at) but which end by drowning me in the dung and the essence of dung, with no sidewalk there at all, and no lamppost to lean on, no café at the corner, no one to call on for help. Abstract ideas are really horrible seducers leading me away from the part of the neighborhood I know, like parents with their arms outstretched who keep moving backwards and then down the stairs. What I always end up in a real heap of, when I am so separated from the real, is self-hatred and disgust, and precisely that feeling that I am out of contact with "reality." All of which makes me wonder if there is not mirrored that fear, too, on all of these postcards, in either a conscious or an unconscious way—that is, a fear that one is not part of a world that is real, and, coupled with this fear, a desperate attempt to project oneself into such a world, a world which has recognizable objects in it, and above all recognizable traits, intellectual, emotional, a world in which it is actually possible for one to "go somewhere," to have definite feelings about this going, and even be liked, hated, or loved a little more or less for these feelings and for one's expression of them. Of course, this "secret" message need not be any more conscious in the writer's mind than the "secret message" of pain and fear we discussed in relation to the postcard woman-from-Auvergne.

> *Inside each person is a doubt*
> *A child comes out*
> *Of mother;*
> *Maybe fear of smother*
> *Causes this,*
> *But whatever it is*
> *The inscription on paper*
> *Of messages, like dots of pepper,*
> *Reassures, if only for a moment, that solace and doubt;*
> *Then later moment death comes turns the lights out.*
>
> *Dear genuineness, I love you!*
> *So come with me*
> *Along these Jackie wastes*
> *And the Billy sea*

Until each from another
One and two
Baby out of mother
Five make three
Dear Calm: I am here, I really am.

Dear, I love you
Of this I have no doubt
Except as of everything
Flower leaf man
And among the every
Noise you hear
As if attuned to them what about a string of butterfly
Twirling in the evening air
Among them there, one you hear
Is the sound of me writing this card,
Am writing you this message
In the Gaston air.

. . . . .

Every card, then, according to my new theory,
Would be an expression of self-hate and a doubting of reality.
It will be a relief, such a relief to go to the Library,
To the Library across the river, and find out something with certainty!

. . . . .

But before I do this I must acknowledge that I have left certain matters up in the air. Because I suggested that obliqueness, self-mocking, self-hating, even, were the most effective attitudes for penetrating another human soul, but I did not prove it, I talked around it, and then I ran away from it into another major subject, which I can't help feeling I got to somewhat slyly and not by a direct path at all, really, that subject being of course the above, the subject of the doubting of reality as being a major factor in all choices of communication, in all communication, and yet I did not treat this subject completely either but merely "jumped" into it and tried to get off with its essence, whereas ideally I should explain it and, not only that, show its connection with the mockery and anti-self motivations that also enter into almost every human action, such as the choice and sending of a postcard. As to what motivates the manufacturers of postcards, that is another subject, whose complexity makes me weak to think of it.

Revenons en arrière! the day is beautiful, the sun is shining, and the glossiest cards glint strangely in the falling light of autumn; soon everything is dusky brown, then green again, a sweet intermingling of colors:

these distinctions between one thing and another actually make you present to me physically, they change what I do, the works of my blood and hands, into a mist of poems.

And what about the maker of this book? But I wish to return to unreality and self-denial. I cannot imagine why I am describing these cards instead of sending them, unless there is a self-mockery, a self-denial in art that is less obvious than that in a blatantly sentimental, stupid card sent off by a sophisticated hand. Art's self-mockery then would be no less real than the other but, if that is possible, even more real for being a part of the very structure of what is said, for being "built-in," as the motor is built into the automobile, and as the epiglottis is built into the body. As far as postcards go, their real absurdity, their built-in self-denial, is the very fact of their existence. Once one accepts the fact that they do exist, then anything one writes on them or anything one intends to communicate by the poem or picture they bear on their front is based on a solidly built-in absurdity but exists above it, as a city exists above its sidewalks and streets and yet cannot exist without them; but in art, ideally, the writer or painter can throw himself into the process at precisely the moment when it becomes arbitrary, becomes absurd, and can thus try to make his houses of the same cement with which he is making the sidewalks, and also the air. When one is confronted with the city of Paris on a photo-postcard, what does one feel? Whatever it is, one is at second remove from the self-destructive and the absurd, which is why it is also sometimes so poignant, like an awareness of tenderness or pain from a great distance. The distance here is psychological. There are moments, however, when these cards, through some secret and exact adjustment of their own, enter into reality with a flash and even a flame. The times I have thought of destroying the collection have been numerous, but the recollection of even one of these wonderful moments has always been enough to convince me that I should save it.

As for the doubting of reality, to the point of doubting one's own existence, which I said I wanted to connect with the self-hatred and self-mockery implicit in communication, I now think the connection is perfectly obvious. Because these feelings are precisely what one needs to convince oneself that one is really alive and there. It is true, however, that the final product is almost always (one can hope that some day one of them will not be!) a disappointment, more! it is a mere piece of paper, canvas, or cardboard, with something scrawled on its face—who has time to look at it or read it? Everyone is walking up and down the streets, with warm thighs pushing upward and outward through pantaloons and dress, faces moving, and the air, the air hovering expectantly over all. What do you want to do to us, air? eat us? Is air a vulture? Is it just waiting until we die? Is it that stink, from that one simple sacrifice alone, that satisfies her? O Messaline Air, or is it love you are thinking of making with all us mortals? Now that, for example, that invocation, is doomed to be lost forever, rolled up and left inside some shuddering flute of time.

"It is very bad for me to be left in here"—so says every message on every card and in every poem in the world. But what way is there to set them loose like swallows?

Again, this is getting too metaphysical, too far away from the cards, though with a reason, and I hope a good one—they always do this to me, and to everyone who interests himself in the collection: there is a liberation, a billowing out and up, resulting in a greater inclusiveness (even love becomes included in the direct postcard argument itself, is no longer a separate thing the cards reinforce or deny, becomes "intellectual" or nearly so in the Platonic sense) which would however have been impossible without minute attention to the cards' particulars. It is as in a garden that spreads out until it covers a city; staring hard at the plants one finally turns one's head and find out one is everywhere and obliged to solve everything. But my ambitions for the moment are more modest. At any rate, let us return to the point that all these communications, represented by the poems and the cards, are disappointments—they do not "equal" the body, or even a headache, effort must be expended to regard them and to read them. Yet somehow one can use their solace, so one continues to write and to send them (ah, how the flower boxes are appearing in the windows)

> *(and a window box) Left punch, right jab*
> *(is appearing in the flowers)!*

> *Excellency, let God appear to us sometime today*
> *(Max Jacob)*

> *Bong! The drums*
>   *Easter cheer*
> *sister swallow*   */And so*
> *there is a*
> *black face appearing in the flowers*

. . . However, it is necessarily true, that after even a limited experience with poetry, with postcards, one begins to know in advance, at least with a part of one's consciousness, that the results will not be satisfying, even though many other benefits may indeed arrive ("accidental aspects")— positions, appointments, the love of beautiful women, all things falling off the shoulder like a shawl made of ice. So that, by the time one is mature (I mean capable of communicating anything beyond a simple desire, though perhaps I have this all reversed), there is, in each communication one tries or decides to make, a built-in compensation for the foreknown fact that the communication cannot possibly have the desired effect. Therefore a little "death" is put into poems, and even into some cards, which can act as an inoculation and make them in effect "deathless." Still unsatisfying, but deathless nevertheless, existing to go on taunting and teasing mankind until all are in a common grave. The essential quality of all these immortal works is that they have annealed inside them "death, time hopelessness, all present and accounted for, Sir." Who? are you calling me "Sir," lovely poem? "Yes, Sir, we have ever treated you with respect, we great poems, but you shall die all the same. May I make your bed?" No, will you just keep handing me those postcards, please; there's a good poem. As William Blake said, "Enough! or Too Much."

In any case now it should be obvious that this built-in sense of or allowance for failure is intimately connected with, if not exactly the same thing as the built-in self-hatred and self-mockery spoken of before. I.e.—dealing with particulars, describing them, touching them, paying for them, sending them, all these things done to reassure one of his existence and of the reality of his feelings and of other things—this effort itself secret, and secretly investing every action (and perhaps most obviously acts of communication) with a kind of death, a mockery, a self-(and on the very highest level too, the level involving existence itself, a sort of twisted form of the metaphysical dissatisfaction expressed by all art—naturally, there, in the midst of praises) despising. Most of the cards, of course, exhibit a far cruder version of these phenomena than do the great works of art I have been using as the secret basis of this discussion.

To return to one or two matters:

I. Is the communication which includes self-mockery and a built-in failure and death the most effective means for the penetration of souls? The question is impossible to answer because in a certain sense there is no other possible kind of communication. It is true that one can, sometimes with a minimum of built-in failure or death, "strike it lucky" both for one's own and someone else's emotional state and for a moment communicate as directly as a bee attacking a white throat. But the soul filled with death is always waiting below the bee and the throat to have its revenge in dreams and in a thousand postcards (thoughts), very many of them sweet as the smell of raw shellfish on a November night.

II. Does the second (i.e. the silver sowing girl) postcard now seem as perfect and sublime as it did before? How can it? The kind of enthusiasm it inspired was obviously an enthusiasm of the moment. If it were really capable of inspiring any other kind (*the* kind, I would say), there would be no point in my continuing this description of the collection. See above. It was not too unlike the "bee sting."

III. In what light now do you view the gyrations of thought which led to the suppositions (that now seem rather naive) about the pain and self-doubt implicit in the writing and sending of the Auvergne postcard? I view them as having been necessary preparation for our present state of illumination. At the same time, I would not renounce them for what they are in themselves, for, dear, they are part of a process, and how can I be sure the flowers will continue to turn and to glow in this now dusty greying air were I to cut off a piece of their stems, not to say anything of their roots.

I will stand up now and cross the Seine.

(Later) There is no Alphonse de la Roche listed in any connection whatsoever with the Mouvement Petits Jeux Floraux de Marseille. If he did not have a pen name (a possibility that just occurred to me, but on which it will be hard to check up), then we are in the midst of a problem again, though fortunately (or unfortunately) by now it is a problem which has begun to seem of less and less importance to me, almost to the point, I mean to say, of fading back into the vast anonymity from which all these postcards, in fact all these words, as the result of a puzzling—if by now, I hope, self-described—and very considerable effort and desire, have been momentarily brought into being.

JOHN LOGAN

The Success

I lived these journeys always with anticipation and with dread, letting my mind race for mooring: preparations, protections, occult cheers, hopes, plans, dialogues. I was afraid to be cast from the jaws of the elevator naked and alone and in a questionable form.

Already in the machine I thought rather desperately of the doctor as *voyeur*, interested in the tabooed places of man, and of a critic like myself as a sort of scatologist, interested in (devoted to) man's effluvia—the invisible dross of his brain and breath cast onto the pages of books. This suggestion so disgusted me that if I were not at the moment rising into the heights toward the holy oracle I would have gone off to a bar. I thought of the one just to the left of the entrance to the building. Remembered I was broke anyway. But how should one protect himself from his own ideas? I was too old to run to mamma like a child afraid of the pictures he had drawn with terrible crayons.

As I crossed the small fourteenth floor court toward the doctor's suite I saw in the marble fountain (sculpted as a boy on a dolphin) a young Jonah on a young whale, and I thought that at that age it is almost as easy for the boy to carry the fish as it is somewhat later for the huge fish to drag the man out to sea. If only one could time things so that he could devour the fish before it got him! Standing in the court before the fountain I knew I had stopped in order to delay my entrance into the doctor's office, but my mind seemed to fill with dolphin images and allusions like a school breaking and leaping in a sea. I was no longer young and had a wife and family to support, but I thought of myself now as a sad youth wafted by dolphins, given to crying with the figures in fountains, constitutionally confusing the devouring shark or whale with the gentle, riding dolphin—and the erotic fish with the Christian one. I wished that any one of those marine animals—or the monster of Tobias, or that of Hippolytus—would come clear and bear me away again.

Having at last crossed that long court I sat in the foyer with its hodge podge of French provincial and modern worked-iron furniture, its foolish books, its view of a garment warehouse where grotesque and naked dummies gestured at the windows like dying women, and its stairway to The Presence—to The Hulk in the Corner that said hello without meaning it, while listening, whirring and watching and listening. The encounter with the doctor imminent as it was, I suddenly thought that the truth about myself was simple: I was a member of the species of Catholic Neurotics—a mediocre group, like most Catholic societies. But I was fairly distinguished myself as a drinker and as a narcissist, fascinated by my own nocturnal images. I was willing to have the doctor look over my shoulder at the pools of my dreams, but it was also necessary to protect oneself. At the moment my defense against the narrowing eyes of the physician, in the process now of recognizing me, was my decision to relate my most recent dream and to keep quiet about my thoughts of the instant, the last of which was a kind of wondering why I always turned to the right instead of to the left as I lay down on the couch—was it because the doctor's stairway had spiraled to the right? (Or was it left?) The doctor himself sat hidden behind my head.

II

A moment of recollection and I was able to get started with the dream, diving into myself at the chosen angle: there were jewels, pearls and exquisitely designed ceramic boxes every detail of which I could remember, and shining large ornate trays which I thought of as Achilles' shields I had myself designed. And there were lucent, glass vases with mythological legends etched on them in excruciating patterns of light on light—Orpheus and the Thracian women, Actaeon and Diana, and others I couldn't remember. Jung's archetypes maybe, I said smugly. The thought of the burrs or the sand on the glass, as I supposed they used, was painful and for some reason reminded me, I said, of a stone going through the ducts of a man's guts cutting fine, colorless lines in which the secretive blood did not appear until sometime later.

As for the pearls, I remembered that one of the secretaries at my publishers wore just such earrings, dew-drop pearls in a golden and baroque set. Or stag-tooth-shaped pearls, slightly curved; wasn't a stag's tooth slightly curved? I now realized for the first time, I said, that the stag's teeth pearls always seem to bite the lobes of the secretary's ear— and I always expected to see blood appear in a moment under the red ringlets of her hair or upon the gold of the jewels. Oepidus stabbed himself in the eyes with his mother's golden brooch, and a brooch is an instrument of sexual attractiveness. Also the piercing earring of the girl, I said, was like the branding iron stuck through the ears of whores and rogues and peasant slaves in *Hamlet*. I didn't mention the historical date of the edict alluded to in the play, because although it came to mind, I was afraid of sounding pedantic. Instead, I said I was now beginning to see the connection of the pearls dream with another I had had the same night. . . .

It occurred to me to pause and see if the doctor had anything to say, but the doctor did not. Still I knew that even if the lips were quiet the slits of the doctor's eyes (which I could not see) changed and changed.

I felt shocked but went on: in this other dream, I said, one of my incisor teeth came out in my hand, having been loosened as I pulled many shreds of carrot from around its root. I thought to myself and did not say that I hated this part of the dream with its connotation of rabbits, silly innocuous and cuddly kinds of rats, and I admired my own virtue and courage as I proceeded. The connection between the two dreams, I said, is that the tooth is a dew-drop pearl—removing the tooth was removing the potency of a playful rabbit, whose nature it is to gnaw with his incisor teeth on carrots. Suddenly I admitted, with a welling up of feeling, my dislike of the rabbit figure in my dreams, but there it was, I said and, regaining control, I added that probably it was something from the Collective Unconscious of Jung.

The doctor was silent.

And the pearl in the ear of the girl, I went on, was the organ of the playful rabbit placed there like poison in the ear of Hamlet's father. That didn't ring right I realized, and growing angry at the doctor's silence, tried again: or the word-swords of Hamlet in his mother's ear. That was better, I thought, and at the same time noticed with a certain delight how much "word" was like "sword" and commented on it. I certainly thought the doctor should speak here, but still there was no sound; only, I knew, the doctor showed his eyes like a pair of powerful teeth.

Or if the tooth is not put in the girl's ear to kill, I went on, then, to get back to the stag—since a stag is a stud isn't it, or a stallion—the stag tooth (which I said I preferred anyway to the rabbit tooth) placed in the girl's ear meant I wanted to do something else to her, maybe to fuck her. I was always uncomfortable saying sexual words in the doctor's presence and went ahead rapidly: I often watched the girl primping in her tiny mirror, I said, and once she had caught me out of the corner of her eyes, which had narrowed. Perhaps she wanted to turn me into a stag and set her dogs on me to rend me with their teeth! The story of Diana, I said, marveling at my gift of finding relations, was one of the legends on the vase in the dream. And the Thracian women tore the poet's flesh, though not with the teeth of dogs. The dog's tooth, I now remembered, is also a violet: Laertes wanted the flesh of his sister to become violets. Suddenly I felt that I was, after all, trying to say something to myself; my composure and my energy seemed to drain from me suddenly, and I almost whispered, "The hyacinth is mournful as the mandrake is."

III

Whatever it was I wanted to do to the girl, I said, after a pause (and in fact somewhat choked), kill her or kiss her, in any case I was being punished, because the tooth or organ being removed represented a form of castration and on one occasion I explicitly thought of castration when I happened to keep a dental appointment in a guilty frame of mind—mortal sin, I said to myself—and found that a tooth I thought was going to be filled actually had to be pulled. Now, the rabbit truth, or rabbit tooth, I corrected myself quickly (and blushing), when it was pulled in the dream had caused me much pain. I had never experienced pain in a dream before, I said, and had waked up moaning and taken an aspirin. I paused.

I thought I was doing extremely well and hoped for some encouragement or some indication of my grade, so to speak. But there was still no sound from the region at the back of my head. In this general area there came to my mind as I paused an indistinct figure, which I killed—a composite man with the ears of a great rabbit and great rabbit eyes, pink as wounded flesh. I then began again without mentioning the bloody battle in which I had just been victor.

As for the pain, I said, I had been worried that the tooth that was pulled would cause me a lot of trouble afterwards, because I felt I deserved it. The dentist had quite a hard time getting the tooth out, hacked and pried it with his tools, and it wouldn't budge until—and I felt a flush as I related it—I had made an act of contrition; then it came out immediately. I said I felt that the guilt I had brought to the dentist's office—it had started with drinking, I confessed, but had already decided not to go into it unless the doctor insisted—was *assuaged*. I repeated the word, lengthening the vowels. As though the dentist had put me in a state of grace, I said. I had never had the nerve to ask the doctor whether he was Catholic but thought to hell with it now. After I left the dentist's I said I had felt that I would never get drunk, etcetera, again, but instead would become a man. I felt, I said strongly, that I was *initiated* by the experience of the tooth pulling, having made—I couldn't help laughing—the rites of passage in a dentist's office. I had started to say "doctor's office," but checked myself in time. But, I admitted, to be made a man by a kind of castration *did* seem strange. Still there was circumcision, excision and such related practices I had read about. These were painful and shocking forms of initiation, like the rites where boys had to crawl across the blood-and-guts-spattered naked bodies of men in order to get to the throne of the king, or the rite—Australia was it?—where the mother squats over the youth and grunts with mock labor before turning him over to the men. I said this seemed particularly brutal. As for castrated heroes, spread-eagling and crucifying were common in myths and religious stories and Jesuit martyrs like Southwell were drawn and quartered alive, a kind of extended spread-eagling, as well as being castrated: a horse pulled on each limb, four of them, like Thracian women, and sometimes their guts were rolled out on sticks. I myself, I said, once had a nightmare—four of them, I thought, one mare on each limb—in which I thought I was being fondled but instead was being stripped and my hands staked to the ground for, I supposed, castration, but had waked up in fright without finding out. I paused. The stakes went through the hands into the natural earth, I said, believing that the phrase "natural earth" as I uttered it had a rather mysterious sound. Raskolnikov bowed down to kiss the earth in expiation after his crime, but he didn't really mean it until in the epilogue of the novel when he first convicted himself in a dream and then, his eyes freed at last of Tobias's scales, was able to look at the beautiful countryside around him. The dactylic rhythms of this last remark I realized were the result of artifice, and I paused for a minute to temper my control over the fantasy, which I was afraid was beginning to sound too much like a poem, or like a critic's gloss on a poem. In any case, I thought, the whole thing was getting away from me a little too uncomfortably. I made myself stop thinking, and a feeling of irritation at the doctor's silence grew stronger as I paused over-long.

IV

The forty-five minutes were nearly gone, I figured. What was the doctor thinking? What were the doctor's eyes and teeth doing? Was the doctor perhaps reflecting that I was trying to treat myself, remembering the cigars in my breast pocket and the new hat on the chair, forced forms of manhood? And perhaps resenting my ability to analyze my own dreams? For which I paid the said doctor a rather penitential sum?—when I could. One time in one of these silences I had point blank asked the doctor what a certain dream of mine meant. And the doctor had answered, "I don't know what it means." This had seemed enigmatic at the time, the awful deceit of a god. Now, today, nothing at all had issued from the corner, nothing since the initial and ritualistic, "What's on your mind today," when, upon entering, I turned to the right (or was it the left, I thought) and spread-eagled myself on the couch. After waiting

in the foyer, I thought, after passing the boy and his beast in the weeping court, after coming to the surface in the elevator. I began immediately to relate the elevator dream I had just remembered.

The elevator was new-fangled, I said, a complicated one, buttons,
lights flashing, levers, numbers. I couldn't operate the machine aright to
get off it and just rode up and down by myself, until someone got in with
me, someone who obviously—the way only things in dreams are obvious
—knew how to run it and who was a kind of authority or official. The
trouble was partly in the floor—there was a zero floor, a number which
puzzled me among the others, I said, and at the same time it seemed to
be the number of the floor I was going to. I said I thought the companion was the doctor. (So it had once turned out in a dream about riding
in a truck through dry brush country looking for the turn to the right to.
the pleasant land.) Now the helper suggested we try to find my floor, I
continued, by starting at the top and stopping at each one in turn. So we
tried that but seemed to slip right past it anyway. What a queer feeling,
I said and immediately wished I had used another word. And we made
the trip several times together, the lights flashing and the new machinery
grinning, or rather glittering. And the dream ended then, I said, a bit
breathless.

I went on to interpret that the floor I was trying to locate, the zero
floor, was my unconscious—unknown, strange, cold in a way, like absolute zero. I realized the weakness of this association as I produced it but
went on, rather courageously I thought: I said the dream meant I needed
the doctor's help and that I couldn't go where I wanted without him.
The doctor was trying to show me that one has to go floor by floor or step
by step to make the unconscious conscious, to drain the Zuider Zee, in
Freud's phrase, I said, or that ocean which Horatio had warned Hamlet
not to go closer to for fear it would make him mad. Not angry, I said,
mad. Suddenly my voice took on excitement and my arms began to flail
like windmills beside the sea: of course, I said, Hamlet found himself by
paying no heed to Jocasta and saying to hell with Calypso. He faced the
coils of the sea, he left the ship that swallowed him, and he returned to
Denmark naked and alone to be king of the court in a graveyard for a
dog's day, like a boy in a court yard who masters the dogfish and sees for
the first time all his mothers in their opened graves. I found my throat
constricting tightly and I choked with phlegm and tears. And I heard the
doctor's voice echoing quietly inside its ancient skull:

"Zero is not unknown, is it? X is unknown." And I could not answer
and did not know what the oracle meant, but the voice pulled at my guts
like a pliers on a tooth tugged from its socket or like the rod on a cage in
the sucking elevator shaft.

The voice continued now, "Zero is *no* place. There *is* no such floor.
You are saying you don't want to go anywhere and you want me to help

you fool yourself. You are satisfied to ride around in the elevator with me, trying the different buttons and the new machinery of the treatment and making the lights flash. You want me to let you believe you are going someplace. You seem to think something will happen to you to change you just by coming here and bringing me your dreams."

Eggs, I thought, but did not answer. Sucking eggs. My dreams are colored, fantastic eggs I bring to calm the sacred snake. And now it rolls its egg-shaped eyes and spits at. . . .

"Your dreams are for you," the doctor was saying, "not for me." I found myself answering, "But I want to give you something. I want you to like me and I know you don't."

"You want to bribe me," the doctor said, "so that you won't have to know yourself. Actually the only discomfort you are willing to suffer is the slightly unpleasant motion of a new elevator, which you would quickly come to enjoy while you waited. You used to wait for a religious miracle to happen to you. Now you are waiting for something scientific to take place. As for your thinking I don't like you—it is you who think you don't like yourself. You see me as you see yourself."

I felt the dragon's bites and knew it was only a matter of time. I was done for, but would fight. "No," I said. "No. You are always right but this time you are wrong. I *do* want to go someplace. I *am* going someplace. I know transportation dreams have to do with a man's desire for change. I have dreamt of buses, cars, trains, and now elevators. I don't know why I never dream of airplanes—I'd like to dream of them—they have so much grace and open air and light around them. They suggest ecstasy. I suppose I am afraid of ecstasy, of being blasted by it, or else I love it too much. Still an elevator is not just a bus or train. It goes up. It's a start toward an airplane, a connection between land and air transportation." My excitement rose as I saw a break in the battle I had lost—"And therefore," I said, "to dream of you helping me take the elevator means you will help me to ecstasy, to happiness, to life . . . the willingness to abandon myself to life as one unafraid of freedom and unashamed of it." (The superior person of Jung, I thought to myself, the one with the necessary moral strength.) "I want you to know me," I said, solidly ending my foray.

"You want me to know you," the doctor said, "because you don't want to know *yourself*, which should be the reason why you are here. You have a misconception of psychiatry."

God, the teeth of the snake! I thought. "But I can prove I need you," I said. "I didn't get drunk (drinking is a means to ecstasy, it occurred to me) for a month and thought I was cured, and then just before this elevator dream I was stinking." (Ecstatic and stinking, I thought. A blasted youth. Real Dionysian.)

The doctor said, "No, your getting drunk was not to prove to me that you needed me. It was to prove that you *don't*. You can leave it alone or take it, you are telling me—go for a month without it if you want or go get drunk if you want. Coming to see me makes you think you're doing something about yourself whereas it's actually providing you with the license to do as you please. You don't want to be responsible for your behavior."

"Good god why do you always make me sound so despicable!" I said, heated and feeling my throat grow tight with sobs again.

"Well, you think I'm criticizing you," the doctor said, "but I'm only explaining you to yourself. You think of me as a kind of priest suitable for adults, who can make you hang your head and who will provide you with feelings of relief for your anxieties and sops for your conscience while you continue to put things off. You want to weep because you want to remain as you are. Children weep to get what they want."

I heard and ignored the last two sentences—"Put off what?" I asked. "Put what off?" I knew the answer to this because it came up in every session and I found myself responding to my own question, "Put off the responsibility that would force me to earn a decent living for myself and my family by my talent. I have let my talents go to my head . . . I mean I have put my genius into my dreams and thoughts instead of into my work, where it might buy bread." I rather liked the rounded way in which the sentences emerged.

The doctor said, "You do not act on the basis of what you have already learned about yourself. You continue to put off. And you do not want to learn more."

Yes, I thought. Yes. I am one of the inferior. I will never unravel the secrets. "But I want to understand the mystery of the flesh," I said sadly.

The snake hissed. "Where's the mystery?" it asked. "You don't want a psychiatrist at all. You just want somebody else in the elevator, a playfellow and a confident. What you want is another rabbit."

I had an image of two giant, friendly rabbits, and heard their teeth click together like the eyeglasses of nearsighted lovers. The dragon's victory was now complete: using its words for teeth it had bridged the gap from its corner lair, attacking from behind and above as was its habit, and it had bit clean through every mask. The hissing was terrible!

I realized slowly that the buzzer was ringing, signalling the arrival of the next patient. My thoughts shaped into lines I did not say:

> *Already the next neurotic*
> *Knocked at the gates,*
> *Crowded his several selves*
> *In the casement, bore his several*
> *Hats and heads at the half open door.*

Emptied of energy, unable to rise yet, though I knew it was over, I struggled for air and for the shapes of words that could be let loose into space. "It's like a figure in Kafka," I said. "I have failed and I don't know why or at what."

The doctor rose from his corner and standing between the couch and the door said: "No, not Kafka. You are like Hamlet. You prefer that anyway, I believe: your visits here are occasions for eloquent and suffering soliloquies, filled with literary allusions, edited for an audience, and actually serving as delays. You have failed at what you do not want to do. Therefore you have succeeded. I believe you might just as well go on as you are, and we'll let the matter of another appointment go for now, at least until you find some way to pay your bill. Good-bye." The doctor touched the knob of the door.

I forgot to check whether the staircase spiraled to the left or the right. My mind went instead to the fountain in the court outside, which would soon be dry for the winter, and there would be white stains on the concrete mould of the basin. I entered the elevator alone and it began its dive: a night journey under the sea, I thought, and said aloud, "But I shall not be born again. I wonder if there is such a thing as a cursed trout, doomed to be drowned."

Suddenly I remembered the doctor's reference to Hamlet, and I decided the doctor was being sarcastic. It had seemed until its mention of Kafka an illiterate snake, never speaking of books often as they came into my reveries. The elevator was docking. "I *have* succeeded," I said to myself, "I shall at least avoid the dragon's eye, pale as ivory buttons that flash by the elevator door like the teeth of a whale."

JAMES MERRILL

Driver

A single lesson converted me. I heard the call and would obey it
happily ever after. This was in the summer of 1919. My father, back
from France, gave me thirty minutes of instruction, after which I was on
my own, learning by experience over a network of frail dirt roads flung
outward from our village into the surrounding farms. I should be able
to describe those roads, those farms. People we knew lived on them. Without question I must have stopped to talk, enjoy a piece of cake or, the
following year, a cigarette, to stroke the long face of a stalled animal before, my own face brightening, I leapt back into the sputtering Ford. But
I have no such memories. That summer of being fifteen, conjured up today, might have passed exclusively within the moving car. My teeth
would clack together over ruts. Off to my right a discoloration of the
windshield made for the constant rising of a greenish cloud. I inhaled a
warm drug compounded of fuel and field. My feet, bare or sneakered,
burned, grew brown, grew calloused. One day at summer's end I noticed
in the rear-view mirror a tiny claw of white wrinkles at the corner of
each eye.

In those days to my embarrassment, as later to my pride, I was not
mechanically minded. Other boys my age preferred the languorous ex-
ploration of parts to the act itself. I took as much interest in what lay
beneath the hood as I did in visualizing my entrails; that is to say,
none.

Quite simply, I adored to drive. Enlarged to the dimensions of my
vehicle, I took on its blazing eyes, its metallic grimace, its beastlike
crouch. Or am I ahead of myself? Were not, at first, humbler qualities
instilled by those early models? They rattled but stood upright in sober

garb. Fallible, they departed like Pilgrims out of faith, theirs and mine. But now I suspect I am *behind* myself: I have no real memory of that Eden of the Model T, in which the car was yet one more patient beast for man to name and rule. Temptations of Power, Speed, and Style were already whistling loud in my young ears. A windshield clearing, I gazed through the forehead of my genie. Other drivers, rare enough still, I hailed silently as having drunk from the same fountain. At night each learned how to lower his gaze, conscious of what blinding foresights were to be read in the oncoming other's. A needle registered the intensity of the whole experience. When I saw my first wreck, complete with police and bodies under sheets, I found in my heart a comprehension, an acceptance of death that has never—or only lately—deserted me.

My parents were amused, if alarmed. "We gave you the wrong name, boy," my father would laugh (I am called Walker after *his* father) but he soon learned to make notes of mileage and to deduct the fuel I was using from my allowance. "Walker, if you're going driving at this hour of the night," my mother would begin. "Your mother's right," my father would add as I rose yawning from the dark oval table where we ate, brushing to the floor, like any destiny they might have arranged for me, a constellation of crumbs. For by then I had ceased to take seriously, or indeed to recall, anything that occurred while I was off the road. The abrupt standstill left me groggy and slow on my feet, as in dreams or on the ocean floor. My parents gesticulated, their lips moved. I cannot explain their helplessness. I was a boy, perhaps in my first year of college: I did not even—but yes! By that time I did have a car of my own.

Once more I have paused to see if I can remember how it came about; I cannot. I can shut my eyes and imagine odd jobs, see my hand, wrist bare and brown beneath a rolled-up cuff, pressing a plunger marked VANILLA—a shiny brownish stream braids downward into the glass; or holding a brush and rhythmically, as if to obliterate any detail that might distinguish such a moment from a million others like it, covering a clapboard wall with ivory paint. I can invent, if not truly recall, the death of a grandparent, a legacy in which I must have shared to the extent of a yellow diamond or dented gold watch immediately pawned. Anyhow, I drove to college in my first car, old-fashioned but sufficient, and finished my education with honors, having been promised a new car if I did.

What is strange is that my teachers complimented me upon my excellent mind. If only I could think of a single occasion on which I used it!

Towards the end of the summer following my graduation the question of what I was to do with my life must at last have arisen with some intensity. Evenings come back, of straight roads traveled in fury, the dog on the seat next to me listening while I rehearsed manifestoes aloud.

"No," I told him. "You may be my father but I refuse to work in the business you have built up. I want to travel, get to know my country. Besides, I scorn both your methods and your product. What are these prosperous times for, if not to . . ." It may be that I ended by delivering this speech to the right audience. More likely it sank without a ripple into those trustful brown eyes fixed upon me through the warm and whizzing night.

I became, in short—but it does not matter what I became. If I am to set down the truth about my life it will not be found in dates and labels but in this brief memoir of my supreme pastime and of those who now and then shared it with me.

My first passenger was the dog I have mentioned. He was brown, short-haired, virtually nameless—we called him Pal. He and I had loved each other for many years. By the time he began to drive with me, habit and trust had taken the place of passionate contact, kisses, exclamations. Neither now had any particular need of attention. Pal's head would be thrust, tongue flapping gladly, into a torrent of sunlit odors. If I reached to stroke him absently he would look round, not displeased but puzzled, then turn with one token thump of his tail back to the window. When I talked, he would, as I have said, listen, especially at night. His face, no longer transfigured by adoration, had grown serious, almost ascetic. I felt he wanted me now merely to illustrate certain still baffling but minor aspects of human behavior, against the day when his own turn came.

A truck hit him, one morning early, in front of our house. The cook kept marveling over how the driver, "crying like a baby," had carried him right into the kitchen. I found him there on newspapers when I came down for breakfast.

I am glad to say that in all my years of driving I have never been responsible for the death of an animal. Nothing pains me more than those little corpses that accumulate on our highways. The first one rarely appears before eight or nine in the morning—a rabbit, or cat, glittering with fresh dark blood—but as the day wears on they become uncountable and unrecognizable, a string of faded compresses dried out by fevers they had merely intensified. All night they are mourned by shining green or amber eyes. And by dawn they have become part of the road itself.

Not long after the death of Pal I left home.

I still preferred to drive by myself. At college, the car had made me popular. Every weekend filled it with classmates, girls, banners, flasks. I drank from the flasks, I waved the banners, I kissed the girls. And yet it was all beside the point. Their emphasis was forever upon *destinations*—the conventional site of waterfall and moon and mandolin; or else of the shabby "club" where liquor could be bought and consumed, where one danced to a phonograph in the red dark. Hours would pass this way, pleasurably no doubt. But I think there were few in which I did not once ask myself: How long will it last? When can we go back to the car?

This is something that happened not long after I left home:

One lovely autumn day I found myself on a road that dipped and rose through golden shrubbery and tall, whitened trunks, when out of nowhere, on a steep curve, two figures appeared. They were all but under my wheels before I could stop: an old country couple patiently signaling for a ride. I let them in the back door. They were brown and wrinkled, dressed in patched blacks and raveling grays. The woman wore knitted stockings. In both hands she held a coffee can planted with herbs. As we drove I would catch sight of her in the mirror, watching them, lips moving, giving them courage. The old man carried on his lap a basket of apples, pocked, misshapen ones which nevertheless had been beautifully polished. Perhaps he had not been in a car before; he kept looking about and moistening his lips. I asked how far they were going. When neither answered I asked again, this time turning to look square in their faces. They looked back. The old man rested his fingertip against the windowglass, appreciatively. I understood his pleasure and was pleased myself to have brought it about. We drove in silence for a number of miles.

Then the old man began to utter noises of unrest. Seeing no house or road, I drove on. His dismay increased. "Mister," said the woman eventually; and when I had stopped the car, "There was a road," she said, and waited. I realized that they had wanted to get out, and rather than cause them an extra inconvenience, I backed some hundred yards to where, indeed, a narrow dirt road forked off.

I followed it without hesitation. An emerald-green ribbon grew between its ruts. Overhead, branches met. I felt a foolish smile cross my face. The road itself soon petered out. We came to a halt in the middle of a cluttered barnyard. Dogs, pigs, doves and a few small, soiled children moved in and out of larger, motionless shapes, a rusty tractor, a cow. One lone peacock trailed his feathers in the hard dirt. To greet us, four young people rounded different far corners and stared taciturn and crimson-eared at the car. Were they all descended from my old couple? I could imagine that, instead of expelling anyone from the garden, God and the angels had found it handsomer to pack up and go themselves, for all that could be done without *their* guidance and example.

My passengers had alighted and were making signs of hospitality. Too young to be gracious, I could only blush and stammer a protest. The poetry of the invitation depended upon its refusal. Each of us, in fact, must have felt as much. In a single gentle movement the old woman set down her herbs, took an apple from her husband's basket, and handed it to me. As I circled the yard they stood waving. A dove fluttered out of my path.

I got back to my original road. The sun, pale and lowering, was waiting for me beyond the first crest. The apple tasted bitter, hard; it could not have been an eating apple. I tossed it away with a shudder. Night fell before I came to a town.

From now on I would offer rides to people. Absently at first, discouraging talk, moved chiefly by the missionary's fervor to acquaint others with Revelation. I drove well—too well, perhaps. As I rounded curves with a graceful one-handed gesture, certain passengers would look admiringly at me instead of at the road. I was young, husky, I had a pleasant face; people told me their stories. Having little to say myself, I became, depending on the occasion, grandson, son, big brother, kid brother, and would do my best not to destroy the illusion while striving to deflect attention back to the main points, those Olympian secrets of Fuel and of the Wheel. Until one day, inevitably, I added to these a role that by its nature and at my age was less easily given up than the rest: the role of lover.

She sat beside me at a counter one early evening, blonde, full-blown and looking heartbroken. She had to go to another town, not far, but had missed the last bus and was I headed that way? Well, she paid for my coffee and I drove her off. Soon she was chatting and patting her hair. "I thought you'd be gone when I came back with my grip. Sure are a nice boy to do this. Shouldn't call you a boy, though. Bet you know more than I do!"

I can smile now at my innocence. She guided me past her town, past the next. Night was falling, I wanted to stop. Even when I understood and drove without protest, indeed with my heart thumping, down the dark dirt road, her hand reaching across me to turn off the lights—even then I had a surprise in store for me. Opening my door, I started out. "Where you off to?" said my friend coyly. I stood frozen with stupefaction. It was going to happen in the *car!* I forced a casual reply and turned from her to the underbrush, lifting my face to the stars, letting her imagine what she liked, while I tried to make sense of my feelings.

I knew that love was made in cars. Mine, though, *my* car—could I put it to these uses? And were the uses high or low? As for love, I can use the word today, but a molten gulf separated its earlier meanings (a girl to be kissed between drinks, an imitative couple in the back seat) from *this* experience, wringing and intense, that within an hour had left the dry track of a tear on either cheek as I drove deeper and deeper into some dark Western state. The woman nodded at my side. I did not know whether I had degraded or fantastically enlarged the road ahead.

That first love rose and set, establishing a pattern others were to follow. First came days, or weeks, during which the fact that we desired, but did not know, one another, kept us both good-humored. Then, gradually, at the woman's insistence, our passion overflowed into rooming-houses and hotels, although with luck I was still able to confine it to the car, reserving our shared bed for sleep. Mornings, we drove on; the woman would not mind, not at first, waiting in the car while I transacted my business. Thinking it over, I shall not emphasize my profession by concealing it. I was a salesman, of countless different things, encyclopedias, garden supplies, trusses, religious texts, all or none of these. I would reach into the back seat for my case. The car door shutting behind me threw a switch. Two minutes or two hours later I would be back, whatever had passed between me and "the lady of the house" forgotten now unless translated into clues: money in my wallet, a thumbnail blackened by a slammed door, more than once liquor on my breath and lipstick on my ear. The patience of the woman in the car came to be tried. We would drive on doggedly, a capsule of discord, she questioning, pleading; myself silent, not guilty, amazed by the recurrence, from one to the next, of the same demands, the same voice first injured then sarcastic before its final sickening fall into a nastiness without nuance or remedy.

I would want only to be rid of her.

I soon learned to avoid these climaxes. At the first sign of strain—when the woman, say, was no longer content to do her nails in the car, but sat making lists of food to buy or friends to surprise with postcards—I would persuade her that I meant to stop several days in a certain town. On being shown to our hotel room, I would make impetuous love to her before going down to "see about the car" (in which I would happen to have left my things) and driving off into the night alone. Those were hours of resolution, of pride in my lonely calling. The renounced woman roared in the motor and wailed in the fleeing dark.

Somewhere I have read that driving is a substitute for sexual intercourse. I am as good an authority as the next man on both subjects, and can affirm without hesitation that for thrills, entertainment, and hygiene the woman is no match for the automobile. There is furthermore the efficient, even temper of the latter, and the fact that you may obtain a younger and more beautiful one as often as you like.

There were bad moments, though. I had no ties. My parents were dead. I was thirty-five years old, one moving body inside another. What does anyone do in my position? I got married.

Muriel.

This poor, foolish, virgin librarian had staked her job, her room, perhaps her entire future, on a summer's trip West. Up to then she had spent her best moments scanning the heavens above Iowa, filling her little heart with the play of clouds and tints, and her little head with the certainty that if once those skies were seen reflected in some vast expanse of water—the Pacific Ocean for instance—all would be changed, life would no longer pass her by, she herself would turn lovable overnight.

Again, that curious faith in destinations.

She never saw the Pacific, she may or may not have become lovable, but life definitely did not pass her by—*I* stopped for her. She had been resting on her suitcase at a crossroads; a placard round her neck read *California or Bust*. She saw the car stop, saw that it was powerful enough to take her where she wanted to go. She was too tired, hungry, and sunburned to wonder about its driver. That came later, offshoot of the basic physical infatuation with the machine.

We *headed* West—my intentions were honorable. We might have gone all the way but for that billboard somewhere in Nebraska advertising a "Motorists' Chapel. Worship in Your Car." My weakness for novel experience within the traditional framework, or chassis, together with Muriel's empty, peeling face, caused me to stop, propose to her and, once accepted, make inquiries that led to the first marriage ceremony ever performed in an automobile. A national magazine paid all expenses. For weeks people recognized us wherever we went. Many wished they had thought of doing the same thing.

My marriage was not unhappy, it was unreal. Legally each other's dearest belonging, we spent, as I might have foreseen, more and more time in rooms, eating places, shops, or under trees with sandwiches and books of verse. "And if thy mistress," read Muriel aloud, "some rich anger shows,

> *Emprison her soft hand and let her rave,*
> *And feed deep, deep upon her peerless eyes."*

Parked up a hill, the car shimmered in waves of heat, gazed wrathfully, peerlessly out over our heads.

Muriel's underclothes hung drying on a cord rigged across the back seat. She wanted to settle down. I tried to dissuade her from this step, the one of all that would lose me to her. Had she forgotten California? Ah, she didn't *need* California now! The denouement can be imagined. One cool blue morning that Fall, or the next, I left our secluded cottage—a last rose blooming by the gate, a letter of farewell written and ready to mail when I stopped, if I ever stopped. I got into the car for the first time in three days. A miniature Muriel waved from the house into my rearview mirror, then staggered abruptly and lurched with a whine out of sight. I was off, life lay ahead once more! In the nearest town faces stopped me. It was the morning after Pearl Harbor.

A voice on the radio was already predicting the rationing of fuel.

I quickly appraised the situation. Six months too old for the draft, I could settle down where I was, with Muriel, in the middle of our continent. This life at best would permit me the daily drive of a few miles to and from some nearby parachute or food-packaging plant. I decided on the spot to enlist in the Ambulance Corps. Weeping over the telephone, Muriel promised to wait. Laughing, I promised to send money. A year later I was driving in North Africa.

I think of landscapes, of roads erased by sand forever rippling under washes of light. A grove of palms, women in veils, the tank burning on the horizon. Above all, a vastness in which hovered black birds of indeterminate size. Whatever the scale, it was not human. This comforted us; we permitted ourselves colorful, passionate acts, at once proving and outweighing our tiny statures.

Made up of volunteers, our company had an odd, aristocratic flavor. Books were passed around—Tolstoi, *Les Liaisons Dangereuses*, collections of fairy tales. These showed me how far I had gone along certain roads never noticed while concentrating upon their macadam counterparts. I found in myself traces of the sage, the pervert, and the child.

Nothing bored me, nothing frightened me. Up from a half-hour's sleep in the shade of a wall, I would face into a warm wind blowing at the exact speed of my life. The laugh and the wound, the word of the wise man and the bullet's sunburst through glass, converged and drove me onward, light as a feather. It became all but superfluous to take the wheel again in search of casualties.

I see now that I did not belong. My heroics were prompted by exuberance, not humanity. My passengers suffered and prayed and died like the natives of a country I was content merely to visit. I had myself photographed smiling in front of grand Roman arches preserved for centuries in that climate. And then I went home. Sand covered them quickly. The war was won and lost, both.

Ours was now the oldest in a cluster of similar bungalows, each occupied by an older couple or single woman waiting, like Muriel, for her hero to return. This colony, having taken my wife to its heart—"you clever, darling child," I heard her addressed with my own ears— welcomed me avidly. Neighbors came to the door bearing covered dishes. Muriel kissed them, led them to where I squirmed. Poor, popular, outgoing Muriel. I was outgoing, too, in a sense. "Sorry," I would say, leaping up. "You caught me on my way to work."

My restlessness neither fazed nor puzzled them. It did me. Often I turned back after an hour on the road. People were buying anything, I could have sold rocks. And yet—

One day I drove home to witness the following scene. A car had stopped, motor running. My wife stood leaning across the gate, talking to the driver. A bleak wind lifted her hair and skirt, she was having to raise her voice. I heard nothing. As her eyes darted my way the car moved on. Its driver had got lost, Muriel said; she had given him directions. I shrugged. We did live off the main road.

Two nights later I heard the truth. We were returning from a drive-in movie. We had sat, not touching, in the car and watched a couple of starlets barely out of grammar school learn "the hard way" (burned biscuits, Madame de Merteuil for a neighbor, a miscarriage leading to a reconciliation under moonlit palms) that it took two to make a marriage. A mile from home Muriel spoke. "Walker, let's stop here." She had to touch my arm. "Can't we stop."

"If that's how you feel."

"I mean the car."

"Of course you do." I pulled uneasily to the side of the road.

"Now let's get out."

"What's got into you? We could be home now."

"Just for five minutes. I want to talk to you."

"All right, talk to me."

"Not in the car. *Please*. I can't think in the car."

"You said you wanted to talk. Make up your mind."

Muriel started to weep.

With my feet on earth, my head emptied automatically. The night stung and shone. Something of that cold clarity may have prompted her words; of those distances, too, without a sense of which the starry sky would be just another town on a hillside, soon to be entered and left behind. I tried to take her hand. These were things she did not need to tell me. At one point a silence fell, long enough for a small oblivious animal to amble past us on the icy road. I looked wistfully after it.

At last we were heading home. "You can keep the house," I said.

"You haven't understood, Walker," said Muriel in a higher, sadder voice than usual. "I don't want you to go. I don't love him—yet. But you're driving me to it."

"Driving you?" I stepped on the accelerator, wanting to turn it into a joke. "You mean like this?"

The car jolted forward.

"Yes!" Muriel screamed. "Exactly like this!"

Then, in our lights, two amber-green eyes were glowing. I pulled out of the creature's way. We turned over.

Muriel was not killed—I have never killed a living thing. But there was no further question of staying together. And early the following summer she and her new husband were drowned in a storm on Lake Tahoe.

Towards my next car, as towards the next and the next and the next,

I felt a kind of disabused tolerance. Each could have been my heavy, middle-aged person—not yet a source of suffering, no longer a source of delight.

In fact I have nothing more to relate except the incident which decided me, some weeks ago, to write these pages. Today I wonder if what I have set down leads anywhere, let alone to that warm, bright morning.

I had bought a convertible—not that it promised to change anything —and had thrown back the top before setting out. It was late June in the South. My road led without warning to a group of old-fashioned buildings, shaggy with ivy and vacant behind pale buff windowshades. A black and gold sign in their midst read STATE TEACHERS' COL-LEGE. I had slowed down for no reason—the place was clearly deserted —when a young man stepped from under a lintel that bore in large block-lettered relief the word POULTRY. He raised a careless hand, as if saying, "There you are!" to a friend.

Although I take no riders nowadays I stopped for him. He was dressed with an undergraduate's nattiness: white shoes and seersucker. In my day he would have carried a mandolin. After we began to move he named a town some fifty miles distant—some fifty miles out of my way, too, if a "way" was what I had—then closed his blue eyes, enjoying the ride, I supposed.

He opened them soon enough and, turning to me, made, in the pleas-antest of voices, a series of wholly uncalled-for remarks. Cars had grown (he began) too ugly for words. So pompous, so unwieldy. He only rode in them when absolutely essential. The seats were no longer covered in cloth or leather, but some hideous synthetic material. The dashboards were cushioned. As for the color-schemes—well, why not put a bedroom on wheels and get it over with? I decided he was a fairy. I suppose *you* fly, I nearly said.

As if he had read my mind he burst into laughter. His name was Sandy, he continued. He had known I was coming. Hadn't *I* felt, too, that something unusual lay ahead that morning? "Look," I said firmly, but he went right on. I could expect something far more unusual than him. A woman, a Princess, was waiting for him—for us. Already I was part of this mission, his and hers. I felt him watching me closely. The Princess was a medium. I knew what that meant? Good. They had been for many months in communion with a guide—did I understand?—a guide who at last had judged them ready to receive and carry out a set of elaborate instructions. They were to fly that very afternoon to the West Coast, thence to an island in the South Pacific. They had been given quite a timetable of duties, contacts with strangers minutely described by this guide as to both appearance and spiritual pedigree—one of the most useful was to be a thirteen year old fisher-boy who in a previous life had been Sandy's grandfather. Just what they hoped to accomplish he was forbidden to say. But the general aim, I might as well know, was to save mankind from annihilation.

I shot him a startled look; he was smiling. Beneath his tanned cheeks the young color danced.

"You've seen the newspapers," said Sandy. "The end gets nearer and nearer. Nobody else is really trying to stop it."

Casting about for a badly-needed plausible touch at this point, it occurs to me to mention his "hypnotic voice." It was nothing of the sort, rather a boyish, matter-of-fact voice, yet I hesitate to put forth any *serious* explanation for what was happening. My early impression of him had vanished. In a strange apprehensive sleepiness I found myself hanging upon his words. I thought of the "missions" of my own youth, the awakenings I dreamed of bringing to my fellow man. Rooted behind my steering-wheel of white, sun-warmed plastic, I had a glimmering of how those others would have reacted, as I did now, half with the drowsy numbness of Muriel's favorite poet, half with a heart shocked by its sudden pounding.

He talked the entire hour. Of that crazy quilt only scraps come back today. Good and Evil existed, pitted against one another. He, Sandy, had seen an angel routed by Lucifer in the New York Subway. The beautiful white yarn of vapor-trails was being used to entangle us all by statesmen, adult impersonators, lurching from one troublespot to the next. Their explosions in the press and on TV caused a kind of horrible psychic fallout in people's living rooms. Forces in the next world were fighting to reach us with messages rarely heard, almost never heeded. The resurrection of the body was at hand; we were no longer to be slaves of—personality? nationality? His exact word escapes me; no matter. We had reached the town. The Princess might or might not see fit to tell me more. Sandy had already implied—with a touch of condescension which, in my increasingly pliable state, turned my very bones to wax—that I had been chosen from among thousands to help them through this stage of their mission.

"A lot depends on what she thinks of you," he said earnestly.

We parked in front of a willow-shaded Tourist Home. From the car I watched Sandy leap up the steps to the porch and into the house without knocking. A fly lit on my face. I could not have driven away.

He held open the screen door for a girl in a black, armless dress. She was using a cane and watching her feet, in sandals, descend the porch steps. At the car door she hesitated, then turned upon me the face of a middle-aged woman, sick-eyed and freckled, but not by this year's sun. I got out to help her. She motioned Sandy into the rear seat and settled herself awkwardly up front.

I looked back at the house.

"No baggages," said the Princess. "This." She patted a bulging leather purse. It sprang open. She took out a scarf of milky chiffon to keep her hair in place. "Everything gets done for us, so we travel light. You are very kind," she added in the same breath, ridding herself as neatly of the obligation as of the unwanted suitcases. "We—I can say?—*anticipate* kindness."

"I think she means," Sandy began.

"He know what I mean," said the Princess grandly. "He understand my English." She gave a formal signal to depart.

Idiotically, I relished my place in their little aristocracy. It was all so effortless! Poor clods (I thought) who had still to rely on telephones and timetables. I drove with my whole heart, bent on getting my passengers to their destination.

The airport was thirty miles farther on. Noon had struck; the plane would leave at half past one. Leaning forward to make himself heard, Sandy pointed out turns. Once on the straight road he announced as if casually, "This isn't a scheduled flight. A DC-4 picks us up at this field and takes us to New Orleans where a connecting jet to San Diego will be waiting."

I nodded too quickly. We were driving through broad fields.

"Oh, not waiting for *us*. We mean nothing to them. Any delay will be dismissed in the usual way—a motor check, a confused weather report. Don't you know what goes *on* at airports? Let me tell you, it's a scandal. They're debasing something pure and rare. I have to say this in spite of times like now, when their obtuseness works to our advantage."

Here Sandy disgressed at length on the subject of flying. I was too much a part of the adventure, by now, to feel the annoyance his earlier speech about automobiles had provoked. Instead, I listened humbly, as ready as not to accept the judgment implicit in his words. I shall not try to reproduce them. The impression he gave was of intense, disquieting enthusiasm for aircraft, for certain models over others, for the view one came, as a pilot, to take of things. In the Islands, he remarked, they would be flying their own plane.

My self-respect spoke up: "But you don't even drive a car!"

I never felt it took great perception to tell the drivers from the rest. All the same, Sandy shouted with delight. "You knew that! What a beginning! Did you hear him, Anya? He's one of us!"

At my side the Princess started—had she been asleep?—and spoke in a new gruff voice whose accents were not hers. "The road first traveled is the longest road," said this voice.

Sandy touched my shoulder. "It's Uncle Sam."

"Who?"

"Our guide. We call him that. She's in a trance."

I looked at her in alarm. Beyond the whipping scarf her jaw hung open.

"Don't worry," said Sandy.

"It is a long and painful road," intoned the Princess. "It will seem shorter and easier a second time."

"Is this message for us, Uncle Sam?" Sandy inquired.

"For your friend. Wait."

"He's such a darling," said Sandy. "He followed the Princess to America last year and *loves* it. He wants to be the fifty-first State."

Suddenly from the Princess came a high, plaintive, uncertain voice: "Walker, have you learned to walk yet?"

I gripped the wheel for dear life.

"I couldn't teach you. Learn to walk, Walker. Learn."

"All right," I said stupidly. "Where are you, Muriel?"

"Here beside you. There's someone else."

"That's the Princess, Muriel."

"Not *her*," the voice giggled. "Someone *here*. Someone who loves you."

I could barely whisper, "Who?"

The Princess whimpered excitedly through her nose.

"It's Pal," said Muriel's voice. "Your little dog."

My throat filled with tears. My hands fell from the wheel. Sandy must have kept us from driving off the road.

We sat there. The Princess was inspecting me with vague, puffy eyes. She gave me a Kleenex from her purse, and shifted her attention to her own appearance where deeper ravages had been sustained. Into a large oval mirror she peered, touching a fingertip to her various features, testing their firmness. Soon she was intently painting her mouth.

Without a word I pressed the starter. They were watching, waiting to bind me closer and closer to them, but I kept gazing straight ahead, mile after mile. I had borne all I could. I already believed.

I believed, too, at the deserted rural airport where I deposited my passengers and waited with them. I believed well after they had exchanged that single faintest of frowns with which one tries to shake a stopped watch into running. When I left at their insistence—as if my presence had thrown the wrench into the works!—I drove away still believing.

The road climbed. At one turning I was able to look back and distinguish, in a dream's deepening light, the two figures motionless outside the locked hangar.

Something glittered on the front seat; the Princess had left her mirror. I peered at myself in it—I am nearly sixty—and threw it down. Phony, hysterical pair! There was no more to be learned from them than from those fat "psychical" studies of the last century, with titles like "Footsteps behind the Veil of Life" and "The Nine Stages: Dante's Vision Corroborated." Though I had never opened one, I have only to think of their Victorian embonpoint, their black or purple bombazines, to invest that whole day with the worst kind of dowdy ineffectuality. Uncle Sam indeed! Would the American Way of Life save mankind from annihilation? Was *that* the level of arcane innuendo from beyond the grave? One thing I knew, though no prophet: their plane would be a long while coming. They might have gone further by horse and buggy.

If I am angry now it is because I still believe, but not in them.

Driving, I kept glancing skyward, prepared, in spite of everything, for the glint of wings. Cross with myself, miles from my road, how gladly I would have hailed an order of machine superior to mine. To this day I cannot see a plane without stopping to wonder, to reenter those last lonely hours in the car—the mirror, face up beside me, shooting provocative flashes into the bare heavens.

W. S. MERWIN

Return to the Mountains

Once, nearly ten years before, I had spent a winter and part of a spring in that bit of high country far away from any cities, and this short return visit was touched with a happiness like the sunlight of the first days of summer: a feeling that was part recollection, part fulfillment.

I had not been married when I had lived in those mountains. I had known a girl in a little town near the top of the valley. She came from a mountain family which owned a small business in the town. They themselves still lived on their farms high up in the cold ridges. The firm was a kind of shipping agency. It had come into being a few generations earlier when her family had felt the need of having someone of their own established in what was then still a village, in order to take care of sending the family products to the markets in the cities. Over the years the fact that the family kept a permanent representative in the town had led other mountain farmers to make use of them, and in time the family had expanded the practice somewhat, and had employed a manager and bought a building in the town. When I knew the establishment it also employed a sallow young spinster who kept the files, and a clean, thin, silent old man who helped with some of the loading and unloading, and with the storing of bags of nuts, wool, piles of hides, and stacks of baskets, who wore a cap with a long visor which dropped nearly to his collar-bone when he dozed in his chair, and who spent a great deal of time sweeping, as it seemed to me, in the dark. The manager I remember only as a tall man in very correct clothes: they were black, long, and out of fashion, and the unshiny parts had a greenish cast. It was said that he was very good, but the meaning of the phrase was never explained, and I never saw much of him because he was seldom around at the hours when

I was there. But the family had never allowed the firm to develop a separate existence: there had always been some descendant of the original founders living in town in order to keep charge of it. The business had no official name, no stationery, and no sign. It was a small brown-shuttered stone house on a narrow curving side street; apart from the fact that the windows on the ground floor had been enlarged during the last century and held the desk at which the spinster sat with her papers, it looked like the other houses in the street.

And the girl I had known had in fact lived upstairs over the office and the store rooms. Later when I recalled visits to the building I remembered at the same time the winter evenings settling into the mountain town which seemed at that hour to be trying to retreat and be a village again: the feeble amber glimmer of the one naked light bulb in the street at the corner, the smell of woodsmoke, the fog that besets those mountains in winter beginning to dilute the few remaining colors, the skirts of broad-bottomed women brushing windows as they turned in their kitchens. Evening is too soft a word: there is no such thing in those regions at that time of year. It was the first part of the night, usually, when I got to the building. And yet often the spinster was still there, and at the beginning she would get up to hurry into her coat as I was shutting the door, and if she was alone in the office she would be torn, as she hurried past me, between a desire to warn me to keep the door locked, and confusion at referring to the situation. Almost always the old man would still be around and would emerge into activity from somewhere in the storerooms. I never understood his hours, and I wondered whether he did not sleep, at least some nights, back among the piled hides and wool, though his red clean-shaven chicken-neck and his boiled and ironed shirts, and the fact that there were only the most rudimentary sanitary facilities on that floor, made it seem unlikely.

I would not have inquired about such things of the girl I came to visit, though she had answered all the questions I had ever put to her about the business and about her family. Her replies had always been made with a calm and matter-of-fact directness which seemed perfectly candid and I believe was meant to be so, but I was always left with the feeling that she had answered some question which was quite different from the one I had asked, and that it would be unfair to her seriousness and her good will to point out the fact or to persist with the subject. There was a certain irony in this: I had met her as a result of pure curiosity. I had been referred to her by a baker with higher yearnings, with whom I used to talk, and who knew of my interest in the mountains and in how the families in the high farms had come to be what they now were. He told me that she owned some old books, or at least that there were some old books in the building, and that she knew more about such things than anyone else he could think of. The books, as it turned out, were of no interest. But I learned in some detail, before the subject filmed over between us, how the old people in her family remembered the change of produce over the decades, from the days of the great lemon harvests on the lower slopes, and the times when different families were famous for their cheeses, until now when those crops were small in comparison with the wool and the hides. It was a change that had come about as the young men, generation after generation, had gone away, and the family had withdrawn higher and higher into the wild treeline pastures that covered whole ranges, where a few hands could tend the great invisible herds scattered on the mountains and in the gorges. The herds had grown as the family had diminished. And as for her, she had come to the town a few years before when an old uncle had been running the firm. She had kept house for him and at the same time had taken lessons in economics from a once well-known professor who had moved to the valley after he had retired. When her uncle had died she had stayed and run the agency, quite as a matter of course.

She did not look dark, but as though she were permanently tanned. I suppose she was beautiful, as I remember her, though I was not conscious of it as a separate fact at the time. She cooked well. If she knew I was coming there was always something special, usually something peculiar to the region since she knew that the fact would add to my pleasure. For a while, if I had not said I was coming, I would take something to eat, along with anything else I might have for her, but she always provided a meal at the usual time and it never included what I had brought. Eventually I came to feel that my provisions were infringing some deep-rooted preference of hers and I stopped bringing things of that kind. But the same was true in different degrees of everything I brought her. If they were books they were seldom referred to again; if they were objects for her rooms they were put away; if they were clothes she almost never wore them. The clothes she usually wore kept within the somber conventions observed by all the local women, and yet hers were worn with decision.

How little we seem to have known about each other, I see now as I recall it. Yet I remember my awareness, from the beginning, of her indifference to the opinion of anyone; it was no deference to others that restrained us from the slightest physical contact when we walked through the empty streets of the shuttered town at odd hours of the winter nights and amazed the dogs, or stood talking on the stone bridge, staring into the water, just at dawn. And it was nothing of the kind, certainly, which kept her from inviting me to visit her family on any of the occasions when we went up into the mountains on sunny afternoons, taking the one-car electric train that had once been an object of pride and was now simply a very dilapidated streetcar built long ago for use in the mountains and battered by the weather and its rough-handed passengers with their heavy shoes and their impedimenta. She must have known all the passengers, by sight at least, on those excursions. But the people of that part of the mountains are not given to showing what they are thinking. They never seemed to be particularly aware of us, and apart from an occasional nod to some older man or woman who perhaps had been on close terms with her family all their lives, she never seemed to be especially conscious of them. She never referred to them when we had left them, for instance when we had got off the car; and she never spoke of passers-by, in the streets. And if I referred to them, what little she told me served only to blur their images for me.

The car was always pointed in the same direction. No arrangements had ever been made for turning it around at the top of the run, and the seats were not reversible, so that as one left the valley all the passengers were facing backward, downhill. It was only on the return descent that one seemed to be facing forward. Leaving the town, the car followed the line of the stream for a few miles, stopping seldom, and then struck off to the west up a ravine at the end of which it made a stop in apparently deserted country, and there at least a dozen passengers always got off, helping each other down with their bundles and crates, into the silence and the air already colder and smelling of height. For some of them there would be men waiting, with or without mules. The tracks—one or two of them with faint ruts, the rest with the grass not even worn off— led upward toward the ridges and clefts on both sides, but there were no buildings visible from where the car stopped. When it started again it began at once to gather its full speed, which it continued to do for a mile or more, with the cement poles rushing past closer and closer together at different angles, and then it suddenly tilted and started a climb at an angle so steep that it seemed impossible that it could continue. But everything had been calculated long before: the car slowed indeed, and at one moment it seemed that it must stop and begin to slide back down the fearful slope in front of us, but just then the angle became gentler and the car ground on. After a time the tracks levelled off and the car stopped again. From there on, she told me, the car climbed very gradually. But it was always there that we got off.

Those slopes must have been pasture for centuries. Even in the spring the earth showed through the sparse, close-bitten brilliant green grass, when one bent down to look. I remember only one afternoon in which the sky was settled, and it was plain that the wintry sun would fill all the slopes with a colorless windless shining until night. That day the passengers had spoken in even quieter voices than usual as they had got down from the car. Perhaps we had done the same. We had started up the slope to the south of the car, away from the passengers who had got off at the same place. She never suggested which way we should go, but waited for me to lead, as though she were in those mountains for the first time. On those days we walked for long stretches in silence, crossing the tilted pastures, winding up into the scree and the snow-filled clefts and into the bases of the crags at the top of the ridge, but it was a silence filled with an unnameable exhilaration and with a tenderness for her such as I felt nowhere else. Even when we lay down, as we did every time, in little grass declivities high up in the scree, with snow drifts and stone rising around us like fragments of something that had gone, we would not kiss or touch, but lie on our backs and talk in low voices, looking down at the corvines and swifts and, from time to time, the kites, flying in and out of the spurs of ice and stone far above us. It was on the cloudless day, lying together in one of those green bowls, that she told me about a brother of hers, about my age, who had been killed in the war. She told me the details as she knew them, the barbed wire, the bombing, the death in a hospital. The story led back into their childhood. He had been the member of her family whom she had loved most intensely. It was he who had taught her to see the animals. Not only the ones whose cheeses and wool and hides they sent to the valley, and the others who guarded them, though he had given those too a sharpness and a depth of existence in her mind which they would never lose. The others too: the ones that the mountain people shot or trapped for their meat or their furs or plumage or their predatory ways or simply because they enjoyed it. And the others, she said; all of them. He showed her what had never been owned, and the tracks. I was surprised, because the people from those mountains, even the women, seem to be born with the senses and knowledge of hunters as well as of farmers, and they take no more interest in the animals than is usual among country people who are their own butchers and tanners. I imagined that what she was telling me revealed more about what she had felt for her brother than it did about what she felt for the animals. I was surprised too because I realized that although I could easily imagine her as a child there were many things that I could not imagine her having learned; I took it for granted that she had always known them. On our first night together I had been aware—as I might have been before that if I had thought about it—that she had never known a man before me. And yet the fact was a fact and nothing more. There was nothing different or startled in her desire, nor in the rush of feeling that came with it and was never spoken of except with her body and her eyes. The first time had been like every other, and the anticipation of her eyes in the room, or of her arms late at night, would have been enough to account for the quickening with which I entered that street on my way to see her, and the difficulty I had in controlling my voice as I said my good evening to the spinster, though it was the thought of her whole elusive presence that tightened my throat every time I set out to go to her, and dissolved time and other circumstances, for me at least, when we were together. On the day I have been referring to she went on telling me of her dead brother, while we lay in the high patch of grass, and she mentioned him again—one of the only times that I saw her laugh—in the streetcar on the way down to the valley, as the feeble lights began to appear far below us and the iron trolley tipped forward at its awesome angle and started to grind slowly down the steep place. It was something he had said about the trolley that had made her laugh, but the noise of the car itself prevented my hearing all of it. When she mentioned him again—and that was seldom—it was with the same grave, measured and yet undeliberate distance with which she spoke of anything else—the news, the small affairs of the town, books, history, the cities.

We never spoke of the future. She seemed to remember everything I ever told her, but when she asked me anything about myself it was done with an air of formality and a sense of the exceptional which endowed my answers with a dignity I could never have claimed for them. At the same time this reserve of hers did not prompt me to tell her much about myself apart from the main facts. What we did know about each other we knew without details but also without doubt. And yet when, in the spring, not more than a few weeks after the trip on which she had talked about her brother, she was suddenly summoned to the city, neither of us had any illusion that we would see each other again. She was needed in a household of a relative in the city, where a child was about to be born, and there was also some question of her being married into another family whose history resembled that of hers. I heard from her once; a message that said she was well. I spent my last few weeks there, between her departure and my own, walking in the mountains above the town, watching the spring come into the pastures and the ice melt, darkening the cliffs, and one last snowfall with large furred flakes. My landlord tried to interest me in carving in horn, which he did very intricately—it is a traditional occupation in that part of the country. He had carved elaborate buttons, portraits, and religious figures, a few favorite saints over and over. I left, as I had planned to do, before the spring was in full flower. He too sent me one card, a few years later, saying that he had heard she was well and had married.

And when I returned to the mountains I was married, myself, and had been for several years. My wife and I stayed in another town a little further down the valley. It was in fact late July but the early summer had been rainy and cold, and when we arrived the light and the colors of the slopes were such as they must have been in May, in other years: bright, lucent, and soft, at least in the valley itself. It is much broader there than in the town where I had spent so much time before. The stream widens out into a shallow lake with rich farms around its shores. The sun shone day after day on the lake and the humid farms and the peach orchards. The colors, even in the weeks we were there, began to turn dusty and tawny. We walked to other little towns and villages. We went up to the town that I had known so well in the winter, and we visited, as I had done then, the reliquary of the local saint: the great face in hammered silver that looks like a battered breastplate with two red glass nipples for eyes. We walked up into the slopes—there are mountains everywhere around there—and heard the cliffs, warmed by the sun, echo when we laughed. We even took the streetcar once and came back down as the long afternoon light was flooding the valley, turning all the stone to brass. And then we walked on down to where we were staying—another five or six miles—as the evening came on, taking the unpaved road that follows the stream and the lake, and stopped at an inn to have dinner out of doors under a vine, looking over the water where the terns were catching their last minnows before dark. Increasingly through those weeks I felt as though the valley had given me my wife, and as though, for all our love before, and our years of marriage, I had come to know her only there. She had never been anywhere near that region and had wanted to see the mountains I had told her about. In those long summer days and the nights that followed them I came to see in her a capacity for happiness such as I had never seen in anyone. Of course we stayed too long there—longer than we had intended to stay. The heat of the delayed midsummer had turned the hay fields pale since we had come, and the farmers on the upper slopes were beginning to complain of drought, and her face had become more deeply tanned than I ever remembered it. We had stayed too long and still had not gone to half the places that, during our first few days, we had planned to visit. We decided to take one last trip into the mountains: another ancient streetcar that went up into a different range. I had never taken it when I had lived in the valley, and had always meant to. We seldom planned trips very far in advance, but this time, so that we should not let the chance slip past, we decided, at the beginning of our last week, what day we would save for the trip into the mountains. And the next morning there was a telegram for my wife. Her mother had fallen sick, and she was needed. We began to pack. But my wife stopped me after a moment to beg me to stay another day or so and take the trip as we had planned to do together. She wanted me to do it, she said, so that the end of our time in the valley should not be simply a rushed journey filled with anxiety. She said that there would probably not be much that I would be able to do to help her with her mother, or not much that could not wait for a few days. She wanted to be able to think of me in the mountains as she travelled toward her family. She said it would help her to be able to leave there what she most loved, for another day or two, and to be able to look forward to my following later, and describing it to her. Whatever shadow of desperation there was in it, the request was born of our happiness that summer, and I could not refuse it.

I saw her off on a train that left early in the morning. When it was gone I had another coffee and then went back to the place where we had been staying, and changed my clothes to go up into the mountains. It was a hot airless morning but I deliberately dressed too warmly and threw a sweater and coat over my shoulder. The streetcar left shortly before noon. I walked down to the lake and took off my clothes in an orchard and bathed in the brownish water and dried in the sun. Then I dressed and walked to the station. It was early. I bought my ticket and got on the car. It was pleasant in the shade of the iron roof. The echoes felt cool. I was thinking of my wife and our summer together, and what she would find in the different life of the city where we had been living, and I paid no attention to the car filling up with peasant women in black clothes, as usual, and I did not hear their voices, any more than I had heard the voices of people on the road beyond the orchard, when I had been swimming underwater in the lake, a few minutes before. The car hissed and clanged and screeched and rolled slowly out into the withering sunlight. It rocked through the back gardens of the town, past the roses and hen coops and pig sheds, and around farms and a loop of the lake, and began to climb. There was a long winding ascent through lemon groves and then through oak woods; then the tracks levelled off in country that had evidently been much more carefully farmed at one time than was now the case: there were overgrown orchards and little meadows where the hay was full of weeds, and there were ruined stone barns and stone houses. Even with all the windows open the heat was terrible in the iron car. It stopped and a few women got off. No one was waiting for them. They called back their goodbyes and the raised voices sounded startling. The car left them. And as the other streetcar had done, this one suddenly began to gather speed and hurtle forward through the remains of half-dead vineyards, and the fields of thistles and brambles, lurching and swinging as though it was about to jump the track, and all at once it tipped upward at a frightening angle and began a climb which seemed even steeper than the one I knew, and even more likely to stall the trolley and send it slithering and crashing back down the slope. As in the other car we were all facing to the rear as we rose from the valley; we were looking back and down. The cement poles appeared from behind our shoulders less often and passed us more slowly. We began to go around a bend, and as we did, the mountain directly across from us came into sight. It was a view of it such as I had never had before, and none of the glimpses of it from the valley or from other slopes would have led me to suspect what the whole of it was like. As the car turned slowly it turned too, huge and, as it seemed, a little below us, rising from a turn of the valley on the other side of the lake, and climbing in one even sweep to a long curving crest. The whole mountain, on the side that faced us, was the shape of an immense mussel lying on its base, and the color was a shade of dark brownish gray between that of iron and that of rust; its surface was crusty, shiny in places and stony in others, with a spongy look like a piece of coke. One could not have been sure, at that distance, but it did not look as though there was anything whatever growing on it, except at the very top, where there were some green stains. Then the car turned another bend; we saw the lake once more as we turned, before the tracks began to level out and the car started a more gradual climb. The country above the steep rise here was utterly empty. I got off at the next stop, a few miles farther up, and most of the other passengers did too. They made off through the brush, following the tracks for a few steps. I turned to look around and when I glanced back they were scarcely visible among the bushes.

It was already well into the afternoon. Ahead of me, in the direction to which I was naturally drawn, there was a stretch of wild upland, rolling and full of dry grass taller than a man, that waved as though the different clumps were responding to different winds. Through the grass I could see patches of bare ground and what looked like marsh and shallow ponds. Great outcroppings of rock the size of houses jutted up here and there. They were like smaller versions of the stone mountain face I had seen from the car: they were all shaped like mussels lying on the hinged side, and they were all pointing the same way. But some of them had tiny dwarfed thorn trees and oaks growing out of clefts in the tops, and ivy and old man's beard and lichens dripping down them and swaying. I walked into the country around them toward the line of dry gray cliffs beyond, which made the top of the ridge. The dry smells of the grass and the rocks were mixed with the smells of stagnant water. What I had seen had indeed been patches of shallow marsh and mud. The first one I came to was marked with the hooves of many animals, though I realized that I had seen none since I left the valley. It must have been an hour or more before I came to the next bit of marsh—it did not seem nearly that long, but judging by the change in the light it could not have been less. There too the ground for yards around the muddy water had been chewed by hooves. There seemed to be not only the prints of sheep and of cows there, but of others as well, and there were paw-marks of different sizes. It was growing cooler. I put on one of the garments I was carrying. Ahead of me the light in the cliffs, where they were broken into gorges, drew me like a window in the dark and I went on. But it was getting to be late in the afternoon; the mid-day stillness ended as the coolness began. I was aware all at once of the stirring of the animals. I heard them in the tall grass. I saw their shadows, immensely long and rapid, hurrying and changing shape, when I could not see them themselves. I stood near one of the large rocks and waited. The shadows slipped back and forth. The light fell from the cliffs. I began to see the animals themselves. Only at a distance at first, looking paler than the shadows, which in turn were no longer so definite. They were hooved, most of them, like elk; they moved in small groups, flitting through the clumps of grass at a rocking canter that I could not hear. The wind rose a little and I saw that dusk had fallen. But as I watched I saw more of them, closer. There were many sizes, some with long necks and horns that curved back over their shoulders. They ran between me and what was left of the light, and from where I stood they all looked to be different shades of gray. There were other animals too, that walked, but whether they were large dogs, or what they were, I could not be sure. It began to grow dark. The moon would rise soon, but the fog that sometimes drifts over those uplands all night in the summer too had begun to gather and to shut out the cliffs and when it did rise the moon would be veiled. When I moved there was a flurry of animal shapes around me as far as I could see. I was moving to go back the way I had come, but I was still looking over my shoulder toward the animals, trying to make out their shapes in the dimness, and as I was looking, one of the large dog-like animals came out of the grass not far from me. There was something of a cat about him, and something high in the withers and long-necked, like the hooved animals. He lay down facing away from me, as a dog sometimes lies down when he wants you to throw a stick for him. All his attention was fixed toward a point beyond him. As I watched him I saw him wriggle his haunches to get into a position of even greater alertness. Beyond him in open spaces in the grass I could see other animals and groups of animals following his example, lying down, facing in the same direction. It was not the direction in which I had been going, but well to one side of it. Then as I stood there I too smelled it. Smoke. And not the smell of bush fires sweeping over the uplands, nor that of chestnut woods burning and writhing at a distance. It was the smell of wood fires in houses, the smell of evenings before dinner-time, in villages. I began to walk toward it. The animals vanished, to reappear at a distance, lying down, showing me my direction. The moon set but I could still see just enough. I put on the last garment. I could no longer smell the smoke, but I had begun to feel a path under my feet.

The dampness got into my clothes. I was coldest just as the fog began to turn from dark gray to a paler color, and as it did the path led me onto a cart track and before long I saw that I was at the beginning of a village street.

It was light enough so that, when I got to the first building, a large gray mass on my left, I could make out the separate swirls of fog in the mud street. There seemed to be nothing on the other side of the thoroughfare—a vegetable garden, perhaps, or a few rows of potatoes, but no building. A sense whose accuracy is sometimes heightened by fatigue led me to believe that beyond the patch of tilled ground there would be nothing, a drop; the village was built on the brink of a ridge. When I went up to it I could see that the building on my left was an immense

Renaissance structure, built in some stone that I was sure had not come from those mountains, but whether it was genuinely old—a palace built with a commanding view of the valley—or whether it was a recent imitation I could not even guess in the fog. The elaborately carved stone ornamentation looked recent, but perhaps it was part of a modern restoration. Certainly the building now had the appearance of an institution. I walked into a paved recess between two wings, wondering whether anyone was awake. At the end of the recess there was a large glass door, three panels of small panes, the middle one with the handle, and the other two, I supposed, for light. As I came closer I saw that there was an old woman sitting in the doorway behind the glass, blocking it so that the door could not open. She was dressed as a peasant but not in black: a red sweater, a faded print tied around her head. She was sewing something in her lap; the bulk of it flowed down from her knees and was partly hidden in her skirts, partly piled up on the floor. She was wearing thick black-rimmed glasses through which she was watching me, without any expression, while she continued her sewing. The needle and thimble never hesitated. I saw what she was sewing. It was the top of a plastic tablecloth wrapped like a caul around the fully clothed dead body of a middle aged woman. The knees were drawn up, but loosely. The arms held them, but loosely. The head was tipped forward. It was smiling, but as though by chance; in the smile one could see that many of the teeth must be gone from inside. I looked around me. All the windows on the ground floor were glass doors of the same kind, and inside each of them there was an ageing woman at the same kind of sewing. The fog was withdrawing, but slowly. There was absolute silence, and it was emphasized by an atmosphere of intense preparation, as though everyone would be too hurried to talk. In the eyes of the old woman there was a bitter reproach, but I could not divine whether it was directed specifically at me or at the whole world of which I was simply a convenient representative. I realized that I should know. Certainly I could not inquire, nor could I ask whether these victims were relatives of the old women who were stitching the cauls, or whether they were the fruit of some sudden disaster or were a continually recurring charge. The tensed grief that seem to breathe out from the building, the quality of shock in the silence around it, seemed to indicate that the catastrophe that had brought so many dead suddenly to the feet of these women with their needles, in the first half-light, must be an exception, must be related to them in some exceptional way that could not be repeated day after day, but the profound bitterness in the old woman's face, and the monastic severity of the building would have led me to suspect that this kind of task was not strange to the place and its tenants.

While I was looking at the face in the caul, trying to catch some glimpse of how it had come to be there, the old woman put in the last stitches and stood up. She seized the plastic sack by the top, opened the door and stepped out, dragging it behind her. I nodded to her as I might have done at a funeral. She glared at me for an instant and then indicated with her head that I should come with her. Dragging the caul at her side, she led me out of the recess, past the other women at their doors, none of them so much as looking up, and around the corner to the left. Here there was a wider entrance to the building. The doors stood open, letting the fog in, but the hallway inside was well lit. The plastic bag squeaked as it slid along the polished yellow tiles of the floor. The sense of some appalling and unusual catastrophe was many times more powerful inside the building. Everything added to it: the doors open onto the fog, the silence of the doors along the hall. The old woman shoved the plastic sack into a place beside a large wardrobe standing against the wall. The first. As she took her hand away from it and straightened up I was certain that the caul contained a relative of hers. At the same moment a woman emerged from a door behind me: a head nurse of some kind. Her gaunt face was smiling. I could not tell whether she was part of some religious order, and I could not at once be sure whether her air of radiant cheerfulness was the heartiness of a gym-teacher, or was an expression of genuine sweetness of nature. She smiled at me, showing several large silver teeth, and strode to the body, nudging it into a position where it took up less space, as a master mason might change the position of the first stone of a wall. She spoke to the old woman in a tone that implied confidence and satisfaction, as a teacher might speak to a good but discouraged student. It had not been decided yet, she said, how big the casket would be. The old woman's face showed no response, though it was apparent that her feeling for the other woman approached reverence. The head nurse caught my eye, as I stood watching her pushing the body into a more compact shape.

"They," she said to me with a smile which I was sure now was the result of sweetness, "they are nothing now."

EDNA ST. VINCENT MILLAY

The Murder in the Fishing Cat

Nobody came any more to the Restaurant du Chat qui Pêche. It was difficult to say just why.

The popularity of a restaurant does not depend on the excellence of its cuisine or the cobwebs on the bottles in its cellar. And you might have in the window ten glass tanks instead of one in which moved obscurely shadowy eels and shrimps, yet you could be no surer of success. Jean-Pierre knew this, and he did not reproach himself for his failure. It is something that may happen to the best of us.

For fourteen years he had served as good *lapin sauté* as was to be found in Paris; and if the *petits pois* were rather big and hard, and the Vouvray rather like thin cider, and you got no more than a teaspoonful of sugar with your strawberries, well, what could you expect for seven francs, all told? Not the world, surely. As for the rest, where else might you, while sitting comfortably at your table under a red-and-white awning, choose your eel, and see it captured for you deftly in a napkin, and borne off, writhing muscularly, to the kitchen, to be delivered to you five minutes later on a platter, fried? That was more than you could do at Ciro's.

It might be, of course, because Margot had scolded him much too audibly. But where was the man among his clients whose wife had not at some time or other addressed him as *saligaud*, or *espèce de soupe au lait*? Let him stand forth.

And, anyway, she had gone now. After fourteen years at his side, stamping the butter, whacking the long loaves of bread, sitting down with a sigh to a bowl of onion soup after nine o'clock, she had gone. She had run off with a taxi driver who had red mustaches that curled naturally. And the place was very still.

Jean-Pierre stood in the doorway with a damp cloth in his hand, and watched the people go by. They all went by. Once he had been sure that all were coming in, but now he knew better. They were going to the Rendezvous des Cochers et Camionneurs, next door.

"*J'ai pas la veine,*" said Jean-Pierre. He stepped out upon the pavement and busily passed the damp cloth over a table which was not yet dry.

A man and a girl went by. Two men went by. A woman went past selling papers: "*L'Intran'! L'Intransigeant! La Liberté—troisième édition! L'Intran'! L'Intransigeant!*" Two young men went by; one was wearing a smock, the other had a painted picture under his arm. A man and a girl went past with their arms around each other. The man was saying, "*Si, si, c'est vrai.*" A very little girl came along, carrying a basket of small fringe-petaled pinks and fading roses. She had a serious face. She held out the flowers earnestly to a woman, with a coat over her arm, pushing a baby carriage; to an old man reading a newspaper as he walked; to two young women, dressed precisely alike, who were hurrying somewhere, chattering.

A priest went by, taking long steps, his black gown flapping about his large shoes, his stiff, shallow hat on the back of his head. He was trying to catch a bus. He began to run. The little girl watched him go by, seriously. Still watching him, she held out her flowers to a soldier in a uniform of horizon-blue. Then she went to the restaurant next door and moved among the tables.

"*Sentez, madame,*" she said without emotion, and impassively thrust a bunch of pinks under the nose of a young woman, with a very red mouth, whose fork dangled languidly from her hand as she conversed with the man across from her.

"*Merci, merci,*" said the woman, and motioned her away without looking at her.

An American boy was dining alone, reading from a yellow book. He looked up from his book, and followed the little girl with his eyes as she moved about the terrace. As she approached him he spoke to her.

"*C'est combien ça, ma petite?*" he asked.

She came up to him, and pressed her small stomach against the table. "*Dix sous,*" she answered lispingly, staring at his forehead.

He put an arm about her while he selected a nosegay from the basket, stood it up in his empty wineglass, and poured Vichy for it. Then he gave her a franc and told her to keep the change.

She stared at him, and went off up the street, holding out her basket to the passers-by.

Jean-Pierre came to himself with a start: the proprietor of a flourishing café does not stand all the afternoon gaping at the goings-on in the café next door. No wonder people did not come to the Restaurant du

Chat: it had an absent-minded *patron*. He hurriedly passed the damp cloth over two of the iron-legged tables, plucked a brown leaf from the laurel which hedged the terrace from the pavement proper, and went back into the restaurant.

"*Ça va, Philippe?*" he questioned jovially of the large eel which was now the sole occupant of the tank.

Not for the life of him could Jean-Pierre have told you why he had addressed the eel as Philippe; but having done so, he was glad. For from the moment he had given the creature a name, it possessed an identity, it was a person, something he could talk to.

He went to the kitchen, and returned with a morsel of lobster from a salad of the night before and tossed it into the pool.

Two men and two women, finding the Rendezvous de Cochers crowded, turned in at the Restaurant du Chat qui Pêche and seated themselves.

They heard Jean-Pierre singing:

> "*Oh, madame, voilà du bon fromage!*
> *Oh, madame, voilà du bon fromage!*
> *Voilà du bon fromage au lait!*"

One of the men rapped on the table with his stick. Jean-Pierre stopped short in his song, caught up the *carte du jour*, smoothed down his black beard, and hurried out.

"Very good, the rabbit," he suggested. And, "What will you have sirs, in the way of wine?"

For half a year there had been only three of them to do the work—he, his wife, and Maurice, the waiter. Maurice had come to them when he was sixteen; but very soon he was nineteen, and the War Department, which knows about everything, had found out about that also, and had taken him away to put him into the army.

Then for two months there had been only two of them, but it was quite enough. Now Margot was gone, and he was alone. But business was worse and worse; and very rarely was he hurried with all the cooking and the serving and the cleaning up.

Jean-Pierre had made few friends in Paris in these fourteen years. He had dealt pleasantly with his clients, his neighbors, and the tradespeople with whom he had to do; but he had been content with his wife. She was a pretty woman from the frontier of Spain and more Spanish than French. He had met her for the first time right over there, in the Luxembourg Gardens. He could almost see from his doorway the very tree under which she had been sitting. She was wearing a hat of pink straw sloping down over her forehead, with many little roses piled high under the back of it; and she was very small about the waist. She was embroidering something white.

Several times he passed the chair in which she was sitting, and every time she looked up, and then looked down again. When she arose to go, he fell into step beside her.

"Mademoiselle, may I accompany you?" he asked.

"No, please," she answered hurriedly, without looking at him, and quickened her step.

He kept pace with her, however, and bent over her and spoke again more softly.

"It is wrong for one so beautiful to be so cruel."

"*Veux-tu me laisser!*" she scolded, tossing her head, and hastened out of sight.

But the next afternoon she was there again.

"You remember my wife, Philippe?" said Jean-Pierre. "Margot of the naughty eyes and the pretty ankles?"

Philippe said nothing.

"You do, all the same," Jean-Pierre averred. "She used to stir the water to make you mad." After a moment he said again, "Philippe, you remember Margot, don't you?"

Philippe said nothing.

"Well, anyhow," said Jean-Pierre, "she's gone."

For three months now Philippe had been alone in the tank. Nobody ate eels any more. The few customers that came ordered rabbit, mutton, or beefsteak and potatoes. It would be foolish to have more eels sent in from the basin in the country. Jean-Pierre had explained that he would need for a time no more eels or shrimps, that he was making some changes.

Every morning when the proprietor of the Chat qui Pêche came down to open the door and put the tables and chairs out upon the pavement, Philippe lay sluggishly on the green bottom of this tank, the sunshine bringing out colors on his back that one had not known were there.

It was an oblong glass tank with brass edges. Fresh water came up through a little spout in the middle of it, and the stale water was sucked away through a pipe in one corner, which was covered with a bubble-shaped piece of netting. Looking into the tank one day, Jean-Pierre wondered why the netting was shaped like that; then he reflected that if the wire had been flat over the mouth of the pipe, it would have been clogged always with bits of dirt and food, which would float up to settle on it. He felt very proud when he had come to this conclusion.

Philippe had been at one time gray-green in color, and thin and very active. Now he was green-black, with a valance standing up along his spine of transparent purple, and with two little pale-green fins behind his head. He was big now, but as lithe as ever.

Jean-Pierre had heard queer tales about eels; he did not know how much truth there was in them. He had heard that their mothers came ashore to give birth to them; that they were born, like little animals, not laid, like eggs. And when they were small they were called "elvers." And he had been told that after they were born, their mothers left them, and went away. And in a little while the elvers started out for themselves in search of pools to live in. And if it so happened that the pools nearby had dried up with the heat, they went farther. And it was said that they have gone as far as twenty miles, across the land, in search of water, thousands of them, an army of little eels. And no human eye had witnessed their sinuous migration. Only from time to time there was found a dead elver in the grass, and people knew the eels had passed that way.

"*Dis-moi un peu, Philippe,*" said Jean-Pierre. "You are a droll one, aren't you?"

The days went by, and nothing happened in them. Every day a few people came to eat there. Once there had been ten at a time, and Jean-Pierre had said to himself that if this kept on, he would have to get a waiter. But it did not keep on.

Every day he missed his wife more keenly. One day he went across the rue de Médicis into the Luxembourg Gardens, and walked up and down past the place where he had first seen her. A young woman was sitting under the tree, embroidering, but she was not Margot. She had two children with her, two little girls, dressed just alike, in very short dresses made all of pale blue silk ruffles. They were chasing one another up and down the walk and calling in shrill voices. One of them lost her hair ribbon, a pale blue silk bow, and ran sidewise up to her mother, holding in one hand the ribbon and lifting with the other a lock of straight blonde hair at the top of her head; but all the time calling to her sister, and pawing the earth with brown, impatient legs.

Jean-Pierre wished very much that his only child, his and Margot's, had not died of diphtheria. She would have been much prettier than either of these little girls; she had looked like her mother. And she would be a companion for him now. If she were here this afternoon, he would take her to the Jardin des Plantes and show her all the different-colored birds. And after that they would go to the Café des Deux Magots and sit outside, and he would have a half-blond beer, and she would have a grenadine. And he would buy her one of those small white-and-brown rabbits made all of real fur that hop when you press a bulb, such as old men are always peddling along the pavement from trays suspended in front of their stomachs by a cord about their necks.

The days went by and went by. May passed, and June passed. One day there came a postcard from Maurice, a picture bearing the title, *Panorama de Metz*. On it was written carefully in pencil, *Bon souvenir d'un nouveau poilu aviateur*. Jean-Pierre was very exited about the postcard. Four times that day he drew it from his pocket and read it aloud, then turned it over and read with happiness his own name on the front of it. Late in the afternoon it occurred to him with pleasure that he had not yet read it to Philippe, and he hastened to do so. But from his wife there had come no word.

It seemed to Jean-Pierre that he would give everything he had in the world if he might once again hear Margot wail from the terrace, "*Un-e sou-u-u-u-u-pe!*" And, oh, to be called once more a dirty camel, a robber, or a species of dog!

He went to the tank and leaned over the quivering water.

"You are my wife, Philippe. You know?" said Jean-Pierre. "You are a *salope!*"

Having delivered himself of this genial insult, he felt happier, and stood for some moments in his doorway with his arms folded, looking boldly out upon the world.

"*Ça va, mon vieux?*" he accosted the eel one morning, and stirred the top of the water with a lobster claw. But Philippe scarcely moved. Jean-Pierre reached down with the lobster claw and tickled his back. The flat tail flapped slightly, but that was all. Jean-Pierre straightened up and pulled at his beard in astonishment. Then he leaned far over, so that his head made a shadow in which the eel was clearly visible, and shouted down to him.

"Philippe, Philippe, my friend, you are not sick, are you?"

He waited eagerly, but there was no responsive motion. The eel lay still.

"Oh, my God!" cried the *patron* of the Chat qui Pêche, and clutched his hair in his hands. Then for the first time he noticed that the surface of the water was unusually quiet. No fresh water bubbled up from the tap in the middle.

"Oh, my God!" cried Jean-Pierre again, and rushed to the kitchen.

There was nothing there with which to clean a clogged water pipe. Everything that was long enough was much too thick. One tine of a fork would go in, but was probably not long enough. Nevertheless, he would try.

He ran back to the window and prodded the tube with a tine of the fork. Then he straightened up and waited, breathless. The water did not come. He rushed again to the kitchen, and scratched about among the cooking utensils. Was there no piece of wire anywhere in the world? A pipe cleaner! That was it! He searched feverishly through all his pockets, but he knew all the time that he had none. It occurred to him that if Margot were there, she would have a hairpin, which could be straightened out, and he cursed her savagely that she had gone.

Suddenly his eye fell on the broom, which was standing in a corner. He went over to it and tore out a handful of splints, with which he rushed back to the tank.

"Wait, wait, Philippe!" he called as he approached. "Don't die! Wait just a very little minute!" And he thrust a splint down into the tube. It broke, and he had difficulty in extracting it. Sweat came out on his forehead. He put two splints together, and inserted them with care.

"Don't die! Don't die!" he moaned, but softly, lest the splints should break.

Suddenly, incredibly, the water came, and dust and particles of food began to travel slowly toward the outlet. Jean-Pierre thrust his hands in up to the wrists, and shooed the stale water down the tank.

The next morning Philippe was quite himself again. Fearfully, Jean-Pierre crept into the room and approached the window.

"*Comment ça va ce matin?*" he questioned in a timid voice, and put a finger into the pool.

The eel aroused, and wriggled sullenly to the other end of the glass.

Jean-Pierre giggled sharply with delight, and all that morning he went about with a grin on his face, singing, "*Madame, voilà du bon fromage!*"

Jean-Pierre hated the room in which he slept. It seemed to have become, since Margot left, every day dirtier and more untidy. For one thing, of course, he never made the bed. When he crawled into it at night it was just as he had crawled out of it in the morning. The thin blanket dragged always to the floor on one side, the counterpane on the other. The sheets grew grayer and grayer, and the bolster flatter. And he seemed always to have fallen asleep on the button side of the square pillow.

Infrequently he drew off the soiled sheets and put on clean ones. But at such times he became more than usually unhappy; he missed Margot more. She had been used to exclaim always over the fresh bed that it smelled sweet, and to pass her hand with pleasure over the smooth old linen. Often she would say with pride, "I tell you frankly, my little cabbage, in many of the big hotels today, rich hotels, full of Americans, they make up the beds with cotton. I don't see how the clients sleep. I could not."

Every morning on awaking, Jean-Pierre groaned once and turned heavily. Then he rubbed the back of his wrist across his eyes, and stared out at the daylight. He saw on the shelf above the narrow fireplace a pale photograph of himself and his brother when they were children. They were seated in an imitation rowboat. Into his hand had been thrust an imitation oar; from the hand of his brother dangled listlessly a handsome string of imitation fish.

He saw also the swathed and ghostly bulk of what he knew to be a clock—a clock so elegant and fine, so ornamented with whorls of shiny brass, that his wife had kept it lovingly wrapped in a towel. To be sure, the face of the clock could not be seen; but what will you? One cannot have everything. Between the clock and the photograph was a marvelous object—a large melon growing serenely in a small-necked bottle. A great trick, that. But Jean-Pierre was very tired of the melon.

He was tired of everything in the room, everything in his life, but particularly of the things on the mantelpiece. And most of all he was tired of the candlestick that stood between the clock and the wreath of wax gardenias—a candlestick which had never known a candle, a flat lily pad with a green frog squatting on it. Jean-Pierre did not know that it was a green frog squatting on a lily pad. It had been there so long that when he looked at it he no longer saw it. It was only one of the things on the mantelpiece.

One morning, however, as he awoke and groaned and turned and looked out with dull eyes on still another yesterday, it so happened that he stared for some moments at the candlestick. And presently he said, *"Tiens! tiens!"* and laid his forefinger alongside his nose.

That morning he dressed hurriedly, with a little smile going and coming at his lips. And when he was dressed he thrust the candlestick into his pocket and ran downstairs.

"Bonjour, Philippe!" he called as he entered the restaurant. "Regard, species of wild man, I bring you a little friend!"

Happily, and with excessive care, he installed the green frog at the bottom of the tank. The eel moved away from it in beautiful curves.

"There is somebody for you to talk to, Philippe," said Jean-Pierre, "as you are for me."

He went to the door and opened it. The morning air came freshly in from the trees and fountains of the Luxembourg.

The days went by and went by, and nothing happened in them. One afternoon Jean-Pierre stood for a long time outside the window of a shop which had the sign up, *Fleurs Naturelles*. It was unfortunate for Margot, he told you frankly, that she had left him, because otherwise on this day she would be receiving a bouquet of flowers, *pois de senteur*, purple, pink, and mauve, and big white *pivoines*. It was the anniversary of their wedding. There were water lilies in the window, too.

Suddenly Jean-Pierre burst into the flower shop with the face of a boy in love, and after much shrugging and gesticulation and interchange of commonplace insults, he parted from the shopkeeper, and went home to Philippe, bearing a long-stemmed lily.

At twenty minutes to one of an afternoon a week later a man might have been seen to walk along the *quai* of the Seine to the Place St. Michel, and then up the Boulevard St. Michel to the rue de Médicis. On the corner of the rue de Médicis he hesitated and looked both ways. Just then a very little girl came up the *boulevard* and held out to him a basket of pinks and roses. He shook his head.

It happened that for that moment these two were the only people on that corner. The little girl stood for a moment beside him, hesitating, looking both ways. Then she tucked her basket under her arm and started up the rue de Médicis. And because she had turned that way, the man turned that way, too, letting her decision take the place of his own. He walked slowly, glancing as he passed at the many people taking their luncheon under the awnings in front of the cafés. He was looking for a place to eat, and it happened that he wished to be alone.

Before the Restaurant du Chat qui Pêche there were six oblong, iron-legged tables, on each of which stood a warted blue-glass vase containing a sprig of faded sweet william and the wilted stamens of a rose from which the petals had dropped. The place was deserted. There was no sign of life anywhere about, saving only that in one of the windows there was a glass tank filled with slightly quivering water, on the surface of which floated a lily, and on the bottom of which, beside an artificial bright-green frog, dozed a large and sluggish eel.

The man seated himself at one of the tables and tapped upon the table with the vase. There was no response. He tapped again.

"*Voilà!*" called Jean-Pierre from the back of the restaurant, and came eagerly out, holding in his hand the *carte du jour*.

"The rabbit is very good," he suggested, "also the gigot. And what will you have sir, in the way of wine?"

"White wine," said the man, "a half bottle. A salad of tomatoes, an onion soup, and an *anguille*."

"*Oui, monsieur*," said Jean-Pierre. "And after the *andouilles*, what?" *Andouilles* are a kind of sausage.

"Not *andouilles*," replied the man with some impatience, "*anguille*."

"*Oui, monsieur*," said Jean-Pierre, trembling. He passed his damp cloth over the table and went back into the restaurant. He sat down on a chair, and his head dropped to one side, his eyes bulging. "*O-o, là là!*" said Jean-Pierre.

Several moments passed. The man on the terrace outside rapped sharply on the table.

"*Voilà!*" called Jean-Pierre, leaping to his feet. Hurriedly he gathered up a folded napkin, a thick white plate, a knife, fork, and spoon, two round bits of bread, and an unlabeled bottle of white wine. With these he issued forth.

When the table was fairly set, he curved one hand behind his ear and leaned down to listen.

"Will *monsieur* kindly repeat his order?" he requested in a half whisper.

The gentleman did so, with annoyance, glanced up into the face bending over him, frowned, and reached for the wine.

Jean-Pierre went away and returned with the tomato salad. It was very pretty. There were green bits of chopped onion scattered over it. Presently he brought the onion soup. This was not very good. It was composed chiefly of soaked bits of bread, and it was not hot; but with grated cheese it could be made to do.

When the soup was finished, Jean-Pierre appeared again and cleared away the dishes.

"And for the rest, sir," said he, fixing the eyes of his client with his own, which glittered meaningly, "It will be necessary to wait a few moments, you understand."

"Yes, yes," said the man, and shrugged. He wished vaguely he had gone elsewhere for his food.

"Because he is living," Jean-Pierre pursued in a clear voice of unaccountable pride, "and it will be necessary first to kill him. See, he lives!" And pulling the man by the sleeve, he pointed with his thumb to the brass-bound tank in the wndow.

The man glanced askance at the window, and twitched his sleeve free.

"*Encore une demi-bouteille de vin blanc,*" he replied.

Jean-Pierre stood for a moment looking down into the water. The eel was stretched along the bottom of the tank, dozing in the sunshine. Once he idly flipped his thick tail, then lay still again. His dark back shone with a somber iridescence.

"*Philippe,*" whispered Jean-Pierre, thrusting his face close to the surface of the pool, "*Philippe, mon petit, adieu!*"

At this, tears rushed from his eyes, and his neck and chest tried horridly to sob, working out and in like the shoulders of a cat that is sick.

"O Holy Virgin!" he moaned, and wound the clean white napkin firmly about his hand.

The eel came writhing out into the air. It was muscular and strong. It struck backward with its heavy body. It wound itself about Jean-Pierre's wrist. It was difficult to hold. It was difficult to shift from one hand to the other while one rushed to the kitchen.

Jean-Pierre held the eel to the table and reached for the knife. The knife was gone. Sweat rolled from his forehead, down his cheeks, and into his beard.

He ran wildly from one end of the kitchen to the other, the eel all the time plunging and twisting in his hand. He could not think what it was he was looking for.

The broom! But, no, it was not that. At length he saw the handle of the knife, Margot's knife, with which she used to kill the bread. It was peering at him from under a clutter of red and white onion skins. It had been watching him all this time.

He walked slowly past it, then turned sharply, and snatched it with his hand. He held Philippe firmly down on the table, turned away his face, and struck with closed eyes. When he looked again, the knife was wedged in the table; Philippe had not been touched. He eased the knife free; the eel struck it with his lashing tail, and it fell to the floor. He stopped to pick it up; the eel reared in his grasp and smote him across the face.

"Ah-h-h!" cried Jean-Pierre, "you would, would you!" Smarting and furious from the blow, he clutched the knife and rose.

"You would, would you!" he said again, between his teeth. His throat thickened. Flames danced before his eyes. "*Eh bien, on verra!* Name of a name! We shall see, my little pigeon!" The flames roared and crackled. His eyes smarted, and his lungs were full of smoke. His heart swelled, burst, and the stored resentment and pain of his long isolation raced through his body, poisoning his blood.

"Take *that* for your lying face!" he cried. "Spaniard! Take *that* for your ankles! *That* for your red mustaches! Take *that*! Take *that*!"

Kneeling on the floor, he beat in the head of Philippe with the handle of the knife.

All the time that the stranger was eating, Jean-Pierre watched him slyly from the door. Twice a small giggle arose to his lips, but he caught at his beard and pulled it down. He was happy for the first time in many months. He had killed the taxi driver with the red mustaches, he had fried him in six pieces that leaped, and the stranger was eating him.

When the stranger had gone, Jean-Pierre gathered up the dishes and bore them to the kitchen, chuckling as he did so. He saw the head of the eel in the corner where he had kicked it, and he spat on it. But when he came back for the wine bottles and the salt and pepper and vinegar and oil, his eyes fell on the tank in the window, with its bright-green frog and its floating lily and its quiet emptiness. Then he remembered that it was Margot that he had killed.

He put his hand to this throat and stared. Margot! Now, how had that happened? He was sure that he had never intended to kill Margot.

What a terrible mistake! But, no, it was not true that he had killed Margot. It was an ugly and tiresome dream. There was sun on the trees in the gardens of the Luxembourg. Was not that proof enough that Margot was not dead, if one had needed proof?

Still, come to think of it, it was a long time since she had been about the house. It was fully a year, if you pressed the point, since he had heard her voice. There was something very dead about her, come to think of it.

But certainly he had killed Margot! How silly of him! He remembered the circumstances now perfectly. They had been out together in a rowboat on a river whose banks were brass. In Margot's hand was an oar, in his a handsome string of fish. At one end of the river was a dam covered by a dome of netted wire. At the other end water bubbled up continuously from a hidden spring.

He looked at Margot. As he looked, the oar slipped softly from her hand into the water; on the other side of the boat the string of fish slipped softly from his hand into the water. Then he noted with disquiet that the water in the river was steadily receding. He looked at the banks; they were like high walls of brass. He looked at them again; they were like tall cliffs of brass. He looked at the river; it was as shallow as a plate of soup.

It occurred to him that if he wanted to drown Margot, he would best be quick about it, as soon there would be no water in which to drown her. "But I do not wish to drown Margot!" he protested. But the man kept rapping on the table with a sprig of sweet william. And even as he said it, he stepped from the boat, seized her by the waist with both hands, and plunged her beneath the surface.

Her lithe body doubled powerfully in his grasp. He was astonished at the litheness of her body. Her feet, in elegant shoes of patent leather with six straps, appeared above the water, the ankles crossed. The top of her head was not even wet. Yet, for all that, the life came out of her. It rose to the surface in a great colored bubble, and floated off into the sunshine.

Jean-Pierre gazed across at the Luxembourg. A child in a white dress passed through a gate into the garden, holding in its hand by a string a blue balloon. Jean-Pierre smiled, and watched the balloon float off.

Over there, under a tree whose blossoms of white and mauve drifted like lilies on the air, wearing a white dress and a pink hat with roses piled beneath the brim, forever and ever sat Margot. Over her head, tethered to her wrist by its string, floated forever and ever the blue balloon.

She was very near to him. It was a matter of a moment only to go across to her and lift the hat and say, "*Mademoiselle*, may I accompany you?"

Save that between them, flowing level with its brassy banks past the curb before his door, forever and ever ran the sunny river, full of rolling motor buses and rocking red taxicabs, too broad, too broad to swim. People went paddling past the window, this way and that way. A priest sailed by in a flapping gown, square boots on his feet. A little girl went drifting by in a basket; her eyes were closed; her hands were full of brown carnations. Two policemen passed, their short capes winging in thick folds.

At the sight of the policemen Jean-Pierre started violently and stepped back from the window. There was something he must be about, and that without more delay, but he could not think what it was. Memories of Margot flew at his mind with sharp beaks. He waved his arms about his head to scare them off. There was something he must be about, and that at once.

Something touched him lightly on the shoulder. He uttered an indrawn scream, and swung on his heel. It was only the wall. He had backed into the wall. Yet even as he said to himself, "It is only the wall," and wiped his sleeve across his forehead, he saw them beside him, the two policemen, one on the left of him and one on the right.

The one on the right of him said to the other, "This is he, the man who drowned his wife in a plate of soup."

But the other answered, "Not at all. He beat in her head with a knife. Do you not see the onion skins?"

Then for the first time Jean-Pierre saw that both had red mustaches, and he knew that he was lost.

"Come, my man," they said, and stepped back, and he was left standing alone.

Suddenly that part of the floor on which he was standing slipped backward like a jerked rug under his feet, and he was thrown forward on his face. There came a rush of cold wind on the nape of his neck.

"No, you don't!" he shrieked, and rolling over violently, leaped into the kitchen and bolted the door.

He knelt behind the door and addressed them craftily through the keyhole.

"*Messieurs*," he said, "upstairs in my chamber is a melon as big as my head, in a bottle with a neck the size of a pipestem. It is the marvel of all Paris. I will give ten thousand francs to the man who can divine me how it came there."

Then he put his ear to the hole and listened, with difficulty restraining himself from chuckling aloud.

In a moment he heard their feet on the stairs.

He counted the stairs with them as they ascended, nodding his head at each. When he knew that they were at the top, he slipped quietly out and bolted the stairway door.

His head was very clear; it was as light as a balloon on his shoulders. He knew precisely what he must do. He must bury the body, remove all traces of his guilt, and get away. And he must lose no time.

He took his hat and coat from the peg where they were hanging, and placed them in readiness over a chair by the street door. Then he went softly and swiftly into the kitchen.

He gathered up from the table six sections of a broken backbone, a large knife, and an unwashed platter; from the stove a greasy frying pan; and from the floor a crushed and bloodstained head. These objects he wrapped in a newspaper, laid upon a chair, and then covered with a cloth.

Hark! Was that a step in the room above? No.

Hastily he washed the table, scrubbing feverishly until the last stain was removed, scrubbed a wide stain from the floor, and set the kitchen in order.

Hark! Was that a step on the stair? No.

He lifted the newspaper parcel from the chair and bore it, shielded from sight by his apron, into the small backyard behind the restaurant, a yard bare save for a tree of empty bottles, some flower pots full of dry earth and withered stalks, and a rusted bird-cage with crushed and dented wires.

There he laid his burden down, and after an hour of terror and sweating toil buried it in a hole much bigger than was required.

The afternoon advanced, and evening came. A light flashed on in the Rendezvous des Cochers et Camionneurs; farther up the street another light. The street was ablaze. Gay people walked up and down, sat at tables eating, talked eagerly together.

In the Restaurant du Chat qui Pêche the dusk thickened into dark, the darkness into blackness, and no lights came on. The door was wide open. The night wind came in through the door, and moved about the empty rooms.

At midnight a policeman, seeing that the door was open and the restaurant in darkness, approached, rapped sharply on the open door, and called. There was no answer.

He closed the door, and went on.

FRANK O'HARA

O the Dangers of Daily Living

George, I said, I hope never to see you again, and with that strode into the thickening dusk. It was April and the smoke of early twilight wreathed slowly around caretakers finishing up their grooming jobs for the day. Sad piles of refuse—papers, weeds, leaves, twigs, rotted blossoms —lay, dotting the park with malignance, putting a period to the day. I was glad of the approaching night. If anyone had asked me two months ago who the oddest person I knew was I would have said Morris Morgan; I would have been wrong, it is George Rose. I shall never forget the night I met him.

MIRIAM: Hello. Hello. Hello. Hello. Oh! Hello.

ME: Hello, Miriam. How nice of you to call me up. I could not get here sooner as I was in Florida with a cold. Who's here?

MIRIAM: Everybody. Just everybody. I don't know what Jake and I are going to do for liquor if they keep coming in. These throngs of people. I know I didn't invite them all.

ME: You invited me, Miriam.

MIRIAM: Yes, dear, I know.

GEORGE: I live upstairs. May I have a drink?

JAKE: Oh. I remember you. You're Lucius Maby, the diamond expert.

GEORGE: Yes, I am. How do you do. How do you do. How do you do.

ME: You have terribly strong hands.

GEORGE: Haha. Haha. Ha.

MIRIAM: I'm locking this door.

GEORGE: Just in time, wasn't I?

MIRIAM: No, you weren't, as a matter of fact.

JAKE: Have you met Fabian Dugan? Hello, Fabian.

ME: No, I haven't. Hello, Fabian.

MIRIAM: Hello, Fabian. How are you?

FABIAN: OK, Mimi. Just a touch of strep, but I've been gargling all day.

GEORGE: I had a friend once who died.

AGNES: Bobo! I haven't seen you since last Christmas when you were drunk at my birthday party.

ME: Sweet! You remembered.

AGNES: I was so in love with you when I was twelve.

ME: Me, too.

AGNES: Fate tricked us, dear. Too young for sex, too old for friendship.

JAKE: This is Annabelle Leach. Say hello, Annabelle.

ANNABELLE: Hello. Hello. Hello. Hello. Hello.

MIRIAM: How is your grandmother, dear?

ANNABELLE: She died a week ago.

MIRIAM: Oh.

JAKE: Another drink?

MIRIAM: Do you mean we have one or would I like one?

GEORGE: I have lots of liquor at my place. I have bitters and menthe and grenadine and kummel.

JAKE: Let's go up to your place.

GEORGE: I'd really love to have you but let me go up first for a minute, and then you come up. In five minutes. What time do you have?

JAKE: Oh, we'll find it all right.

MIRIAM: He's the nicest man. Isn't he the nicest man, Bobo?

ME: No, he is not. Morris Morgan is.

MORRIS: Hello, Bobo.

ME: Hello, Morris.

MORRIS: Hello. Hello. Hello. Hello.

AGNES: So your name is Morris. I thought it was Lud.

MORRIS: Lud? Oh, no. Oh no.

AGNES: I could have sworn it was.

MORRIS: Oh, no. It's Morris.

AGNES: How nice.

MIRIAM: Are the five minutes up?

JAKE: Yes. Let's go.

FELICE: Let me come, too. My husband never takes me anywhere.

MORRIS: I think I'll come, too. And you won't mind if I bring my secretary, Knute Lipsk?

KNUTE: Hello. Hello. Hello. Hello. Hello.

MORRIS: He's sort of a business associate.

JAKE: I didn't know you were in business.

MORRIS: These stairs are terribly dark.

FELICE: I just saw something. It brushed past me.

MIRIAM: His apartment has a purple door. The maid said he must be artistic.

JAKE: Oh, he is. Terribly.

AGNES: What's your name again?

KNUTE: Knute.

AGNES: Oh. Mine's Agnes. I always used to say newt.

KNUTE: No. It's knute.

AGNES: Yes. Isn't it.

FELICE: Do you suppose we'll ever get there? I'm scared. Frightened, I mean.

JAKE: Why?

FELICE: Ladies never get scared. They get frightened.

ME: I saw a wonderful painting once. It was called *Lady in a Frightened Lavatory*. Vermeer. Or somebody.

MORRIS: I had an aunt once who slept with him. He was dull.

MIRIAM: He paints divinely.

MORRIS: My aunt didn't think so. She just would say Vermeer is a dull tool from one end of the day to the other. She was jaded.

FELICE: My father knew your aunt. They met in Venice.

MORRIS: How nice.

FELICE: What was your aunt's last name?

MORRIS: Abercrinch. Boost-Abercrinch.

FELICE: What Boost-Abercrinch?

MORRIS: Agatha.

FELICE: Oh.

MORRIS: This reminds me of *The Temptation of Saint Anthony*.

KNUTE: Why, Morris?

MORRIS: Now don't copy this down. Because I always think of sex on stairs.

FELICE: How difficult.

ME: You're so odd, Morris.

FELICE: Who made that noise?

JAKE: It was a what.

FELICE: A what?

JAKE: I didn't see it.

MIRIAM: Have you been to Fisby's lately?

ME: No. I imagine you asked that for a purpose. You think I am breaking up their home. I am not. I like their children better than I do them. Platonically. Julius Fisby is a boor. Mitzi is a sweet girl when she's been resting. The two children, Hrothgar and Bob, are very athletic. I had wished they might be brought up more normally. But I never once, not once, butted in. I minded my own business. They were not my children. Julius drank a good deal and Mitzi took to burlesque, but they were not my children. Afterward, when the house burned down, I did my best. I bedded them in the garden house for three years. But Julietta wanted to give teas there. She began to suspect me of having an affair with Mitzi and took to staying in the hedges all night to watch the garden house. Something had to be done. I did it. Mitzi and Julius are very happy now even though the children are miserable. I have minded my own business and Julietta no longer watches the garden house. I resent your questioning me.

JAKE: You might make an effort to be more polite, Bobo.

ME: You are all against me.

FELICE: I felt something. Near my groin.

MIRIAM: After all, Bobo, what good is a friend if you can't ask him questions?

AGNES: Some women are such cats.

MORRIS: Now girls.

KNUTE: Miss Janine Poisson once told me that stairs did things to her.

JAKE: Then or once?

KNUTE: I don't remember. Then, I think.

FELICE: OHH!

JAKE: Was it a what?

FELICE: No. It was a who.

MIRIAM: How odd.

JAKE: I wonder what the stairs did to her.

KNUTE: I didn't know her very well.

ANNABELLE: I've been thinking.

MIRIAM: Oh. We thought you'd stayed downstairs.

ANNABELLE: No. I've been thinking. There is something peculiar about this landing. I don't think the stairs are leading anywhere. Does anyone know where we are? Wait till I'm finished. I've been thinking. Who ever heard of a purple door? This is an illusion. I studied them in college. I have known for the past two flights that Felice is really Janine Poisson. I went to school with them both. She is feeling nothing. It is just her fixation.

MORRIS: Oh no it isn't.

KNUTE: Morris!

ME: I think you are all perfect beasts. I am going home.

FELICE: OHH!

And so it was that when George Rose came up to me in the park that April evening and asked me what time it was, I did not so much as look at my watch, but fled into what was soon to be the night.

SYLVIA PLATH

Johnny Panic and the Bible of Dreams

Every day from nine to five I sit at my desk facing the door of the office and type up other people's dreams. Not just dreams. That wouldn't be practical enough for my bosses. I type up also people's daytime complaints: trouble with mother, trouble with father, trouble with the bottle, the bed, the headache that bangs home and blacks out the sweet world for no known reason. Nobody comes to our office unless they have troubles. Troubles that can't be pinpointed by Wassermanns or Wechsler-Bellevues alone.

Maybe a mouse gets to thinking pretty early on how the whole world is run by these enormous feet. Well, from where I sit I figure the world is run by one thing and this one thing only. Panic with a dog-face, devil-face, hag-face, whore-face, panic in capital letters with no face at all—it's the same Johnny Panic, awake or asleep.

When people ask me where I work, I tell them I'm assistant to the secretary in one of the outpatient departments of the Clinics Building of the City Hospital. This sounds so be-all, end-all they seldom get around to asking me more than what I do, and what I do is mainly type up records. On my own hook though, and completely under cover, I am pursuing a vocation that would set these doctors on their ears. In the privacy of my one-room apartment I call myself secretary to none other than Johnny Panic himself.

Dream by dream I am educating myself to become that rare character, rarer, in truth, than any member of the Psychoanalytic Institute: a dream connoisseur. Not a dream-stopper, a dream explainer, an exploiter of dreams for the crass practical ends of health and happiness, but an unsordid collector of dreams for themselves alone. A lover of dreams for Johnny Panic's sake, the Maker of them all.

There isn't a dream I've typed up in our record books that I don't know by heart. There isn't a dream I haven't copied out at home into Johnny Panic's Bible of Dreams.

This is my real calling.

Some nights I take the elevator up to the roof of my apartment building. Some nights, about 3 A.M. Over the trees at the far side of the Common the United Fund torch flare flattens and recovers under some witchy invisible push, and here and there in the hunks of stone and brick I see a light. Most of all, though, I feel the city sleeping. Sleeping from the river on the west to the ocean on the east, like some rootless island rockabying itself on nothing at all.

I can be tight and nervy as the top string on a violin, and yet by the time the sky begins to blue I'm ready for sleep. It's the thought of all those dreamers and what they're dreaming wears me down till I sleep the sleep of fever. Monday to Friday what do I do but type up those same dreams. Sure, I don't touch a fraction of them the city over, but page by page, dream by dream, my Intake books fatten and weigh down the bookshelves of the cabinet in the narrow passage running parallel to the main hall, off which passage the doors to all the doctors' little interviewing cubicles open.

I've got a funny habit of identifying the people who come in by their dreams. As far as I'm concerned, the dreams single them out more than any Christian name. This one guy, for example, who works for a ball bearing company in town, dreams every night how he's lying on his back with a grain of sand on his chest. Bit by bit this grain of sand grows bigger and bigger till it's big as a fair-sized house and he can't draw breath. Another fellow I know of has had a certain dream ever since they gave him ether and cut out his tonsils and adenoids when he was a kid. In this dream he's caught in the rollers of a cotton mill, fighting for his life. Oh, he's not alone, although he thinks he is. A lot of people these days dream they're being run over or eaten by machines. They're the cagey ones who won't go on the subway or the elevators. Coming back from my lunch hour in the hospital cafeteria I often pass them, puffing up the unswept stone stairs to our office on the fourth floor. I wonder, now and then, what dreams people had before ball bearings and cotton mills were invented.

I've got a dream of my own. My one dream. A dream of dreams.

In this dream there's a great half-transparent lake stretching away in every direction, too big for me to see the shores of it, if there are any shores, and I'm hanging over it looking down from the glass belly of some helicopter. At the bottom of the lake—so deep I can only guess at the dark masses moving and heaving—are the real dragons. The ones that were around before men started living in caves and cooking meat over fires and figuring out the wheel and the alphabet. Enormous isn't the word for them; they've got more wrinkles than Johnny Panic himself. Dream about these long enough, and your feet and hands shrivel away when you look at them too closely; the sun shrinks to the size of an orange, only chillier, and you've been living in Roxbury since the last Ice Age. No place for you but a room padded soft as the first room you knew of, where you can dream and float, float and dream, till at last you actually are back among those great originals and there's no point in any dreams at all.

It's into this lake people's minds run at night, brooks and gutter-trickles to one borderless common reservoir. It bears no resemblance to those pure sparkling blue sources of drinking water the suburbs guard more jealously than the Hope diamond in the middle of pinewoods and barbed fences.

It's the sewage farm of the ages, transparence aside.

Now the water in this lake naturally stinks and smokes from what dreams have been left sogging around in it over the centuries. When you think how much room one night of dream props would take up for one person in one city, and that city a mere pinprick on a map of the world, and when you start multiplying this space by the population of the world, and that space by the number of nights there have been since the apes took to chipping axes out of stone and losing their hair, you have some idea what I mean. I'm not the mathematical type: my head starts splitting when I get only as far as the number of dreams going on during one night in the state of Massachusetts.

By this time, I already see the surface of the lake swarming with snakes, dead bodies puffed as blowfish, human embryos bobbing around in laboratory bottles like so many unfinished messages from the great I Am. I see whole storehouses of hardware: knives, paper cutters, pistons and cobs and nutcrackers; the shiny fronts of cars looming up, glass-eyed and evil-toothed. Then there's the spider-man and the web-footed man from Mars, and the simple, lugubrious vision of a human face turning aside forever, in spite of rings and vows, to the last lover of all.

One of the most frequent shapes in this large stew is so commonplace it seems silly to mention it. It's a grain of dirt. The water is thick with these grains. They seep in among everything else and revolve under some queer power of their own, opaque, ubiquitous. Call the water what you will, Lake Nightmare, Bog of Madness, it's here the sleeping people lie and toss together among the props of their worst dreams, one great brotherhood, though each of them, waking, thinks of himself singular, utterly apart.

This is my dream. You won't find it written up in any casebook.

Now the routine in our office is very different from the routine in Skin Clinic, for example, or in Tumor. The other clinics have strong similarities to each other; none are like ours. In our clinic, treatment doesn't get prescribed. It is invisible. It goes right on in those little cubicles, each with its desk, its two chairs, its window, and its door with the opaque glass rectangle set in the wood. There is a certain spiritual purity about this kind of doctoring. I can't help feeling the special privilege of my position as assistant secretary in the Adult Psychiatric Clinic. My sense of pride is borne out by the rude invasions of other clinics into our cubicles on certain days of the week for lack of space elsewhere: our building is a very old one, and the facilities have not expanded with the expanding needs of the time. On these days of overlap the contrast between us and the other clinics is marked.

On Tuesdays and Thursdays, for instance, we have lumbar punctures in one of our offices in the morning. If the practical nurse chances to leave the door of the cubicle open, as she usually does, I can glimpse the end of the white cot and the dirty yellow-soled bare feet of the patient sticking out from under the sheet. In spite of my distaste at this sight, I can't keep my eyes away from the bare feet, and I find myself glancing back from my typing every few minutes to see if they are still there, if they have changed their position at all. You can understand what a distraction this is in the middle of my work. I often have to reread what I have typed several times, under the pretense of careful proofreading, in order to memorize the dreams I have copied down from the doctor's voice over the audiograph.

Nerve Clinic next door, which tends to the grosser, more unimaginative end of our business, also disturbs us in the mornings. We use their offices for therapy in the afternoon, as they are only a morning clinic, but to have their people crying, or singing, or chattering loudly in Italian or Chinese, as they often do, without break for four hours at a stretch every morning is distracting to say the least. The patients down there are often referred to us if their troubles have no ostensible basis in the body.

In spite of such interruptions by other clinics, my own work is advancing at a great rate. By now I am far beyond copying only what comes after the patient's saying: "I have this dream, Doctor." I am at the point of re-creating dreams that are not even written down at all. Dreams that shadow themselves forth in the vaguest way, but are themselves hid, like a statue under red velvet before the grand unveiling.

To illustrate. This woman came in with her tongue swollen and stuck out so far she had to leave a party she was giving for twenty friends of her French-Canadian mother-in-law and be rushed to our emergency ward. She thought she didn't want her tongue to stick out, and to tell the truth, it was an exceedingly embarrassing affair for her, but she hated that French-Canadian mother-in-law worse than pigs, and her tongue was true to her opinion, even if the rest of her wasn't. Now she didn't lay claim to any dreams. I have only the bare facts above to begin with, yet behind them I detect the bulge and promise of a dream.

So I set myself to uprooting this dream from its comfortable purchase under her tongue.

Whatever the dream I unearth, by work, taxing work, and even by a kind of prayer, I am sure to find a thumbprint in the corner, a bodiless midair Cheshire cat grin, which shows the whole work to be gotten up by the genius of Johnny Panic, and him alone. He's sly, he's subtle, he's sudden as thunder, but he gives himself away only too often. He simply can't resist melodrama. Melodrama of the oldest, most obvious variety.

I remember one guy, a stocky fellow in a nail-studded black leather jacket, running straight into us from a boxing match at Mechanics Hall, Johnny Panic hot at his heels. This guy, good Catholic though he was, young and upright and all, had one mean fear of death. He was actually scared blue he'd go to hell. He was a pieceworker at a fluorescent light plant. I remember this detail because I thought it funny he should work there, him being so afraid of the dark as it turned out. Johnny Panic injects a poetic element in this business you don't often find elsewhere. And for that he has my eternal gratitude.

I also remember quite clearly the scenario of the dream I had worked out for this guy: a Gothic interior in some monastery cellar, going on and on as far as you could see, one of those endless perspectives between two mirrors, and the pillars and walls were made of nothing but human skulls and bones, and in every niche there was a body laid out, and it was the Hall of Time, with the bodies in the foreground still warm, discoloring and starting to rot in the middle distance, and the bones emerging, clean as a whistle, in a kind of white futuristic glow at the end of the line. As I recall, I had the whole scene lighted, for the sake of accuracy, not with candles, but with the ice-bright fluorescence that makes the skin look green and all the pink and red flushes dead black-purple.

You ask, how do I know this was the dream of the guy in the black leather jacket. I don't know. I only believe this was his dream, and I work at belief with more energy and tears and entreaties than I work at re-creating the dream itself.

My office, of course, has its limitations. The lady with her tongue stuck out, the guy from Mechanics Hall—these are our wildest ones. The people who have really gone floating down toward the bottom of that boggy lake come in only once, and are then referred to a place more permanent than our office, which receives the public from nine to five, five days a week only. Even those people who are barely able to walk about the streets and keep working, who aren't yet halfway down in the lake, get sent to the outpatient department at another hospital specializing in severer cases. Or they may stay a month or so in our own observation ward in the central hospital, which I've never seen.

I've seen the secretary of that ward, though. Something about her merely smoking and drinking her coffee in the cafeteria at the ten o'clock break put me off so I never went to sit next to her again. She has a funny name I don't ever quite remember correctly, something really odd, like Miss Milleravage. One of those names that seem more like a pun mixing up Milltown and Ravage than anything in the city phone directory. But not so odd a name, after all, if you've ever read through the phone directory, with its Hyman Diddlebockers and Sasparilla Greenleafs. I read through the phone book, once, never mind when, and it satisfied a deep need in me to realize how many people aren't called Smith.

Anyhow, this Miss Milleravage is a large woman, not fat, but all sturdy muscle and tall on top of it. She wears a gray suit over her hard bulk that reminds me vaguely of some kind of uniform, without the details of cut having anything strikingly military about them. Her face, hefty as a bullock's, is covered with a remarkable number of tiny maculae, as if she'd been lying underwater for some time and little algae had latched onto her skin, smutching it over with tobacco-browns and greens. These moles are noticeable mainly because the skin around them is so pallid. I sometimes wonder if Miss Milleravage has ever seen the wholesome light of day. I wouldn't be a bit surprised if she'd been brought up from the cradle with the sole benefit of artificial lighting.

Byrna, the secretary in Alcoholic Clinic just across the hall from us, introduced me to Miss Milleravage with the gambit that I'd "been in England too."

Miss Milleravage, it turned out, had spent the best years of her life in London hospitals.

"Had a friend," she boomed in her queer, doggish basso, not favoring me with a direct look, "a nurse at St. Bart's. Tried to get in touch with her after the war, but the head of the nurses had changed, everybody'd changed, nobody'd heard of her. She must've gone down with the old head nurse, rubbish and all, in the bombings." She followed this with a large grin.

Now I've seen medical students cutting up cadavers, four stiffs to a classroom about as recognizably human as Moby Dick, and the students playing catch with the dead men's livers. I've heard guys joke about sewing a woman up wrong after a delivery at the charity ward of the Lying-In. But I wouldn't want to see what Miss Milleravage would write off as the biggest laugh of all time. No thanks and then some. You could scratch her eyes with a pin and swear you'd struck solid quartz.

My boss has a sense of humor too, only it's gentle. Generous as Santa on Christmas Eve.

I work for a middle-aged lady named Miss Taylor who is the head secretary of the clinic and has been since the clinic started thirty-three years ago—the year of my birth, oddly enough. Miss Taylor knows every doctor, every patient, every outmoded appointment slip, referral slip, and billing procedure the hospital has ever used or thought of using. She plans to stick with the clinic until she's farmed out in the green pastures of social security checks. A woman more dedicated to her work I never saw. She's the same way about statistics as I am about dreams: if the building caught fire she would throw every last one of those books of statistics to the firemen below at the serious risk of her own skin.

I get along extremely well with Miss Taylor. The one thing I never let her catch me doing is reading the old record books. I have actually very little time for this. Our office is busier than the stock exchange with the staff of twenty-five doctors in and out, medical students in training, patients, patients' relatives, and visiting officials from other clinics referring patients to us, so even when I'm covering the office alone, during Miss Taylor's coffee break and a lunch hour, I seldom get to dash down more than a note or two.

This kind of catch-as-catch-can is nerve-racking, to say the least. A lot of the best dreamers are in the old books, the dreamers that come in to us only once or twice for evaluation before they're sent elsewhere. For copying out these dreams I need time, a lot of time. My circumstances are hardly ideal for the unhurried pursuit of my art. There is, of course, a certain derring-do in working under such hazards, but I long for the rich leisure of the true connoisseur who indulges his nostrils above the brandy snifter for an hour before his tongue reaches out for the first taste.

I find myself all too often lately imagining what a relief it would be to bring a briefcase into work, big enough to hold one of those thick, blue, cloth-bound record books full of dreams. At Miss Taylor's lunchtime, in the lull before the doctors and students crowd in to take their afternoon patients, I could simply slip one of the books, dated ten or fifteen years back, into my briefcase, and leave the briefcase under my desk till five o'clock struck. Of course, oddlooking bundles are inspected by the doorman of the Clinics Building, and the hospital has its own staff of flatfeet to check up on the multiple varieties of thievery that go on, but for heaven's sake, I'm not thinking of making off with typewriters or heroin. I'd only borrow the book overnight and slip it back on the shelf first thing the next day before anybody else came in. Still, being caught taking a book out of the hospital would probably mean losing my job and all my source material with it.

This idea of mulling over a record book in the privacy and comfort of my own apartment, even if I have to stay up night after night for this purpose, attracts me so much I become more and more impatient with my usual method of snatching minutes to look up dreams in Miss Taylor's half hours out of the office.

The trouble is, I can never tell exactly when Miss Taylor will come back to the office. She is so conscientious about her job she'd be likely to cut her half hour at lunch short and her twenty minutes at coffee shorter if it weren't for her lame left leg. The distinct sound of this lame leg in the corridor warns me of her approach in time for me to whip the record book I'm reading into my drawer out of sight and pretend to be putting down the final flourishes on a phone message, or some such alibi. The only catch, as far as my nerves are concerned, is that Amputee Clinic is around the corner from us in the opposite direction from Nerve Clinic, and I've gotten really jumpy due to a lot of false alarms where I've mistaken some pegleg's hitching step for the step of Miss Taylor herself returning early to the office.

On the blackest days when I've scarcely time to squeeze one dream out of the old books and my copy work is nothing but weepy college sophomores who can't get a lead in *Camino Real*, I feel Johnny Panic turn his back, stony as Everest, higher than Orion, and the motto of the great Bible of Dreams, "Perfect fear casteth out all else," is ash and lemon water on my lips. I'm a wormy hermit in a country of prize pigs so corn-happy they can't see the slaughterhouse at the end of the track. I'm Jeremiah vision-bitten in the Land of Cockaigne.

What's worse: day by day I see these psyche-doctors studying to win Johnny Panic's converts from him by book, crook, and talk, talk, talk. These deep-eyed, bush-bearded dream-collectors who preceded me in history, and their contemporary inheritors with their white jackets and knotty-pine paneled offices and leather couches, practiced and still practice their dream-gathering for worldly ends: health and money, money and health. To be a true member of Johnny Panic's congregation one must forget the dreamer and remember the dream: the dreamer is merely a flimsy vehicle for the great Dream-Maker himself. This they will not do. Johnny Panic is gold in the bowels, and they try to root him out by spiritual stomach pumps.

Take what happened to Harry Bilbo. Mr. Bilbo came into our office with the hand of Johnny Panic heavy as a lead coffin on his shoulder. He had an interesting notion about the filth in this world. I figured him for a prominent part in Johnny Panic's Bible of Dreams, Third Book of Fear, Chapter Nine on Dirt, Disease, and General Decay. A friend of Harry's blew a trumpet in the Boy Scout band when they were kids. Harry Bilbo'd also blown on this friend's trumpet. Years later the friend got cancer and died. Then, one day not so long ago, a cancer doctor came into Harry's house, sat down in a chair, passed the top of the morning with Harry's mother, and on leaving, shook her hand and opened the door for himself. Suddenly Harry Bilbo wouldn't blow trumpets or sit down on chairs or shake hands if all the cardinals of Rome took to blessing him twenty-four hours around the clock for fear of catching cancer. His mother had to go turning the TV knobs and water faucets on and off and opening doors for him. Pretty soon Harry stopped going to work because of the spit and dog droppings in the street. First that stuff gets on your shoes, and then when you take your shoes off it gets on your hands, and then at dinner it's a quick trip into your mouth and not a hundred Hail Marys can keep you from the chain reaction. The last straw was, Harry quit weight lifting at the public gym when he saw this cripple exercising with the dumbbells. You can never tell what germs cripples carry behind their ears and under their fingernails. Day and night Harry Bilbo lived in holy worship of Johnny Panic, devout as any priest among censers and sacraments. He had a beauty all his own.

Well, these white-coated tinkerers managed, the lot of them, to talk Harry into turning on the TV himself, and the water faucets, and to opening closet doors, front doors, bar doors. Before they were through with him, he was sitting down on movie-house chairs, and benches all over the Public Garden, and weight lifting every day of the week at the gym in spite of the fact another cripple took to using the rowing machine. At the end of his treatment he came in to shake hands with the clinic director. In Harry Bilbo's own words, he was "a changed man." The pure Panic-light had left his face; he went out of the office doomed to the crass fate these doctors call health and happiness.

About the time of Harry Bilbo's cure a new idea starts nudging at the bottom of my brain. I find it as hard to ignore as those bare feet sticking out of the lumbar puncture room. If I don't want to risk carrying a record book out of the hospital in case I get discovered and fired and have to end my research forever, I can really speed up work by staying in the Clinics Building overnight. I am nowhere near exhausting the clinic's resources, and the piddling amount of cases I am able to read in Miss Taylor's brief absences during the day are nothing to what I could get through in a few nights of steady copying. I need to accelerate my work if only to counteract those doctors.

Before I know it I am putting on my coat at five and saying good night to Miss Taylor, who usually stays a few minutes overtime to clear up the day's statistics, and sneaking around the corner into the ladies' room. It is empty. I slip into the patient's john, lock the door from the inside, and wait. For all I know, one of the clinic cleaning ladies may try to knock the door down, thinking some patient's passed out on the seat. My fingers are crossed. About twenty minutes later the door of the lavatory opens and someone limps over the threshold like a chicken favoring a bad leg. It is Miss Taylor, I can tell by the resigned sigh as she meets the jaundiced eye of the lavatory mirror. I hear the click-cluck of various touch-up equipment on the bowl, water sloshing, the scritch of a comb in frizzed hair, and then the door is closing with a slow-hinged wheeze behind her.

I am lucky. When I come out of the ladies' room at six o'clock the corridor lights are off and the fourth floor hall is empty as church on Monday. I have my own key to our office; I come in first every morning, so that's no trouble. The typewriters are folded back into the desks, the locks are on the dial phones, all's right with the world.

Outside the window the last of the winter light is fading. Yet I do not forget myself and turn on the overhead bulb. I don't want to be spotted by any hawk-eyed doctor or janitor in the hospital buildings across the little courtyard. The cabinet with the record books is in the windowless passage opening onto the doctor's cubicles, which have windows overlooking the courtyard. I make sure the doors to all the cubicles are shut. Then I switch on the passage light, a sallow twenty-five watt affair blackening at the top. Better than an altarful of candles to me at this point, though. I didn't think to bring a sandwich. There is an apple in my desk drawer left over from lunch, so I reserve that for whatever pangs I may feel about one o'clock in the morning, and get out my pocket notebook. At home every evening it is my habit to tear out the notebook pages I've written on at the office during the day and pile them up to be copied in my manuscript. In this way I cover my tracks so no one idly picking up my notebook at the office could ever guess the type or scope of my work.

I begin systematically by opening the oldest book on the bottom shelf. The once-blue cover is no-color now, the pages are thumbed and blurry carbons, but I'm humming from foot to topknot: this dream book was spanking new the day I was born. When I really get organized I'll have hot soup in a thermos for the dead-of-winter nights, turkey pies, and chocolate eclairs. I'll bring hair curlers and four changes of blouse to work in my biggest handbag Monday mornings so no one will notice me going downhill in looks and start suspecting unhappy love affairs or pink affiliations or my working on dream books in the clinic four nights a week.

Eleven hours later. I am down to apple core and seeds and in the month of May, nineteen thirty-four, with a private nurse who has just opened a laundry bag in her patient's closet and found five severed heads in it, including her mother's.

A chill air touches the nape of my neck. From where I am sitting cross-legged on the floor in front of the cabinet, the record book heavy on my lap, I notice out of the corner of my eye that the door of the cubicle beside me is letting in a little crack of blue light. Not only along the floor, but up the side of the door too. This is odd since I made sure from the first that all the doors were shut tight. The crack of blue light is widening and my eyes are fastened to two motionless shoes in the doorway, toes pointing toward me.

They are brown leather shoes of a foreign make, with thick elevator soles. Above the shoes are black silk socks through which shows a pallor of flesh. I get as far as the gray pinstripe trouser cuffs.

"*Tch, tch,*" chides an infinitely gentle voice from the cloudy regions above my head. "Such an uncomfortable position! Your legs must be asleep by now. Let me help you up. The sun will be rising shortly."

Two hands slip under my arms from behind, and I am raised, wobbly as an unset custard, to my feet, which I cannot feel because my legs are, in fact, asleep. The record book slumps to the floor, pages splayed.

"Stand still a minute." The clinic director's voice fans the lobe of my right ear. "Then the circulation will revive."

The blood in my not-there legs starts pinging under a million sewing machine needles, and a vision of the clinic director acid-etches itself on my brain. I don't even need to look around: the fat potbelly buttoned into his gray pinstripe waistcoat, woodchuck teeth yellow and buck, every-color eyes behind the thick-lensed glasses quick as minnows.

I clutch my notebook. The last floating timber of the *Titanic*.

What does he know, what does he know?

Everything.

"I know where there is a nice hot bowl of chicken noodle soup." His voice rustles, dust under the bed, mice in the straw. His hand welds onto my left upper arm in fatherly love. The record book of all the dreams going on in the city of my birth at my first yawp in this world's air he nudges under the bookcase with a polished toe.

We met nobody in the dawn-dark hall. Nobody on the chill stone stair down to the basement corridors where Jerry the Record Room boy cracked his head skipping steps one night on a rush errand.

I begin to double-quickstep so he won't think it's me he's hustling. "You can't fire me," I say calmly. "I quit."

The clinic director's laugh wheezes up from his accordion-pleated bottom gut. "We mustn't lose you so soon." His whisper snakes off down the whitewashed basement passages, echoing among the elbow pipes, the wheelchairs and stretchers beached for the night along the steam-stained walls. "Why, we need you more than you know."

We wind and double, and my legs keep time with his until we come, somewhere in those barren rat tunnels, to an all-night elevator run by a one-armed Negro. We get on and the door grinds shut like the door on a cattle car and we go up and up. It is a freight elevator, crude and clanky, a far cry from the plush one in the Clinics Building.

We get off at an indeterminate floor. The clinic director leads me

down a bare corridor lit at intervals by socketed bulbs in little wire cages
on the ceiling. Locked doors set with screened windows line the hall on
either hand. I plan to part company with the clinic director at the first
red exit sign, but on our journey there are none. I am in alien territory,
coat on the hanger in the office, handbag and money in my top desk
drawer, notebook in my hand, and only Johnny Panic to warm me
against the Ice Age outside.

Ahead a light gathers, brightens. The clinic director, puffing slightly
at the walk, brisk and long, to which he is obviously unaccustomed,
propels me around a bend and into a square, brilliantly lit room.

"Here she is."

"The little witch!"

Miss Milleravage hoists her tonnage up from behind the steel desk
facing the door.

The walls and the ceiling of the room are riveted metal battleship
plates. There are no windows.

From small, barred cells lining the sides and back of the room I see
Johnny Panic's top priests staring out at me, arms swaddled behind their
backs in the white ward nightshirts, eyes redder than coals and hungry-
hot.

They welcome me with queer croaks and grunts as if their tongues
were locked in their jaws. They have no doubt heard of my work by way
of Johnny Panic's grapevine and want to know how his apostles thrive in
the world.

I lift my hands to reassure them, holding up my notebook, my voice
loud as Johnny Panic's organ with all stops out.

"Peace! I bring to you . . ."

The Book.

"None of that old stuff, sweetie," Miss Milleravage is dancing out at
me from behind her desk like a trick elephant.

The clinic director closes the door to the room.

The minute Miss Milleravage moves I notice what her hulk has been
hiding from view behind the desk—a white cot high as a man's waist
with a single sheet stretched over the mattress, spotless and drumskin
tight. At the head of the cot is a table on which sits a metal box covered
with dials and gauges. The box seems to be eyeing me, copperhead-ugly,
from its coil of electric wires, the latest model in Johnny-Panic-Killers.

I get ready to dodge to one side. When Miss Milleravage grabs, her
fat hand comes away a fist full of nothing. She starts for me again, her
smile heavy as dogdays in August.

"None of that. None of that. I'll have that little black book."

Fast as I run around the high white cot, Miss Milleravage is so fast
you'd think she wore roller skates. She grabs and gets. Against her great

bulk I beat my fists, and against her whopping milkless breasts, until her hands on my wrists are iron hoops and her breath hushabys me with a love-stink fouler than Undertaker's Basement.

"My Baby, my own baby's come back to me . . ."

"She," the clinic director says, sad and stern, "has been making time with Johnny Panic again."

"Naughty naughty."

The white cot is ready. With a terrible gentleness Miss Milleravage takes the watch from my wrist, the rings from my fingers, the hairpins from my hair. She begins to undress me. When I am bare, I am anointed on the temples and robed in sheets virginal as the first snow. Then, from the four corners of the room and from the door behind me come five false priests in white surgical gowns and masks whose one lifework is to unseat Johnny Panic from his own throne. They extend me full-length on my back on the cot. The crown of wire is placed on my head, the wafer of forgetfulness on my tongue. The masked priests move to their posts and take hold: one of my left leg, one of my right, one of my right arm, one of my left. One behind my head at the metal box where I can't see.

From their cramped niches along the wall, the votaries raise their voices in protest. They begin the devotional chant:

> *The only thing to love is Fear itself.*
> *Love of Fear is the beginning of wisdom.*
> *The only thing to love is Fear itself.*
> *May Fear and Fear and Fear be everywhere.*

There is no time for Miss Milleravage or the clinic director or the priests to muzzle them.

The signal is given.

The machine betrays them.

At the moment when I think I am most lost the face of Johnny Panic appears in a nimbus of arc lights on the ceiling overhead. I am shaken life a leaf in the teeth of glory. His beard is lightning. Lightning is in his eye. His Word charges and illumes the universe.

The air crackles with the blue-tongued, lightning-haloed angels.

His love is the twenty-story leap, the rope at the throat, the knife at the heart.

He forgets not his own.

MURIEL RUKEYSER

The Club

That was the day when he decided what it was he had to do. It was fortunate that he was not a nervous man, for this was Monday, and the wait between Monday and the weekend is too hard for the resolve of nervous people; that is what he thought as he looked down at the pens and pencils, the gold pen and the mottled green one in their groove, and the two mechanical pencils with their metallic colors among the red company pencils in their groove on his fancy inkwell. The inkwell was a present from Gracie.

But it was two minutes to three, and he had better put the whole matter aside until four thirty. At three the time-study man was coming for his appointment. The whole office, all the branches, and the plant itself might be reorganized. At four thirty, after the time-study man, after Mr. Greenwood, and Miss Brosnac, he would be free to find the place.

And now it was three o'clock. There was his door opening, the shadowless lights of all the fluorescent overheads in the main office were falling through the doorway, the shoulder of the time-study man was darkening the heavy pebbled glass of the door whose surface he loved, and he said, "Good afternoon."

"Good afternoon, Mr. Stainer," said the time-study man.

It was nearer to a quarter of five before he got away. But on this day of April, the blue-green of the McGraw-Hill Building was still brilliant, almost white, with the sunlight. There was beginning to be a strength in the sun.

He got his car out of the garage in the second cellar of Two Hundred West; he was in the tunnel within ten minutes. The roar of enclosed noise was, this time, a happiness to him; he felt that he was living in a trumpet; the exultation and the light were still there as he came to surface on the New Jersey side.

He headed north almost at once. Seven traffic lights, two red, one green, one red, three green. Why should they run that way? he thought in irritation, and realized he had turned several corners. Why should I be counting? he thought.

He looked again at the road map. For none of these roads, none of these towns, were known to him. When the transfer had finally been announced, four months ago in Salt Lake City, he welcomed it; the eager, confirmed man at the high moment of his life. New York! The main office! He and Gracie were ready to leave in three weeks, their train pulled out a month to the day after his notice arrived.

And now here he was, in the gathering darkness, looking at the last lap of the journey as it lay on the map in crude green and yellow and the decisive black.

The road was even better marked in reality than on the map. The traffic circle after Paterson; Butler, and now it was really dark, and hardly any cars. He could use his full headlights. He liked the red dot over the speedometer that showed now, when the headlights were on full. A careful man, I'm a careful man; it gave him pleasure to say that of himself; and my pleasures are all the keener for my care.

This driving alone was one of the excellent pleasures. During all his office life, of course, people could come in at any time. And much as he wanted to be left alone, much as he disliked associating himself with random people, he was exposed to that always. In a car, by himself, he had freedom; as long as he wanted it that way, the doors opened in one direction only: out.

Butler, and Newfoundland, and then any old road. Better than he had hoped; this dark way up the hill, and it must be over a thousand feet. Before and below him in its shining, the reservoir, its darkness gleaming under a colored moon. With a swift floating movement the moon cleared a flat edge-lit cloud. Time's going, Mr. Stainer thought. It won't be dark. It will be bright and green; the leaves are out, they are bright. I'll kill her here, he thought.

He was walking upstairs and turning the key in the apartment lock at the usual time. He had a usual time, a little later than homecoming in Salt Lake City; but the smells were almost the same as he opened the door. Lamb and potatoes, and he could sort out mint, and no, that was the cedar on the floor oil, and was that asparagus?

There was Gracie's smell, flowery and unlike her, a moment before he put his arms lightly around her arms and back, and, mechanically, kissed the flatness of her mouth.

Gracie's mouth was not flat. He knew that when he looked at her; he really knew it, of course. But it was as though he had not looked at her since he came to his decision; for months before that, too. Perhaps for two whole years, if you counted what had happened on Easter Sunday two years ago.

He had understood, that day, the full extent of her refusal. It was a refusal to see how all his suffering derived from her denial, refusal to see his drive for separation which she would not allow, for divorce which she would not allow, for anything to break this life. And now here she was, talking about the trip as if she were going to go.

"Flora is so excited," she was saying. "She went to the consulate and found out a lot . . . all French towns, you know, and the Gaspé . . ."

He made her voice fade out. He could do that at will. And it was because he could make her image fade that he could feel as if he no longer saw her. As for dreams: he had not dreamed about her since before he had married her.

Yes, it was all about sex. Whatever anyone said, that was the whole answer. What other answer was there? He said what she expected him to say. There! it was said, and they were going in to dinner, the last dinner at home.

People could say that money, economics, dominated our lives, that society always had a hand; but take their own case. If things had been right between them. Anything. Any one thing. But her flat mouth. When he kissed her these days, it was as if her lips were flatness of—not flesh, not meat, more like potato, he thought. His fork went into the little new potato on his plate.

In Salt Lake City he had been able to manage. Even if her mouth was flat, he had—his legs tightened. He was advancing in the company— the automobile business was in a curious position and suddenly he, Paul Stainer, had been able to predict and maneuver and move freely in his business life. A sort of fog light for the company, in that period. People who talk of economic reasons! With, all the time, his personal life shot to pieces.

He could say that Gracie had been awful when the vice-president came to dinner. Better to stay away from people altogether than have that kind of evening. Better not to identify yourself with any group. He had never been a joiner. However, the vice-president . . . But he got his promotion, didn't he? The raise and the transfer? She had been nervous, weeping and pink-faced, and then weeping and red-faced, in the bedroom, later.

Everything was so bad between them. Abomination, he thought, this curse, nonexistence! He couldn't make her feel it. She never could see that the lack was an active cause. But it worked in him, night after night, day after day.

It wasn't so bad in Salt Lake City. He had been able to manage. First, there was Miss Aydelotte; then there was little Miss Kenmore, who had even added a henna tint to her hair; and then, right up to the day they left, Miss Dietz.

New York was different. Even forgetting how awful Gracie had been the night the vice-president came to dinner. He himself liked only the society of the well-bred, the handsome, the powerful. Gracie was ill at ease with people at that level. He was resigned to all that. But the chances here, the range, the rival excitements in the air; this fierce spring in the vertical stone city, at the nerve center of the company, a kind of open fighting and open creation. Life stronger than he had ever felt.

In business, that is. The rest of it . . . He could not, he could not; he was overpowered. Gracie, the company, the city. Whatever it was, it came out in the open that night at the hotel. With the neon striking the hotel room red one instant, black and dark the next, red the next. Striking the terrified face of Miss Walters, so moving in its panes (a modern, metropolitan face, he thought, even without its freshness of color and passion, even twisting in fear and disappointment, and that bud of horror, her mouth), striking her face and young breasts and the long fair legs first red then black.

It was all Gracie. While she was there, he was done for—as done for with anyone else as he was with her. And no children. No life in them. No life before them . . .

He put his hand out for another slice of lamb. He would have his life; nobody would keep him from it. He could be himself, come into his own powers, whatever they were, that had been kept from him. Some part of himself was out of reach. He would reach it.

"But, Paul," she was saying. "I don't know how I can do this without you. It's been two years since—oh, I suppose—but to be separated—"

Finish your sentence, he was saying to her, although his teeth locked, his voice closed on the words, the little muscles hardened over his jaw. He was not a big man, but when his face darkened with blood, and his muscles rose, he seemed almost tall, almost broad.

Soon they were lying in their bedroom. The last, he thought. And the dim, level affection she was showing was worse for him than nothing at all . . .

Sunday morning was a real spring morning. The chimes woke Gracie; Paul was wide-awake, and started as his wife woke and sat up, all in one movement.

"The picnic!" she said, in her moaning singsong.

"Let's just get out of town," he said, as he shut the apartment door, "and not decide where we're going. Let's go some place we never went before."

From then on it was easy. They were on top of the big hill. Under them, the reservoir, steely, and its cold walls.

It was at that point he had his only bad moment. I will be my only weapon, he thought, looking at his thumbs. She will never again stare her frigid terrible stupid empty frightening fiery vegetable stare, he thought; the brain lies unprotected directly behind the eyes.

But he got hold of himself. That was a satisfaction he was not to have. And when he pushed her into the reservoir, and she went down almost at once, her hair going reluctantly down after, he knew he had been right not to use violence.

He jumped in almost at once and swam about, although he hated this part. And soon he was dripping in the farmhouse parlor, his teeth beginning to chatter, hearing himself say, "An ax—" and he almost began to laugh—"there's been an accident."

He went through the next three days as if he were drunk. People were very kind. Flora was a great help at the funeral. And the work of mourning, he discovered, turned into, actually, a kind of mourning. Work was being done on the image of Gracie. More than she had ever faded in life, she faded to whiteness after her death; and quickly; and to a kind of benevolence, so that he began to lose his hatred.

But he was attracted to the place.

He went to stay with Flora and her husband after the funeral and they talked very little about the tragic accident. They were glad he had himself so well in hand; they did not protest to the point of annoyance when he left early Sunday afternoon. He would be going back to work the next morning, anyway; he had some things to do.

On the bus he fell asleep. The sleep was a powerful drink to him, he had been thirsty for this for weeks. He woke on the road leading to that hill, he realized the murder for the first time, and he knew he must not go back.

With an effort he stayed in his seat. He felt as if some change were taking place in him. He was learning something, that was all he knew, as the bus drove steadily into the green spring countryside.

He got off in the first town with a railway station. He was surprised to find, in the Men's Room of the restaurant where he went to inspect his clothes and his face, that he looked and felt no different. There was no difference at all. "You're supposed at least to want a drink," he said to his reflection in the square glass above the wash basin. For the sake of form he left by way of the bar, where he drank most of a Scotch and soda.

There was not long to wait. He got on the New York train and opened the magazine he had bought on the platform. As the train started and he settled down to his story, he realized that the feeling he

had had for months, the sense of things losing substance, fading before
his eyes, the sense of unreality and fear amounting to insanity, had
disappeared. All apprehension had gone. The pressure on his chest and
head, the unease of feeling followed by her look—these too had been
abolished. The set of acts had been frightful, yes; but necessary; and the
trouble was gone.

The magazine story was in front of him, letter by letter and word for
word. It *stayed*, as nothing had stayed before him all this time. He read
with concentration and considerable relish. It was not much of a story;
but it was a pleasure to him to follow the events and motives of simple
people, wearing their habits, behaving in lightness and love, and moving
inevitably toward the prescribed ending. It would be a happy one. He
turned to the last page of the story. Yes, it was a happy one.

He looked up into the eyes of the passengers on the slow local. The
man was watching him with a summary stare; he did not now blink or
avert his attention. The man looked as though he thought he knew Paul;
but Paul was certain he had never met this passenger.

Paul often forgot the names, and indeed the faces, of guests at cocktail parties or of brief visitors at the office. But this passenger could never
have been at the office or at any party the Stainers would have attended.
The passenger had the face of, say, a small grocer: dark-stubbled, fleshy,
notable only for the eyes, around which were bunched the folds which
develop after years of critical appraisal or uncorrected nearsightedness.
However, the look which met Paul was not critical; it was as if the
passenger were reading something with appraisal and withholding any
final opinion; and what he was reading was Paul's face.

As Paul came to this conclusion, he judged also that he did not care
for the stare, nor indeed the face which stared. It was a rather ugly,
unapproachable, repellent face.

Just at this moment the passenger began a nod of recognition. Paul
looked away.

Why did I do that? he thought with a rush of consternation. Suppose,
he went on, with a real taste of panic, suppose this man I cannot place
has reason to remember me on this train. He must be some night clerk at
a delicatessen, or an elderly newsboy I pass everyday.

And he saw how he might give himself away. However, he thought,
there is nothing to give away. He looked back at the face, which by now
he hated cordially. But the other passenger was looking out the window
at the flats, whose tender green showed over the deep browns and ochers
of the earth.

Only in the tunnel, lit by the black-yellow light, just before the train
got in, did their looks meet. This time the delicatessen man did nod at
him.

Once in the station Paul rushed to the escalator and walked the moving stairs. He could not wait to ride to the top. On the lower level he searched for a restaurant; he was awfully hungry by now; but he did not wish to face the glare of the health bars and the soda fountains. He went on to the Savarin and felt much better after a hot roast beef sandwich and a cup of coffee. He took more cream than he was used to, and drank a pony of brandy after his meal.

Out on the street he paused for the first time. He knew he must not go home until after the office on Monday. He knew that he must buy an overnight bag and some shaving things and a toothbrush—and a couple of paperback mysteries, he supposed—and go to a hotel that he would choose at random. But he must make the random choice count. First he would find a drug store.

He was thinking very clearly. It was almost as if he had been insane for two years, and now was at last sane.

He was startled out of his musing plans by a woman who stood before him, weaving slightly, a very tall woman with a thin round face. Her eyes had something of a look he had seen somewhere before. Recently. On the train. Her appraisal was open, and she went further than the passenger: she said, after a moment, in a breath that carried a strong current of cheap whiskey, "Take it easy, fella."

"Of course." Paul clipped off the syllables and walked away. Damn fool, you damn fool! You needn't have answered at all!

He hurried to the big drug store down Thirty-Fourth Street, bought a zipper bag, and filled it with toilet articles, paperbacks, and a bottle of eau de cologne whose heraldic stopper he had admired for a long time. He walked back to the station and straight through, with his executive stride, to the opposite doors. Then he crossed the avenue, got on a downtown bus, and rode to the end of the line.

The nearest hotel was across the little square, over the travel agency. He lay in his small green-gray room, hearing the voices outside. At first he imagined he had scrambled the words. They were speaking a language he had never heard a word of, and languages were what he had been keen on in college. He read a mystery novel, shaved carefully and bathed, read another mystery instead of going out to dinner, and fell into an early dreamless sleep.

He woke with heat on his face; the sun, combed through the slats of the venetian blinds. What language could it be? he thought. And then— Gracie. He must see a paper. For the only time he felt that someone might have been watching the reservoir that Sunday.

At the hotel desk, where steamship tickets were also sold, he asked what language he had heard in the halls. The boy behind the desk was happy to inform him. "Basque," he said, and smiled with his dark mouth.

"Have you got a *Times*?"

The boy sent Paul up the side of the square to a newsstand. Nothing on the front page: a headline about a union row. Nothing on the back page: an attempted suicide by mother of four, illness of a Nobel prize-winner. All the way through, nothing.

Things went well at the office. He had a large morning mail, got it all out of the way, talked to Detroit, and looked at his calendar. The time-study man was due at eleven thirty.

It was not until the time-study man had been talking to him for almost ten minutes that Paul was fully aware of the evil in his face. A week ago he had seen him as a very effective, rather pushing, blond man, with saturnine eyebrows and lines going straight down his cheeks. A statistical mind, he had thought, a man who is himself not much more than a labor-saving device.

But this week the time-study man, seen clearly, conveyed the most extreme corruption with every feature and every gesture. Or was it simply the manner in which he was regarding Paul, seeming to give a double meaning to everything he said?

Just then the time-study man drew a breath, interrupted what he was explaining about methods in the middle west to mutter to Paul, in an entirely new voice, "We trust you, you know," and went on with the Terre Haute report.

"What do you mean?" he said like a schoolboy.

"The sort of person you are," said the time-study man.

"How do you—"

"How do you think?" the time-study man answered, inflecting the words curiously. Then he picked up his brief case and his hat, and left.

It had been a remarkably stupid conversation. But for a minute Paul thought the man meant that he knew about what had happened that picnic afternoon. Paul went to the office library and opened a copy of *Fortune*. But he could not have known! Paul smiled at what he was reading: here was an article praising the beauty of design in certain new industrial buildings. (It must have been something about the company that he knew; something evidently flattering to Paul.) The article included photographs of some of the buildings. Handsome they were: long low windowless factories, great round turrets, and the radar tower just built in (no, of course he meant what he seemed to mean) New Jersey.

Yes. The time-man knew. And the only way he could know was by seeing something that had given Paul away.

But what was there? There was not a clue to that day. The map? Destroyed, thrown over the railing of the George Washington Bridge. And what would the map have meant? Plans for a picnic. No. Someone would have had to see the thing itself. He had taken that chance. By this time he was safe. Completely safe.

Paul thought he had better go home. It was lunchtime—an early lunch, well, yes, but just the same.

But at home, on the way back, during the rest of the office day, there was nothing that did not go smoothly.

It was a routine afternoon until just before closing, when the inter-office gadget announced Mr. Dought. For a second Paul could not remember who that was, and then, before he remembered, he jumped, his skin leaped. The time-study man!

"Mr. Stainer," he heard, "I have only come back to be friendly. You seemed nervous this morning, alarmed."

"I'm not alarmed," Paul said.

"Of course not," the answer came. "You are not to be. We want you to understand that you can trust us."

In bed that night Paul began to see.

He took the subway to work the next morning. There, facing him, he saw the one who brought it home to him. Stupid, thick-faced, filthy, he was smiling and rolling his head at Paul as if he had found a long-lost brother. Paul thought the man had the worst face he had ever seen, the most brutal hands; the foulest, most broken shoes.

After two stops, when still no one stood between them to cut off his view, Paul leaned forward and said across the aisle, "Why do you pretend to recognize me?"

The man drew back, hurt. A stricken look passed over the thick features; then a defensive changing expression, and that gave way to the most disfiguring mask of all—jocular, intimate, and in a low defaced way, witty.

"Well," said the thick man, and the bullying creature came through in its full force, "take it easy. We're all in this together, you know."

It would not end. He was pulled into a group, doomed to a herd at last, to a group doom. Tighter, more stable, more demanding than any clan he had ever imagined. And the rasping or weak or timbreless voices; the brute masks, stupid and sly and always less human; the knowledge in all their eyes of his fall, his fault, the fact of his unaccepted guilt.

This is the worst, he thought.

But it was not the worst. That was not to come for almost a week or more, when, again in the subway, he saw the young white-faced boy, the eyes that looked through the windows at the blackness of subway tunnel and the sudden fever-bright station platforms, the mouth that only occasionally trembled, the feet, one pressed down hard on the laces of the other shoe. He knew at once: a murder has just been committed. And he saw the streak of half-dried blood on the dark ragged cuff.

And then he comprehended: it was not only that he would be recognized, and taken in and befriended by those, and only those, who saw his crime, all his life long. It was that they recognized him because of their own crimes.

And it was more: it was that he too would recognize all those, and only those, who had committed such violence against human spirit and flesh, such murder of assault or treachery against life, all his life long.

JAMES SCHUYLER

Life, Death and Other Dreams

They are known as *They*
Kenward Elmslie

They lived like Shakers, with a slight difference: they didn't leave anything out, and they didn't let anyone in.

2

*"I love all beauteous things,
I seek and adore them . . ."*

"No wonder the old grouch got to be such a crab. He was travel tired: footsore, weary and blue."

"Footsore? English shoes really are very well made. At least they used to be. They called them, boots."

Robert Bridges led them up the garden path, which was lined on either side by narrow beds of white pinks. The moist green English air was charged to saturation with a smell like cloves, only more so, and better. They were making a sensuous scene. Nearby, the towers of Oxford glittered and flashed in the starless night like the lumps in a bottle of rock and rye.

3

"All things are relative. I mean, all things are relatives. 'There's a wee bit o'gold in the gray of your hair,' i.e., trace element."

"What a downer. Stop rapping and lie on top of me. Move down a little further. No, up a little more. Right."

"I'm . . ."

"Stop rapping."

4

"Say, or, by the way, or, look, or, hey, you, Chihuahua: Didn't somebody write something called, *Wishes, Lies and Dreams?*"

"Could be. Then there's that spick who wrote *La Vida es un Sueño.* Christ, how I hate words like 'spick.' "

They talked dirty.

5

They put on the most driven, the ugliest recording of *La Traviata* they could find (Toscanini's). They put French sleeping wax in their ears. They went to the control panel and turned everything hard right, except the bass, which they turned hard left. The night was bronze. They flipped the switch. At the first note the neighborhood awoke with a start, under the impression that Chamfort was reading aloud to them in a raging sewer. Thumps, yells, execrations, poundings from all sides, from below, from above. A POOR WOMAN, stated the last Trump, or the Great Darning Needle, whatever it was, IN THIS POPULOUS DE-SERT THAT THEY DO CALL PARIS. Many, perhaps all, phoned the police, who had other fish to fry and were good and hungry. Fumes drifted about the room in an interestingly gauzy way: they were in a bathosphere of love, submerged in a sea of hate. When Alfredo threw the bag of money at Violetta's feet, Etna lost its cool, and the neighborhood was spared—or denied—the ultimate effect: The Cough.

6

"What a fuck! moving, and deeply felt."

7

"Let's get rid of the junk."

"Get rid of the junk!" ?!?!

"Not that junk: all the other junk."

They sold the basalt tea service, the Wedgwood mourning ware (place settings for eighteen), Robespierre's curl, the Brunelleschi floor plan, the this, the that. They were comfortably off.

8

"What are you reading?"

"Dear only knows."

9

"Wanna try it with the lights off?"

10

"And now, I'm going to scrub you down with the Milan Cathedral."

11

They shaved. They went out. They dined, they drank, they took a walk, they bought an oriental calculating device and dropped it in an ashcan.

"What is this place anyhow?"

They were encircled by straight lines.

"Slab City."

12

"I wouldn't care if I dropped dead tomorrow."

"Not a possible state of mind."

"It's mine, at the moment."

"To sustain."

"I didn't say, 'I wouldn't care if I dropped dead *today*:' I mean, I *like* life that much. And I don't love life, I like it: a more constant feeling."

"You lost me."

"Then I want to die now, this second. I wish I had, just before you spoke. I would not have heard that."

They hugged and kissed and threw the plastic bleach jug full of popper juice out the window. It bounced when it hit and the loosely secured cap came off, creating unanticipated turmoil among some passing protesters. Placards on sticks were everywhere. They were inscribed:

> O'HARA PAPERBACK POEMS
> NOT COMPLETE WORKS KILL KILL
> P*E*A*C*E B*A*B*Y
> Vote for Bella Abzug

Clothing in fashionable muted tones mingled with the dog shit, the car farts and the activity at a nearby fire.

"Litterbugging."

"Truly a trip, and a rare one."

"Not since we made it with Lytton Strachey in Ottoline Morel's gray drawing room, its long windows streaming with yellow taffeta curtains. Even the light came."

aside: "Did you know that her grandfather, the Duke of Portland, was mad?"

not aside: "I never found him so."

"Time to break out the *Château Yquem*."

"No .... it's a good trip—but it's not a great one. Or even if it is a great one: I'll put it this way: Get the *vin de paille*."

"You're always right and you're never wrong."

13

"Did you know that Catherine the Great died, straining at the stool?"

"So did George II. Now may I go on with my book?"

Watch it fellows: The best laid relationships can deteriorate—a strain here, a strain there.

14

Their forged prescription slips were the unsung wonder of the day.

15

"Funny, our being the only two—or one, for the matter of that—who know, in precise detail, the event chain immediately preceding the recovery of the drowned King Ludwig of Bavaria, his foolhardy and equally drowned doctor clutched in his (Ludwig's) powerful embrace."

Taste flew out the window, along with a Sense of Values, The Stern Daughter of the Voice of Time, and a set of William Dean How . . . —Please! no personalities.

"Some scholars think one thing, others another, and at least one has an open mind." A distant—but no less hideous for that—shriek of pain was heard. By them. They lashed Richard Wagner to a gilded date palm (San Carlo Opera House) and the overture to *La Gioconda* struck. About Noon in "The Dance of the Hours" R.W. went into catatonic shock. They relented, unlocked the padlock, wrapped him in burlap and mailed him home, along with some squid and a few sea urchins for Cosima. They went up on stage and joined the soprano in a rousing rendition of, *Suicidio*!

> . . . *in questi*
> *Fiere momenti*
>
> ★ ★ ★ ★ ★ ★ ★
> *Ultima croce*
> *Del mio cammin.*

The harmony got pretty close. The Neapolitan fatties in their homemade silks were sent way out there, far, far beyond i Fariloni, Capri and the bourne.

"Get the piss cubes, the toe jam and . . ." surely, informed and gentle reader, these things need not be spelt out? Detail is such a drag.

17

"I want a mixmaster."

"Baby, I am at your side."

18

"Dig a little leather?"

Shrug.

They got into their Chesterfield sofa drag, hung swastikas around their necks (swastikas with the arms going the other way: what a put-down! a genuine send-up) and creaked off to Lasher Lane. THE DIVINE MAR-QUIS: BARS AND GRILLS: walls hung with hangman's knots and trophies of chain and motor hog parts; buzz saw chandelier; busts and statuettes of fun-loving figures of history: Torquemada; Nero with matchbook; Sawney Bean; Papa Doc. The Ilse Koch bridge lamp was possibly a fake; though an able one. A giant tinted photograph of the late Joseph Stalin loomed and smiled beneficently down. Autographed too: *With abiding love from your Uncle Joe*. But who reads Russian? Printed mottoes:

TOO MUCH IS JUST
NOT ENOUGH

SUFFER, LITTLE CHILDREN

BEYOND THE PLEASURE
PRINCIPLE

BE A BLOOD DONOR

and so on. Oh yes. A set of Felicien Rops illustrations for *The Chinese Torture Garden*. The sawdust reeked of—never mind.

"Classy. Harmony in bruise tones. Bold, but not too bold."

"Heard on the gropeline that Headless Hannah got a mint. For doing it."

"Yeah. A mint compounded of Spanish fly, Absorbine Jr. and cholera lice."

Clank clank: the bartender. "Your wish, master?" he pleaded.

"Budweisers—on the rocks and straight up, slave." Ear Indian burn: beatific grin.

A few of the boys were there, playing dress-ups and shooting pool. One had his mouth taped shut. "Piss up my nose, Mister?" They could not quite make out what he was saying.

They fed the juke box: "Beat me, Daddy, 8 to the Bar"; the great great Mickey Rooney at his greatest, "Treat me Rough (Muss my Hair)"; and unforgettable, "Primitive Man." They turned respectful ears to these classic laments—then intrusion intervened.

Thus to them addressed a blond asp with cloudy eyes these words:

"Got a cabin cruiser: care to join me and a couple of buddies and head out from Montauk?" They replied in Stoney Stares. "Sea bass are running," added the albino Dragon Lady. His slim long fingers—they had a few superfluous joints and the nails were à la Camorra: sharp points, tipped with industrial diamonds—tenderly scratched at a large economy size bag of Portland cement.

They delivered their blackout line as in one voice: "Get away from me before I slice you up into ladies' leather wallets." It was a swiped gag, it was an old gag, they had used it often—and it never failed.

19

"Violence is never right—outside the home, that is, of course."

"You're the milk in my cambric tea but you sure are ONE DUMB DORA."

20

They paid a visit to the nicotine pit. They got it up to a couple of brace of Larks a day (i.e., two cartons each per demi-diem) and went cold turkey. *My dear, I tell you . . .*

"Visit the Met Museum."

"You're on."

Niagaras of sweat and all atremble "like aspen leaves upon a lute" they got as far as the bannered hall of metal men and were promptly asked to leave. The carbon steel armour was breaking out in rust spots. Slashing great footprints behind them, like Abominable Snowmen in a thaw, they reached the porch and stumbled and fell down the steps, scarcely noticing what have got to be the world's worst fountains (giant trough urinals with reverse piss). They yelled and screamed and moaned at flocks of illuminated cabs. Understandably, none stopped. They were arrested by a heavy-set gentleman in blue, hustled to the station, charged with: creating a disturbance; loitering with intent; possession of a silver flask containing a suspicious fluid (*eau de vie de framboise*); addressing an officer in ill-chosen words; and hurled into the Tomb. The service was not all that great. At a later date, they were let out again.

21

"I'm not so sure I liked that. Once you've been in jail, there is a, well, kind of stain on your name, so to speak. In some people's eyes, anyway; and even if their eyes have sleep crowns in the corners, I mind; a little."

"Forget it."

22

They took in a musical. On the marquee it said, in melancholy letters on a white ground:

B O O S T I N G

Long loud cheesy overture.

CONDUCTOR: Cool it.

The band plays on and stops when good and ready. Up the great gold curtain. Thunder, lightning flashes, light drizzle on audience. Inner crimson velvet curtains sweep apart. Release Brazilian killer bees. Asbestos curtain rises: *lento lentissimo*.

Scene: An emporium, totally crammed with objects, some more choice than others. THE PROPRIETOR, a buxom woman in the midst of life, is alone on stage. Enter A MAN.

MAN: Porcupine quill pen and don't keep me waiting I'm in a rush. (He fondles her ass.)

PROPRIETOR: Easy on the bakemeats, buster. (She picks up a machete and deftly severs the offending hand from its wrist. While she is thus distracted the MAN pops into his off-side pocket small articles: Rolaids, a Lady Bulova watch, etc. Here the actor may improvise—*up to a certain point*. MAN departs hastily. PROPRIETOR picks up turkey feather duster and commences to dust.) Enter CHORUS OF TEN. Possibly that from the old Cotton Club, or possibly not. THE CHORUS is played by one giant show girl. She must convincingly indicate presence of other nine non-present show girls. It does not matter how she does this. However, *should she fail*—CHORUS (title song):

> Boosting
>
> Boosting, boosting
>   boo boo boo boo
> Boost boost boost
>   troubles away
> Boost boost boost
>   part of each day etc.

Thus the slow progression toward the inevitable intermission.

23

The velvet curtains—possibly real velvet, loomed in Leeds by a Loiner—dense with dust and star-clutch curtain-call sweat, swept closed. House-lights. Shuffle blatter shove.
"Your ass is in my face, madame."
"You need not, therefore, chew my girdle. Desist. You are danking my Dior."
"Christ! My beads!"
"Eff your effing beads, babe, and take that stiletto heel out of my bunion."
"Why don't you go back where you came from you—you alien."
". . . bartender bartender bartender . . ."
"Bee Man's Pep Sin? What's? That?"
". . . curtain going up curtain going up . . ."
". . . bartender bartender I beg I implore . . ."
"That is one pack of filter tip double Queen length Lady Rhodas in the floral pack. That you want. Which will be, $2.75. Plus tax. At 6%. It is a fact: I cannot do my multiplication tables in my head: mumble buzz: do

you use matches? My boy, he collects matches. The folders, that is. He is forty-nine and dreams of finishing high school. At home. With me. In a moment, *sir*: can you not see that I am occupied in serving this *gentleman*? We live off Riverside Drive on . . ."

"Eleven sidecars, a Singapore sling and . . ."

"Curtain going . . ." Smoke puff cough choke gag spit cigar-butt-urinal charm.

"We got Sacramento Valley rye, flat fizz and chlorinated sump water. Snap it up. I haven't got all night."

"Curtain going, curtain going: do I hear $275,000?"

". . . shoved the whole shebang off the shelf, cooled it at a grand a share, *nor* skipped he off to Rio."

"Oh wow."

"Mints? *You* are asking *me* for a *bag* of after-dinner *mints*?"

". . . gone gone gone . . ."

"I wish a gin and tonic. Make it a double. And skip the fruit wedge George or I will feed you through this transistorized platinum pocket parsley mincer."

"Yes! Sir!"

Scream.

"There is PHLEGM on my TRAIN! It is got YIK on it!"

24

"How many ways do I love you? Clad, half-clad, starkers, erect, recumbent, tumescent, down right limp. Snoring. Smiling—as now—eyes shut, almost asleep. I love your fingers. They unlax, they unfurl. You are floating away from me on a dark, salt, refreshing tide. I will tell you softly and more softly still of the many ways I love you and gently ease my voice to a thread, to an all but invisible strand of silk loosened—so lightly—from the cocoon of sleep, unseen, within you. Dream. I love you, a whole dream world away from me, far as Mars and further than the Pleiades, who are seven. You no longer hear my voice: its "baltering torrent is shrunk to a soodling." I will, all loving all of you, cease, now, to speak."

"Go on. I'm listening."

"Dear heart!"

25

They contracted childhood diseases. Their immunities became intense.

"Nothing ever changes."

"Whine whine."

They practiced what they would have preached had they been preachers
and soon had mouth-to-mouth resuscitation down to a soft-shoe shuffle.

26

They received an invite to mingle with some upper hoi—. It did not
have gilded edges. It didn't need any. You just knew it was there: the
chocolate candy coins skinned with gold foil, the mazuma mazuma, the
what it takes to get up out of bed and take a shit in your own best
crockery (unless you wanna do it in the gutter: that's your trip, baby):
yes, folks, they had IT, the curly cress that tastes of ink and horny
fingers, printed on Crane's best notepaper, the kind with nosegays of
zeros in each corner, preceded by a digit.

A minor general hustled to open the door of the cab they had long since
left. They did not tip him. He cursed them up, he cursed them down, he
cussed them out: *in brogue*. They toiled across the lobby. O quarries of
travertine, will you never run out? Or is it you who are the hint, the key,
the clue, perhaps the Thing itself: the (seemingly) impossible: inexhaustible supply. In truth, it was all sleazy bleached Kasota stone—who
cares. They did. Distantly a kettle drummishness gave them a twinge of
ear freak: some tons of prisms had hit the deck, one and a ½ light days
ago. Upward whizz. Mountain sickness. Ninetieth floor, all of it,
trimmed with Terror Terrace (nylon thread balustrades). An automaton
—the masterwork of a raft of mastercraftsmen and the wizard of Menlo
Park: The Hostess. Arms of chryselephantine lifted and parted, palms
down: one hand each to do with as each pleased: squeeze, lick, pat, slap;
but not exactly shake. The eyes—lavender transplants, the best—were
wet with joy, the costliest. The lips parted. Click. "This is a prerecorded
message. 'I am so HAPPY you could 'COME!' If you have anything to
say—and it better be good—wait for the beep."

Upon these hands they lowered eyes like fish-eye lenses: the gaze of a
beads, gems and watches connoisseur who really knows his stuff and
don't take no lip from nobody, most of all when nobody ain't said
nuthin'. They studied the collection.

"Uhnn."

"Not top."

"The blue ruby knuckle duster?"

"*That* is THE most famous FAKE in the entire world, plus Saturn, Mars and Jupiter . . ." Rage stutter. "FOOL! CRETIN! IDIOT!"

They raised gazes and looked at its face. The smile had grown merely a little warmer, but the eyes had subtly changed. Out of them streamed the aurora borealis, smoking hot.

Their faces reddened, peeled, healed and darkened to the desired tan: a ruddy, healthy glow. They split.

"Better than Bermuda: cheaper, no hit-and-run bicycle riders. . . ."

"Bermuda? Who needs it, Tweedwits. Domenica."

27

"Reality starts in a checkbook."
"Speak for yourself, Miles."

28

They stopped for a traffic light. So did a Rolls. It was *that* shade of green—you know, the one that isn't black—or maybe it was maroon. They could scarcely tell, so turned on were they by the attar of roses clouds of its exhaust. An imported, hand-picked chauffeur graced the wheel. He too was a human being. On the back seat, cloistered in the regal solitude it so richly deserved, reclined a throw pillow. Petit point. Imperial yellow ground. Edged with red, the reddest red. Not a thin red line, not a thick red line: just right. In orange Bodoni:

THIS IS MY CAR
AND I'LL SIT
WHERE I DAMN
PLEASE

"Molotov cocktail time?"

"Embroidery is an honorable hobby, like any other."

The light changed. The car rolled forward, clashing its gears.

There they stood, too zonked to move.

29

"Read the directions."

"I can't even read my palm in this murk. Put on the strobe. That's besser, baby. Says here it says, 'to ball for eight continuous hours . . . something something . . .' What it boils down to is, get a light liquor high, throw in the upper of your choice, toke away at the Nepalese Blue Streak Hash, and keep the amyl handy."

"Nothing about henbane, belladonna or angel dust?"

"One can but try."

30

They went to the Rainbow Room, and groveled at its wondrous décor. They had the whole dump to themselves and made the most of it. All around the twilight lay shattered into mauve, canary and blue tourmaline. No clouds troubled its repose as the day died into itself. They issued forth upon a balcony. They addressed the night.

"O Alva! Alva!"

"O flow! budding out in fragile glass"

"as though the living and the dead had fled, leaving phosphorescent shells."

"O Steinmetz, Steinmetz, Steinmetz!"

"And waterfalls that change and charge the night with fatal 'don't chew on me' wirings!"

"O monotony, peopled invisibly"

"Parks, offices and murderous squalor"

"Here and there lights go on . . ."

"and the unperceivable is seen . . ."

"in the rhythm of the swelling and subsiding sea . . ."

"no wave breaks"

"O Davy Davy Davy"

"O blue TV"

"and Waring blender, automated pencil sharpener, burglar alarm, electric toothbrush"

"O wattage"

"fluent and tappable"

"O phone"

"Alexander Graham Bell and Mrs Bell"

"And everyone, all talking at once or snoring or suckie-fuckie"

"City, you name it, you got it"

"She thinks, I can no more, and shakes the pills into her palm"

"She thinks, so many years to wait for love and Oh boy, was it worth it"

"He thinks, did I give, or get, a bum steer?"

"Darkness darkens and struggling against its tug more lights come on and more"

"water lilies whose stems the water drags and they flower"

"lights beyond all flowers!"

"O flowering flux!"

"O. Henry! O. Henry! O. Henry, O. Henry!"

"He said 'Turn up the lights; I don't want to go home in the dark' "

"And died"

"Bright embroidery of sound"

"Taxis, limousines, the common hog or 'motorcycle,' Vespas and motor-skates"

"All this splendor and it is not ours"

"I would groove in silence"

"If I could: lights! lights! lights!"

"And roomy rainbow"

"flashing from blue steel: guns, and knives and terror"

"Squeal?"

"Was that an accident?"

"Or a near thing?"

"There is no one to question, there is no one to ask"

"About the afterlife: have you a thought?"

"City called Miracle, what do you think?"

"If this is very heaven, how acceptable to the senses might be . . ."

"It is such a little thing to be born of woman"

"O hard-faced death with Grecian nose"

"Are you Miss Liberty?"

"Answer! Answer! Answer!"

"O free will! honey, baby . . ."

"Flipping switches"

"Randomly at large"

"It is such a little thing"

"To be born of woman"

"And to die. O shining city"

"O fatal sting"

"All that is strongest and most frail"

"honors you"

"O New York City"

'O secular sublime"

31

They took a trip and crossed the Natural Bridge. Below, in the chasm, the gulf, the rain engorged arroyo, were pearly depths, in whose whorls lurked hideous monsters that snapped and harrowed (by monsters is meant: the neighbors—the man who comes to read the meter—a lady in galoshes selling raffle tickets, etc).

32

They invited Holly Woodlawn to join them in a visit to the Necropolis. She was busy, starring. They went anyway. There were an awful lot of people there, tucked up to the chin and beyond, only the headboards of stone bedsteads poked through the blades.
"Like sooty dominoes."
"Nonsense."
And each in the ghetto of his choice: Jew bones by Jew bones, recusant by recusant, Neuter Baptists, Moondog followers, Hutterites, Millerites, Seventh Day Adventists (women who gave birth once a week), Pickled Pig Fat Eaters, Slaves of the Lotus, Worshippers of the Squishy Banana.
"Shall we honor the dead?"
"What for? They're a thankless crew."
They split a rainy day pill. (It was not about to rain: that was the name of the pill.) Nothing much happened, unless you count the neon liana thread webs and the sun, whose fingers nervously clutched and grabbed at them for about eight hours, a hailstorm or two, the lightning bolt bundles, the edible Goodyear blimp. They downed on sheepshit, encapsulated in gelatin of a thrilling transparency.
"Pretty sluggish ride, all in all. Better than *Gone With the Wind*, maybe?"
"STOP COMPARING."
"O, wow, man. When you raise your voice to me—and you never do—it

turns me on to *Written on the Wind* and I'm it: Dorothy Malone,
Daddy dying, Rock Hudson and Robert Stack, the oil derricks, all of it,
all of it."
Crunch.
They broke a widgeon off the High Holy Hash, got out the meerschaum
—its bowl, a bust of William Tell—and had a smoke. Moonlight seeped
into the room, between the floorboards.

33

They sent a nice note to Sir Basil Liddel Hart, thanking him for his
history of World War II. They told him how much they enjoyed it.
Excessive praise, but sincere. The note arrived in time for the funeral.

34

"Ought we not go to Russia and spit on the graves of Mayakovsky and
Pasternak, Pushkin, Tolstoy and Tuytchev? Not out of hate—out of
contempt for fame."
"No, we oughtn't. Wait. You may have something there. Get the kerosene and we'll discuss it."

35

They put on their sox, sat back, relaxed and lit up a Camel. You can
imagine how the creature felt. This one was by Stieff, out of F.A.O.
Schwartz. It cost—well—plenty. It was the money they wanted to burn.

36

Inveterate nighters—first nighters, closing nighters, by-pop-demand-
absolu-last-chance nighters, middle of the flop nighters—they frequented
matinees and previews where their presence went unnoted, save by Carl
Van Vechten: him, they intrigued. The deliciously wicked Mr. Van V.
made an intriguingly naughty pastiche *à propos de ces gens-là* (pastiche?
de Sade, a few nodding-out thoughts of Anatole France, the Russian
ballet midout Nijinsky, Karsavina, Fokine or the sets) and sent it to a
friend in Europe.
Mr Firbank put aside a grape, a grape of dawn-pale green, the morning
mist of its bloom brushed and untroubled by prints, fingerprints: *"per-
ceptuably upon the lea were reeds,"* opened the envelope, extracted the
letter and held it, gingerly, at arm's length, not unnear his knee. Distinctly, yes, there was an (his nostrils troubled not to quiver) aroma: a
railway station sandwich scent: prosciutto on something unchewable:

thick prosciutto. From an hotel balcony arose thin wings of air-mail stationery blue (a kind of gray), the letter, fluttering to join some doves in their evening peregrination of the sky.

He also mentioned them, *en passant,* in a book length missive to Miss G. Stein. In reply, Alice B. toasted a postcard: "Dear V.V.'s Eyes, Can the prattle and make with the steam. Tender B.'s is the topic, Mable the Dodge the subj't. G.S. fit to be tied and dyed. May you walk with God. Miss Toklas." Thus it was they experienced a mixed media marathon of some length. Sample: The letter aria from *Onegin*: love, love, love, orgasmic love: cut to silent movie lawyer's office tough kewpie doll blonde in satin and poils: Title:

> *I want you should take the*
> *old geezer for every last*
> *red cent he's got, Hymie.*
> *Them letters is red hot:*
> *they are the goods.*
>
> *I believe we understand*
> *each other, Miss LaVerne.*

37

They took the green pill bus trip to Vermont. How gray it was that hot summer! All roads were dust and dust was everywhere. Most notably on the gray and giant mullein whose yellow flowers were obscured in an ashes-to-ashes look.

"King's candle."

A nothing gesture was the reply, one expressive of: "It is not humanly possible for you to shut up, anywhere, ever, is it. Oh. Well."

They found that village boneyard with the stone which was the objective of this fleeting tour.

HERE LIES SILENCE
HIS WIFE

The green pill has little staying power, so: they popped some uppers, toked at the Blue Streak, stipped, sloshed down a bottle or so of Uncle Fredleigh's Apple Wine and wheezing, sneezing, eyes awash with hay fever gunk, did it in the dust. They called it, *The Mortal Storm*. A fine time was had by all.

38

A pause for reflection.

39

What with paying the pusher, coughing up for the contact, all the little sundries of Wistful Vista, the cash ran low. They needed—no, they wanted: records, books and Brooks Brothers suits. Also some haberdashery. So they wrote a best seller. It was easy. It was not one of your flash in the pan fancy Dan type best sellers either: it was the real Britannica. They called it, *The How Book*. And I tell you Heloise, if a lot of jokers got off some good ones at their pseudonymous expense—"The Fanny Farmer of the Funny Farm"—it was jake with 'Myrtle Tilbush' because it is a fact, a silver dollar *will*

> roll upon the ground
> because it's round.

Other sorts of currency more or less floated, drifted and strolled into varied accounts and wound up, nicely spaced on paper that is hard to bend, in the village stocks. Another stream from the inscrutable source wended into a tin box, which was not stashed under the bed. The box, to its intense content, lived in a serried row with others of its kind, beyond a thick round door off which the light flashed. A nice door, a hand-made door, and one of many parts: tumblers, pratfalls: all that's needful to keep good paper from the damp.
How's about a sample or so?

40

from: *Attending a Job Interview*
Job: *Your name, I take it, is Mr Hoare.*
Mr Hare: *Approximately. My name is Augustus J. C. Hare.*
Job: *You are not, perchance, a connection of Alfred A. Hoare, author of*
A Short Italian Dictionary, *an invaluable work to which I frequently refer, published by CUP? A distant, possibly a remote, cousin?*
Mr Hare: *I am appreciative of the compliment you would, it appears, wish to intend. Indubitably, that Mr Hoare is a species of cousin, one as remote, I trust, as the nearest banana munching baboon. My own Italian is superb. The word, by the way, for which you so vainly fished is not author: it is compiler. I myself would hesitate to use 'compilation' of that egregious concatenation of foreign scribblings followed by—HAH! —definitions of which I will not speak. To be lucid, I would not touch Hoare's Short, no, not even with a ten-foot mamba.*

Job: *I see, I see. You understand Mr Hoare that, though a certain vacancy exists among our researchers here on our staff, within this monolithic dream (Rockefeller Center, I cannot clasp thee close enough! Gilt Prometheus! Skaters upon the cat's ice of my mind! Many chambered heart! You dazzler you!), there also exists a stockpile of the anxiously over-educated upon which we may freely draw. We pay dirt: they are overjoyed to haunt our stacks by day and by night and by artificial light and do our bidding. It's the free air conditioning that does the trick. Now, Mr Hoare, would you tell me a little about yourself?*

Mr Hare: *Gladly. Nay, willingly. I was a child. Quite a young child. I had a pet. A pet rabbit. Or a dog or a cat. I forget, that part becomes confused. I had been bad. I was a bad child, a very bad child. I was too fond of my pet. I deserved to be punished. They meant no wrong. I swear to you that they did no wrong. I don't know what happened. They took it, my pet, out into the barn and hung it with a rope. It died. It strangled. I—Calvin! Calvin! my pet, where are you?—I—*
Job: *Mr Hoare, kindly arise from the floor and, without bothering to count to two, turn round and leave my office. O-U-T spells out.*
Mr Hare: *I will leave, toad, in my own good time. My name is Augustus J. C. Hare. You may read about me in my* The Story of My Life *(six vols.). My ghost stories are sheer witchery. My spacious handbooks, such as* Walks Near Rome, *even in these dilapidated days are found by many—by the few who count—viable, more viable than any* Italy on a Nickel a Day *drool liable to issue—but I grow rude. I, sir, in my time, was never deemed other than a gentleman. Would that I might say as much of you. Bedlamite, good day.*

41

Dressing Wounds
Sphagnum moss makes a fine dressing for wounds.

42

Dressing for Dinner
No longer done.

43

Old Fashioned Turkey Dressing
Follow directions on Bell's Poultry Seasoning box.

44

From the chapter, Pitching Woo
Dear Desolation of My Heart,
I can be sad, so very sad, and over such little things. Our love is not a little thing, no more than the idea of a god, or electricity, or learning Greek in order to read Hesiod.
These few flat flowers (see enclosure) I gathered where your skirt has brushed. I went out at night with my Eveready flashlight and, flicking it on and off, hastily picked these dying moments where, from the sewing room window, I thought I saw you pause, en route to the mill and your job. I am sad that I cannot know, for certain, that these are the pallid blooms that you stopped to regard. Or perhaps you stopped, unseemingly, to muse? At times you notice so little, and at other times, so much. It makes me sad, not knowing.
You say that you love me, that my great love for you is returned with a bonus: you even said that, if it were possible, you would not mind seeing me, from time to time. I told you I ask no more, and indeed I am filled by your words, your nods and infrequent becks, with a great joy, a joy far greater than any sadness these clumsily pressed mementos betoken.
And yet. And yet. I am so sad today. You are not mine: we have considered this in all its aspects, and in accepting all provisos and prohibitions, I felt a rising radiance like that of an artesian fountain or a riderless pony baring its teeth to the wind. I am sorry I am sad, I know it irks you. You said, by word and by deed, that only joy, happiness, good health and smiles are acceptable to you.
I should destroy this letter. Perhaps I will.
And yet. In the prairie of my love for you, extending beyond any visible horizon, there are these gopher holes of small gloom: warrens of skinny sadness. Sadness is a meager emotion, and in telling you of it, I may lose all, thus making it a terrible and great thing, a love gone wrong. The thought of it fills me with terror and irritation. Truthfully now, would you wish me to go always about with the fixed grin of rigor mortis? It would frighten the wits out of my grandchildren to see their normally gloomy granny in such a state.
Yes, I must risk all and take this letter to our own oh! so private letter drop in the blasted oak. Sad or happy, I am yours.
(Inscribed, to Mabel from her Mavis)

45

Among other chapters:
GETTING THE MOST OUT OF WELFARE
MONOCHROMATIC COOKERY

ARSON
SANDALS AND SADDLERY
THE BLUES (1)
   "   "   (2)
AGNOSTIC BURIAL SERVICES
THE COW, USES AND ABUSES
SECULARITY
TO GROW AND HARVEST FLAX
BUILD YOUR OWN VIBRATOR
THE ART OF DISGUISE
   "   "   " DISH DISPOSAL
ART (all phases)
TEACH YOURSELF DEAFNESS
ESP AND THE INVESTOR
POISONOUS HOUSE PLANTS
TRANSLATIONS AND APPROXIMATIONS
*From the latter, comes this approximation of a translation of Tyutchev,
based on his name, and an interesting book by Gregg.*

46

Clump Birches

*Pale arms, bruised and scarred and with sooty rings, raised and opened
to embrace!*

*Wandering chalk lines on the black and soppy woodland of my heart,
among you I pass unseeingly and the distant train goes hoo, in echo of
the abandoned one's thought. Growing crookedly (it is not your fault!)
and hung with leaves that fall in haste and with dispatch fade from
lovely colors, quickly as the loved one's love for the beloving one failed,
so quickly as to question whether said love ever existed save in the
quondam lover's strolling bemusement. Is it possible, white birches, that
he ever loved and moved among you, seeing spring green on white, a
celebration of the youth of love in the heart of one who, in diplomat's
garb, he—the one of serious mien—saw white and green as living em-
blems of the vessel of his empty heart so suddenly aslosh with May
wine?*

*It is the winter of the year and of one's life, a hopeless case, and yet, this
too must be borne with, as must this snow scene in which your trunks
rise, smirched. "I have been too happy," she said, trailing away, an egret
in search of its true clime. Birches! birches! how filthy you look in the
snow!*

And if I were the Czar, and truly, I long to be he, my first unreasonable
command would be, "Cut down the birch trees, saw them into logs."
Then, this scene I see would hold a mirror to my heart: the murk of
evergreens, home of fly agaric and the vestal death cup amanita, for its
white is truly the white of deception, to kiss and flee away, oh short-lived
as love, clump birches.

47

"I've been thinking about the orgasm."

"And?"

"Oh nothing. I've just been thinking about it."

48

"It will soon be winter."

"Frozen slush."

"A feeling of discontent pervades the money capital."

"Capitol?"

"Our days pass pleasantly enough—people die and move away, going
west—and the appropriate emotion comes, so to speak, to hand. What we
do or do not feel, is appropriate because true."

"Yes, it is a good some while since I thought, 'Oh dear, another goner. I
ought to feel more (or less) than this blank surprise.' "

"True. You are not so nice as when I met you. Niceness stood in the way
of evolving into yourself, not that there will ever be a static you, un-
changing as a seated green bronze Fitz-Greene Halleck."

"Oh I wouldn't care for that at all."

"Do you feel the need of a hobby?"

"Why no. Do you?"

"You know me better than that. Turn over. I want to examine your back
through the magnifying glass. A blackhead may lurk among the freckles."

"So long as it's not the other way round. You wouldn't prefer to take a
long stroll among the office workers and the rising towers, the fenestrated
phalli of, well, this place?"

"Mah-jongg?"

"Cribbage?"

"Parchesi? Scrabble? Double solitaire? Pounce?"

"Honeymoon bridge?"

"Brooklyn Bridge is more like it. A heartening tooling among the gulls,
the pigeons and their droppings. A view of the tugs among the mercan-
tile fleet, burrowing away like voles with their voracious need to unceas-
ingly eat."

"Look, rooster, let's talk turkey: only on condition you won't pretend
you're going to hurl me off the bridge and into the harbor."
"Sure. Promise anything. You know I don't keep promises. And what
makes you so sure I was pretending? I may simply have changed my
mind."
"Then for sure it's mah-jongg."
They dressed and went out.

49

"So what am I supposed to do: get down on my knees and thank The
Finger for dreaming up the impossible dream, Adolf the red-nosed rug
chewer? 'That'll be a spritzer—club soda and gypsy blood, shtoopid—
and a broiled Jew chop. *Und* don't forget the mustard sauce *oder, Maxie
ich mach mit einem Dachau fahrt.*' "
"How about some stein songs from *Der Freischütz*?"
"God is thank God only another sick figment of Man (Dreaming Lips)
Kind's endlessly ingenious gift for dreaming up yet fresher way to delude,
entrap and torment—not himself: mankind is not a self—one another.
You, me, each of us. Too much and too long. Kill the professors. Take
the church down stone by stone. Ditto the Capitol: all the Capitols: the
white Capitol, the one in Albany, the red Capitol, the State House, the
House of Burgesses, City Hall. Money, religion and art. Venice? Don't
let it sink into the sea, push it in. It is stone, cement, bronze, glass, cloth
and a very little paint. It is in the way. Get rid of it."
"Why, that's mere anarchy!"
"Watch it, or you could get to be the first to go. Anarchy! If that's all we
got left, gimme."
"You turn my stomach. I'm sorry I ever let you pick me off the meat rack
under the blue park lamps. You're worse than a dose of bleeding piles."
"Good. You're mad. Maybe you're waking up. Blood. If that's what it
takes to clean up the mess, then blood is what it's going to be. Blood.
Blood on the sheets, on the walls, in the streets and the subways, in the
water cooler and the ladies' room: and not just blood on a whiter than
white vaginal insert. Somebody's fingernails; somebody's bleeding ripped
out tongue; somebody disemboweled and bleeding and if you don't
know what disemboweled means, it means I pick up *this* knife, and shove
it in your belly right *here*, like *that*, and yank it up and pull it out—
throw away the toy, *there*—and reach my hand in and get a fistful and
drag out your bloody hot shit-filled guts: and they do not come loose all
that easily. How does that grab you?"
"I would give my blood, my mind, my soul whatever that is, whatever
love I ever felt or could have felt—and that's a lot—if, for a minute, for
one split second, I could believe in an after life and die in the certainty

that you would burn in the pit of hell for all eternity, just like an electric barbecue spit somebody forgot to turn off. Turn off! you totally turn me off."

"Good. At last. Maybe we can make it: because kid, don't kid yourself, you can't leave hate out. It's there, like blood. Here. Take this Lady Schick injector stainless steel blade with the plutonium edge, keener than keen, and cut my arm. Right here. Flesh is flesh and flesh bleeds. I want you to see it bleed and know, for once if not for all, that blood and hate are real, red and real as roses. Take it and cut."

"No."

"Do it."

"Never. Good day, good morning, good afternoon, good evening star, and, good night. Tootle loo goodbye. *Je pars*: I go: *pour toujours*: Forever."

"Bye bye, Manon, bye bye. But don't count on big brother making with the shoulder and the hankie when you take the final zonk down in the dismal swampland and start in on the, '*Ah, le beau diamant!*' whine."

"Up your freaked off arse gratia arsehole head, you busted-brasier-eared gorgon."

"Miss worm turns. You sure took your time about it, Shirley: loveable, pokable you. Dreamer, dream on."

And so on. They, too, had their little spats.

50

"You look sad."

"I am."

"Why?"

"I was thinking, what will become of me if anything happens to you?"

"Is that a wish?"

"No. An excuse to indulge my sadness. I'm never sad with you."

"How about the time I went to the store and didn't ask if I could bring you anything."

"That wasn't sadness. That was pique."

"If you say so. Do you want anything from the store? We're fresh out of French ticklers."

"Ditto Lubriderm."

"Isn't there something personal, just for you, you want?"

"Not a thing. Though I'm rather hurt that you don't ask me to come with you."

"Well, sometimes I like to be alone."

"To the store and back isn't much in the way of solitude."

"OK. Come with me."

"Never. I mean, not today."

So they put on their coats and watch caps and went out. A blizzard was in progress. Stalled cars everywhere: the snowplows couldn't get through. They helped one man rock his car until it got out of the icy ruts and crawled forward a few yards. The Pleasure Chest was shut, but the walk was invigorating and blew the cobwebs away.

"Myriad flakes."

"A single whiteness."

"Desperate for the destitute."

"But beautiful."

"The sun shines and we can't see it."

"The snow stops, the moon rises, looters approach the stalled cars for leftovers."

"A family dies because of a snow-blocked exhaust."

"But we don't die."

"No. Not today."

51

"You're bleeding."

"So I see."

52

"Welcome to the transit strike," said one to the other. Heavy men (thin ones, too) stood around blocking subway entrances and exits and telling people at bus stops to move on or. . . . No trains or buses were running so the shoving and hustling was all in fun. Rough fun, but wholesome.

"I urgently wish to go north—what is it, two hundred blocks?—and give the unicorn tapestry a reprise."

"Everyone here is so happy when anything breaks down. It brings them out of themselves, into the streets."

"We could interview a few bystanders."

"OK. We can start with ourselves."

"I think it's a good day for a cook-in. The slush is getting up the legs of my pants and over my boot tops and, thence, on down."

"Better go barefoot."

A group—fairly large—of religious fanatics went by chanting that the end was passed and this, this was very paradise enow. All had their hair cut Iroquois style, a single bristling rib surrounded by waxed baldness.

"I wouldn't care to appear so conspicuous. There's a white sale at Altman's."

Instead they took in the fruitessence counter at another large store. Clerks were squeezing atomizers at all who hove within range and yelling the brand names of their costly wares. On an upper floor they found an interesting exhibit of glass chairs and stuffed rugs.

"Do we have a charge here?"

An elderly woman assured them that to buy a room divider was pointless, the drivers of the delivery vans having walked out in sympathy with the transit strikers. "I wouldn't want to say *when* you'd receive *that*," she said and shook her head like a dice cup as she gave the offending article a good kick.

"Did you notice? She spoke in italics."

"Everyone does. That's what conversation is all about. Though it's mighty bad form in writing."

"*Yes.*"

"Food."

"Is of the essence."

They addressed themselves to the store cafeteria and plates of broiled and flaming weenies.

53

"Few things are smarter than a black and white sunset. What with the snow, ermine, diamonds and soft coal soot."

"More like a copy of *The Times*, I'd say. One that the cat shat on."

54

From the diary, or Housekeeping Book.

Mon.   Took wash to Wash-o-Mat.
Tues.   Picked up wash.
Wed.   Found dry cleaners closed for inventory.
Thurs.   Cleaners still closed. Fear they have absconded with the Shetland sweaters.
Fri.   Hung around the house.
Sat.   Special ordered two pair golf shoes without cleats. Saw a film.
Sun.   Went downtown to savor the quiet. Statue of Liberty looking very well in the rain.
Mon.   Took wash to Wash-o-Mat.
etcetera

55

They decided to look into psychotherapy, and having decided, proceeded to do so. Oh the books, the books!

And chats with a few practitioners, none of whom seemed interested in

taking on a group limited to two. Until they came to a small Frenchman
who took in the situation, if that's what it was, at a blink. In high and
rapid tones he held forth on *folie à deux*. They were not uninterested.
Until, borne away on the wind of his oratory, he got onto *folie à trois*,
which he seemed to think both a good idea and a feasible one. They
slipped silently away, careful not to break the thread of his thought.

56

Food was of no great interest to either of them. Some fruit, choice vino,
frozen fish cakes—things along those lines satisfied them. They preferred
to spend their time doped—not always *utterly* doped: they had their
subtleties—listening to their fabulous stereo. It took up a whole wall.
And part of another. It was as sensitive as a ripe touch-me-not seed
capsule. Touch. Split. Spurt. By great good fortune one of them was an
engineer: a *graduate* engineer. That *was* fortunate. Their residence was
not troubled by the comings and goings of costly so-called stereo fixers
with long greasy hair.
Their taste in tapes and discs was catholic. They would buy anything,
provided it fitted in with the current kick. The worst days were during
their early recordings spell. The de Rezkes recorded under the stage of
the Metropolitan. Like someone whistling for his dog during a cow
stampede. Art. Yes, art was what they lived for, that, and their love.
There, too, their taste was catholic. It included everything except the
more refined forms of abstention. That, they did not practice. It might
have seemed to some that theirs were empty days. Not to them, however,
not to them by any means at all. Why only the day before they had gone
to the International Flower Show, wearing concealed tape recorders.
They collected the full flat flavor of flower show chat and added it to
their holdings.
The flowers, they were wilted. Unspeakable the much admired ferny
corner: dank smelly sod, a pool with a stone frog in it, a young weeping
beech that wept with reason. Only some bromeliads, adhering to a rotting
log, past muster. Alas, they were not for sale. Distinctly, the boat show
was more fun. Yes, yes.

57

"Death is not quite like anything else."
"Wake up, dear, it's only you."
"Pushing daisies is a mug's game."
"Wake up, you're singing in your sleep."
"Will these bones live? Cowshit I know, asshole him."
"All right, I'll do that."

Shake, punch.

Growl, object.

"Let me sleep."

"You weren't letting me sleep."

"I thought you didn't care about sleep."

"Mostly I don't, but when I do, I care passionately."

"What did I say?"

"I've already forgotten."

"You might have fetched the cassette."

"Yes, I might have. But I didn't. Care for a snack? Fried eggs?"

"What time is it? In a general way."

"Noon—at a guess. Or midnight. One of the twelves."

"It's amazing how you keep your looks. We're both still personable men."

"Flattery won't butter any toast, and buttered toast is what I want."

Outside, people went about their business in the unseasonable weather. And not all their business was all that nice. Mugging was the least of it. If the grocer didn't know you there was small chance of his unlocking. Strangers could starve on the doorstep of their choice. A cloud-smeared sun beamed down on the filthy city and its rumbling traffic.

"Buttered toast with poached eggs on them, like bazooms."

"Fix yourself whatever you want. I'm going bye bye back to sleep."

"Crypt."

"Musk ox."

58

The white geranium of a cloud lost a few petals which drifted off on their own. The mother cloud did its foaming Niagara imitation. Clear on its southern flank was the profile of an Indian chief in full feather. It wasn't going to rain, and the breeze was balmy.

"Do you remember the opening night of Carnegie Hall, when Tchaikovsky conducted?"

"Vividly."

"What was your favorite record when you were thirteen?"

"Stokowski's *Afternoon of a Faun*."

"You still like that."

"I don't stop liking things: I just find more things to like."

"People?"

"Well . . . I've never *dis*liked people. I know that's not enough, but it's all I've got to give."

"What foods do you like best?"

"Lamb chops, peas and fresh fruit in season."

"Not winter raspberries?"

"I really don't care."

"You use the word 'really' a good deal. Isn't that a bit of a cliché?"

"Do you think what I say would be truer if I left it out?"

"No, not really."

"You see?"

"No, not really."

59

They took a ride on the Reading. All the windows had been shot at or struck by stones (in most cases, the latter). There was neither heat nor food. The other passengers sat in stupefaction. As dark came, the lights flickered and went out. This made the patterns of shattering in the window glass clearer. It was nostalgic, riding a train. The conductors, who now and then announced an up-coming stop, had neither shame nor courtesy. Unless not hitting people or pushing and shoving them can be called courtesy. Perhaps it can.

The desolate landscape slid by, made cozy by small houses with lights on them. The lighted rooms were kitchens at this time of day, where someone was preparing the evening meal for one or more persons who soon would be coming home. A surprising number of uncultivated fields sported dead automobiles and in a small woods a refrigerator lay rusting on its back, its door open to the elements. The wind rose and all sorts of trash went fluttering about, restless as birds feeding.

Speaking of feeding: they had brought a box lunch, which showed foresight. Tuna salad on white had never tasted better. Eventually the train reached its last stop. There, they rented a car for the trip back. Enough is as good as feast, and they had had the train story.

60

They cut each other's hair, but not each other's nails.

61

They were invited to a gathering—and what is more, they went. A maid in a uniform collected wraps and shuffled them onto hangers. A youth in a tarboosh sloshed potent liquors into tumblers and filled with the mixer of the victim's choice. It was not a large room, though an attractive one, and a hundred guests created what could justly be called a babel. Since they never reciprocated invitations, it was with reason, if without manners, that a portly figure in shades of canary said, "Well, and what are you *two* doing here?"

Easy to handle. One of them mouthed a reply, as though speaking a shade too softly, while the other firmly set down a brackish glass of rye and demanded club soda, with a twist. All about them discussion raged: the latest reading, the latest trattoria, the high cost of taxis, how to find an apartment, where to go in the winter and why not to go there, how to have fun, whether to step into the bedroom and join the heads. The quality of the lox was praised by all who partook of it.

The furor created a kind of silence through which, in magic manner, threaded a recording of the late Povla Frisjch—something of Grieg's which the artist caused to transcend itself. A vase of eucalyptus leaves was upset—the high point of the evening, just the slow slosh of water and the piercing voice of the lieder singer.

"It was not a beautiful voice," one was heard to say, "but she was tops."

A bit later, when a woman with foxy hair sought for our protagonists, she found them gone. They weren't much for parties. In fact, it was a miracle they were ever asked.

62

Then life—she is no lady and she sure is a button-lip—slipped them a Mickey.

They tripped.

They fell.

They crashed.

They went—or were sent—away. It took a long, long time, a very, very, very long time.

63

When they came out their therapists put their heads together and said they thought it wiser for them not to live together. So they rented lofts in the same building and opened an antique shop. They had never had friends so happily they did not have to drop any, on the grounds of bad influence. But frequenters of antique shops are a chatty crew, and they soon had a wide acquaintance—progressive bridge one night, and often a brunch on Sunday.

They went in in a small way for what used to be called good works. One of them gave up one night a week to recording light novels for the blind. The other escorted wayward boys who had attained a status of trust at the Home on visits to the zoo, and such.

As they will, the years passed, and as it will, mortality made good its claim. First the one, then the other. They were interred side by side, and from beneath the green green grass of home one might have heard, as in a dream, their voices speak as one: "Dear reader! How we love you! (I think)."

ANNE SEXTON

All God's Children Need Radios

Roses

Nov. 6, 1971

Thank you for the red roses. They were lovely. Listen, Skeezix, I know you didn't give them to me, but I like to pretend you did because, as you know, when you give me something my heart faints on the pillow. Well, someone gave them to me, some official, some bureaucrat, it seems, gave me these one dozen. They lived a day and a half, little cups of blood, twelve baby fists. Dead today in their vase. They are a cold people. I don't throw them out, I keep them as a memento of my first abortion. They smell like a Woolworth's, half between the candy counter and the 99-cent perfume. Sorry they're dead, but thanks anyhow. I wanted daisies. I never said, but I wanted daisies. I would have taken care of daisies, giving them an aspirin every hour and cutting their stems properly, but with roses I'm reckless. When they arrive in their long white box, they're already in the death house.

Trout

Same day

The trout (brook) are sitting in the green plastic garbage pail full of pond water. They are Dr. M's trout, from his stocked pond. They are doomed. If I don't hurry and get this down, we will have broken their necks (backs?) and fried them in the black skillet and eaten them with our silver forks and forgotten all about them. Doomed. There they are nose to nose, wiggling in their cell, awaiting their execution. I like trout, as you know, but that pail is too close and I keep peering into it. We

214

want them fresh, don't we? So be it. From the pond to the pail to the pan to the belly to the toilet. We'll have broccoli with hollandaise. Does broccoli have a soul? The trout soil themselves. Fishing is not humane or good for business.

Some Things Around My Desk

Same day

If you put your ear close to a book, you can hear it talking. A tin voice, very small, somewhat like a puppet, asexual. Yet all at once? Over my head JOHN BROWN'S BODY is dictating to EROTIC POETRY. And so forth. The postage scale sits like a pregnant secretary. I bought it thirteen years ago. It thinks a letter goes for 4 cents. So much for inflation, so much for secretaries. The calendar, upper left, is covered with psychiatrists. They are having a meeting on my November. Then there are some anonymous quotations scotch-taped up. *Poets and pigs are not appreciated until they are dead.* And: *The more I write, the more the silence seems to be eating away at me.* And here is Pushkin, not quite anonymous: *And reading my own life with loathing, I tremble and curse.* And: *Unhappiness is more beautiful when seen through a window than from within.* And so forth. Sweeney's telegram is also up there. *You are lucky,* he cables. Are you jealous? No, you are reading the Town Report, frequently you read something aloud and it almost mixes up my meditations. Now you're looking at the trout. Doomed. My mother's picture is on the right up above the desk. When that picture was taken, she too was doomed. You read aloud: *Forty-five dog bites in town.* Not us. Our dog bites frogs only. *Five runaways and five stubborn children.* Not us. Children stubborn but not reported. The phone, at my back and a little to the right, sits like a general (German) (SS). It holds the voices that I love as well as strangers, a platoon of beggars asking me to dress their wounds. The trout are getting peppier. My mother seems to be looking at them. Speaking of the phone, yesterday Sweeney called from Australia to wish me a happy birthday. (Wrong day. I'm November ninth.) I put my books on the line and they said, "Move along, Buster." And why not? All things made lovely are doomed. *Two cases of chancres,* you read.

Eat and Sleep

Nov. 7, 1971

Today I threw the roses out, and before they died the trout spawned. We ate them anyhow with a wine bottled in the year I was born (1928). The meal was good, but I preferred them alive. So much for gourmet cooking. Today the funeral meats, out to Webster (you call it Ethan Frome country) for a wake. *Eat* and *Sleep* signs. World War II steel helmets for sale. There was a church with a statue of a mother in front of it. You know, one of those mothers. The corpse clutched his rosary and his cheek bumped the Stars and Stripes. A big man, he was somebody's father. But what in hell was that red book? Was it a prayer book or a passport at his side? Passports are blue, but mine has a red case. I like to think it's his passport, a union card for the final crossing. On the drive back, fields of burst milkweed and the sun setting against hog-black winter clouds. It was a nice drive. We saw many *Eat* and *Sleep* signs. Last night the eater, today the sleeper.

Mother's Radio

Nov. 8, 1971

FM please and as few ads as possible. One beside my place in the kitchen where I sit in a doze in the winter sun, letting the warmth and music ooze through me. One at my bed too. I call them both: *Mother's Radio*. As she lay dying her radio played, it played her to sleep, it played for my vigil, and then one day the nurse said, "Here, take it." Mother was in her coma, never, never to say again, "This is the baby," referring to me at any age. Coma that kept her under water, her gills pumping, her brain numb. I took the radio, my vigil keeper, and played it for my waking, sleeping ever since. In memoriam. It goes everywhere with me like a dog on a leash. Took it to a love affair, peopling the bare rented room. We drank wine and ate cheese and let it play. No ads please. FM only. When I go to a mental hospital I have it in my hand. I sign myself in (voluntary commitment papers) accompanied by cigarettes and mother's radio. The hospital is suspicious of these things because they do not understand that I bring my mother with me, her cigarettes, her radio. Thus I am not alone. Generally speaking mental hospitals are lonely places, they are full of TV's and medications. I have found a station that plays the hit tunes of the nineteen-forties, and I dance in the kitchen, snapping my fingers. My daughters laugh and talk about bobbysocks. I will die with this radio playing—last sounds. My children will hold up my books and I will say good-bye to them. I wish I hadn't taken it when she was in a coma. Maybe she regained consciousness for a moment and looked for that familiar black box. Maybe the nurse left the room for a moment and there was my mama looking for her familiars. Maybe she could hear the nurse tell me to take it. I didn't know what I was doing. I'd never seen anyone die before. I wish I hadn't. Oh Mama, forgive. I keep it going; it never stops. They will say of me, "Describe her, please."

And you will answer, "She played the radio a lot." When I go out it plays—to keep the puppy company. It is fetal. It is her heartbeat—oh my black sound box, I love you! Mama, mama, play on!

Little Girl, Big Doll

Nov. 10, 1971

Out my window, a little girl walking down the street in a fat and fuzzy coat, carrying a big doll. Hugging it. The doll is almost as large as a basset hound. The doll with a pink dress and bare feet. Yesterday was my birthday and I excised it with bourbon. No one gave me a big doll. Yesterday I received one yellow wastebasket, two umbrellas, one navy pocketbook, two Pyrex dishes, one pill pot, one ornate and grotesque brown hamper. No doll. The man in the casket is gone. The birthday is gone, but the little girl skipped by under the wrinkled oak leaves and held fast to a replica of herself. I had a Dye-dee doll myself, a Cinderella doll with a crown made of diamonds and a Raggedy-Ann with orange hair and once on my sixth birthday a big doll, almost my size. Her eyes were brown and her name was Amanda and she did not welcome death. Death forgot her. (For the time being.)

Daddy Sugar

Nov. 15, 1971

O. called the night before my birthday, sticking his senile red tongue into the phone. Yet sentimental too, saying how it was forty-three years ago, that night when he paced the floor of my birth. I never heard of my father pacing the floor—a third child, he was bored. Isn't pacing limited to fathers? That's the point, isn't it! Maybe O. is my biological father, my daddy sugar and sperm. It ruined my birthday, to be claimed at forty-three by O. Just last Christmas, around the twentieth of December, he arrived out here with a secret package—my photo at sixteen (I never gave it to him. Mother must have given it to him!) and a lock of my baby hair. Why would Mother give a lock of baby hair to bachelor-family-friend-O.? He said, "I don't want to die with the evidence!" And then he drove off. Later, on the phone we promise to meet for lunch and have a confession hour. But I shy away. I am like Jocasta who begs Oedipus not to look further. I am a dog refusing poisoned meat. It would be poison he pumped into my mother. She who made me. But who with? I'm afraid of that lunch—I would throw up the vichyssoise if he said: "Happy birthday, Anne, I am your father."

Brown Leaves

Nov. 16, 1971

Out my window: some wonderful blue sky. Also I see brown leaves, wrinkled things, the color of my father's suitcases. All winter long these leaves will hang there—the light glinting off them as off a cow. At this moment I am drinking. At this moment I am very broke. I called my agent but she wasn't there, only the brown leaves are there. They whisper, "We are wiser than money; don't spend us." . . . And the two trees, my two telephone poles, simply wait. Wait for what? More words, dummy! Joy, who is as straight as a tree, is bent today like a spatula. I will take her to the orthopedic man. Speaking of suitcases, I think of my childhood and MUTNICK FOREVER. Christmases, every single year, my father tearing off the red wrapping and finding a Mark Cross two-suiter, calf, calf the color of the oak leaves—and thinking of the wool supplier, Mr. Mutnick, who gave him this yearly goodie—he'd cry, "MUTNICK FOREVER." That sound, those two words meant suitcases, light tan, the color of dog shit but as soft as a baby's cheek and smelling of leather and horse.

Breathing Toys

Nov. 18, 1971

The gentle wind, the kind gentle wind, goes in and out of me. But not too well. Walking a block—just say from Beacon to Commonwealth—or over at B.U., I lean against the building for wind, gasping like a snorkel, the crazy seizure of the heart, the error of the lungs. Dr. M. wants me to go into his hospital for tests, come January. He's a strange one, aside from his stocked trout pool he keeps saying, "I want to save a life!" The life being mine. Last time we met he said, "You'll be an old hag in three years!" What does he mean? A yellow woman with wax teeth and charcoal ringlets at her neck? Or does he only mean the breathing—the air is hiding, the air will not do! An old hag, her breasts shrunken to the size of pearls? My lungs, those little animals, contracting, drowning in their shell. . . . Joy is still down. Meals float up to her. (I am the cork.) She lies on her mattress with a board under it and asks, "Why me?" Her little toes wriggling on the roof, her head lolling over the TV, her back washing like sand at low tide. As I've said elsewhere: the body is meat. Joy, will you and I outlive our doctors or will we oblige, sinking downward as they turn off the flame? As for me, it's the cigarettes, of course. I can't give them up any more than I can give up Mother's radio. I didn't always smoke. Once I was a baby. Back then only Mother smoked. It hurts,

Mama, it hurts to suck on the moon through the bars. Mama, smoke curls out of your lips and you sing me a lullaby. Mama, mama, you hurt too much, you make no sense, you give me a breathing toy from World War II and now you take it away. Which war is this, Mama, with the guns smoking and you making no sense with cigarettes?

Dog

Nov. 19, 1971

"O Lord," they said last night on TV, "the sea is so mighty and my dog is so small." I *heard* dog. You say, they said *boat* not *dog* and that further *dog* would have no meaning. But it does mean. The sea is mother-death and she is a mighty female, the one who wins, the one who sucks us all up. *Dog* stands for me and the new puppy, Daisy. I wouldn't have kept her if we hadn't named her Daisy. (You brought me daisies yesterday, not roses, daisies. A proper flower. It outlives any other in its little vessel of water. You must have given them to me! If you didn't give them to me, who did?) Me and my dog, my Dalmatian dog, against the world. "My dog is so small" means that even the two of us will be stamped under. Further, dog is what's in the sky on winter mornings. Sun-dogs springing back and forth across the sky. But we dogs are small and the sun will burn us down and the sea has our number. Oh Lord, the sea is so mighty and my dog is so small, my dog whom I sail with into the west. The sea is mother, larger than Asia, both lowering their large breasts onto the coastline. Thus we ride on her praying for good moods and a smile in the heavens. She is mighty, oh Lord, but I with my little puppy, Daisy, remain a child.
Too complicated, eh?
Just a thought in passing, just something about a lady and her dog, setting forth as they do, on a new life.

Thanksgiving in Fat City

Nov. 25, 1971

The turkey glows. It has been electrified. The legs huddle, they are bears. The breasts sit, dying out, and the gizzard waits like a wart. Everyone eats, hook and sinker, they eat. They eat like a lady and a bear. They eat like a drowning dog. The house sits like the turkey. The chimney gasps for breath and the large, large rock on the front lawn is waiting for us to move into it. It is a large mouth. Autograph seekers attend it. They mail it letters, postage due. They raise their skirts and tease it. . . . It is a camera, it records the mailman, it records the gasman, it records the needy students, it records the lovers, serious as grandmothers, it records the sun and the poisonous gases, it records the eaters, the turkey, the drowned dog, the autograph seekers, the whole Hollywood trip. Meanwhile I sit inside like a crab at my desk, typing pebbles into a boat.

A Life of Things

Dec. 2, 1971

They live a life of things, Williams said. This house is stuffed like a pepper with things: the painted eyes of my mother crack in the attic, the blue dress I went mad in is carved on the cameo. Time is passing, say the shoes. Afrika boots saying their numbers, wedding slippers raining on the attic floor. The radiator swallows, digesting its gall stones. The sink opens its mouth like a watermelon. Hadn't I better move out, dragging behind me the bare essentials: a few pills, a few books, and a blanket for sleeping? When I die, who will put it all away? Who will index the letters, the books, the names, the expendable jewels of a life? Things sweat in my palm as I put them each carefully into my mouth and swallow. Each one a baby. Let me give the jar of honey, the pickles, the salt box to my birthday. Let me give the desk and its elephant to the postman. Let me give the giant bed to the willow so that she may haunt it. Let me give the hat, the Italian-made Safari hat, to my dog so that she may chew off her puppyhood. Finally let me give the house itself to Mary-who-comes. Mary-who-comes has scoured the floors of my childhood and the floors of my motherhood. She of the dogs, the army of dogs, old English Sheep dogs (best of show), fifteen altogether, their eyes shy and hidden by hair, their bodies curled up wool. Mary-who-comes may have my house: the Lenox for her dogs to lap, the kitchen for breeding, the writing room for combing and currying. Mary will have a temple, a dog temple, and I will have divorced my things and gone on to other strangers.

Found Topaz

Dec. 10, 1971

The sherry in its glass on the kitchen table, reflecting the winter sun, is a liquid topaz. It makes a tinkerbelle light on the wall. Sea light, terror light, laugh light. . . . There is less and less sherry, a cocktail sherry, very light, very good. It keeps me company. I am swallowing jewels, light by light. To celebrate this moment (it is like being in love) I am having a cigarette. Fire in the mouth. Topaz in the stomach.

Oatmeal Spoons

Same day

I am still in the kitchen, feeling the heat of the sun through the storm window, letting Mother's radio play its little tunes. Dr. Brundig is away, a week now, and I'm okay, I'm sanforized, above ground, full of anonymous language, a sherry destiny, grinning, proud as a kid with a new drawing. I'm flying invisible balloons from my mailbox and I'd like to give a party and ask my past in. And you—I tell you how great I feel and you look doubtful, a sour look as if you were sucking the ocean out of an olive. You figure, she's spent fifteen years attending classes with Dr. Brundig and her cohorts, majoring in dependence. Dr. M. (trout man, lung man) asked me, "What is your major problem? Surely you know after fifteen years?"
"Dunno."
"Well," he said, "Did you fall in love with your oatmeal spoon?"
"There was no oatmeal spoon."
He caught on.

Angels Wooly Angels

Jan. 1, 1972, 12:30 A.M.

I feel mild. Mild and kind. I am quite alone this New Year's Eve for you are sick: having fallen in love with the toilet, you went on an opium voyage and fell asleep before the New Year. I heard it all down here in the kitchen on Mother's radio—Times Square and all that folly. I am drinking champagne and burping up my childhood: champagne on Christmas Day with my father planting corks in the ceiling and the aunts and uncles clapping, Mother's diamonds making mirrors of the candlelight, the grandmothers laughing like stuffed pillows and the love that was endless for one day. We held hands and danced around the tree singing our own tribal song. (Written in the eighteen hundreds by a great, great uncle.) We were happy, happy, happy. Daddy crying his MUTNICK FOREVER and the big doll, Amanda, that I got. . . . All dead now. The doll lies in her grave, a horse fetus, her china blue eyes as white as eggs. Now I am the wife. I am the mother. You are the uncles, the grandmothers. We are the Christmas. Something gets passed on—a certain zest for the tribe, along with the champagne, the cold lobster hors d'oeuvres, the song. Mother, I love you and it doesn't matter about O. It doesn't matter who my father was; it matters who I *remember* he was. There was a queen. There was a king. There were three princesses. That's the whole story. I swear it on my wallet. I swear it on my radio.

See, Mother, there are angels flying over my house tonight. They wear American Legion hats but the rest of them is wool, wool, that white fluffy stuff Daddy used to manufacture into goods, wool, fat fleecy wool. They zing over the telephone wires, their furry wings going *Hush, hush*. Like a mother comforting a child.

JON SWAN

The Invisible Nation

We could choose whether we wanted the walls painted bright yellow or sky blue. I wanted it bright in there so it would look like the sun was shining even when it wasn't. There were only three votes for bright yellow. The rest of the class was for sky blue. That was the same day they said there was a new principal. We were glad to hear there was a new principal, but they shouldn't have asked us about what color we wanted the walls if they knew they weren't going to paint them. Instead, they said the money would go into buying playground equipment, something every child could use and enjoy, and an outdoor drinking fountain since we didn't have one. The walls in our room are yellow, but not bright yellow. They're closer to brown. The ceiling is full of long cracks. Flakes fall when there's a fire drill or when the whole school has to get down on the floor under their desks. When the drill's over you'd think it had snowed and the snow had got dirty on the way down.

I wish that instead of getting a new jungle gym and a fountain they had got a new art teacher. I can't draw very well, but I love drawing horses, so sometimes I put a horse in a house looking out a window. She says that I'm old enough to know better, and what I don't say is that if I'm old enough to know better maybe I do. People don't know what to do at home. They're always telling you to be quiet or to pick up, or watching TV, but horses would have fun in a house. If they got bored they could kick down the walls and in one jump be out in the country. So now I put people in my houses, but she doesn't like them very much either. She says they look ugly. What I don't say is that my people are her.

We got in the bus today and there was a new driver. He didn't know where to let us off and we didn't tell him either, so we drove for hours and hours, up the long hill and around all the back roads. He kept

asking if we lived here or there, and we all just shook our heads and
went on singing, and by then it was night and his lights didn't work. So
he got out, and said he was going to walk to the nearest house and phone.
Then he shut the door from the outside, and locked it so we couldn't get
out, and walked off. As soon as he was gone we opened the windows and
climbed out. We played hide and seek until we couldn't see each other
anymore. We were way out in the country where nobody had ever been
before. We turned the bus into a house. We hunted, and the girls cooked.
We spent the whole day out hunting. When we came back our clothes
were all torn, so the girls made us clothes out of deerskins. I was the only
one who knew how to make a fire. I wasn't the chief though. When I said
I knew how to make a fire, I said I would make it on one condition, that
we would never have a chief, or if we did, then just for a day. A chief
doesn't have to listen to anybody if he doesn't want to, I said, and that's
why people want to be chief. When our old principal used to talk to me
he never listened to a word I said, or else he would tell me what I meant
when I said something, and he was always wrong. That wasn't what I
meant, but you can't talk to people when you know they've got a ruler in
the top drawer. Even if he doesn't even take it out you get so scared you
say the wrong thing every time. Which is why I didn't want us to have
any chief. When I explained this everybody agreed. I gave my speech at
night, around our campfire. We didn't stand up when we spoke. Sometimes you couldn't tell where the voice was coming from. I used to wish
the fire would speak. It did once, all about colors and how they felt and
where flames are trying to go when they fly up, and that fire was our
friend, our best friend on earth together with water, and that most
people didn't know this until the minute they died, when they turned
into fire and water and dirt. We all sat around the fire, listening to the
fire telling its story, and now maybe you wonder if any of this is true,
and it isn't. I was just telling a story too, about the day our bus got lost.
It never got lost. We always get let out at the right place, and when a bus
stops all the cars behind it have to stop too.

When I asked the teacher what indivisible meant, she said it was
something you couldn't divide. Then she said it meant one, but what I
didn't say was you can divide one too, and that she had taught us how
herself. I used to think it meant invisible, like God, which comes right
after that, and that we lived in an invisible nation under Him. My
mother says you can see God when you're dead though. When she turned
out the light I thought it would be funny if He couldn't see us when
we're alive either. I would like to be invisible sometimes, even if only to
God. In geography class, when the teacher starts talking about some
faraway place like India, sometimes I shut my eyes, and feel myself

getting smaller and smaller until I'm not in the room anymore but over in some city she's talking about, and as long as I keep my eyes shut and can see the shops and the people and the holy monkeys and the people lying in the streets, I feel I'm invisible to everybody in class because I'm not there. As soon as she starts talking about crops and climate though, there I am right back in that crummy room. Instead of buying us a new jungle gym they should let us all go over to India. We would learn more that way. I would keep my eyes wide open! Yesterday I shut my eyes too long and fell asleep. I guess the bell rang before the teacher noticed because nobody called my name or pulled my hair. When I opened my eyes the walls looked red. Everybody looked red, including our teacher.

Three of us have races around the building sometimes. One stands by the back door and one runs around the building one way and the other the other way. You're really only supposed to play out on the playground behind the school, but that only makes us run faster so nobody will see us. A ramp goes up each side, and there aren't many windows on the sides, so you don't need to worry too much about anybody seeing you there. It's around the front where you really have to run. There are lots of windows and only a few bushes and then the front stairs. You can usually tell who's going to win by where you meet in front. If you've already passed the stairs and he's only made it to the flagpole, you can be pretty sure you're going to win. But you can't slow down because anything can happen. The janitor can come out the side door, or one of the teachers may be standing out there, like the one who was crying once when I ran past. Then you have to slow down and pretend you're looking for something. Like you lost your lunch money or a milk ticket or something. But nobody came out, and I was running hard, and when I came around the back I knocked a girl over and she fell down and started crying. Some teachers came running over, including our gym instructor, who looked at the girl and then started shaking my shoulders and asking me questions. I didn't even know the girl's name. One of the teachers led her away. The gym instructor walked away too, but the bigger boys, who'd been throwing a football with him, stayed behind. They put their arms around my shoulders like we were all pals and led me over to the drinking fountain. They said, how could I do such a thing? I said I didn't mean to and that I didn't even know the girl's name. Then they made a circle around me so nobody could see, and then three of them picked me up and laid me down with my back against the sharp point in the middle of the drinking fountain. Then the one who was holding my arms pushed down and the other two pulled my legs down. It felt like the point was digging a hole right into my backbone. They said if I yelled they'd do it even harder. But finally I couldn't help it. I screamed.

They all started laughing very loud as if it was all a joke and let me down and walked away. My back hurt. I tried not to cry. My shirt was all wet in back and so were my pants, but when I touched myself my hand wasn't red. It was only water. Actually, this didn't happen to me at recess. They did it to me one night when my father and I went to a basketball game. They caught me out in the hall on my way back from the boy's room. They chased me all the way down the hall and out into the playground, and that's when they did it. But I could never figure out why, because they all went to high school and I'd never seen them before, and maybe if I hadn't started running they never would have chased me and hurt my back like that. When I tell the story I make it happen right after I knocked that girl down, because then it makes sense.

After that, I started picking worms up off the driveway after a rain. I throw them back onto the grass. I know they don't have backbones and that you can even cut them up and parts of them will live, but they look helpless lying there on the asphalt or on the sidewalks downtown, and it only takes a second to bend over and pick them up and toss them back onto the grass. I thought my father would laugh at me but he didn't. He says they help air out the earth, which needs to breathe too, and that when they die they make the earth richer. I'd never thought of the earth breathing. It must be asleep. I like to think of it dreaming about those cities I go to when I shut my eyes in geography. Except, where would they be if it ever woke up? In spring, all the country roads break up. They call what happens frost heaves. Some are so deep the driver has to stop and shift to get across, but when he's in a hurry and goes over fast, we all bounce until our heads practically bang against the top. You can tell something's alive down there. If it can break an asphalt road apart when it's sound asleep, think of what it could do if it ever woke up! I wish it would. We have the news on when we eat at six.

Riddle: What has three feet and can't walk?

(A yardstick.)

Riddle: What light has three lights and only one works at a time?

(A traffic light.)

Riddle: If you were in a cave and a big boulder that was too heavy for you to move fell over the only way out, how would you get out?

(Be a big bore and get out that way.)

I read the first one in a book. My friend made up the second one. And I made up the last one in class when I was staring up at the ceiling. With all those cracks it looked like a cave that could cave in any minute.

Sometimes, when a jet goes over low enough, like they did on makeup day, big chunks fall out. We were all out on the playground when they went over. It was on a Saturday. We were making up for all those days we lost because of the snow that was so deep the regular snowplows couldn't handle it and they had to use bulldozers. My father and I were walking down the road to pick up some eggs and milk at a neighbor's farm when suddenly we heard a tremendous noise, but we couldn't see where it was coming from. Then we saw a whole mountain of snow coming at us down just below the curve. You couldn't see the bulldozer. All you could see was this big wall of snow moving along very slowly. We had been snowed in for five days. When the bulldozer got close we had to get way off to the side, practically in the woods. We saw a hole in the snow. My father said rabbits lived in there in a little cave they dig and that this was only one tunnel. Then the bulldozer went by and it was easy to walk and when we came back with the milk and eggs the whole road up to our driveway was plowed out. My father said, well that's the end of that road! The bulldozer had scraped up rocks and cut some right in two. Some of the banks, on the sides, were ten feet tall. I made lots of angels. My father wrote words in the snow with a stick. He said that when the snow melted the words would sink into the ground, or run off to the sea, or go up into the clouds, since we were made out of dirt and water and air, and so were our words, but our best words turn into fire. Sometimes I start a story like that and he goes on with it, or he starts one and I go on with it, but on the way down he didn't want to talk. He said snow made him want to be quiet. It was when we heard the bulldozer that he started talking, and we made up those stories about what the rabbits would do if they couldn't get out and about angels and words.

Anyway, on that makeup day we were all out on the playground when three jets came over. I've never heard anything like it. The bulldozer wasn't half as loud. They came over so low it looked like they were going to hit the trees and crash in the playground. I was swinging. It looked like my feet were going to hit the bottom of the middle jet. I got off the swing fast. You saw them right overhead, and then the noise came. They came over three times. Everybody looked scared. I thought it was pretty dumb of the teachers to just stand there. You're supposed to run for shelter, or lie flat on the ground, or hide behind something like they do on TV. We all talked about it back in class. My teacher said there was no reason to hide or take shelter because they were our own airplanes and were just practicing. I said we should have practiced too. Practiced what? she said. Practiced hiding. She said there was no reason for that, that there was no reason to be frightened except for the noise, and that anyway, they hadn't meant to scare us. They probably hadn't even seen us they were going so fast. Then she told us to put our heads down on our desks and rest for three minutes, and she put on a record, and we all rested. When I woke up I looked at the flakes on my desk, and this time when I opened my eyes the flakes looked white as snow, and the walls looked white, and my teacher's face was white as chalk, and I thought, I told her we should have hidden, because now we were all dead.

MAY SWENSON

Mutterings of a Middlewoman

It fascinated and horrified me at the same time. Well, actually, the fascination came first. Because had it been repulsive rather than attractive (in appearance, I mean, and when quiet) I would have left it alone, I would have gone away.

I had taken off its hood and was sitting in front of it, touching various levers and keys, trying to find the one that turned it on, when Sandra came in. She was the other girl in the office; I was the new girl. Mr. Cobb was in his office dictating onto his Talk-a-Belt already. He had been there when I arrived (10 minutes before 9, because I hadn't known how long it would take to get to my new job from home). Mr. Robert L. Roberts, the head of the firm, hadn't come in yet.

This place is in mid-town on 5th Avenue, in that building with the square archway that looks like it's made of big gold ingots. It's only brass, of course, but very swank. From across the street it looks like the entrance to a giant safe, people instead of money rolling in and out. Or closer to it would be to say, a beehive, with workers and drones trooping through it, and a queen bee once in a while, in mink, getting out of a cab and dreamily tottering over its threshold. The worker bees are mostly male and the drones female. That is, the former go and come as they please, in their process of gathering honey (money) to be fed to the queen, while the latter stay in the hive (safe) from 9 to 5, to take care of things and make the wax. Coincidentally, this *was* a wax products firm I was employed in: The Robert L. Roberts Company, Paraffin, Ceresin & Micro-Crystalline Waxes.

Now where were we? Oh, yes, at the point where Sandra comes in. But let's not have her come in just yet. Because I want to explain how I felt about IT—the personal, subjective relationship there seemed to be between me and it—even while it stood humped there silent, cool and asleep. I turned on the blue cathode light over it. It was huge, rugged, squarish but with rounded edges, of light-gray pebbled steel with chrome trim. Cleanly molded, sturdy, smug-looking. It had all kinds of attachments beside the 4-deck keyboard: buttons, triggers and various-shaped switches marked with abbreviated names.

There I sat on the specially made stool affixed to it (like a jockey's saddle? a pilot's cockpit?). Anyhow, a seat of importance and adventure. Its name was inscribed on it: The Atom-atic Typer.

Only a typewriter. All right. That's its function. But think of a peasant's plow (a wooden handle, a single blade) as against a Bulldozer tractor with all its appendages: cultivator, mower, thresher, baler, loader. See now what I mean about a *difference*? And it was handsome! Nice to look at, and to touch. It thrilled my fingers wandering over it while it was still cool and unconscious. Like sometimes you come to a big smooth rock in the woods that's so solid, calm and confident-feeling. So dependable and simple-looking. But what's going on inside, if you could be aware of its atoms whirling? Remember, everything in the universe is in motion, in rotation; nothing is static; *nothing ever stops*. It's an awful thought, in a way, but there's a necessity for it, I guess. You may as well assume that the way things are is the way they should be.

O.K., so here was this machine, a rock, or the opposite of a rock, in the woods of commerce, and I was to run it. I only had to find out how to turn it on, to see what it would do, what it would make. I adjusted the little microphone in my ear, I put my feet on the pedals, and my fingers on the keys. I was all ready, when Sandra came in. And she immediately showed me that the switch was hidden under the right hand edge of the Atom-atic. I touched it, and the little window there flashed the word, ON, in red. There was a low humming.

Now, don't be mad if, in this story, nothing happens really. Nothing terrible, nothing exciting. I know it might sound as if, the way I've told it up to now, we're going to another world, me and this strange contraption. Or that I'm trying to say it's a symbol for something psychologically wacked-up about our metropolitan way of life, the industrial age, or the gadgeteering craze, or what-not. I don't mean anything like that. What happened was just what happened inside of me, I recognize that, and nobody even knew about it but me. The place didn't blow up or anything; I didn't disappear, didn't discover a new dimension.

It's just that I'm a typist, and a good, accurate, fast one. Now, ordinarily, when you hit a key it prints a letter, and the speed with which the letters appear on the page depends on how often your fingers hit the keys; each letter appears *after* you hit its corresponding key, and the carriage shifts when and/or *if* your hand rises to the jigger, there, and pushes it. In short, your hands control the machine. On the Atom-atic, however, my fingers were barely posed above the keys, getting *ready* to touch them, when they began to type, at unbelievable speed. Those keys made my fingers fly at their pace, and I had to keep up with them; they jolted my fingers into action, instead of the other way around. And when we got to the end of a line (which took a fraction of a second) my left pinky finger was nudged, lightly as a breath, by a shift key that tossed the carriage to the beginning of the next line. Hickety-dickety-ho—a line; hickety-dickety-ha—another line. As swift as that.

Effortless. Nice. Maybe I should only give into it, go along with it? But the darn thing didn't care what it typed, whether it matched with the words coming through the microphone in my ear or not. Those were Mr. Robert L. Roberts' words, and he expected them to appear on his desk, in neat block-form on his very white water-marked bond, 6 onion skin copies to each original, plus the Yellow file sheet, each letter (with copies) attached with paper clip to addressed envelope, and another clip attaching this to the file folder containing previous correspondence to the addressee, with a typed slip noting the cross-reference files, as well as any file changes he might dictate in connection with adding or removing wax product prospects to, or from, the various files, according to the incoming correspondence as it indicated what particular lines of wax and wax products they might be in the market for; also, if in the course of dictating a letter, he thought of points of discussion to be taken up with these prospects at lunch or at a sales conference, these were to be typed on small sheets of Pink paper and appended to the correct file; and incidentally, would I remember to water the plants in the reception room the minute I came in each morning: "Ask Sandra for a key to the office in case you're the first one in In fact it would be a good idea to try to *be* the first one in The cactus plant not to get *too* much water Don't flood it The begonia to get a full glassful And while I think of it ask Sandra to explain to you how each night before closing up everything goes underground That is nothing left on tops of desks Everything in drawers The machine covered and be sure to turn it *off* as we can't have the generator running all night and please wipe off your desk with a piece of Kleenex so it looks shipshape for next morning and no butts left in ashtrays please Put these instructions on a Blue slip and initial it please and pass it to me and I'll initial it and pass it back to you for your own personal file to be kept in your lower left hand drawer then we'll understand each other O.K.? From time to time I'll give you further

instructions to add to your personal file Now back to letter to Zigoni of
Dappletan Wax in Rochester It says: Further to our letter of April 28
This is the second paragraph Oh by the way this should go on the
Specialty stationery for the original instead of the All-Purpose stationery
I said at the beginning of the belt Ask Sandra to explain when we use
one and when the other so you won't waste paper or time doing let-
ters over O.K.? All set now? Paragraph Further to our letter of April
28. . . ."

The Atom-atic wasn't recognizably typing any of this, although we
were already near the bottom of the page, my fingers still going lickety-
heck. Well, here, and there, you could make something out, like "our
lettttr of Aprl 2888/" and "We ould deee plyap pppreciate/y our frwdg
us alistof y ourr equi rements/" The thing to do was to back-track to the
beginning of the belt, start all over, on Specialty stationery this time,
and take it slow and careful. If possible.

Also, I had already learned that the placing of the alphabet, the
numerals, punctuation marks and other signs on the Atom-atic, weren't
in all cases the same as on an ordinary typewriter, and that the back-
spacer was where I was accustomed to finding the tabulator key. Or was
it that my fingers were put on wrong? It did seem as though it would feel
more familiar if I crossed my hands, as when, occasionally, you'll see a
pianist playing the bass with the right hand, while the left runs into the
treble. The troubling thing was that I couldn't, for the moment, lift my
hands to try this. The machine went on, and my fingers dithered up and
down with the keys, receiving their impulses, which felt like little electric
pricks and ticklings. Not unpleasant, except for the compulsion to accelerate the speed. I did wish I could remove the little finger of my right
hand, which seemed perversely lazy and tried to sit down on the ?and/
key, so that the slant bar got printed at the ends of some of the words. I
curled it up like a bird's claw in flight, but this made my other little
finger curl too, and then all the a's dis ppe red from the copy.

I was trying to imagine I was holding a teacup in my right hand, so as
to cause my pinky finger to crimp (which ought to work, as I rarely hold
a teacup in my left hand; it would be on the same principle as thinking
of squeezing lemons makes your mouth water) when Mr. Robert L. Roberts came in.

In a way I was glad I was going great guns; I certainly looked busy.
He and Sandra exchanged breezy greetings, and he said to me:

"Well, Gal, how's it going?"

Sandra saw my embarrassment at not being able to stop to say Goodmorning, and she reached around from her desk and turned off the
machine. My hands plonked down, dead as dropped marionettes, on the
keyboard. That mesmeric humming was gone. It should have been a

relief, but it wasn't. I felt acutely uncomfortable with my hands still, and my spine settling down onto the stool, and having to turn my neck from its forward-march position to look up at Mr. Roberts.

I did say, "Fine, thanks," and managed a grin, but I felt it freeze on my face and stay there, even after he'd swished around into his office and closed the door. The buzzer on Sandra's desk sounded, and *she* went into his office and closed the door.

Naturally I pulled the 8 atrocious sheets out of the machine, tore them across and slid them into the wastebasket under the desk. Sandra popped back out.

"Mr. Roberts wants all correspondence on the first belt on his desk by 10, and in the meantime wants me to show you how we handle the phones so you can take his and Mr. Cobb's calls whenever I'm out. Now, these little buttons here are the connections with the two offices. This one's for holding the call while you announce who's calling. For that you switch to the Local button, see? And the buzzer which is a slightly different tone from the phone (please don't get it mixed up with the phone because I did when I first came and he got very annoyed) well, when it rings *once* you go in, and when *twice*, it means he wants to talk to you on his connection, and if it rings 2 times and then a little pause and then a third ring, that means Mr. Cobb wants you in his room to pick up a belt. Always do Mr. R.'s dictation first, no matter how Mr. C. stomps around. But they both like all their mail out by 5, nothing hanging over for the next day. Sometimes when it's a heavy day, rather than ask you to put on more speed, Mr. R. will let you stay late to finish up (he can be very sweet that way) but he'd rather we all leave when he does. Now, the way he works is, he always does tomorrow's belts today, so there'll be some for you to start on when you come in in the morning. In case he gets in late. Sometimes you'll get stuff on the belt about doing shopping for his wife on your lunch hour. Now, on that, you can pass it on to me because I love to shop, and I'll do it when I go out for coffee, and you can take care of the phone. If Mr. R. ever asks where I am, and it's not my lunch hour, tell him you couldn't find whatever it is his wife wants at Altman's or wherever he said, and that I offered to go to Bloomingdale's for it. It'll be too much for you to have to take care of the shopping with everything else you'll have to do. OK.?"

I hate to shop, so I said, "Thank you." Then the phone rang.

"You take that," Sandra suggested. "Let's see how you make out."

I'm not going to go into that. My fumbles on the phone would make any receptionist reading this brand me a nitwit. It wasn't a switchboard, only a dinky little inter-com system. Nothing unpredictable about it like the Atom-atic. But I'm just a typist. A good typist. I've never been a receptionist.

I felt my main relationship was with that machine: my job was to run it, or learn how to give in to it—it felt like *that* was the secret. So we could turn out perfect and immediate letters together. Plus, of course, all those other incidentals: notes, agendas, file changes, reminders and things on the colored sheets. I hate to have things sloppy myself, and I admired Mr. Roberts' organization of all the innumerable details a head of a business (and a home) must have on his mind.

So when I made errors on distinguishing the sounds of the buzzers and bells, and rushed into his office when the phone rang, or picked up the receiver (first I had to rip the microphone off my ear and unhitch myself from the seat and lunge over to Sandra's desk) to say "Robert L. Roberts Company Wax Wax Wax Goodmorning" when it was only Mr. Cobb buzzing to have me pick up a new belt; or forgot that Mr. R. was *never* in to Mr. Claridge, so that when that gentleman appeared at the reception window I opened Mr. R.'s door and, professionally for once, showed him right in, I didn't let the consequences disturb me greatly. Except to tell myself that it was pretty decent of Mr. R. to keep giving me one chance after another to do it right the next time, considering the number of errors I made in one morning.

Truth is, it was only my mistakes on the Atom-atic that cut deeply with me. I like to be precise in my typing, and I generally am, on an old-fashioned standard machine.

But, by lunch time—I could hardly believe it—I'd made tremendous progress. It was a matter of keeping your fingers just the right smidgin of an inch *above* the keys (like playing the Theremin, probably) and sensing with your fingertips how to respond to the electrical pulsations. You free your hands from the current by whipping them up and off. Hard to do, because that machine, while on and humming, sounded so ambitious, as if it wanted to, *had* to, be making something. Its energy and eagerness were contagious.

I used all my will power, however, and my performance did improve. Sandra showed me the newest method of erasing. You use a piece of chalk over the rubber erasure to whiten the spot. But then you have to induce the keys to strike your fingers *hard* to make the impression match the rest of the copy in blackness, and with several carbon copies to be erased too, that slows you up, so the best is to concentrate on no errors. Lifting a finger a little higher above the key makes it strike harder, but if you lift it too high, it stabs a hole through all the copies. Now, there *is* a way to correct that, even. Mr. R. invented it himself (showing how close he is to the grass roots of his business)—then, too, of course, he hates to have his paper wasted. You use a little dispenser of RLR Liquid-Quick-Adhesive-Paper-Patching-Wax. But this is a heck of a chore requiring an absolutely steady hand and lots of practice.

I didn't get time to catch on to that. I could have, though, if the

Buried, the Unforeseen, the Incalculable hadn't cropped up. Because I'm a very determined person.

I guess I should have described Mr. Roberts and Sandra before now. Mr. Cobb wouldn't matter. He's just a husky sort of voice on the Talk-a-Belt—slow, uncertain, rather easy-going. Kind of a blimp. Can't imagine him "stomping around," as Sandra put it. Now Mr. R. is a different proposition. I'd like to call him the newest model in executives: unlimited power and drive, engineered for action, free-wheeling. He has an eel-smooth voice, rich, vibrant, that *glides*, never gallops; a voice that has all these superb features, plus the ability totalkfastersaymoregetmorestuff onaTalk-a-Beltinlesstimethanyou'dthinkhumanlypossible. I describe him chiefly in terms of voice because that's how I knew him best, in our brief but intimate association. You do feel close to a person whose actual words, hot off the tongue and onto that red strip of plastic, come directly into your ears, with all their cunning nuances such as sneezes, snorts, cigar-suckings, chuckles, or parenthetical exclamations like "Oh H——" or "Shoot" or "Forget that letter, that s.o.b.'s in Bermuda chasing a piece."

As to what he's like in *person*, well, when I'd go into his office, answering his ring, I'd be so confused, usually, that there was a sort of haze in front of me, and all I saw, behind a long, flossy mahogany desk, was a head squeezing a phone receiver against a shoulder, and a cigar oscillating at the corner of a mouth. Sometimes, though, when he'd jet out of his office to squat down at the file cabinet beside my machine, I'd get a closer look. He has a strato-power chassis, with great road-hugging stability, a slab-sided fender line, and a bold front snorkel. But his clothes, I'd say, really type him as a sports convertible.

The few seconds he'd be parked there on a level with my knees, riffling through a file, I'd make a slew of mistakes and have to do a lot of scrubbing with the eraser and chalk. I'm sure I was only projecting, but it *felt* like he was looking at my calves, down there only 3 inches or so from his face; and I know it's crazy, but the idea came into my head he might bite me. I guess it was just that he was in a position to, and *could* have. Being more objective, it was probably that the Atom-atic tended to act up whenever Mr. R. was in its vicinity. As if it got an extra charge out of him. Or maybe it resented him as a competitor, which would be only natural. Or their respective electronic wave lengths were incompatible. I don't know much about these mysteries. Shouldn't be expected to. I'm only a typist.

About Sandra. She was all *right*. A real little crackerjack, Mr. R. called her, and so do I. She looked like a Receptionist. Everybody knows what that is. Like if someone says "chair" it isn't necessary for them to add "a seat, a back and 4 legs," although they might want to be specific and say "lounging chair." And carrying it further, in Sandra's case, they might say a Floating-Comfort Lounging Chair. With a long, blond, page-boy bob.

By 12:15, I felt like an old member of the firm already. Sandra gave me the kind nod to turn off the Atom-atic, it was time for lunch. I got up and took the key to go to the Ladies Room. Couldn't understand why I felt so bushed. My feet would hardly move along the corridor, which seemed to be tilting uphill. An optical illusion absolutely, because when I came back to check in the key and get my coat, it tilted uphill *again*, running the opposite way. It was too bad I had to walk so slowly, since I had only 30 minutes and really needed to sprint to get to the cafeteria, eat, and get back by 1.

I was the only one getting into the elevator from my floor, the 45th, next to the top, and the boy must have recognized me because he gave me a nice smile. It made me feel as if I belonged. To be friendly in return, I asked him if he liked his job. I was scrunched up in a corner of the car holding onto both handrails, swallowing quickly with my eyes closed, as we plunged.

"It has its up and downs," he said, and I thought that was cute.

"I've never been in one that goes sideways," I said, trying to be clever too.

But it was no joke. The elevator was scudding along horizontally, simultaneously with dropping vertically, according to my stomach. In a few floors, though, it accumulated enough people to keep me bolstered upright; and going through the lobby and along the street for 3 down-town blocks, around the corner East to the nearest cafeteria, the crowd was so solid that, fortunately, I couldn't fall down. With the lunch time mob shoulder-to-shoulder moving at a lope, half one way and half the other, I felt like that little knob in the middle of a roulette wheel, smothered among clumps of chips all whizzing past me counter-clock-wise.

I looked up at the sky, and that helped. It was astonishingly empty, and as flannel-soft and blue as a new-born baby boy's blanket. Jabbing up into it, way above the other buildings that made a V-shaped wedge of the avenue (like the configuration on a business graph or fever chart) was the Empire State. That example of sovereign and enduring priapism that symbolizes, for me at least, the superior vigor and stamina of this, our fair city, the greatest on earth. A volt of vicarious pride, mixed with humility, suffused me. As if that great hypodermic tower had injected a shot of No-Doze into my blood. And I was able to straighten up, adjust my shoulder bag resolutely, and wriggle through traffic like a scroll-saw through soft pine.

I crammed myself into the revolving doors of the cafeteria, collected a tray and hardware at the counter, snarled my order (Swiss cheese on rye, butter, lettuce *and* pickle), slid the tray down the nickel rods, and accepted a half-full cup of coffee in a brim-full saucer, instantly poured and handed to me by a girl who could see by my manner that I was in a hurry. I jostled my way expertly to the only table with one chair empty (in the back between the Rest Room entrance and the kitchen).

Three other girls at my table, office workers by their conversation, were nearly finished with their 70c sandwiches, chewing awfully fast, talking a blue streak, combing their hair, applying fresh lipstick and smoking their cigarettes all at the same time. And without my noticing it, or tasting anything, not even the pickle, I found I had eaten my lunch and was all through the same time they were. They got up and left, and I was alone at the table heaped with dirty dishes. I looked at my watch. Only 12:35. I could relax for a whole quarter hour almost! After getting out the right change for the check, I lit a cigarette, and crossed my legs.

Since this was the first time my spine had touched the back of a chair and my hands had been still since morning, it should have been lovely to lean back and ruminate about my new job and its future behind the gauze of my first cigarette. So what the heck was the matter? My crossed leg jiggled up and down, my hand went to the back of my neck and around to my forehead and down my face and over my chin, and I felt a little muscle there, making my mouth go twitch-twitch-twitch without my wanting it to. I guess it was all the other people in my line of vision, with their jaws chomping, and the noise they made trying to be heard by each other above the cloudburst of silverware and crockery slamming into trays, the Musak playing La Paloma, the bus boys prowling through it all with their wagons and pyramids of saucers sliding off and smashing on the floor, not to mention the traffic frisking past me in and out of the Rest Room, phone booths and kitchen.

But this was *natural* to me, a typist, who always ate in crowded cafeterias. It had never brought itself to my attention before. Far as I was concerned, I never *heard* noise unless I chose to listen, or saw what was going on unless I deliberately *looked*. Now, for no reason I could think of, in these few minutes I should be tranquilizing both my psyche and soma (I had made a practice of this during lunch hour on past jobs) so as to go back to the Atom-atic refreshed and single-minded, I was over-alert and all involved with everything around me. I found myself examining the stuff on the table as closely as if it were a Still Life in a museum. Or, as if I were boning for a test and had to memorize every object there. Besides the plates and cups with their leftover blobs of food, the filled ashtray in which was a wet teabag, the soggy napkins on the table, was a Lazy Susan bolted to the center, and on it was a mustard pot with a wooden dip, ketchup and chili bottles sticky around their tops, sugar dispenser, salt and pepper shakers . . . and in the middle of *that*, a foot-high bud vase containing an artificial pink sweet pea, with real laurel leaves wired onto its stem. Peeking out from under the edge of the Lazy Susan was a dried dollop of gum, with teethmarks in it.

All the tables were accoutered in this way, but I had to make *sure*. So my eyes flicked from table to table, taking note of the bud vase (like a flagpole or lighthouse) planted on each one. It disturbed me that I couldn't see around to the front where all the rest of them were. I wanted to get up, take a few steps, and check that part of the cafeteria too, but I restrained myself. Then I noticed that the wallpaper, which was pink and black, with ballroom couples dancing, some upside down and some rightside up, hadn't been pasted together correctly on the wall across from me, so that some of the dancers were chopped in two. I wondered if the missing strip was under the overlap, and I wanted to go over there and see if there wasn't something I could do to fix it. I felt I'd be more comfortable if I could set it right.

I looked at my watch, and it was 12:40, and I just couldn't *stand* it anymore. The best thing to do was to go back to that quiet neat little office, and my big new beautiful machine, where I could concentrate on just *one thing*, the main thing, really. And, with that thought, I felt *so* much better. We'd learn to understand each other, the Atom-atic and I, before the day was over. We'd be real buddies, and nothing else would matter.

As I opened the grain-glass door (without having to knock, even) with the light behind it outlining in simple purity the words, ROBERT L. ROBERTS CO., I did sort of hope Mr. R. would notice I was back early. But Sandra said he had gone to lunch. She was eating hers, having had it sent up, and spread on her desk were several current magazines: QUICK, SLICK, FLICK, CHIC, SNICKER and PIC, among others. I turned on the machine, and wanted to get right to work; there were 6 new belts, plus the one I'd left unfinished. But Sandra wanted to talk while she ate and read, and I didn't think it would be polite to not listen. She said she was getting married in two weeks, and that then (had Mr. R. told me?) I'd have to take over *her* job along with my own for a while, until I got a new gal trained. Therefore, I'd better familiarize myself with all the procedure of the firm, and get some practice in it, so that not only could I teach it to the new gal but show Mr. R. that I was capable of being his Gal Friday, which was the position *she* held, so that if he decided, after a year, say, to promote me to that title, he'd be convinced I was worth the raise. I didn't like to ask what the raise might be. Some firms are touchy about employees discussing this, especially behind the boss' back. So I just asked her the best way to learn about the business. And she took a thick folder out of the file marked: BACK-

GROUND & OFFICE PROCEDURE, and said I could take it home and absorb it after hours.

I couldn't help, out of curiosity, starting to read it while she went on talking, and I gathered roughly that RLR was a sort of middleman, or, specifically, a broker *for* middlemen in the Wax Industry; the middlemen being promotion and sales representatives (not *sales*men, that's something else) between manufacturers and wholesalers, or wholesalers and retailers. As we know, manufacturers sell to wholesalers who sell to retailers who sell to the ultimate consumer. Or this is how it used to be, when merchandising was in its infancy. *Now*, in between these buyers and sellers are the subsidiary outfits, the middlemen—and in between them comes a firm like RLR & Co., which, obviously, doesn't handle the product itself, but does so figuratively, that is, on paper. And this is a very important function in the total merchandising process, as it largely determines the prices and costs of production, as well as distribution.

So what did that make me? What little link was I in the chain? I asked myself. Because I believe in trying to orientate myself in a new job, and find out just where I fit. I looked at my Atom-atic crouching there so seemingly self-sufficient, purring energetically to itself.

I was the mid-woman between the mid-middleman and the machine.

By no means a dispensable or expendable link. Because, as yet, the Atom-atic could only transcribe, and not interpret Mr. R.'s words; especially in view of his spontaneous and dynamic way of dictating, with everything coming wrapped up in something else, having been incorporated inside the first thing, which might be a letter or long memo, so that sometimes the beginning of the beginning thing at the beginning of a belt would have the commencement of the final conclusion several belts later; and then the P.S.; and often the cancellation of parts, or of the whole—that is, the outer shell (while the inner layers, consisting of other unrelated bits and pieces, were to remain) would come a couple of belts further on.

Now, machines are durable and inexorable, more so than the human mind, but they are not elastic, adaptable and selective, and that's why I'd never have to worry about having a job of some kind, no matter how the marvels of technology multiplied and improved—at least while I had my youth.

Mr. Cobb came out of his office to go to lunch, with a shy smile for both of us, as he deepened the crease in his hat and put it on, and I took this as an excuse to start typing. Right after that Mr. R. catapulted back with a brilliant smile, for Sandra. And a tail end of it left over for me.

The machine and I spanked along like pretty much of a team that afternoon. Although I still had to do frequent erasures, and got fouled up with the different colors and grades of stationery that were specified and then unspecified, by and large, I (or I should say *we*) co-ordinated to turn out clean, dark, accurate copy, manifestly did it faster and faster. The problem of editing came up, as for instance, when Mr. R. used "appreciate" 4 times in 2 paragraphs, and I asked Sandra if I should maybe change one of them to "would be very glad if." She said:

"Ask him, if you want. I wouldn't be in a position to know. But if I were you I wouldn't. He doesn't like to have you make as if he isn't always entirely right. But if he calls *you* on it, asks you why you repeated yourself—what's the matter with your vocabulary—just say you're sorry, and *then* change it."

As I say, we zipped along famously until 3:30 or so, and I found I didn't want to do anything else. It was so sort of satisfying and secure-feeling to entrust myself to, and fall in with, the romping rhythm of the machine. If I'd stop for a minute with the idea of lighting a cigarette, I'd feel all jittery and tense and functionless. I found I felt stable as long as my fingers were constantly and rapidly drinking up those electric vibrations transmitted to them from the keys, and my ears were sorting out RLR's versatile and magnetic sizzle of words. I even regretted having to stop and go to the Ladies Room when it was time. There was too great a contrast between sitting with feet on pedals and hands on console, being *carried* in smooth momentum, and then stumbling under my own puny power through that uphill hall, with a sort of heavy stagnant silence pouring into my head. When I came back, I must have been pale, because Sandra said:

"You look like death warmed over. Why don't you punch the Tune-Tonic key? It'll give you a lift."

I thought she was ribbing me, but as I climbed onto my stool, my eye was simply *guided* to a kidney-shaped button on the uppermost deck marked T.T. I had thought it was the Touch Control and hadn't bothered with it. Sandra was watching me, so I couldn't put it off and make the discovery in secret. Pretending I knew all about it, I . . . pushed.

Well, for Pete's Periwinkle! Music, just like Muzak! A rippling tune with an imperious percussive beat funneled into my ear just behind Mr. R.'s voice. A kind of private serenade to flatter the typist out of her blues—how *sweet*, really.*

As I mentally adjusted my goggles, tested the flaps, started the propellers, taxied to the end of the strip, gave her the gun, pulled on the stick and took off like a scalded cat, I noticed that the rhythm of the Tune-Tonic began to accelerate just a wee bit over the speed the Atomatic was setting for my fingers, and when we'd synchronized with that, it

---

* Interesting Footnote: The Sunday after I wrote this down, I found the following bit in the paper: "A California bee keeper has been regaling his bees 14 hours a day with broadcast music. Result: More honey from his 1200 hives. The bees like the music so much they get restless and swarm if it is turned off."

accelerated just a *wee* bit more. The arrow on my m.p.h. dial pinged around to the right. Next thing I knew I was over Schenectady.

And the *next* thing I knew, I was home in bed with a 103° fever; my pulse was 120 and my blood pressure 205. The doctor had just left. My body was a boat—an old rowboat, not a yacht or a cruiser even—all alone in the middle of a choppy lake, and I'd lost one oar; and inside of me green bilge water was sloshing, mounting higher inch by inch. I wished I had a can to bail with. The doctor had left a basin on the bed table—*kidney-shaped*—reminded me of something. I used that to bail with, but it wasn't big enough. Things started coming back, but backwards, like back-tracking on the Talk-a-Belt (aha, another clue).

Well, face it. I'd have to reconstruct the crime in order to prepare my defense. (To myself, understand. Everything that happened, as I said before, happened inside myself. It was my own fault—I'm not blaming anything or anybody.)

I back-tracked. I'd just got off the 5th Avenue bus. There lay Washington Square, comparatively somnolent in the afternoon sunlight. My feet were rounded on the bottoms, like old-fashioned desk blotters. No, they were long and curved like on a rocking chair. No, I have to amend that once more: They were ice skates (and I can't skate) and the two blocks between me and home was a flashing stretch of ice; its thick slickness continued up the stoop, into the foyer, and coated the stairs of my 3-floor walk-up.

Next (back-tracking another strip), I was in the subway station at 42nd and 5th, where on one side the trains go to Queens and on the other to Times Square. One was coming in and the other going out. Now, there's a peculiar sensation you get, even under normal circumstances (if you're sensitive) when one roaring projectile is swooping toward you on one side, and an identical one streaming away on the other, and you're stationary in the middle. When the trains are gone, there are two long black silent trenches that seem to *widen*, swiftly narrowing the platform between them to a rail, to a tightrope, to nothing! That's why I had to climb back up to the pavement and take a bus instead.

I back-tracked some more. I was getting to the awfullest, the most shameful part (or so I thought *then*, in my state of partial amnesia). I was standing in front of The Lions, waiting for a bus to stop that had room on the step to fit a toe into. The ones that were not full surged by in the middle of the street, and the ones that were jammed piled up at the curb like elephants trunk to tail. The bulbous cars crept uptown, downtown and crosstown so close together a ballet troupe could have done Swan Lake on their tops, and yanking in and out between the blacks, cobalts and grays of chauffeur-driven motors were the yellows, mauves, peaches, vermilions, magentas, cerises and checkered black-and-greens of cabs and private cars. Why couldn't they be made of rubber, I thought, so when their bumpers collided and their fenders swiped, there wouldn't be that noise? The 8-million-headed rush-hour mob coiled by me endlessly, like a monster made of congealed molasses. There, above it all, serene in the blue, soared, leapt, projected, reared, ejaculated (take any one of them) the Empire State. And I caught myself commanding it (out loud, but no one let on they heard me) to contract, deflate, narrow, shrink, dwindle, shrivel, wither, wizen, crumple up, collapse, drop dead.

Now, how I could harbor such a wish within me even for one unbalanced moment, let alone voice it, fills me with guilt. It bares the deep dichotomy in my soul, I guess, but honestly, I didn't, I don't now, really mean it. I know it resembles a terribly significant symptom, and every girl is supposed to suffer with it, unconsciously at least. But I've *never* wanted to deny that women are, well, secondary, to men. I believe every active principle necessarily has its passive component, and that Man constitutes the former. I do, I do, I do, and nobody's going to make me say I don't, even with a lie detector. It would also seem to show an unconscious desire not to go to work. But I *want* to work, and I need to work, and I'm a *good* typist. I have always agreed that "only through work does the individual achieve wholesome social contacts, express his creative interests, make a contribution to society, and achieve status in his community."*

The word, Work, the shape and sound of it, like an anchor pitched into the lake of my recapitulative daydream jolted me back to the present. I looked at the clock. It was 10 A.M. of the next morning. . . . I hoped it was only the next. There were great gaps in my recollection still, but my roommate must have called the doctor before she left for her office . . . I must have moaned something to her. . . . Never mind that now, I had to get Sandra on the phone.

I managed to reach it on the bed table and dialed the number. My heart felt like a whale's having coronary thrombosis as I waited for her to say: Robert L. Roberts Company Wax Wax Wax Goodmorning. When I'd made her understand it was me (my voice was quavery and hoarse from the fever) she gave an explosive pop to her gum, and said:

"You certainly left me in a spot. I had to promise Mr. R. to postpone my honeymoon a week. And the *goons* that've been trooping through this office from the Agency. They just won't *do*. They refuse to learn the machine. Mr. R. is giving birth to bulldogs."

Jeepers, Joseph and Harry! that meant I was out of a job. What terrible thing had I done? It almost came into consciousness and I grabbed for the bailing can.

"Want me to put Mr. R. on?"

* Same paper, same Sunday, Editorial Page.

"No, please!" I started to plead. "*You* tell him how sorry I am, and that I'll always remember his . . ."

But it was too late. Mr. Roberts was already talking into my ear. My left hand went out to twist the dial on the Talk-a-Belt to Slow—an empty gesture.

"It's a little early in the game to be taking sick leave don't you think? Now you didn't work the whole day yesterday or it would have been $12 even gross Now the deduction for Withholding is $2.43 Old Age 58c Disability 20c State Payroll Tax 24c and that leaves just enough to pay for cleaning the rug. I'm explaining this to you in detail in case you're quitting and expect a check. I warn you don't go to USES and say I fired you I never fire anyone And remember you have a key to the office I'd like it back if *you're* not coming back I will say this I had great plans for you I'm a shrewd judge of character and when the Agency sent you over I had a hunch yours was the right temperament for the job. You and the Atom-atic would get on nicely in time It's a new whimwham Aren't many like it around Too many firms reluctant to move up to date. RLR is one of the few in the forefront It's a continual shove-shove-shove to stay there but I mean to do it. There are only a few operators as yet *built* for a sensationally-efficient machine like the Atom-atic They have to be shock-resistant and I sensed that you were one of them Now I'd consider putting you on contract for say 10 years By the way how old are you now? and somewhere along in there I shouldn't be surprised if you'd become useful to me. You take the day off and think it over Without pay but next time you're sick after six months and not exceeding one day I'll pay you half-time Fair enough? So long now be good see you in the morning Or send back the key."

"Yes, Mr. Roberts. Thanks . . ." I whispered. But he'd hung up.

"See you in the morning" or "Send back the key" See you in the morning or send back the key Seeyouinthemorning or Sendbackthekey. I depth-dived into blissful sleep. Those codeine pills are really wonderful. Just before my blunt nose touched the roiling bottom, I remembered how I'd thrown up about 4 P.M. on Mr. R.'s dark blue Blodroom—no, Broadloom rug, while he was in confab with three important prospects and all. He'd buzzed for me to bring in copies of the agenda on Pink paper.

Now it's late in the afternoon. I'm awake, sitting up, and feel better. I decided to tinker around with my roommate's portable (a Quiet De Luxe) just to see how it feels. It feels pretty odd—clumsy, slow, like going back to the plow. A 1-handle one—not even an ox in front of it.

It's kind of peaceful though. Makes queer, subversive ideas come into your head. What if everything were to stop? (Just what-if. What-if isn't a crime, is it, as long as it's only in your head, and you don't try to do anything about it?) All the cars that look like refrigerators with their round-angled, substantial, yet rocket-shaped contours, their dazzling trim, their clean flowing lines, their superior maneuverability; and the refrigerators that look like cars—what if they were to stop? There are so many other objects I could work into this, but I'll just cite those two for examples. What if the whole colossal business were to stop stock-still right where it is and grow green hair. And the city would be covered up after a while with moss and fern. And people be turned into furry animals (say, rabbits—they're so gentle) nestling in the green.

Now, that's retrogressive thinking, the worst kind, and I know I'm still sick or I wouldn't be typing these things. But, INERTIA. It's such a nice word. Try saying it. Like letting your breath out in a happy sigh.

Should inanimate things be made to move? What if scientists had never found out that a rock has molecules, and that all atoms in molecules vibrate, and that each vibration has a particular frequency, just as a tuning fork emits a note of a particular pitch?*

On the other hand (and that makes me wonder whether, if I only *had* one hand, and one hemisphere to my mind. I could make it up more easily) what about my beloved Atom-atic, with its luxurious superstructure, its wondrous power and supersonic speed, the potentialities for accomplishment it had begun to instill me with? Why not move into the future? *With* it—as part and parcel of it. Financially it wouldn't make any difference whether I stayed with the plow in the backwash of progress, or not. And rightly so, because eventually, once you'd adjusted to it, the Atom-atic was *easier* to operate. No pushing and shifting, no muscular effort involved—simply a matter of teaching your blood, bone, tissue and nerves to *give in* to its dominating current, and tool along.

As a woman, I was peculiarly adapted to this role in the technological scheme—with my smaller, biologically more nimble fingers, my more malleable nature, and my greater longevity. There *was* the hazard that one might reach what seemed an ultimate speed limitation, and hence frustration. But, surely future engineering would remedy that. For a small office like RLR's, where there was no competitive factor, such as a lot of other gals at other machines to furnish added incentive, maybe an attachment like Cineramic Television could be developed. You punch the C.T. key and a small 3-D screen, but panoramic, with stereophonic sound, would give you a forest of typists at a forest of Atom-atics, in full color, operating at a frequency or two faster than you.

Here I am, belly-whopping off the deep end again, this time at the opposite extreme (I can't swim, either).

"See you in the morning or send back the key."

Which?

* Same paper—Science Page.

MONA VAN DUYN

The Bell

If Mother were less large, or if the whole front room were not already filled with Mother's things, each with its value or its taboo so inescapably put on it, then the voices from the kitchen would not make her own dressing of Lily, the doll, so jerky and awkward. If she were in the garage playroom, for instance, Mother's voice quarreling with Grandma's would come out as far as her window and stay outside there, like the bees that would not hurt you if you let them alone, and it would be only the good smells from the kitchen that would come out and claim her as one of the people who lived inside, not the voices. It was not like that in the front room, however. There were things like the enormous picture over the davenport of an Indian Squaw trailing her big toe in the river and thinking of the little shadowy warrior riding beside her head; though she herself might look at it for any length of time, wiggling her own bare toe as if the cold water were running over it, still it was never hers but always really Mother's by rules of ownership and happenings that went outside herself like wedding anniversaries and presents from old relatives who died. In this room, the circle of doll's clothes she had around her was too small to keep the voices out. And if she heard Grandma saying, "Ach, the Kleine—such a little one yet . . .," as if Mother wanted a big one now and must be told that it was not so, she knew it was she that they were talking about. But the sound of Grandma's voice, which was somehow protecting her from something, did not make her feel warm and good now and ready, as she sometimes was, to jump up and down high in the air in front of Mother and Dad and Grandma and say, "Look how big I am! Look how big I am!" She

245

could tell by the muffled and smacking sounds of the words that Grandma was talking as she brushed her false teeth. Always on other mornings she would come running to watch Grandma spit out the whole top of her mouth, pink and shiny white, and hear her say, "Ain't Grandma funny looking, though. My, I wish I had Janie's nice white teeth." But she did not do so now. She instead continued to dress the doll, noticing that Lily was smaller and needed more help than she, who could dress herself to the last slippery back button in the morning. And she could hear Mother say, out loud and with a scolding sound which, in a way, put herself and Grandma together as little ones, "Now, Ma, you don't know anything about it. Why I was reading in the paper just the other day . . ." before the voices went down again. And several times Mother's voice rose with some special words and came in through the circle of doll clothes, "After all she's an only child . . . an only child doesn't get to. . . ."

When the voices stopped, as they did suddenly, it would be the one who won who would come out of the kitchen and into the front room to speak to her to do something with her—or perhaps, if Grandma won, rather than Mother, no one would come at all, and she could presently go through the kitchen where Grandma was warming up the old coffee and cutting a piece of Apfelkuchen for her second breakfast and Mother was washing dishes, so that she could slip out of the back door to the playroom without being noticed and before anything was changed. But the banging of pans in the cupboard was so loud that to her, still as a mouse in the middle of the floor, it seemed that whoever it was that got to come did not want to, but was showing the other, by clattering the pans, that there was more important work to be done before she could go; just as she herself would cause the scissors to make great snapping noises when she was called to dinner in the middle of cutting out a Ladies' Home Journal lady, however much the fine ridges of the lady's hair or feet might suffer for it.

It was Mother, after all, who came out of the kitchen and walked so fast and heavily through the dining room that she could feel the floor quivering under her, and there was no time to start humming to Lily as she tied the ribbon of the bonnet under the doll's chin, so that it would not seem as if she had been listening or had been disturbed. But Mother stopped in the doorway and said crossly, "What a mess!" looking at the doll clothes once, although Jane knew they were not a real mess at all, and then going across the room to straighten the picture of Dad's sister, Aunt Grace the missionary in China. And when Mother said, "How is Lily today? I see she has a new bonnet on," she herself said nothing, feeling mean and hard from the long wait on the floor. When Mother sat on the davenport and said with a queer embarrassment, "Come here, Jane. Mother wants to tell you something," she got up slowly, pretending that her knee still hurt, though the scab had long ago fallen away and she could only tell where the skinned place had been by a ring of slightly deeper pink and the slick feeling of the new skin when she touched it with her finger.

"Now listen to Mother, Jane." But she would not look up from Lily, the doll, sprawled back now with one leg kicking into the air, in the middle of a little circle of doll clothes where she herself had been sitting and waiting. "Jane, remember the old mother cat we had last year? Remember the little yellow kittens we found with her?" But even then she could not give any help, since mingled with the clutch that came in her throat for the little yellow kittens that had to be given away, one by one, no matter how softly they mewed at night or how neatly they drank their milk from a tin dish, and for the mother kitty who was killed by a car right afterwards, was a fear of the dark place on the other side of the question; into that she would somehow will herself to enter by an admission that she remembered. She did not answer at all, but still looked at the doll, small and defenseless on the floor. The silence did not seem to make Mother angry, as it did sometimes when it was a deliberate keeping back of an answer that Mother had to know in order to decide something or to punish. For if this were a plain question then Mother must surely know already, without an answer, that she remembered the kitty, in whose name she still claimed all yellow cats who came to the house, saying that this might be Muffin, who might still, somehow, be alive. It seemed rather that the silence was going to give them both reprieve, for Mother said "Oh well," and moved to get up from the couch. But then, at the very moment when the words were almost spoken that would set them both free and send her, unscathed, to the playroom outside, she heard Mother's yell, "Ma, you get out of here!" loud and angry, and saw Grandma's gray face peeking at them around the dining room door before she turned and went back to the kitchen, mumbling the "Ja, ja," that never seemed to mean "Yes, yes" at all, but only that Grandma did not know what to do.

If Mother was angry now, the anger seemed not so much to do with herself as with all those things outside, not so much to do with Grandma either, though Grandma was going clear outdoors, she could tell by the bang of the screen door, to get away from it. Mother sat down again, bouncing so hard that her own cushion at the other side of the couch heaved her almost off balance for a moment. But it was not going to be about the kitty, now. "Listen, Jane," Mother said, pounding each word at her, "I'm going to tell you something and I don't want you to ever forget it. Do you hear?" But the rush and energy of Mother's voice was so impressive and she had so given herself to being tossed by it, as she had been tossed by the bounce of Mother's cushion on the couch, that the important words were almost by when she heard them: ". . . tell you about your conscience. Your conscience is a little bell in your head that rings when you've done something naughty."

Even while the shock of what she had heard made her sit up straight and stare at Mother to see if she had really said the words, she knew it was not to be denied, though even the heart that pushed blood back and forth clear to her toes, or the round sack of a stomach for food, or the kidneys, however strange to consider at first, had never seemed so disturbing as a bell in her head, which sounded hard and unfriendly toward her. "So now Mother won't have to worry about you any more, because the bell will tell you when you're doing something wrong." When the questions came crowding up, What kind of a bell? Like the alarm clock? or, Is it loud? Do I have to keep listening for it? or, How does the bell know when I'm naughty? she hardly knew which ones to choose, for Mother was already jiggling the two gold rings on her finger together, in sign that she wanted to go back to the kitchen again. But Mother did not like the ones she picked to ask, and it was clear that something was wrong, though she could not see where it was, for it was Mother that she was always to believe, and not Grandma, who had told her when she was little that a black man would get her if she was not good, so that she screamed and screamed at the Negro who came to the door until Mother had to take her away and tell Grandma never to tell stories again.

Still, she had to ask why she had never heard the bell before, for perhaps hers was broken and she would be held responsible for all the warnings that never came, and Mother said it was because she was not old enough, before she got up to go. And now, when she sought for questions that would keep Mother there at any cost, for if the room were big and queer before, surely Mother must see how terrible it would be to be in it with the strange bell in her head, which might ring and ring until she was dizzy and no one could make it stop, the questions would not come. Only one did and she caught Mother on her way out of the room with it, "Can other people hear my bell?" begging her silently to say no, for this would be shame almost too deep to bear, worse than throwing-up in the kindergarten room. Mother said that they could not, and that she herself must listen carefully for it, before she went back to the kitchen and the screen door banged again to show that Grandma had come back in.

Through the intentness of her inward listening, as she moved softly and carefully to the doll clothes and knelt to break the circle by the folding of each garment away into a neat pile, came the questioning murmur of Grandma's voice and the anger of Mother's "No, I didn't!" snapping shut at the end so that Grandma could not get in. But Grandma said, "Ach, well . . . such a little one, enahow . . ." and she heard Mother's loud "Oh shut up, Ma, she's not your kid," though all this was lulled and far away to her because of the silence of the bell, which filled her whole head and covered it over like the paper sack mask she wore on Halloween. And with Lily, lying tipped backwards on the floor, there could be no friendship until she had made peace with the bell, all by herself, for Lily's head was as round and empty as a darning gourd, and, being a doll, she could not ever really be naughty or good at all.

How faint or how loud the ringing of the bell would be she did not know, and thought that if she pressed both hands against her ears to shut out all the outside, then perhaps the sound might come. But oh, this was wrong, for in the midst of her listening she saw Mother's face, frowning and sad, peeking at her, as Grandma's had, through the open doorway; and though she quickly moved her hands, pretending to be pushing some stray hairs back behind her ears, Mother was not appeased, and she heard in a moment after the face had gone again, the knocking and banging of Mother's broom, striking hard against the stove and table legs. Yet, in all the sorrow of her own failure, when she heard Grandma saying, "Ja, child, ja, child," with the lullaby tone that she herself received and coveted after punishment, she knew that this time, however strong and fierce the knocking of the broom, it was Mother who was the child that she was comforting.

Although Mother said he was too fat, and indeed his stomach grew in a long gradual slant out from his chest, so that when he would lie on his back on the floor and she would sit straddling on top of his middle it was like the coasting hill where they went in winter with the little sled, yet at supper time Mother and Grandma always filled the plate two or three times for Dad, with big mounds of potatoes and gravy and round steak. And tonight Grandma said, as she always did, "Why don't you eat nice like Daddy, then?" although she was already eating as hard as she could in order to make the mounds on her own plate get small enough to satisfy them. Right after supper, if she was good and did not get too excited to eat her food, she was to ride down to the gas station with Dad, who had to work on his books tonight, and could play in the pile of sand the cement men left there until Dad was ready to come home.

When it was all accomplished, with only the scare of the very last moment at the door, when Mother had said that she must take her sweater along and that Dad must remember to make her put it on when it got cool, and Dad had said if she wasn't old enough to know when to put her own sweater on he couldn't be bothered with taking her, making her stomach turn tight and hard until they were satisfied with her own promise to remember, she sat in the front seat of the car, like Mother, as they rode downtown to the station. And if Dad said, "It's a nice evening, isn't it?" as if she were as grown-up as Mother and as able to consider the quality of weather, she would say, "Yes, it is," and look out of the window at it knowingly, for the room of the car was small and had no particular feeling or possessions, so that it could be made all hers and Dad's simply by their being in it together. And that she could behave like a "little lady" with Dad, rather than with Mother, whose anxiety made her feel reckless and unsure, had also to do in some manner with his lack of blame for her, for it was clear that he did not feel what she did was his fault but only her own and Mother's.

At the station she got out of the car and went straight to the sandpile as if she too had come on business that must be dispatched, feeling the responsibility of not bothering Dad with questions of how she could amuse herself, for even when he said, before he went in and left her, that she must be careful not to play near the greasing pit and fall into it, it was not as if he would worry all evening that she might, but only as he would remind Grandma of the loose step on the porch, knowing that once told she could be trusted not to stumble on it. But really the sand was too big to play with, and rolled under her feet so that she could hardly move, refusing to pack together into cakes or hold up into caves when she dug into it, so that she grew scratched and dissatisfied when hardly any of the time had been taken up at all. It was when she had almost given up and was sitting at the edge of the sandpile, tracing with a finger the indented marks the sand had made in her knees and palms, that she saw the little boy, standing on the parking on the other side of the street and looking at her. She turned her head away and began digging in the sand again, so that her need of him might not be shown so openly and yet he might see that the sandpile was attractive to play in, and when she glanced up again he was looking to left and right to see if the cars were coming and then walking slowly across the street toward her. When he came to where she was and stood looking down at her with his hands in his pockets, he said that his name was Keith and she answered that hers was Jane, so that the thing was settled, the pact offered and accepted, before he sat down beside her and they began playing in the sand together.

If he knew how to make the sand work as he wanted it to, even carrying water in his hands from the faucet outside to pour on it, always allowing her to make the first sand cake and watching her pat it flat with her hands and begin drawing designs on the top with a stick before he went to get water again to make his own, his superiority did not make her feel clumsy and angered, as Mother's did, but, indeed, somewhat proud, as if her own importance rather than her failure caused him to offer help. And later, when the sand grew cool and the lightning bugs came out around them, they caught those, running and jumping into the air like big birds, and holding the little bright insects carefully in their fists so that their lights would not be smashed out, and sniffing each other's palms to catch the warm green smell of where the bugs had been when they let them go. And still later when Dad came out of the station to write down the numbers on the gas pumps, he saw them running together and said, "Well, I see you've found a playmate, Jane," commending her with his tone; and then he said "How would you kids like an ice cream cone?" taking out two nickels and giving them to Keith instead of to her, so that when they walked up the block hand in hand to the drug store, and she heard him jingling the nickels together in his pocket with the hand he kept over them so they would not be lost, she felt important and proud again, since it was her own Dad who had given him his pleasure.

When they walked back with their cones, both the same, for when she said she wanted chocolate he had said that he did too, it seemed that she could hardly keep from skipping all the way in the excitement of his company and the flickering of the lightning bugs, which flashed on and off, first before their eyes and then far up in the trees, so that they could not see the movement of their bodies when the lights went out, and might imagine it was all the same bug zooming up and down in the dark air so rapidly and madly. Yet, when they got back, though they licked the ice cream slowly, catching up drops that ran over the edge of the cones with their tongues, she was worried about what they could do after the cones were gone, for she could see through the window that Dad was still busy at his desk, and could not bear for Keith to go home and leave her alone by the sandpile again. And he, though he would not follow her own economy of eating the very last tip end of the cone, throwing his to the sidewalk and spinning around and around on it with his heel until it was powdered, seemed also to be uneasy, as if, perhaps, it was her place to offer him further excuse for staying, since in a way he was her guest. It was he, though, who after a moment made the suggestion that would prolong his visit, for he said, "I know what let's do. Let's kiss each other, shall we?" and she said, "I don't care," feeling the excitement of the new game beginning to tingle through her.

Still, even after it had been decided, they could only stand and look at each other. She herself could not make the first step to come toward him, and he did not move either except to scuff with his toe at the smashed tip of the cone on the sidewalk. But after a while it was he, again, who directed them saying, "Well, where shall we go?" as if he too recognized that it was impossible to do it abruptly in the big openness of the sky and trees, and that there should be a place, a definite place, to fold it around and give it its importance. And when he said, "How about behind the sandpile?" and they went and sat down side by side on the cold gravel that bit into her bottom and legs, she knew before he spoke his own dissatisfaction, that it was still too big and open. When they got up again he went and looked into the oil pit, but said, "It's too dirty down there," pointing to her own light dress, although she thought that if it had a lid over the top of it instead of the sky still reaching far up past the trees, dark and sprinkled with the flashes of lightning bugs, so that people could not come and look down into it and see them, it would be just the place.

As they walked, hunting, in the moist grass back of the station they came to the big brick warehouse beside the alley, where Dad's tires and supplies were, and she thought that perhaps the dark place of the door-step would be good and led him there. When they sat down on it they were a little apart, and even here neither seemed willing to make the first move. And though he said, "Well, shall we?" and she said, "I don't care," again, still she could not look up toward his face, nor even imagine taking hold of his hand as she had when they walked after the cones, for the actual touch of their skin together had become a thing so solemn and ceremonial that she felt hardly big enough to bear the thought of it. Then suddenly they heard footsteps coming, crackling on the gravel in the alley toward them, so that they jumped up and she ran with him, her heart jumping like frogs, in a wild hide-and-seek terror, to hunch down in the shadows on the other side of the warehouse until the footsteps had gone away. While they squatted in the grass there the kiss could be almost forgotten, as if the real game were the breathless running and hiding away, and she wished that someone were hunting for them so that they might have to run again to cover, perhaps behind a tree or around the other side of the warehouse; but no one else came down the alley, and they had to come out and walk back toward the station again. Then she thought of just what they were looking for. "Let's get in my Dad's car," she offered him, and he agreed that it would be the very place.

Now they were dark and safe in the back seat of the little room of the car, and she could take her place as hostess, telling him to put his feet up on the seat if he wanted to and showing him the ash trays that pulled out of the arms, where he could pretend he had a cigar and tap off the ashes with his little finger. But after all this was done and he had tried the springs of the cushions with a bounce or two, she knew that the kiss was still more remote than before, and he knew it too, for he was quiet, seeming to be trying to think of something else that they could do, now they were in there. Yet when he turned to her and said, "Well, I know something that might be fun," she had to ask him "What?" two times before he could answer her, though she could tell he was not being mean but was considering something to himself. What he said next was, "Have you ever seen a boy?" and she was startled at first, before she realized that this must be the funny kind of question that did not mean what it said, and she said, "No," hoping this was the right answer to begin the game, for really she did not know whether she had or not at all. Then he said, still slowly and solemnly as if he were being careful of her like Mother, "Well, shall we?" and when she did not say anything but only looked at him, knowing still less what to answer for this, he saw her wonder and added, "I mean take down our pants."

It was quite a long while before she answered him, for at first an awe at the utter novelty of the proposal, his great cleverness at thinking up this adventure, more different and strange than any she had even imagined to herself, sitting alone with Lily in all the wonders of the pretend-world, quite overwhelmed and silenced her; and then, when this went away and the decision was to be made, the strange wavering began in her, a pushing backward and forward under her mind that grew to such proportions that she could only sit still and let it carry itself out, not needing to will the contest to come out either way, as if she herself had no favorite in it at all. Back and forth they pushed, the one that wanted to see and wanted his game to be successful, and the one that was not a fear exactly, of Keith or of whatever it was that might be there if she looked, but rather something that wanted to be left alone or was not ready yet, until it seemed that she was held motionless, almost perfectly balanced between them. And then one of them grew stronger and she could say, "No, I don't think I'd like to." And Keith said, "Well, I don't really care," to show he was not mad.

When they got out of the car she found that it was cold and pulled her sweater out from the front seat to put on, with Keith helping to untangle the arms and pull it down in back. And when she heard the station door slam and saw Dad starting across the pavement toward them she knew that it was over and time to go home, and taking hold of hands again peacefully, they went running to meet him. When Dad smiled and said, "Well, did you kids have a good time?" they both said yes, and when Keith asked if she might come down again to play Dad smiled again and told them he wouldn't be surprised. Even after the car was started and moving down the street they waved and called goodbye to each other, so that when they turned the corner toward home she caught a last sight of him, standing and looking after her and waving still.

In the car with Dad she leaned back against the seat and shut her eyes to keep in this warm and important evening, which in memory was colored delicately, not of the darkness of the actual night but with gold tinglings of excitement, and when Dad said, "He's a nice little boy, isn't he?" she said yes, feeling sure and proud. And now, going back, she need not pretend that she was Mother in order to feel secure and equal to Dad, for her place in the car had been earned by her own decision, the enactment of her own business in it, so that she sat comfortably and without fidgeting as, side by side, they rode on together through the town.

Received into the house and enfolded again by the concern of Mother, who had worried because they did not come home until so late, she walked out through the kitchen to the bathroom where water had been set running for her bath as soon as Mother had seen the headlights of the car turn into the driveway. But all the while, in the dazzle of house lights that nearly blinded her and made her vague to the questioning of Mother and the reportings of Dad about her own behavior, she held in the glow of the evening, and the clothes came undone under her fingers and slipped to the floor as smoothly as banana peelings, as they did in dreams sometimes where there were no buttons or hooks that stuck and angered her.

The warm water lapped her and lulled her, so that when she heard Dad say, "No, she wasn't any trouble. She played with the little boy across the street all evening," the image of Keith came up before her, so clearly that she could see the big white buttons where his suspenders fastened on and the cluster of hairs that stood straight up at the back of his head. When Mother came in to wash her back the questions had to be answered again, and if Mother said, "Did you get too tired out?" or, "Did you have a good time?" or, "Did you bother Daddy?" she must be given a reply, however softly it was spoken so as not to break the picture, even though Mother knew already what all the answers were. And when Mother wanted to know if she had remembered to put her sweater on as soon as it got cool, she said yes, for surely she had been warm herself up until the last moment before they came home, and had put the sweater on immediately.

Still, when Mother was not satisfied completely and asked again if she was sure she had put it on soon enough, the worry began to joggle in her own mind, since the problem of whether she had been good or bad seemed often to be a question of whether words meant exactly the same to both of them. And then—suddenly—she remembered. All the feeling of the morning, which seemed now like one from a long ago time instead of today, came whirling back, and she remembered the bell, the terrible watching bell in her head, which sometime in the afternoon she must have forgotten, though all morning long and even after lunch she had waited and listened for it, making Mother cross by not hearing when she was questioned or spoken to.

But now she turned hot from shame, and guilt for the enormous crime went spreading through her like the milky film of soap through the bath water, for what sin could be greater than the forgetting of the bell itself, her conscience, on the very day, indeed, that it had been set free to ring for the first time by Mother's pronouncement of her own maturity? And by no magic could she destroy it, saying to herself, if Mother hurts my ears or back three times with the washcloth and I do not say it hurts, the badness will go away. The water sloshed cold and oily across her back and, hardly able to bear the large accusing presence of Mother, whose voice went on probing with the questions, she was in more agony still because of the violation of the bell, so intimately close in her own head, for surely it must have rung at least once during the long undirected evening and she had not listened for it—she had not listened for it at all. If Mother asked if she had found someone to play with, and who it was, and if she had a good time with him, she answered only "yes" or "Keith," since Mother really knew already and besides might merely think that she was tired if she said no more, but all the while she was concerned with the real and giant problem, of when it was that the bell might have rung, of whether the bell had tried to tell her to put her sweater on before she did, so that by admission of the wrong it might be satisfied. Yet if the questions were disturbing, the silence of Mother while she herself was being dried was suddenly worse, seeming to hover over her, a warning of something ominous, as if perhaps her own thoughts had been revealed and Mother was waiting to be told. Instead, after a moment it was Mother who spoke again, having another question, "Was he a nice little boy?"

It was strange that she could not, this time, say the yes that she had spoken with Dad, for somehow the question was different and there was something queer in the way Mother's voice said "nice," so as to set worry joggling in her again and to bring back again the morning's fear and sense of mysterious darknesses on the other side of what any word might seem to say. And while she was waiting there rose again the still unanswered demand of the watcher in her head, now become so huge that surely the sweater would no longer satisfy it, and she must offer up the very greatest and most important accomplishment of the evening in forfeit to the bell. To bring the whole heavy attention of Mother in tense focus upon her by saying, "Mother . . . I've got something to tell you . . ." was hard, but once she had started the very eagerness of Mother seemed to reach out and take the words from her before they came, so that, "Keith wanted me to take off my pants," was spoken almost before she knew it. Mother's hands hurt her shoulder when she said, "He *did!*" and, quickly, "Did you do it?" but released her again when she answered that she had not. And it was not until Mother had said, "Why didn't you, Jane?" and it was done, the denial of her own will-lessness in the matter, the gift to the bell, her own reply, "The little bell told me not to," that the feeling began to come over her, so that it seemed as if Mother were fading, withdrawing far, far away and she herself was growing huge and fat like Great Aunt Ella in the smelly room at the boarding house. Even the queer great jubilance of Mother's approval, "That's right, honey! Oh my, that's a *good* girl!" or Mother's roar that rang in her own ears like thunder, "Ma! Ma, come here quick!" did not stop the feeling, the horrible and unnatural growth that seemed to be swelling her out in folds of flesh, like something evil and overripe, so that she stood naked, by the bathtub, not daring to move.

When Grandma came hurrying into the kitchen with the crochet hook still in her hand and her glasses sliding down her nose, saying, "Lord, girl! What's the matter, then?" Mother jumped up and went to meet her, beginning to talk in German, so that at least she herself did not have to know what was being said. But when Grandma cried out, "Gott im Himmel!" Mother said in English, "Well, what did I tell you?" as if what was done no longer had anything to do with her, but had become in some way a triumph of Mother's, and she was glad to have been forgotten, wishing indeed that she could hide completely. But as soon as Mother had finished, Grandma saw her and came in to her, leaning close with her face all red and wrinkled like a witch and hissing through her teeth, "Ja, them dirty, nasty little boys! Then dirty, sneaky little devils, all the same, every last one of them!"; and though she tried to pull away in terror from this strange, fierce face, the cords of the neck that stood out, and the horrible hot smell of Grandma's breath in her own face as she spoke, still Grandma held her and hissed at her, "I guess our girl ain't going to do anything like that, is she? Rotten, dirty little boys, enahow!" until Mother said, "That's enough, Ma," in warning, and pulled her away.

Then Mother said, "Come on, honey, let's go tell Daddy what a good girl you are," and though always before on bath nights if it was warm enough in the house Mother would take her in to where Dad was sitting in the old leather chair in the den and reading the *Saturday Evening Post* and say, "Look how solid she is, Daddy," and Dad would turn her around and pinch her bare bottom and say, "Yep, she's getting big, all right," yet this time she could not go. It was not that she would feel embarrassed at having brought blame upon him for not watching her and keeping her from this terrible thing, for what she did could never be blamed on Dad, but it was as if Dad himself must have changed, the stomach that she used to sit on become swollen and bulbous, and his legs fleshy and unpleasant hanging from the chair. So she said, "No, I'm cold," seeing, sure enough, when she looked the goosepimples standing out on her arms; but Mother was too excited anyway to make her go, and said only, "Hurry and put your nightie on," before going out of the kitchen so fast that she bumped against the cabinet by the door and the pans rattled and rattled after she was gone.

When Grandma said, "How would my girl like a piece of candy?" and got out the paper bag of peppermints in the cupboard, from which she and Grandma each got two pieces after lunch, and from which she had once caught Grandma taking an extra piece in the morning and had not told, she could take the one held out to her and eat it, though its sweetness made her stomach quiver. And when Grandma had eaten her own piece and said, "Want to watch Grandma brush her teeth now, do you, Janie?" she looked at it, though the circle of white teeth in their flesh-colored rubber going back all wet and glistening into Grandma's open mouth this time made nausea swell up again inside her.

At last she was in bed, for they were anxious now to please her and allowed her to walk, slowly and stiffly as if her body belonged to someone else and must be directed even how to move its legs, up the stairs without saying goodnight to Dad, telling each other over and over what a good girl she was and how she was all tired out. Yet still, through the open register in the floor of her room came the sounds of the strange celebration she had caused, and when she heard Mother's voice under the floor where Dad's den was, saying, "Well, I guess I'm not so dumb about raising our kid," it seemed to her that surely the hot clinging of the covers against her and the sickness in her body was too big a price to pay for Mother's pleasure, however great it was. When she closed her eyes, though the lids became wet for the little boy who would wait for her and she would not come, the picture of Keith would not return any more for her at all, no matter how still she might lie or how many times she might sniff at her hands to catch again the smell of lightning bugs, though all that was left there now was the sharp antiseptic smell of Mother's soap. But after a while the voices stopped and she seemed to go to sleep.

How much later it was that the thing began to happen she did not know, for the sound seemed to begin in her head, softly at first, and then growing outward in the spongy substance of her dream like bread dough swelling on top of the stove, until the whole room was rocked and shaken with it. And louder, louder it grew until if she could have screamed to Mother her voice would have been as lost in it as a sparrow's cry, and louder still, until she knew her own head had become the steeple where all her life long it would be resounding. And if she woke, as she tried, muffled and smothering, to do, and if she found it was only the town clock striking twelve, still it did not quiet at all that monstrous bell, clanging and clanging against her for whatever had been betrayed.

RICHARD WILBUR

A Game of Catch

Monk and Glennie were playing catch on the side lawn of the fire-house when Scho caught sight of them. They were good at it, for seventh-graders, as anyone could see right away. Monk, wearing a catcher's mitt, would lean easily sidewise and back, with one leg lifted and his throwing hand almost down to the grass, and then lob the white ball straight up into the sunlight. Glennie would shield his eyes with his left hand and, just as the ball fell past him, snag it with a little dart of his glove. Then he would burn the ball straight toward Monk, and it would spank into the round mitt and sit, like a still-life apple on a plate, until Monk flipped it over into his right hand and, with a negligent flick of his hanging arm, gave Glennie a fast grounder.

They were going on and on like that, in a kind of slow, mannered, luxurious dance in the sun, their faces perfectly blank and entranced, when Glennie noticed Scho dawdling along the other side of the street and called hello to him. Scho crossed over and stood at the front edge of the lawn, near an apple tree, watching.

"Got your glove?" asked Glennie after a time. Scho obviously hadn't.

"You could give me some easy grounders," said Scho. "But don't burn 'em."

"All right," Glennie said. He moved off a little, so the three of them formed a triangle, and they passed the ball around for about five minutes, Monk tossing easy grounders to Scho, Scho throwing to Glennie, and Glennie burning them in to Monk. After a while, Monk began to throw them back to Glennie once or twice before he let Scho have his grounder, and finally Monk gave Scho a fast, bumpy grounder that hopped over his shoulder and went into the brake on the other side of the street.

"Not so hard," called Scho as he ran across to get it.

"You should've had it," Monk shouted.

It took Scho a little while to find the ball among the ferns and dead leaves, and when he saw it, he grabbed it up and threw it toward Glennie. It struck the trunk of the apple tree, bounced back at an angle, and rolled steadily and stupidly onto the cement apron in front of the firehouse, where one of the trucks was parked. Scho ran hard and stopped it just before it rolled under the truck, and this time he carried it back to his former position on the lawn and threw it carefully to Glennie.

"I got an idea," said Glennie. "Why don't Monk and I catch for five minutes more, and then you can borrow one of our gloves?"

"That's all right with me," said Monk. He socked his fist into his mitt, and Glennie burned one in.

"All right," Scho said, and went over and sat under the tree. There in the shade he watched them resume their skillful play. They threw lazily fast or lazily slow—high, low, or wide—and always handsomely, their expressions serene, changeless, and forgetful. When Monk missed a low backhand catch, he walked indolently after the ball and, hardly even looking, flung it sidearm for an imaginary put-out. After a good while of this, Scho said, "Isn't it five minutes yet?"

"One minute to go," said Monk with a fraction of a grin.

Scho stood up and watched the ball slap back and forth for several minutes more, and then he turned and pulled himself up into the crotch of the tree.

"Where you going?" Monk asked.

"Just up the tree," Scho said.

"I guess he doesn't want to catch," said Monk.

Scho went up and up through the fat light-gray branches until they grew slender and bright and gave under him. He found a place where several supple branches were knit to make a dangerous chair, and sat there with his head coming out of the leaves into the sunlight. He could see the two other boys down below, the ball going back and forth between them as if they were bowling on the grass, and Glennie's crew-cut head looking like a sea urchin.

"I found a wonderful seat up here," Scho said loudly. "If I don't fall out." Monk and Glennie didn't look up or comment, and so he began jouncing gently in his chair of branches and singing "Yo-ho, heave ho" in an exaggerated way.

"Do you know what, Monk?" he announced in a few moments. "I can make you two guys do anything I want. Catch that ball, Monk! Now you catch it, Glennie!"

"I was going to catch it anyway," Monk suddenly said. "You're not making anybody do anything when they're already going to do it anyway."

"I made you say what you just said," Scho replied joyfully.

"No, you didn't," said Monk, still throwing and catching but now less serenely absorbed in the game.

"That's what I wanted you to say," Scho said.

The ball bounded off the rim of Monk's mitt and plowed into a gladiolus bed beside the firehouse, and Monk ran to get it while Scho jounced in his treetop and sang, "I wanted you to miss that. Anything you do is what I wanted you to do."

"Let's quit for a minute," Glennie suggested.

"We might as well, until the peanut gallery shuts up," Monk said.

They went over and sat cross-legged in the shade of the tree. Scho looked down between his legs and saw them on the dim, spotty ground, saying nothing to one another. Glennie soon began abstractedly spinning his glove between his palms; Monk pulled his nose and stared out across the lawn.

"I want you to mess around with your nose, Monk," said Scho, giggling. Monk withdrew his hand from his face.

"Do that with your glove, Glennie," Scho persisted. "Monk, I want you to pull up hunks of grass and chew on it."

Glennie looked up and saw a self-delighted, intense face staring down at him through the leaves. "Stop being a dope and come down and we'll catch for a few minutes," he said.

Scho hesitated, and then said, in a tentatively mocking voice, "That's what I wanted you to say."

"All right, then, nuts to you," said Glennie.

"Why don't you keep quiet and stop bothering people?" Monk asked.

"I made you say that," Scho replied, softly.

"Shut up," Monk said.

"I made you say that, and I want you to be standing there looking sore. And I want you to climb up the tree. I'm making you do it!"

Monk was scrambling up through the branches, awkward in his haste, and getting snagged on twigs. His face was furious and foolish, and he kept telling Scho to shut up, shut up, shut up, while the other's exuberant and panicky voice poured down upon his head.

"*Now* you shut up or you'll be sorry," Monk said, breathing hard as he reached up and threatened to shake the cradle of slight branches in which Scho was sitting.

"I *want*—" Scho screamed as he fell. Two lower branches broke his rustling, crackling fall, but he landed on his back with a deep thud and lay still, with a strangled look on his face and his eyes clenched. Glennie knelt down and asked breathlessly, "Are you O.K., Scho? Are you O.K.?," while Monk swung down through the leaves crying that honestly he hadn't even touched him, the crazy guy just let go. Scho doubled up and turned over on his right side, and now both the other boys knelt beside him, pawing at his shoulder and begging to know how he was.

Then Scho rolled away from them and sat partly up, still struggling to get his wind but forcing a species of smile onto his face.

"I'm sorry, Scho," Monk said. "I didn't mean to make you fall."

Scho's voice came out weak and gravelly, in gasps. "I meant—you to do it. You—had to. You can't do—anything—unless I want—you to."

Glennie and Monk looked helplessly at him as he sat there, breathing a bit more easily and smiling fixedly, with tears in his eyes. Then they picked up their gloves and the ball, walked over to the street, and went slowly away down the sidewalk, Monk punching his fist into the mitt, Glennie juggling the ball between glove and hand.

From under the apple tree, Scho, still bent over a little for lack of breath, croaked after them in triumph and misery, "I want you to do whatever you're going to do for the whole rest of your life!"

Notes on Contributors

John Berryman died on January 7, 1972. *Dream Songs* is his most important work. The first part, *77 Dream Songs,* won the Pulitzer Prize in 1965, and the second, *His Toy, His Dream, His Rest,* the National Book Award in poetry in 1969. Since Mr. Berryman's death, several posthumous books of poetry and prose have appeared. The most recent are *Henry's Fate* and *The Freedom of the Poet.*

Elizabeth Bishop was born in Worcester, Massachusetts, but spent a good deal of her childhood in Nova Scotia. Besides her poems, she has published translations of Brazilian poetry, and *The Diary of Helena Morley,* also a translation. *Poems* was awarded the Pulitzer Prize in 1955, *Questions of Travel* a National Book Award in 1970, and *Geography Three* the National Book Critics' Circle Award in 1977. She received the Books Abroad/Neustadt International Prize for Literature in 1976.

Louise Bogan died in 1971. For more than twenty years she was the poetry critic of *The New Yorker.* Her reviews and essays have been reprinted in *Selected Criticism* and *A Poet's Alphabet,* and a selection of her letters in *What the Woman Lived.* Her last collection of poems, *The Blue Estuaries,* has just been reprinted by the Ecco Press. In 1954, her *Selected Poems* was awarded a Bollingen Prize.

Jean Garrigue was born in 1913 in Indiana and died in December 1972 in Boston. She is the author of a prose fable, *The Animal Hotel,* and the editor of a book of translations by American poets. A posthumous volume of poems, *Studies for an Actress and Other Poems,* was published in 1973.

John Hollander was born in New York City in 1929, and now teaches at CUNY. He is the author of two critical studies of poetry, *The Untuning of the Sky* and *Vision and Resonance,* the editor of an anthology titled *Poems of Our Time,* and coeditor of *The Oxford Anthology of English Literature.* His most recent book of poems is *Reflections on Espionage.*

Josephine Jacobsen and her husband travel widely, and she is particularly familiar with the West Indies. A book of new and selected poems, *The Shade-Seller,* was recently published, and she is coauthor with William Mueller of *The Testament of Samuel Beckett.*

Donald Justice was born in Miami in 1925 and teaches at the University of Iowa. His most recent book of poems is *From a Notebook.* He is the recipient of many awards, including the Lamont Prize in 1959, a Ford Fellowship in the Theater in 1964, and an award in literature from the American Academy and Institute of Arts and Letters in 1974.

Caroline Kizer's Midnight with My Cry—Selected Poems was published in 1972. She was the first director of the literary program for The National Endowment of the Arts. *A Slight Mechanical Failure* is her first published story.

Kenneth Koch teaches at Columbia University and is the author of many books of poems, the most recent being *Duplications.* A book on teaching poetry to children, *Wishes, Lies and Dreams,* was published in 1970, and *I Never Told Anybody: Teaching Writing at a Nursing Home* in 1977. They are considered landmark works in educational as well as literary circles. Mr. Koch received a Guggenheim Award in 1961 and an Ingraham-Merrill Grant in 1969.

John Logan is Professor of English at the State University of New York at Buffalo. He is a critic and a short-story writer as well as a poet. His most recent book is *The Zig-Zag Walk.*

James Merrill lives part of the year in Stonington, Connecticut, and part of the year in Athens, Greece. He is the author of two novels, *The Seraglio* and *The Diblos Notebook,* a full-length play, *The Immortal Husband,* and a one-act play, *The Bait.* He received the National Book Award in Poetry in 1967, the Bollingen Award in 1973, and the Pulitzer Prize for *Divine Comedies* in 1977. He is currently working on further episodes in the same work.

W. S. Merwin now divides his time between New York City and his farm in Lot, France, with recent excursions in Mexico and Hawaii. He is as well known a translator as he is a poet. Works as diverse as Chamfort, Mandelstam, Follain, and *The Poem of the Cid* have been made available to English-reading audiences through his efforts. A new translation of *Iphigenia at Aulis* is about to be released, as well as a new book of prose pieces, *Houses and Travelers.* Mr. Merwin has been awarded the Pulitzer Prize in 1971 and the P.E.N. Prize in Translation in 1968. His most recent book is *The Compass Rose.*

Edna St. Vincent Millay was born in Maine in 1892 and died in 1950. She was probably the most popular poet of any serious achievement in the United States. A Vassar graduate, Village bohemian, and expatriate for a while, she was a romantic figure as well as a writer. She is probably best known for her group of love sonnets *Fatal Interview,* but she also translated Baudelaire and wrote plays and a libretto, as well as stories and articles under the pseudonym of Nancy Boyd. She was awarded the Pulitzer Prize in Poetry in 1923.

Howard Moss has been the Poetry Editor of *The New Yorker* for many years. A critic as well as a poet, he is the author of *The Magic Lantern of Marcel Proust* and *Writing Against Time.* His play, *The Palace at 4 A.M.,* was produced in 1972. In the same year his *Selected Poems* won the National Book Award in Poetry. His most recent books are *Buried City* and *A Swim off the Rocks.*

Frank O'Hara was born in 1926 in Baltimore and tragically killed in an accident on Fire Island in 1966. He was associated with the Poets' Theater in Cambridge and with the Museum of Modern Art in New York. A presence and also a source in the New York worlds of painting and poetry, he is the editor of many important art catalogs and the author of *Jackson Pollack. The Collected Poems of Frank O'Hara* was posthumously awarded the National Book Award in 1972. Several volumes of poems and of art criticism have been published since his death.

Sylvia Plath was born in Boston in 1932 and committed suicide in London in 1963. Her book of poems *Ariel,* published posthumously, established her as one of the chief figures in contemporary poetry. Her earlier work was collected in a book called *The Colossus.* Transitional work, discovered over the past years, has been published in several volumes, a selection of letters to her mother has recently appeared. She is also well known for her autobiographical novel, *The Bell Jar.*

Muriel Rukeyser was born in New York City, where she still lives. She studied and taught at Vassar, has translated the poems of Octavio Paz, and written prose studies of Willard Gibbs and Wendell Willkie. She is also the author of a novel, *The Orgy.* She has written many books of poems, the most recent being *The Gates* (1977).

James Schuyler is the author of several books of poems, the latest titled *Hymn to Life.* Like Ashbery and O'Hara, he is associated with the painting world and has written art criticism as well as a novel, *Alfred and Guinevere.* He collaborated with John Ashbery on another novel, *A Nest of Ninnies.* In 1977, he received a grant in literature from the American Academy and Institute of Arts and Letters.

Anne Sexton was born in Massachusetts and died on October 4, 1974. She left behind many unpublished poems and a completed manuscript, *45 Mercy Street,* which has been edited by her daughter, Linda Gray Sexton, and published in 1976. She is the author of a play with a similar title, *Mercy Street,* many books of poems and several excellent short stories. She was teaching at Boston University at the time of her death.

Jon Swan was born in Iowa and now lives on a farm in Connecticut with his wife and children. He was on the staff of *The New Yorker* for many years and published his first book of poems, *Journeys and Return: Poems,* in the seventh volume of Scribner's *Poets of Today* series. He is also the author of *3 Plays* published in 1968, one of which, *Football,* was produced at the Seattle Repertory Theater's Off Center Theater in the same year.

May Swenson was born in Utah, lives in Long Island, and has been a reporter and a teacher as well as a poet. She has won many awards for her work, including the Shelley Memorial Award, the Brandeis University Creative Arts Award, and the Bryn Mawr College Donnelly Fellowship.

Mona Van Duyn was born and educated in Iowa and now lives in St. Louis. She was a founder of *Perspective* and its coeditor for many years. *To See, To Take,* a book of poems, won a National Book Award in 1971, and Miss Van Duyn has also been the recipient of the Bollingen Award. Her most recent book is *Merciful Disguises.* Her story *The Bell,* won second prize in the *Kenyon Review* short story contest of 1945.

Richard Wilbur was born in New York City and lives with his wife and children in Cummington, Massachusetts. His translations of the Molière plays *The Misanthrope, Tartuffe,* and *The School for Wives* have been acclaimed on the stage and in print, and his lyrics for the Hellman-Bernstein *Candide* are widely admired. Mr. Wilbur's poems have been awarded a Pulitzer Prize, a National Book Award, and a Bollingen Prize. His recent books are *The Mind-Reader,* poems, and *Responses,* a group of essays and reviews.

Acknowledgments

John Berryman, "The Lovers": Reprinted with the permission of Farrar, Straus & Giroux, Inc. "The Lovers" by John Berryman, copyright 1944 by John Berryman, copyright renewed 1972 by John Berryman. First published in *Kenyon Review*, Winter 1945.

Elizabeth Bishop, "In Prison": Reprinted with the permission of Farrar, Straus & Giroux, Inc. First published in *Partisan Review*, March 1938.

Louise Bogan, "Journey Around My Room": Reprinted with the permission of the Estate of Louise Bogan. Copr. © 1933, 1961 The New Yorker Magazine, Inc.

Jean Garrigue, "The Snowfall": Reprinted with the permission of the author and of Kenyon College. First published in *Kenyon Review*, Fall 1944.

John Hollander, "In the Creep Block": Reprinted with the permission of the author. First published in *Partisan Review*, Spring 1969.

Josephine Jacobsen, "On the Island": Reprinted with the permission of the author and of Kenyon College. First published in *Kenyon Review*, Fall 1965.

Donald Justice, "The Lady": Reprinted with the permission of the author. First published in *The Western Review*, Winter 1950.

Carolyn Kizer, "A Slight Mechanical Failure": Reprinted with the permission of the author. First published in *Quarterly Review of Literature*, Vol. XV, Nos. 3/4, 1968.

Kenneth Koch, "The Postcard Collection": Copyright © 1964 by Kenneth Koch. First published in *Art & Literature #1*, 1964.

John Logan, "The Success": Reprinted from *New Letters*, Spring 1972; copyright 1972 The Curators of the University of Missouri.

James Merrill, "Driver": Reprinted with the permission of the author. First published in *Partisan Review*, Fall 1962.

W. S. Merwin, "Return to the Mountains": Reprinted with the permission of the author. Originally published in *Evergreen Review*, Vol. VII, No. 31, October/November 1963. Copyright © 1963 by Evergreen Review, Inc.

Edna St. Vincent Millay, "The Murder in the Fishing Cat": Reprinted with the permission of the Estate of Edna St. Vincent Millay. First published in *Century Magazine*, March 1923.

Frank O'Hara, "O the Dangers of Daily Living": Reprinted with the permission of the Estate of Frank O'Hara. First published in *The Harvard Advocate*, March 1948.

Sylvia Plath, "Johnny Panic and the Bible of Dreams": Reprinted with the permission of Olwyn Hughes. © Ted Hughes 1968. First published in the *Atlantic Monthly*, September 1968.

Muriel Rukeyser, "The Club": Reprinted by permission of Monica McCall, IFA. Copyright © 1950 Muriel Rukeyser. First published in *Tomorrow*, August 1950.

James Schuyler, "Life, Death and Other Dreams": Reprinted with the permission of the author. First published in *The Paris Review*, Fall 1972.

Anne Sexton, "All God's Children Need Radios": Reprinted with the permission of the author. First published in *MS.*, November 1973.

Jon Swan, "The Invisible Nation": Reprinted with the permission of the author. First published in *The Atlantic Monthly*, October 1970.

May Swenson, "Mutterings of a Middlewoman": Reprinted with the permission of the author. First published in *Discovery No. 5*, 1955.

Mona Van Duyn, "The Bell": Reprinted with the permission of the author and of Kenyon College. First published in *Kenyon Review*, Fall 1945.

Richard Wilbur, "A Game of Catch": Reprinted with the permission of the author and *The New Yorker*. Copr. © 1953 The New Yorker Magazine, Inc.